TWISTED CRAVINGS

The Camorra Chronicles, #6

Cora Reilly

Copyright ©2021 Cora Reilly

All Rights Reserved. This book or any portion thereof may not be reproduced or used in any manner whatsoever without the express written permission of the author except for the use of brief quotations in a book review.

This is a work of fiction. All names, characters, businesses, events and places are either the product of the author's imagination or used fictitiously.

Cover design by Hang Le

TWISTED CRAVINGS

TRIGGER WARNING

Twisted Cravings deals with many sensitive topics such as drug abuse, child abuse, violence and torture, so please be aware of that.

PROLOGUE

Adamo

BLOOD COATED HER LIPS, A STREAK OF COLOR AGAINST HER PALE skin. Even the flaming red of her hair paled in comparison.

She lay motionless on the cold stone floor, her wide eyes directed at the ceiling but unseeing of what lay before her.

I dropped the knife. It landed with a clatter, blood splattering around it. For a second a sliver of my face reflected in the only clean spot on the sharp blade. For the first time in my life, I understood the fear people harbored when they heard my name.

Falcone.

Today my expression justified their terror.

Bloodshed was in my genes. All of my life, I'd fought this craving deep in my veins, had dimmed it with drugs and alcohol, but its call had always been present, an undercurrent in my body that threatened to pull me under.

I hadn't let it. Instead I'd thrown myself headfirst into its depth, had followed the current to the darkest part of my soul. For so long, this day had been my greatest nightmare, a fear beyond measure. But fuck, today felt like a rebirth, like a homecoming to my true self.

My palms were sticky with her blood and it felt perfect.

No street race could ever compete with the thrill, the absolute high of a kill, and even less with the power rush of torture.

Denying one's nature was living a lie. Only drugs in all shapes and forms had made it possible in the past. No more.

People finally had a reason for the nickname they gave my brothers and me.

The monsters of Las Vegas.

My monstrous side had come out to play but the revelry had only just begun.

ONE

Adamo

THE SUN BURNED DOWN ON THE DRY EARTH, MAKING THE AIR flicker, distorting the shapes of almost two dozen race cars lined up at the abandoned road stop. It was only the end of April but not far from Death Valley, the temperatures already reached unbearable heights in the afternoon. I killed the engine of my yellow BMW M4 and got out. Sweat almost instantly broke out on my skin, making my white tee stick to my skin. I was familiar with heatwaves, having grown up in Las Vegas, but the unmoving air in this part of the country still often made me breathless. The heat wreaked havoc on the race cars and drivers all the same, which was why we chose the area for our qualifications.

Many familiar faces nodded at me through the windows of their cars, staying in the cool shelter the indoors provided. Some of them never got farther than the qualifications, but others displayed serious talent. My steps faltered briefly, my gaze magically drawn to a streak of flaming red. For a moment I was sure this was a fata morgana. Slowly, more and more of the red streak of color took shape. A long mane of red hair framing a pale face. Her red lips, the color of dried blood, curved into a smile around the cigarette dangling from her mouth. The smile wasn't flirty or particularly friendly. Challenge lay in her eyes. It was too soon for pit girls and groupies—they mostly stuck to the final races or swarmed around the winners of the qualification races after the finish line—and even if it weren't, I'd have known she wasn't one of those girls. The way she perched on the hood of a neon-green Toyota Supra told me it was her car and she'd be racing today. Women rarely made the cut into the finals. My brother Remo thought they lacked ruthlessness and ambition, but they were probably only more sensible than us men. With this girl, I had a feeling she might surprise us.

I dragged my eyes away from the redhead and moved toward the gas station.

A generator spluttered beside the run-down shop, powering a small AC unit inside the decrepit building. I entered our makeshift headquarter, where Crank was already going over the registration sheets piling up on the desk. The heat was marginally more bearable inside but the small AC unit didn't stand a chance against the almost hundred degrees blasting down on us. The broken gas station window certainly wasn't helping either.

"Any new arrivals?" I asked, shaking Crank's outstretched hand. I knew about at least one, and I was awfully curious about her.

"Three," Crank said. "A girl and her brother. Plus another guy with a big ego."

"He can't be worse than our favorite egomaniac?" Racing was a magnet for a certain type of person, but some displayed an over-boarding amount of self-centeredness.

"Not sure yet, but he's close."

I held out my hand for the info sheets Crank had dug up about the newbies.

I narrowed my eyes as I read what Crank had found on the girl and the guy with her—her supposed brother. Nothing. No arrests. Squeaky clean with generic names. "This stinks," I muttered. Mary, really? This girl wasn't a Mary. The only way any Mary probably got close to her was in a glass as a Bloody Mary.

Crank nodded. "Fake names, definitely. That guy, he's got the hint of an accent. Eastern European or something like that."

Eastern European. The only time I ever dealt with Eastern

Europeans, they were Bratva guys trying to mess with business or kill me. The races weren't their main target though. Drugs and prostitution were their most successful business areas after all.

I went in search of "John" and "Mary".

The qualification race would start in an hour. If this girl and her companion proved trouble, I wanted to know in advance and make sure they stayed the fuck away—unless it was the fun kind of trouble. The redhead still leaned against the hood of her car, smoking. By now her cigarette had burned down to a small stub. She flicked it away with her fingers. Given the red of her lips, I would have expected her nails to have the same color but hers were short and painted in a dark, almost black color.

The guy beside her with the buzz-cut stomped out her cigarette as it landed before his boot-clad feet. I had a feeling that was their usual dynamic. I strode toward them. "John" said something to "Mary" but she only smiled at me. Her eyes didn't hold nervousness as I stopped in front of them. She lit up another cigarette. Maybe this was a small sign of unease, but it was difficult to say with this girl. Usually the Camorra tattoo on my forearm made most people shit their pants, even some of the people who knew me well, and they didn't even register with false names in my races.

"Mary, John," I said with a hard smile.

A bare nod from the guy.

The girl took another deep smoke before she squashed it under a heavy black leather boot.

"What lovely names…"

"Actually, it's Dinara."

Fake John threw her a warning look. "Mary, what—"

There was a certain edge to his words that belied English wasn't his mother tongue. "Give us a moment, Dima." She never took her eyes off me. Dima gave me a harsh look, promising me retribution, and something in his blue eyes made it clear that he wasn't unfamiliar with the act of causing others pain, but neither was I. He shoved away from the hood and stalked toward his car, a blue Nissan Silvia.

"Dinara?"

She gave me a tight-lipped smile. "Mikhailov. Dinara Mikhailov."

She said the name as if it meant something, or should mean something to me. I didn't make a habit of getting too involved in all the business areas of the Camorra. Organizing and driving the races was a full-time job.

"Sounds Russian." And not just that, it was the name of the fucking Pakhan in Chicago, Bratva royalty. Mikhailov was a common name in Russia though, so this didn't mean anything.

"It is."

"Why the fake names if you give them up at the first chance you got?"

She shrugged. "Dima insisted, and it got me your attention."

As if she would have needed fake names for that. This girl was hard to ignore.

"A Russian name would have had the same effect."

Her smile widened, white against the luscious red of her lips. "You don't like Russians?"

I walked around her car, taking a closer look at the paint job. Viper was written across the passenger door and a snake curled along the side of the hood. "Just a certain kind of Russian."

She never took her eyes off me. I couldn't tell if it was due to worry that I'd do something to her car, or because she had trust issues in general. Probably both. "And what kind of Russian would that be?"

I stopped beside her and leaned against the hood of her car, an open provocation. You didn't touch another's car without permission and you definitely didn't use it as a chair. "You want to race?"

She smirked. "Quick thinking."

I stifled a smile. I liked her sass. "That takes courage. Few girls ever make the final cut. It's a rough game. People get hurt. People *die*."

She rose from the hood, making herself taller than me. A flicker of anger lay in her eyes. "I'm not like other girls."

"I have no doubts." I stood, towering over her again. This was my territory and everything followed my rules, even this girl would have to learn this. "Good luck with the qualification race. Don't get yourself killed."

"I'm hard to kill."

I nodded then with a smirk toward Dima who hadn't let us out of his sight for a second, I headed back to Crank in the gas station. He'd gotten rid of his T-shirt, revealing his scarred, naked back. Since a car accident last year, the burn wounds marred his back and left arm.

"And?" he asked, looking up from one of the laptops. Wi-Fi could be spotty but we tried to keep track of incoming bets. Nino and a couple of accountants handled most of the betting, but if things went too slow, it sometimes required us to make the races a bit more challenging to drive up the excitement.

"As we suspected. Not their real names."

Crank grimaced and picked up their registrations. "So what do you want to do? Kick them out with a warning? Or…?"

"I'll have to give Remo a call. Maybe he knows what's going on."

"Only forty-five minutes until the race."

"It won't take long. Remo hates chit-chats."

I threw a glance out of the window. Dinara observed me too. If she was involved with the Bratva, she was playing a dangerous game. The days of our truce had elapsed. If she was a spy or wanted to manipulate the races, I'd have to deal with Dima and her. The thought didn't sit well with me but a time when qualms held me back from doing the necessary were long over.

Dinara

I'd done my research on Adamo Falcone. Anything else would have been foolish. But he still surprised me. The photos I'd found of him in the Darknet had made him look younger, more sunny-boy like with his unruly, slightly curled hair and the trimmed beard. Like the surfer boys I'd watched during a vacation in Portugal. I'd expected a spoiled brat who threw around his last name like a grenade, trying to impress, and with a name like Falcone he would have been certain to succeed.

I'd met more than enough men of that type before but I could already tell he wasn't one of them. I'd seen a couple of videos of him in the cage. There hadn't been many but I'd had trouble linking those brutal fights to the sunny-boy smile photos in the Darknet. Now I got it. Something dark lurked behind those brown eyes. I had a feeling he could switch from easy-going to ruthless brutality in a heartbeat. A Falcone after all. Their reputation carried far beyond their borders. Fear wasn't my strong suit, so I'd never understood the reverence in the voices of so many people when they talked about the monsters from Vegas.

I didn't doubt he carried the name Falcone like a weapon if required, but he seemed confident enough to control the racers with his own charisma. I watched him return to the shabby gas station. A couple of pit girls who'd gathered in the shadow of the roof followed him with their hungry eyes. A powerful name, money and the aura of a bad boy with the indisputable fact that Adamo had a body few girls would dismiss drew them in like a moth to the flame. His sweaty shirt clung to his chest, revealing the lines of muscle and an impressive six-pack, and his ass in the dark blue jeans wasn't shabby either.

I knew he'd be calling Vegas now, asking for further instructions. Adamo may be the organizer of the races but his oldest brother and Capo Remo Falcone was a control freak and would keep a watchful eye over everything. Two Russians showing up in their territory definitely required a family chat. My pulse picked up thinking of Remo but I squashed my anxiety. This wasn't a sprint, it was a marathon.

Dima stalked toward me. *"This is bad. You know that, right?"* he whispered in Russian.

"We'll see," I replied, not bothering to lower my voice. Soon everyone would realize we were Russians, why try to hide it?

"We should call your father in case things go badly. I can't protect you alone."

"No," I clipped. "Remember your promise, Dima."

"I do. And the first oath I ever made was to protect you."

"We'll be fine." I didn't feel the same amount of confidence my voice conveyed. Adamo hadn't been overly hostile, and I had a feeling Remo wouldn't hurt me. I wasn't completely sure about Dima's safety, but every attempt to make him leave my side had been futile. Torture or death weren't my main concern though. I didn't want to be sent away. I needed to get to know Adamo Falcone, get him to trust me so he'd tell me everything I wanted to know. But for that to happen, I had to become part of the race circuit.

TWO

Adamo

Remo wasn't answering his phone, so I called Nino.

"What's the matter? You never call so shortly before a race unless it's urgent."

Of course, Nino was already ahead. "It is urgent. We might have a problem here. Two new racers. Fake ID. Russian origin. Dima Antonov and Dinara—"

"Mikhailov."

I was used to Nino knowing everything so I wasn't overly surprised. "You know her?"

Nino was silent for almost a minute, which meant this was really bad. "Talk to Remo. He can tell you more."

"If he knows, you know. What's the big secrecy about?"

"Dinara and Remo have history."

"History, what the fuck is that supposed to mean?" Dinara was younger than me, my age tops, so history couldn't mean he'd fucked her, but that had been pretty much his only interest in the female species before he found his wife Serafina.

"Talk to Remo."

"Isn't he around? Why don't you hand him the phone?"

"Give me a sec. He's in the cage with Nevio." My nephew was only six, almost seven, but Remo and he often trained in the cage, mainly to control Nevio's outbursts and his hyperactivity.

Rustling sounded, then the line went quiet. I waited impatiently. It used to bother me a lot that my older brothers kept secrets from me, but now it mostly just annoyed me. Remo and Nino had gone through a lot together. They shared many secrets I'd never be privy on. Another rustling in the line, then Remo's deep, out-of-breath voice. "Adamo, you want to talk?"

I doubted Nino hadn't filled him in on what I wanted to talk about but by now I knew Remo's games. I leaned against the wall, my eyes following the redhead through the broken window. "Two Russian racers joined the circuit today. Dima Antonov and Dinara Mikhailov. I'm wondering if it's a coincidence that Dinara shares the same last name with the Pakhan of the Bratva in Chicago?"

Her eyes briefly met mine and again that challenging smile hit me, as if she knew what I was doing and whom I was talking to. She didn't look worried at all. That either made her very brave or very reckless. The latter would explain why she was into illegal street racing.

"No coincidence, no. She's his daughter."

"His daughter?" I repeated in disbelief, mostly because Remo didn't sound shocked by the news or even worried. I'd hoped for some distant relative. But his daughter?

Fuck.

"And what the fuck is she doing in our territory? Playing car racer? Don't tell me this a coincidence."

"Did you talk to her?"

"Yeah, she registered with some fake ID. She and a Russian guy with her."

"Probably her bodyguard. I doubt Grigory would allow her to walk around by herself."

"You think the Pakhan knows his daughter is in our territory?"

"I think Grigory makes sure he knows about Dinara's whereabouts at all time."

"How about you tell me why she isn't afraid to be in enemy territory? Why she revealed her name without batting an eyelash?"

Remo was silent on the other end. While Nino had done it to think things through, Remo probably only wanted to play with me.

I lost my patience. "Nino said you and her got history. History how? I'm taking a guess that you didn't fuck her at some point. You don't fuck minors and I doubt you'd cheat on Fina."

"Careful, Adamo."

"Just spill the beans. I don't have time to tear every answer out of you. I have a race to set up."

"Then do it. I don't see a problem."

Oh, he didn't?

"You want me to detain her and that guy with her? As leverage against the Bratva?"

We hadn't been at open war with the Russians in Outfit territory. They weren't our concern but the Bratva in Camorra territory definitely was. They'd attacked our restaurants, had killed the father and grandma of my brother Savio's wife Gemma. He was the least vindictive of my older brothers, but he definitely held a huge grudge against the Bratva. Not to mention that Remo had declared war on Grigory for not helping him when the Outfit kidnapped me. Having a Bratva princess in our territory, especially participating in our races seemed like a particularly bad idea.

Remo was silent for a while. "No, let her stay. I see no harm in letting her drive in our races."

"You see no harm? You sure Grigory will share your belief?" I muttered. If Dinara got hurt, or even killed in our races—even if deaths happened rarely—Grigory would raise hell.

Remo was keeping things from me. Again. Did he still think I couldn't handle shit? Hadn't I proved I wasn't a goddamn pussy anymore since I'd returned from New York? These last three years, I'd done everything necessary to make the races in our territory even more profitable.

"I'm sure Grigory would interfere if he had concerns."

"That's what I'm fucking worried about, and I'm a bit confused why you aren't, unless he didn't give a fuck about his kid."

"Oh, he gives a fuck, trust me."

"Just stop the fucking games and tell me what the fuck happened?"

"You remember Eden?"

"That whore working in the Sugar Trap?" I'd never talked to her, much less touched her, but my friend with benefits C.J. had mentioned her a couple of times. They both sold their bodies for money.

"She's Dinara's mother. Ran off from Grigory with Dinara and eventually wound up in Vegas, asked for help to stay hidden from Grigory."

"So what? You made a deal with Grigory and handed his daughter back to him on a silver platter and forced Eden to work as a prostitute to make her pay for kidnapping her own daughter? Savio once mentioned Grigory asked you to make her life hell."

"You always think the worst of me." His words dripped with sarcasm. My relationship with Remo had been bad for a while, especially in my early teenage years, but we'd gotten past that point, even if we still fought on occasion.

"Why did you get your hands dirty? Why didn't you let Grigory handle her?"

He laughed darkly. "You think she would have met a kinder fate at his hands?"

"No, but I'm wondering why you'd take it upon yourself to have her punished."

"I'm a sadistic, twisted bastard, remember?"

"Damn it, Remo. That's bullshit and you know it."

"So you're saying I'm not sadistic and twisted?"

"You are but you always do things for a purpose."

Remo didn't say anything for a long time. "Keep an eye on her."

"You think she's trying to get closer to us to reconcile with her mother? Find out the truth about her past that you don't want to share with me?"

"I'm sure the past is the reason why she's there. As long as you keep an eye on her and make sure she doesn't get herself, *or you* killed, we're fine for now. Keep me updated."

His dismissal rubbed me the wrong way. I was used to his cryptic words by now, but sometimes they still drove me up the wall.

"I'll keep you updated, Capo."

Remo chuckled. "You better do. How's the racing business going?"

"Good. Didn't Nino give you a report with the numbers? We've been growing these last couple of years, especially with the expanded qualifications races. But I don't have time to chat now. I need to tell Dinara the good news."

I hung up and my gaze returned to Dinara and Dima. Remo's lack of worry regarding their sudden appearance worried me. He loved the provocation and thrill of a conflict, even now that he was a married man, maybe more so. Maybe he saw the appearance of the Russian princess as a perfect chance to bring some heat into our life. I, on the other hand, wanted to keep my racing business running smoothly. It was my baby, one in which I invested my heart and soul. I needed to find out why Dinara and Dima were really here and if they'd prove a problem. If they were, I'd make sure they'd leave our territory. Remo could figure out another way to make his life more interesting if torturing enemies and cage fights didn't do it anymore.

Dinara still perched on the hood of her car, her red hair fluttering in the early evening breeze. Dima stood beside her with crossed arms, giving the surrounding racers suspicious looks. Not surprising given the looks they were giving Dinara. Some of them were only amused and derogative, others flirting or downright leering.

They thought she was a nice piece of ass who had no chance in the race and would be impressed by their racing skills. Some of these guys probably even thought they'd have a chance with her afterward.

Dinara pushed away from the car and stalked toward me, tossing her cigarette stub in her path and stomping it out. I smoked occasionally, but this girl was a chimney in comparison to me. I waited for her, pushing my phone back into my pocket. She was stunning with her high cheekbones, plump lips and long legs. The fire in her eyes and that confident smile curling her lips made her look like a fierce goddess, especially with that red hair flaming up in the sinking sun.

She stopped right in front of me. "And? Did we pass the inspection? Are we allowed to participate in your race *circus*?"

I smirked. "You're allowed to participate in the qualification race today. If you make it into our racing camp that's up to you and your driving skills."

Dinara tilted her head. "I'm not worried about my driving skills, Falcone. What about yours? When was the last time you did a qualification race? You're set in the main races, aren't you?"

She had quite a mouth on her and bravado, I had to give it to her. Most people, even in the racing camp, either kissed the ground I walked on or tried to stay clear of my path from fear.

"I'm a part of the camp, because I'm one of the best drivers, Dinara. If I'd join the qualification race, that would only mean that fewer new drivers would get a chance to qualify." The racers who participated in all the main races in the season were part of our racing camp, which was what the name promised: a camp where we all lived in the months of the races.

She leaned closer, giving me the chance to really admire the blue-green of her eyes, a shade I'd never seen. "Then why don't you join the race today? Show off your amazing driving skills. Let's see what you got, Falcone."

I usually wasn't easily baited but Dinara had me on her hook. I wanted to impress her, and I wanted to know why she was here. What her endgame was. "All right," I said, grinning. "I'll race today but don't come crying to me afterward because your brother didn't make the cut."

"Dima's a big boy. He can handle himself. Don't underestimate him."

"I don't underestimate either of you. But you better not underestimate me either. I'm a Falcone, winning runs in my blood."

"Arrogance too?"

I smiled. "I think you and I both don't lack confidence when it comes to racing. Now let's stop the chitchat and prove we aren't just words."

Dinara stood on her tiptoes, leaning even closer and bringing her lips close to my ear. "Yes, let's do that, Adamo."

She stepped back and turned around, walking away, giving me a perfect look at her ass in her tight pants. I ran a hand through my hair. She *was* a hot piece of ass, but I preferred less trouble in my sex life. Hooking up with grid girls or the rare racer girl had proven a hassle in the past, so I'd stopped reacting to advances. Business and pleasure better stayed separated.

I hadn't participated in a qualification race in forever. Twenty-five drivers were set in the racing camp and five more could qualify to be part of it through a qualification race, but only the racers with the best positions throughout the year stayed in the camp for the next season. I was always among the best racers, had been for years, so qualifications hadn't been necessary. Yet, I had to admit I felt a giddy kind of excitement about being part of a qualification again. The atmosphere was different, less dominated by money and bets, more free-spirited.

I grinned. This would be fun.

Dinara

Dima's face flashed with disapproval. His go-to mood lately. "We're good to go," I said.

"So, we got the official blessing of the Falcone clan?" he scoffed in Russian.

"Don't know about their blessing but they don't mind us racing. Or rather Remo Falcone doesn't mind because he's the one pulling the strings."

"He'll have his little brother keep taps on us. They have to suspect there's more behind this than playing racers."

"Of course, they do. I'm sure Adamo will do his best to extract information from me."

Dima regarded me, gray eyes slanting to slits. "Don't let his charm lower your guards."

I burst out laughing. "What charm? Only because you have the sunny-boy persona of frozen bread doesn't mean any guy capable of smiling is a Casanova on the hunt."

Dima didn't crack a smile. I bumped my shoulder against his. "Don't worry. I can handle myself."

"I know you can, but don't underestimate the Falcones, not even the *youngest. They don't take it lightly if they're being played, and out here we're in their territory. Grigory would send the cavalry but it wouldn't go over well with our men."*

I rolled my eyes. "Don't conjure up ghosts, Dima. There won't be a reason for the cavalry or any other rescue missions." I kissed his cheek. "And I got you, don't I?"

He sighed. *"Just be careful. You know what your father will do if he finds out about this. One day he's going to dump me in an oil-barrel."*

"He likes you too much for that. He'll give you a quick end," I said with a twisted smile.

Dima let out a sharp laugh. *"Glad you find it funny."*

"Everything will be all right."

"Eventually, you'll have to put the past to rest, Dinara, or it's going to swallow you."

"It's already chewed me half up. The only way I can put it to rest is to find the full truth. We both know my father was selective when he told me what happened."

"He wants to protect you."

"He can't, nor can you. Nobody can. This is my fight."

The roar of engines filled the air. I'd always loved speed. The thrill of it. Dima and I had raced against each other, bikes at first, later cars, but never on a professional level, or with as many competitors.

Adamo pulled up in his car beside mine, flashing me a confident smile.

Unlike most of the other guys, he didn't look at me as if I was delusional for thinking I could race a car. Most of the girls who were part of the racing camp wore hotpants and lolled about on car hoods. Their only goal was to get in bed with a racer and better yet: become his official girlfriend.

One of these pit girls appeared on a podium off to the left with a start flag. Her hotpants didn't even cover the underside of her ass cheeks, but I had to admit she could pull it off.

Dima came to a stop in his car to my right, sending me a warning look. "Don't do anything stupid" was what his expression said. I rolled my eyes at him. We were here for a reason and nothing would stop me from reaching my goal.

My attention drifted over to my left where Adamo parked in his yellow BMW M4. His window was down and his muscled arm rested casually on his door. His eyes met mine and one corner of his mouth tipped up. My heart sped up and I narrowed my eyes at him, not liking my body's reaction to the overconfident Falcone baby brother. But fuck, he looked all man, trouble and danger, how he lounged in his seat as if that was the place he was meant to be. His kingdom.

I revved the engine once, a challenge. I wasn't easily intimidated. Adamo was a force to be reckoned with on the racetrack, but he wasn't the only one who had speed in his veins. The sound of two dozen engines filled the silence, like a wolf pack growling in unison. Goose bumps rose on my skin and my fingers around the steering wheel tightened. I'd never been part of a race with more than a couple of drivers.

The pit girl raised a flag above her head, smiling daringly. Adamo nodded at me as if to say good luck.

I smirked. I didn't need luck. I had skill, and the advantage of being underestimated by most of my opponents.

The second the pit girl dropped her arm with the flag, I slammed my foot down on the gas. Viper shot forward with a roar, dust rising up and hiding my surroundings from me. For several seconds I didn't see my opponents or the street before me, only the impenetrable sand storm awakened by spinning tires. I steered the car straight ahead blindly, my foot on the gas not easing. Then finally the dust settled and my surroundings came into focus and with them, Adamo's BMW which was a car length ahead of me. Dima was still on my right and another car had taken the spot where Adamo had been. We all drifted into the first bend in the road, but I barely reduced my speed, even as my car rammed into my unknown opponent. I sped up the second my car left the curve, my hands clutching the steering wheel to control Viper. Adamo was still ahead of me but I thought my risky maneuver had brought me closer.

My opponent on the left rammed my side, almost sending me flying off the road. Obviously payback. "Fuck you!" I raged. My foot on the gas became heavy from the force of the pressure I put down. Dima let himself fall back then slid over behind me and positioned himself behind my aggressive opponent. Then he drove into his trunk.

Grinning, I returned my focus to Adamo ahead of me. Dima would deal with the vengeful idiot.

I was slowly catching up to the BMW when Adamo suddenly slowed until we were hood to hood, and I could see his face. He grinned.

I cocked an eyebrow. A sharp curve lay ahead of us, much worse than the one before. Adamo raised his brows before he focused on the street and sped up again. The bastard had slowed to check on me. No matter how hard I jabbed my foot down on the gas, Adamo stayed half a car length in front of me. I entered the curve less than a second after him and my back tires broke out. I held on fast and carefully steered the wheel in the other direction before I sped up once more and catapulted Viper and me out of the dangerous bend. Four cars were only half a car length behind me, one of them Dima. We'd left most of the other racers behind, but only five of us would make it to the final race and I had a feeling Adamo wasn't going to be on the losing side. He was too good and his car too damn fast.

Twenty seconds later, Adamo crossed the finish line first and I came in after him. I let out a battle cry. Pulling up beside Adamo's parked car beside a makeshift winner's rostrum, I let down my window. Adamo was already getting out of his car. The sinking sun had turned the sky into a fiery blaze behind him. He pulled out a cigarette packet from his jeans.

"Nice race, Falcone," I shouted over the sound of the incoming race cars.

His lips twitched around the cigarette and he strode toward me. Again I couldn't stop admiring his sun-kissed, strong forearms and the outline of his six-pack through his thin white T-shirt. As if he knew what I was thinking, his smile turned cocky. He held out the packet to me through my window and I gingerly snatched up a cigarette. Shoving the door open, I got out.

"You risked a lot," Adamo said.

I shrugged, stepping closer to him. "Can you give me fire?" I put the cigarette in my mouth. Adamo leaned closer with the lighter, one of his hands protecting the flame from the breeze. Out of habit, because I always did it with Dima, I guided his hand with mine so the flame touched the tip of my cigarette. His hand was hot and strong beneath my palm. His eyes met mine and for a moment we were both frozen in the moment, in the realization of our sudden closeness. The second my tip kindled, I withdrew from Adamo and took a deep drag.

My eyes scanned the other cars, worried about Dima.

"He made it," Adamo said as if my thought process was an open book to him. It was unsettling. "Fourth. But Kay won't be happy with the way you two rammed him. He'll file a complaint."

I rolled my eyes. "This is illegal street racing. If he can't stand the burn, he should stop playing with fire."

Adamo chuckled and nodded. "His complaint will fall on deaf ears of course."

"Because you want me in the final race," I said, smiling challengingly.

"Because risky maneuvers raise the bets. And I have a feeling you'll provide more reckless moves like today."

"It's all about the money, huh?" I leaned against my car, blowing out a plume of smoke. I was familiar with the business Adamo and his brothers dealt in. Money and power were all that mattered, but Adamo gave the impression that this was about more than that.

"The price money for winning a main race is 25k. Winning the season, it's 250k on top. Except for a few speed junkies with rich parents who never win anyway, every racer wants that price money. But that's not why you are here, Dinara, right?"

Considering that he and I both came from money, his derogatory words seemed hypocritical but I got what he meant. He searched my eyes, trying to dig deeper. I wondered what Remo had told him. Maybe half-truths like my father. If he knew everything, he wouldn't look at me like this.

I smiled. "No, money isn't what this is about. That's what connects us."

Dima advanced on us, expression hardening when he spotted Adamo beside me. "*You risked too much,*" he said in Russian.

"Some things are worth risking everything for," I said in English, my eyes boring into Adamo's.

Adamo inclined his head with a tight smile. "Congrats to you both for making the finals. Crank will send you the details of our camp so you can join us for the next race. If you don't show up without a good excuse, you'll be disqualified for the rest of the year."

I nodded. "We'll be there."

Without another word, he turned around, heading toward the guy Crank, who'd registered us.

"*He's suspicious,*" Dima murmured. "*This could be a trap.*"

I bit out a laugh. "You're paranoid, Dima. There won't be a trap for us. And I would have been disappointed if he weren't suspicious. This makes for a more interesting game."

Dima shook his head. "*Don't forget what's at stake.*"

I glowered. "Nobody knows what's really at stake except for me."

THREE

Adamo

THE FIRST RACE OF THE SEASON WAS SCHEDULED ALMOST TWO weeks after the qualification race where I'd met Dinara. We had forty races in total spread out over the year. Stepping out of my tent, I sucked in a deep breath of the still fresh desert air. Dozens of tents were set up around me, all of them circling a bonfire and barbecue area where the racers and pit girls gathered at night. Our camp always traveled from one starting point to the next. Many racers spent the entire year in our racer camp, their only home. Some compared it to the Burning Man festival, but the rivalry between some drivers made it less of a free-spirited and relaxed place.

It was the day before the race, the deadline when all drivers had to appear in camp. My eyes registered a neon-green Viper at the very edge of the camp. I stifled a sigh. Dinara was the last to show up and last night I'd worried she wouldn't. I wasn't even sure why I cared. Her presence meant trouble.

Our camp cook was flipping pancakes on a mobile gas stove and I grabbed a plate with a stack of steaming pancakes before I headed toward Dinara's car.

I didn't see her anywhere, only Dima who hunched over a cup of coffee, leaning against the hood of his car. I gave him a curt nod, which he barely returned. Stuffing a pancake into my mouth, I walked back to my tent. From the corner of my eye, a streak of familiar red caught my attention. Turning my head, I spotted Dinara. She came from the direction of the mobile showers one of our race workers transported on a truck from one camp stop to the next. Her hair hung in damp ringlets down her shoulders and she didn't wear any makeup. A too-big Van Halen T-shirt was knotted above her belly and her jean shorts hung low on her hips, revealing a belly button piercing which made me want to discover the rest of her body to find out if there was more body jewelry hidden beneath her clothes.

Noticing my attention, she gave me a confident smile before she made a beeline for me.

Her black biker boots looked huge on her, as if they weren't meant for delicate female feet, and no matter how much Dinara acted like a tough guy she looked delicate by the simple fact of her body's measurements. "Are those your brother's? Don't you think sharing clothes takes sibling love a bit too far?"

Of course, I knew by now that Dima wasn't Dinara's brother but she had never really retracted on the original lie.

Dinara stalked toward me and perched on the hood of my car without asking. It was expected to ask another driver before you even touched his car, but she obviously didn't care about the rules as she'd displayed before. Good thing I didn't either.

I held out the plate with the stack of pancakes to her but she shook her head.

"Dima?" She pulled out a cigarette and lit it.

"Yep. The tall, lanky guy giving us the stink eye."

Dinara didn't look his way. "You still think he's my brother?"

I leaned beside her, arms crossed, trying to look as if I didn't care either way as I stuffed another piece of pancake into my mouth. "He's not?"

"No," she said with a hint of amusement. "He's not."

She held out her cigarette pack to me. Usually I didn't smoke this early in the morning but I took one anyway and slid it into my mouth. "Got fire?"

A grin flitted across her face but just as quickly it vanished. She held up the lighter, the flame fluttering in the soft breeze. I set the plate down on the hood before I leaned closer until the tip of the cigarette dangled over the fire and lit up. Our gazes met and she held mine steadily. Many girls tried to be coy or batted their lashes, some even looked away because the name Falcone had that effect on people. But Dinara looked at me. I got the feeling that she was trying to see beyond what I wanted other people to see, and yet, she kept up her own guards. Whatever she had to hide, I'd figure it out.

"I guess it makes sense you don't travel around without a bodyguard," I said. "I'm actually surprised your father allows you to have only one."

"I don't need bodyguards and my father knows I'd never let anyone cage me in. I chose Dima and he's the only one I accept."

Something familiar and protective was in the way she spoke about the guy, but I had never seen them exchange any physical intimacies, so that gave me hope there wasn't actually something going on between them.

Dima was still watching us. Something about the way he looked at Dinara raised my suspicion. I wanted to have Dinara deny it. "He's your boyfriend?"

She blew out smoke, staring up at the sky. "No, but he used to be. A while ago."

"Looks like he wished he still were."

Dinara gave me a wry smile. "You're awfully curious about my relationship status."

"I prefer to know everything about the people who drive my races."

"Even their bed stories?"

"Even those, especially if they involve the Bratva princess. Intel on you is a high commodity."

"I bet," she said. "Did Remo ask about me?"

The way she said his name made me pause. My brother spread fear in the hearts of even the bravest man. Dinara's voice wasn't scared. She sounded as if she were talking about an old acquaintance, someone she wouldn't mind seeing again. They had unfinished business of some sort. Maybe I was her way of getting closer to my brother, even if it really wasn't hard to find him and he wasn't really prone to avoiding people who meant trouble. I wasn't sure how I felt knowing that she might only be seeking my closeness to get revenge on my family, or whatever else her pretty head had in mind.

"You've read up on my family, I guess," I said.

She laughed. "As if that's necessary. Your family's reputation isn't really a secret. Even in other parts of the country."

I narrowed my eyes, trying not to look at her belly again. "Even in Russia?"

She dropped the cigarette and squashed it. "In the according circles, of course, but I spent most of my life in the States."

I shrugged. "We work hard to keep up our reputation." It wasn't long ago when I'd wanted nothing to do with my brothers' business and the Camorra. I'd even considered refusing the tattoo. Of course, Remo didn't allow it. Now I was glad. This life was really all I knew, and allowed me to follow my passion: racing.

"And it's a spectacular reputation," she said.

"Most of it is thanks to Remo."

"One of the most fascinating tales about your family came to be thanks to you if I'm not mistaken. You are the mother murderer," she said. Her teal eyes snapped to mine, arresting me.

Coming from her mouth, she made it sound like I deserved accolades. "I didn't kill my mother. My brothers did."

"You stabbed her. You wanted to kill her and you would have if your brothers hadn't been quicker."

She made it sound like a race too. It hadn't been. It had all happened as if in slow motion. I didn't like to think of that day, but it occasionally visited my dreams.

"You would have killed her, right?"

I searched Dinara's eyes, wondering why she wanted to know. Most people felt uncomfortable with that particular topic. Killing your mother just wasn't a good small-talk topic.

I nodded. It hadn't been a conscious decision to stab my mother. I'd acted on pure instinct and the fierce determination to protect my brothers and their families.

"What about your mother?" I asked.

A shadow passed Dinara's face. "Dead. She was killed."

I nodded, wondering if she was lying or if she didn't know the truth. Eden's life could hardly be considered living but she definitely wasn't dead.

She leaned in closer. "Do you still think of that day? Do you regret it?"

"My mother's brutal death is what fascinates you most about me?" I asked, my voice harder than before.

"It is fascinating. Children are supposed to forgive and forget the wrongdoings of their mother. They are supposed to love and cherish them despite their faults. But you Falcones aren't about forgiveness, huh?"

Challenge rang in her voice.

I put the cigarette out in my palm, a spot that wasn't sensitive to pain anymore after I'd made a habit out of killing my cigarettes like that as a teen. Dinara's eyebrows rose a fraction. "No, we aren't in the business of forgiveness, Dinara." I stood, towering over her. She didn't move from her spot on the hood, only threw her head back to look at my face. "That's something you should always remember."

She hopped off my hood and pushed past me. Throwing me a dark smile over her shoulder as she strode away, she called, "Oh I know, Adamo, and I won't forget."

I shook my head. She was something else. My eyes followed her to-die-for body until she arrived at her own car. I had a strict no sex with other racers policy but I had a feeling Dinara wouldn't stay in the camp for long, only until she realized she couldn't get what she wanted or I kicked her out. It had been a long time since a woman had caught my attention like this, that I'd felt such a strong urge to conquer someone.

But if I wanted to play Dinara's game, I needed to find out more about her and the reason for her appearance.

C.J. might know more about Eden. They'd worked together for a while, even if they'd never been close. I had been wrapped up in my own problems back then so I'd never paid much attention to the friendships between the prostitutes. If I wanted to understand Dinara, I needed to find out more about her mother first, and it was clear that neither Dinara nor Remo would be helpful in that endeavor.

I was on the road with the race camp most of the year, but we had several family occasions that required me to return to the Falcone mansion in Las Vegas. In the first few months of me living the nomad life, I'd resented coming home where I was still the youngest brother and would always be, where everyone remembered me as the unstable fuck-up and would probably always do. I'd enjoyed the freedom of a new life racing had offered me, but eventually I'd realized I missed my family and our crazy gatherings, even if Remo knew how to push all my buttons. Maybe it was payback for my teenage years.

I pulled up in front of the ginormous white mansion, and for the first time in a long time, I almost turned back around and returned to camp. For some reason, I didn't want to be away from Dinara, as if she might vanish into thin air if I left her out of sight. Seeing her drive in the main race for the first time and holding her own, finishing in the top ten despite the strong competition, my admiration for the redhead had only grown. I wasn't sure what she'd done to wedge herself into my brain like that, and it needed to stop. Maybe a couple of days with my family would give me the chance to stifle my fascination for the redhead and at the same time gather more information about her—if Remo was in a generous mood.

I got out of my car. The front door flew open and my nephew Nevio stormed outside. "Adamo!" he screamed. He barreled toward me and collided with my middle not five seconds later. The air rushed out of me from the impact. "Happy birthday," I said, tousling his black hair. He pulled back to look up at me with his dark eyes. Every time I saw him, he looked a little more like my oldest brother Remo, his spitting image inside and out. I dreaded to think what kind of trouble he'd cause once he got a little older.

"Where's the rest of the circus?" I asked.

Nevio stepped back. "In the garden. Will you fight with me for my birthday?"

I laughed as we headed toward the front door. "I doubt your mom will appreciate it if I kick your scrawny ass on your special day. Let's do it another day."

"That's what you said last time," Nevio complained. And he was right. I usually didn't stay long enough to make time for cage fights with my nephews. Camp always called too loudly to me.

Like Nevio had said, the rest of the family was in the garden. Nevio rushed away toward his cousins Alessio and Massimo who were doing some kind of sword fight with sticks. Shaking my head, I joined my family at the big table. Before greeting anyone else, I went over to Greta, Nevio's twin sister. She perched on Remo's lap, eating a piece of the spectacular cake throning in the center of the table. "Happy birthday, Greta."

I kissed her cheek and she beamed up at me. "Thank you." She was the complete opposite of Nevio: shy, careful and peace-loving.

"Long time no see, little brother," Remo said, his dark eyes boring into mine as if he wanted to extract answers to unasked questions from me. I had a feeling his curiosity was linked to Dinara. Kiara motioned at the cake that she'd undoubtedly baked. "Chocolate cream. Want a piece?"

"I wouldn't miss it," I said, giving her a warm smile.

Savio got up and hugged me briefly. Our once tense relationship had improved considerably with distance.

"Still in a monogamous relationship with a whore?" Savio asked as his way of greeting, keeping his voice low so Greta, and Aurora who sat on Fabiano's lap, didn't hear.

Fabiano narrowed his eyes. Savio obviously hadn't succeeded.

His wife Gemma punched his belly but he only grinned and shrugged.

"C.J. and I are friends. Whatever happens behind closed doors isn't your business." I clapped his outstretched hand.

"That means yes," he said, rolling his eyes as he sank down beside Gemma once more.

"No, it doesn't but whatever."

Nino stepped out on the terrace. "Kiara, I think your lasagna is ready to be taken out." He gave me a nod in greeting.

Kiara quickly rushed back inside, followed by Gemma, who often helped her with cooking for bigger family gatherings. They were the best cooks in the family. Serafina and Fabiano's wife Leona were usually responsible for keeping the kids in check.

"Cake before lunch? What kind of anarchy is this?" I asked, sinking down on one of the empty chairs between Fabiano and Savio.

"Nevio's wish. Anarchy is his middle name," Fina said, rolling her eyes.

"My wish too," Greta said softly.

Fina gave her daughter a patient smile. "Yours too, but we both know you always say yes to Nevio's wishes."

"Not always," Greta said even quieter.

"Too often, mia cara," Remo said, kissing her temple.

Kiara and Gemma came back, both carrying casseroles with steaming lasagna.

"One of them is vegetarian with antipasti and lemon-ricotta, and the other is a more traditional lasagna with pancetta and minced beef," Kiara explained. She and Greta both didn't eat meat, but the rest of us did, even if we'd gotten used to more vegetarian meals since Kiara had married Nino.

"The food is ready! Sit down!" Fina screamed to be heard over the boys' rough swordplay.

Alessio was the first to drop his sword and began trotting over to us. Massimo and Nevio kept clanging swords.

"Nevio!" Remo called.

Nevio's head swiveled around and he lowered his sword. Massimo had already done so and together they rushed over to us. Alessio gave me a smile but like Greta he wasn't an overly touchy-feely kid, at least with most people. Nino touched his shoulder and the boy sank down beside him. Nevio and Massimo followed shortly after and plopped down in the two remaining vacant chairs.

Massimo smiled broadly at me, sweat glistening on his face. He looked more and more like Nino every day.

We finally dug in. Of course, dinner wasn't a quiet affair. Even when it had been only my brothers and me many years ago, that hadn't been the case, but the topics and entertainment had become less explicit and more PG-13.

After dinner, I stepped away to smoke. Remo hated it but I wasn't a kid anymore. Kiara came over after a moment. "How are you? You look happy."

I smiled, lowering my cigarette and blowing the smoke in the other direction. "I am, what about you?"

Kiara's face glowed with happiness. "How could I not be happy being surrounded by family? We miss you."

I gave her a one-armed hug. "I miss you too. But I belong with the racers."

"I know."

Remo stepped up to us. Kiara being the clever woman that she was realized he wanted to talk to me. She excused herself and went over to the girls.

"So how are things going with our Russian princess?"

"She doesn't act like a princess. Smokes like a chimney, and can drink any man twice her size under the table. She's a damn good race driver too."

Dinara and Dima were still mostly on the fringes of camp life but they'd participated in the after-race-party, and Dinara had drank half a bottle of gin by herself without any outward signs of being drunk. I hadn't talked to her since our conversation about my mother even it had cost me plenty of restraint to stay away.

"You sound fascinated," Remo said with his twisted smile.

"I'm wary. I don't need trouble in my races."

"Trouble can bring us money."

"Depends on the kind of trouble. Maybe I should talk to Eden. She might be able to give me important information on Dinara."

Remo's face hardened. "Stay away from Eden. She won't be able to tell you anything of worth about Dinara."

"Because you forbade her to talk? What's your endgame, Remo? Why are we keeping a Pakhan's ex in our brothels? And why does Dinara think her mother is dead?"

Something flickered in Remo's eyes, a hint of realization maybe. I wished he'd share that insight with me. "She talked to you about her mother?"

"She questioned me about the day we killed our mother is more like it. Will her mommy issues come back to bite us in the ass?"

Remo's expression had shut off even more at the mentioning of our mother. He'd hated her with a fiery passion before we'd killed her, and his feelings hadn't improved since then, especially now that he was surrounded by good mothers like Fina, Leona and Kiara.

"If she wants to discuss her mommy issues, send her to me."

That was the last thing I wanted to do before I knew what was going on. If Dinara wanted to save her mother and worse avenge her, she'd be in more danger than she could ever anticipate. Maybe a reasonable Capo would hesitate to hurt a Pakhan's daughter, but Remo had never shied back from insane maneuvers. After all, he'd kidnapped the niece of the Outfit's Capo and even made her fall in love with him.

Even if Dinara had ulterior motives for joining the races and for seeking my closeness, I didn't want her to get hurt. I loved Remo, but I didn't agree with everything he did, and many of his actions had me worried, especially in the past.

FOUR

Adamo

C.J. SMILED BRIGHTLY WHEN SHE OPENED THE DOOR AND embraced me. "I missed you." She lived a thirty-minute-drive from the mansion and after the festivities were over, I headed over to her. We hadn't seen each other in four weeks, which was a long time. I usually tried to return to Vegas every other week for at least a night or two.

"I missed you too," I said and kissed her lips. She was dressed in a sexy purple negligee that left little to my imagination and her brown hair hung in smooth curls down her shoulders. We both knew what our companionship was about after all. Why try to be coy about it? Despite what Savio thought, I wasn't in love with C.J. but I enjoyed her company and the sex even more, and it was the same for her. "How are things at work?"

"Rough," she said. "The last few days were a real shitshow. Only asshole customers. At least, I used the time while I got them off to think about my own bar."

She took my hand and led me into the small living room of her apartment. It was a comfy but tiny place because C.J. saved most of her money to open her own business one day. I'd suggested to help her but she didn't want to accept money from anyone else. She was close to having enough money soon, and I was glad when she'd finally stop sucking off assholes for cash. C.J.'s beginning in the business was one of the topics Remo and I had the most fights about.

C.J. was ten years older than me. She and the other girls I'd fucked on occasion had all been older than me. Dinara was the first girl around my age that caught my interest in a long time, another point that made her all the more fascinating. I followed C.J. toward her small kitchenette and accepted the glass of red wine she held out to me. But I was distracted by my thoughts about Dinara, and judging by C.J.'s erect nipples, she was distracted by the very thing I was here for. She stepped closer, taking another sip of her wine before she peered up at me with a seductive smile. I set down my glass and kissed her, waiting for my lust to banish any thought of Dinara.

I put even more passion into our kiss, answering to C.J.'s need. She rubbed herself against me and I slipped my hand under her gown, finding her sopping wet. "It's been a really shitty week. All I could think about was this," C.J. admitted in a whisper. I knew she hadn't been with any guys except for the johns for work in the time since we'd started fucking. She'd always assured me it was because her job didn't allow for other relationships with men but sometimes, I worried it was more than that. I fingered C.J. until she exploded after only a minute. C.J. sank down on her knees and began sucking me deeply into her mouth until my balls hit her chin. I groaned, my eyes fluttering shut. Over the years, I'd been with several girls, still far less than my brothers, but enough to know that C.J.'s skills were out of this world. An image of Dinara's challenging smile popped up uninvited. I shoved it away. That wasn't fair toward C.J.

I still remembered my first time with C.J. vividly. I'd been attracted to her from the start but after the thing with my first girlfriend Harper who'd cheated on me and made fun of my lacking sexual skills, I had been worried about being with anyone again. Of course, I couldn't really talk to anyone about my issues. My brothers wouldn't have understood. They'd all lost their virginity at a younger age and fucked their way through enough women to practice when they were my age. I didn't really want to fuck random girls but I also didn't want to risk another relationship so I was at an impasse.

C.J. had noticed how I'd constantly checked her out. Eventually I'd asked her if we could spend some time together. At first, we'd only talked but eventually I just wanted more. C.J. was sexy, and she was safe, but I didn't want to use her. So I'd insisted she showed me how to get a girl off and that's all we did the first few weeks until we finally fucked. The first few months I certainly wasn't a good fuck and C.J. probably only enjoyed half of the time we spent together but I was a quick learner and determined to give her a good time.

I kept my eyes on C.J. as she sucked me off, worried I'd see another face again if I closed my eyes or looked away. After I came in her mouth, she straightened and ran her hands through my hair, her expression full of need. We talked and fucked. That's how it had always been. We weren't exclusive but we shared a special bond. Maybe it was this bond that made me wonder if I could keep up doing this with Dinara thrown in the mix. There was nothing between Dinara and me, except for rivalry, fascination and taunting, but I wanted more, and I had a feeling she wasn't completely turned off by the idea.

"Is something the matter?" C.J. asked carefully. She was sexy and she'd had a hard week. So had I. We both needed this. She smelled of her vanilla shower gel, not something Dinara would use. "I'm fine." I kissed her again and as before she answered with passion and need. We fumbled our way to her couch, already shedding the rest of our clothes on the way.

I tangled my hand in her hair and gently pulled back, considering to stop this after all. Her gaze snapped up, and her lips pulled into a needy smile. Fuck. I gripped her arms and shoved her onto the sofa.

To this day C.J. was the best lay I'd ever had, and much more than that, but these last few weeks all of my fantasies had revolved around a redhead. I knelt before her and raised her heels onto my shoulders before I plunged into her. As always when we met after a long time, we fucked all night until we were spent. That's when we started talking about everything that bothered us, but this time I had a more important topic to discuss than race car driving.

"What do you know about Eden?"

C.J. lifted her head from my shoulder, looking surprised. "Eden? Why are you interested in her?"

"I'm interested in her backstory. Remo won't share details with me but I have a feeling something important happened. It might be useful for our fight against the Bratva."

Lying to C.J. wasn't something I enjoyed doing, and usually I just skidded around topics she wasn't allowed to know anything about.

C.J. sat up slowly, looking thoughtful. "Most of the other girls and I kept our distance to Eden. In the beginning because your brother ordered us to ignore her and then later because she really preferred to be on her own. I haven't worked in the same place as her in a while. I think she's now stationed in a dingy little club outside of Vegas."

"You girls talk. Did you never speculate about the whys for her special treatment?"

"Donna was one of the few girls who were there when Eden first appeared in Vegas. She always said that Eden pissed off Remo majorly."

That's what I'd gathered. No new information really.

C.J. smiled apologetically. "Sorry. I wish I could help you. Maybe you should talk to Donna. She's waiting tables in the Red Lantern if you want to go looking for her."

Talking to C.J. was one thing but going around questioning other prostitutes about Eden would definitely make Remo furious. The more I pissed him off now, the less likely he'd listen to me if I put in a good word for Dinara in case she ever showed up in Vegas to do whatever she had in mind.

The next day, I decided to give Remo another try. I joined my brothers in our gym in an abandoned casino for fight training. Savio had been surprised when I'd asked him if I could drive with him. Nino and Remo were already inside the fighting cage when Savio and I entered the vast hall.

Most people who stepped into our gym, but few were allowed, couldn't stop staring at the chandelier dangling from the ceiling above the fighting cage. Remo and Nino stopped fighting when they noticed us. Savio and I strolled over to the cage. Fabiano was waiting for his turn and kept himself busy doing bench-presses.

He sat up. "Hey stranger."

I gave him a short wave. Nino was already climbing out of the cage, making room for Remo's next opponent. Fabiano rose from the bench but I gripped his shoulder.

"It's my turn," I said. He cocked an eyebrow then shrugged and sank back down. "Knock yourself out. Though, Remo's going to do that."

"That's right," Savio agreed, chuckling.

I didn't react. I wanted answers, and Remo had avoided giving them to me. In the past we'd shared some of our most honest conversation in the fighting cage. I hoped it would be the same today.

Remo's smile widened knowingly when I stepped into the fighting cage. It was difficult to trick Remo into doing anything. He was a trickster himself. But I wouldn't back down this time. I was sick of fishing around in the dark.

"That look in your eyes is a good start for a fight," Remo said.

I didn't bother taping my hands, raising them instead. "You ready to fight?"

"Always."

I was usually a cautious fighter, keeping my defenses up a long time and not one for risky moves, but today I immediately went into attack mode. Remo took me up on my offer and our next few hits bounced off our respective defenses before Remo landed two hard punches in my stomach and one in my kidneys. Then I got my first hit in. I raced more than I fought and Remo was still the best fighter because he made sure to be in the fighting cage as often as possible and not just for training. He fought against real opponents for money. If I wanted to keep this fight going long enough for answers, I needed to bring my A-game.

Ten minutes later, both he and I were covered in sweat and blood. I was bleeding from a cut in my lower lip and Remo from one in his eyebrow where I'd opened up part of his scar marring one side of his face. We did a water break, leaning against the mesh of the cage beside each other.

"Ask," Remo muttered between gulps of water.

"Why does Dinara think her mother's dead?"

"Rest is over," he declared and I barely had time to put away my bottle before he sent a jab toward my face but I dodged the hit.

"Because he thinks he can protect her," Remo grunted as he avoided my upper cut.

"Protect her from what?"

"From herself, I assume." Remo sent me a wry smile. "But we both know protecting someone from themselves is fucking impossible, right?"

I hopped out of his arm's length. Remo had tried to save me from my drug abuse and wrong friends when I was younger. He'd only succeeded when he'd sent me off to New York, *away from his protection*. Sometimes the risk of falling without a safety net was necessary, that's what Remo had learned from this experience.

"For fuck's sake, why can't you tell me what the fuck is going on?" I growled, sending a hard jab toward his face which he blocked.

Remo tilted his head with a dark smile. "There's something going on between you and Dinara."

I glowered. Remo always knew more than he should and he enjoyed it. "It's none of your business but there's absolutely nothing going on."

Yet. Not that I hadn't imagined it...

"Some people might disagree with you. After all, Dinara is part of the Bratva through her family. You're fraternizing with the enemy."

"Like I said there's nothing going on, and don't play holier than thou. Fina used to be the enemy too and now she's your wife."

Remo's smile became more dangerous. "You're right. But I was the one who was pulling the strings when I met her. Make sure you are too."

"It would help if you could tell me what I'm up against. Is Dinara out for revenge?"

"Once she finds out the truth, definitely."

I grimaced. "What the fuck did you and Grigory do? I should tell Dinara that her mother is alive."

"Yes, you should."

I paused, narrowing my eyes. "What's your endgame, Remo? I don't want Dinara to get hurt."

Remo shook his head. "You have a complicated taste in women."

"That's something we have in common."

Remo chuckled. "Go tell her and see how she reacts."

"I don't like this. I don't want Dinara to become a pawn in your war with Grigory."

Remo didn't say anything.

I considered punching his face but he probably anticipated the move. Instead I gave him a smile in turn. "This fight is over. Let Fabiano have a go at you. I need to return to camp."

Remo leaned against the corner of the cage, his eyes never leaving me. "I'm not the villain here, Adamo. My intentions are pure for not telling you."

I couldn't help but laugh as I climbed out and Fabiano took my place in the cage instead. "The word pure and you are at odds."

Nino came toward me before I could leave the gym. "You should join us at the pool in the afternoon. We'll have a barbecue and enjoy the good weather."

I shook my head. "No thanks, I've had enough of Remo's mind games."

"He's not the only one at fault. Whenever you're here, you're looking for a topic to fight over."

"I don't have to look. Remo and I disagree on many things."

"He and I do too, but you only focus on your disagreements and try to ignore the good. Remo loves you and always does what he thinks is best for you."

"I really need to return to camp now. The next race is in only a week. I have plenty of things to set up."

Nino nodded and allowed me to pass. I felt a pang when I left. But it wasn't only because of Remo. The next race was the start of a number of races in short succession, all of them without a day for rest between them. I had plenty to organize and make sure my car was in top condition.

And I was eager to see Dinara again.

FIVE

Adamo

THE FIRST TRAILERS AND TENTS CAME INTO VIEW IN THE distance, and I couldn't help but smile. Living the nomad life wasn't very comfortable, especially the sanitary options sometimes left a lot to be desired. But we preferred to be among ourselves instead of staying in motels. Of course, some racers opted for the comfort of nearby hotels and only joined us the night before a race, especially those who were sponsored by their rich parents and didn't do this for the money. Luckily there weren't many of them. With the upcoming seven races in only one week, everyone would have to camp or sleep in their car.

I parked my car at the edge of camp and got out. Crank's rustic trailer was in the center with everyone else's makeshift homes set up around it. He was the go-to guy when I wasn't there and his trailer was often our business home-base.

It was late in the afternoon and tomorrow was the last day to get everything in order before our seven-day-race, especially drill the rules into the participants. I already knew a few people I'd have additional chats with to make sure they really got the message.

A fire burned in the center in preparation for nightfall and the scent of meat smokers and barbecues filled the air. I set up my tent, a small two-person thing that I attached to my car. I preferred to keep a close eye on my BMW. Sometimes strange accidents occurred.

"How was Vegas?" Dinara asked close behind me, just when I'd zipped the tent up. I turned around to find her standing very close with her arms crossed over a cut-off AC/DC T-shirt, revealing that tantalizing piercing again. It was a tiny red and golden egg. For once Dinara wasn't in boots but flip-flops, revealing dark-red painted nails. "And what happened to your face?"

My lip was slightly swollen from Remo's punch. "A friendly grapple with my brother. And Vegas is the same it always is. Loud, flashy and dirty," I said, tearing my eyes away from her body and meeting her knowing gaze. Dinara seemed perceptive, but even if she weren't, she would have noticed me checking her out by now. It was really difficult not to do so. Her confidence alone drew me in.

Dinara's brows rose as she leaned against my car and took a sip from a Styrofoam cup. "Someone's holding a grudge against his hometown."

I glared off into the distance. She held out the cup to me. "You look like you need it more than I do. Why did you fight with your brother?"

I took it without asking what it was and swallowed a big gulp. The bitter burn of Vodka bloomed in my mouth and traveled down my throat. I hated the stuff. I'd never understood the reason for drinking it pure. Dinara's lips twitched as if she knew what I was thinking. "Dima brewed it himself."

I handed the cup back to her, ignoring her previous question. "You sure it's safe to consume?" My eyes scanned the circuit for her buzz-headed shadow, and of course, I found him beside his car, watching us.

"You don't seem like someone who shies back from taking risks."

"I'm not. I'd just rather not die from consuming homemade Vodka. There are far more interesting ways to leave this planet."

She took a sip before her lips pulled into a teasing smile. "Like dying in a car race or being killed by an enemy bullet?"

"Something like that, yes."

I reached into the open passenger window and pulled out a clean T-shirt. I'd been wearing this one on the drive from Vegas and while setting up a tent in the burning afternoon sun. I dragged my sweaty shirt over my head and tossed it on the hood beside Dinara. She eyed it briefly but then her gaze moved on to me, definitely checking me out. Her eyes lingered on my abs before she scanned the scars on my body, ending at my marred Camorra tattoo.

"Seems like you aren't a stranger to dancing with death."

I shrugged. I didn't want to talk about the time when most of these scars came to be. I put on a clean white shirt and leaned beside Dinara. Some of the pit girls who shared tents with their respective racer boyfriends or affairs gave us curious looks. A few of them had tried to get it on with me but I hadn't taken them up on their advances. Dinara followed my gaze. "Got your eye on one of them?"

I chuckled. "No. I don't mix business and pleasure."

Dinara tilted her head. "What an un-Falcone-like thing to do. Why limit yourself when you make the rules? You are kings in your territory."

"Remo is king. The rest of us are his vassals." I could have kicked myself at the note of bitterness in my voice, making me sound like a fucking sulking teenager, but I was royally pissed at Remo for keeping Dinara's past a secret from me.

"You are many things but not a vassal. Sounds like you have ambitions to become a regicide to grab the crown for yourself."

Fury raced through my veins at the accusation. Even when Remo sometimes drove me up the wall, he was my Capo and my brother. I loved him and would rather chop myself to pieces before betraying him like that. I masked my first reaction, realizing it gave me the chance to figure out Dinara's true intentions. If I left the door open to me betraying Remo, she might see me as an alley to confide in her possible revenge plans. I stared off toward the horizon, leaving the question hanging between us. Dinara regarded me closely but her expression was impossible to read.

"Did you give your brothers a report about the Bratva princess while you were in Vegas?" she asked after almost a minute of silence. More and more people were gathering around the firepit, sitting down on logs arranged around it, and the aroma of smoked ribs now drifted unmistakably into my nose. Music was turned up, a colorful mix of hits from the last few years because tastes varied greatly in the group.

"There isn't much to report, is there?"

She shrugged and fixed me with a look as if she didn't believe me.

"I don't know why you're here. You're a mystery and so are your reasons for seeking my closeness."

"Someone's overconfident. Maybe I just want to enjoy the thrill of racing."

"Big coincidence that you're joining the racing camp that's in the territory of the Camorra. You have history with us and so does your father."

"What do you know about my history with the Camorra?" she whispered harshly. For the first time a crack in her beautiful mask showed. She hadn't been overly emotional so far.

I was taken aback by her outburst but I kept my cool. I shrugged. "I know that your mother works as a whore in one of our brothels."

Dinara froze, slowly lowering the cup from her lips. Blatant disbelief played across her face. "My mother's dead." Her voice sounded…terrified and elated at once.

"No, she's not. She is alive and in Las Vegas, working for us."

Dinara tore her gaze away, frowning. She emptied the cup and set it down on the hood. I wished she would allow me to see her eyes but she kept them carefully turned away, not willing to let me see her emotions, but the rest of her body gave me an inkling of her turmoil. Her hands shook when she reached into her pocket and took out a joint. She lit it and took a deep, shaky breath. "You sure?"

The familiar sweet aroma of marihuana filtered into my nose and a deep craving settled in my body. I'd given up on harder drugs during my time in New York after Luca broke a few of my ribs when he found me drugged, but giving up joints was harder, especially because many people smoked them at the after-race parties and barbecues.

Maybe I should have backtracked, but Remo wanted me to tell her for whatever insane reason. Was I risking his life or Dinara's by telling her? But it was too late to back down now.

"Yes. I've met her several times over the years." That was an exaggeration. I'd never actually talked to her, only seen her in passing. I didn't remember much about her, not even if she'd been as beautiful as her daughter. She was a hazy shadow I couldn't focus on.

"Fucked her too if she's one of your whores?"

I grimaced. "No."

Dinara rolled her eyes. "Don't play indignant. I know how things work. Mobsters often seek the services of whores and many of them even lose their V-card to one. I'm familiar with the business. The Bratva and the Italian mob aren't that different when you break it down." The way she said Bratva, I almost developed an appreciation for the word.

"I didn't fuck your mother, Dinara. I'm not in the habit of sleeping with every available pussy."

I couldn't speak for my brothers though. Remo had definitely fucked her in the past. I wasn't sure about Nino and Savio, but the latter had dipped his cock into anything before Gemma tied him down.

Dinara nodded but didn't say anything. She looked upset. Dima had pushed away from his car and was slowly coming closer. A true protector. I wanted to kick his stupid Bratva ass. His expression wasn't that of a bodyguard, and not a brotherly friend either.

She jerked to her feet and dropped the joint before stomping on it. I felt a pang I tried to ignore.

"I need to leave the camp and return to Chicago."

I shook my head and stood as well. "Tomorrow evening the first race of the seven-day circuit starts. You need to be present in the afternoon to set up everything. If you miss the first race in the circuit, you can't join the race at a later point. Every race builds up on the previous. And if you miss seven races, your chances of staying in camp are close to nil." I didn't want Dinara to disappear so soon. I wanted to keep her close, to find out more about her history, and her.

"I'll be back in time," she clipped and started to move away.

I touched her arm. "We're almost 1400 miles away from Chicago."

She gave me a sardonic smile over her shoulder. "Don't worry. I won't miss tomorrow's race. We aren't done yet, Adamo."

With that, she walked away and I was left to stare at her back, wondering if her last words were warning or promise.

Dinara

Dima hurried toward me. "What's—"

"I need a private jet from Salt Lake City in thirty minutes. Set everything up."

Dima stared at me. He opened his mouth but I wasn't in the mood to talk.

"I don't have time for questions. Get a jet. We need to leave now. We're taking my car."

Dima didn't try to extract more information from me. Instead he picked up his mobile and pulled a few strings with contacts before he gave a terse nod. "Done."

We settled in my car, and I hit the gas. We'd have to hurry if we wanted to reach the small private airport in time. It sat right outside of Salt Lake City.

It was half-past five, so if everything went to plan, we'd board the jet around six.

"What's going on Dinara? Are you in danger? Did anything Falcone say upset you?"

Upset didn't even begin to cover my feelings about the news Adamo had given me. My mother was alive. For years, I'd thought she was dead. Everyone had led me to believe she was.

My fingers around the steering wheel tightened even more until it hurt. I wasn't in the mood to talk now. My head was a mess full of whirring thoughts, a thunderstorm slowly building up and about to unleash its destructive power. Deep inside of me, my dark craving began its enticing chant, a siren's call I'd resisted for ten months now.

Dima gave up on talking to me for the rest of the drive and when we pulled up at the airport with only five minutes to spare before the scheduled departure, I breathed a sigh of relief. After Dima and I had boarded the private jet and settled down on seats facing each other, the stewardess served us drinks and snacks. "This could be a bumpy ride. A thunderstorm is brewing over Chicago."

I gave her a quick smile. "That's perfect." Obviously set aback by my reply, she excused herself. I took the glass, and sipped at my Gin & Tonic while the plane began moving and soon we were air-bound.

Dima never took his eyes off me. "Won't you tell me what's wrong?"

"Did you know about my mother?"

If Dima knew what I meant, he hid it well. His blond brows pulled together. "What about her?"

The problem was Dima was my father's man, would always be. He'd sometimes bent the rules for me but ultimately, he'd never betray my father outright.

"That she's still alive, not dead like my father said."

Dima shook his head. "How do you know? Did Adamo put that idea into your head?"

I leaned forward, narrowing my eyes. Something in his voice was off. Our close bond made keeping secrets from each other a difficult endeavor. "Did you know? Why would Adamo lie about something like that?"

"Because he and his brothers are masters of manipulation. They are the enemy, even if you get cozy with Adamo."

"I'm not getting cozy with anyone," I gritted out, but I couldn't deny the mutual attraction between Adamo and me. I'd noticed the way he checked me out, and I'd ogled him more than once too. "What could they gain from making me believe my mother's alive, hmm?"

Dima leaned back in his chair, his gaze moving to the window. Was he buying time? A subtle tension had entered his body, but I wasn't sure if it was because he knew more about my mother or because he was jealous of Adamo. "Maybe they hope you'll come to Vegas to find her. It could be a trap to get you in their hands. It wouldn't be the first time that Remo Falcone kidnapped a high-ranking woman."

"If he wanted to kidnap me, he could ask Adamo to do it. And I doubt Adamo's the only racer with close ties to the Camorra. He wouldn't have to lure me to Vegas to get his hands on me."

Dima's mouth tightened and he avoided looking my way. I rose from my chair and sank down beside him. His gaze met mine. "Dima," I said softly, imploringly, and put my hand over his that was resting on the armrest. "*If you know, you have to tell me. I need to know. You know I do.*"

Dima's face, which was usually all hard lines, like a piece of cubism art, softened. "Dinara." The way he said my name reminded me of our past. He turned his hand and closed his fingers around my hand. I swallowed. I didn't want to use Dima's feelings, or whatever feelings he tried to convince himself of having, to get what I want, but this truth could change everything. I needed to know.

"*Tell me,*" I implored.

He leaned a bit closer as if to kiss me. I tensed. I didn't want to have to push him away. I didn't have to. Dima scanned my body and retracted a few inches. His fingers around mine loosened and his smile turned pained. "*What are you going to do with the truth?*"

"*The same I've always wanted, get closure.*"

"*And revenge,*" Dima said quietly. "*I'm not sure you'll find closure on the path you're on.*"

Revenge was daily business in our circles. Every man lived and breathed for revenge if they'd been wronged, but women were supposed to let others handle their problems like helpless damsels in distress.

"*Dima.*"

My path was my business. I'd walk it alone if I had to. Dima let his head fall back. "*She's alive. Falcone told you the truth.*"

"*Why did you lie to me?*" I asked, hurt. Dima was my closest confidante. We'd shared everything, or at least I'd thought so.

Dima tilted his head. "*Because your father ordered me to lie to you and because I wanted to protect you.*"

I snatched my hand away. "*I don't need protection from the truth!*" I got up, unable to sit still. I began pacing the aisle, my pulse pounding. A tiny part of me had remained doubtful after Adamo's words, but now the truth glared brightly at me. It was my turn to accept it and decide how to proceed. "*It's my right to decide what to do with the truth. My fucking right.*"

Dima nodded. "*Your father might not agree. He'll be furious if he finds out I told you.*"

"*You didn't tell me. Adamo did.*"

Dima let out a bitter laugh. "*Your new hero.*"

I glared and sank down on the seat. "*Adamo's not the hero in this story. Nor are you or my father. I'll be the hero in my story.*"

I turned my gaze to the window, admiring the grim sky that matched my emotions tragically. Soon the clouds thickened and rain pestered the plane. I ran my palms up and down my thighs, lingering on familiar ridges high up. The siren's call now rang in my blood. My dark craving was a strong opponent, my greatest foe, but also balm and friend in my hardest hours. He made the unbearable bearable, if only for a few hours.

"You are stronger than it," Dima said into the silence.

He knew my body language too well. I gave a terse nod. "*I'm stronger than you and my father think.*"

Thirty minutes before the estimated landing time, I grabbed the bag with my Chicago clothes and went to the bathroom to change. This had become habit, letting go of my style and freedom when I returned home, and becoming the girl my father wanted and needed me to be.

A black limousine was waiting for us when we landed on a Bratva-affiliated airport outside of Chicago. I got in without a word and let the ride pass in silence as well. I'd sent Dad a message shortly after we'd boarded the plane, announcing my arrival. Judging by his lack of surprise, Dima had informed him before I could.

We didn't enter Chicago. Dad had bought four acres of land about twenty miles outside of Chicago because the home he had in mind needed space. The gilded gates slid open as we approached them. A long driveaway with grounds reminiscent of Versailles led up to a splendid white and blue mansion. It had taken almost two years to build this smaller version of Catherine The Great's Palace, which Dad and I had visited in Saint Petersburg many times.

I wondered if it gave Dad a sense of home living in a mansion like this or if it only reminded him of what he was missing. Sometimes it was harder to live with a lesser version of what we missed than to lose it altogether.

The limousine parked at the base of the majestic staircase leading up to the front door where Dad was already waiting for me in his usual dark suit. A member of the staff opened the door for me and I slid out of the car. It always took a few seconds to find my balance on my champagne-colored pumps after days or weeks of living in boots. I smoothed down the silk and cashmere dress that matched my heels and headed toward Dad. Dima stayed back, but the hard look Dad sent him concerned me.

Dad smiled but it was strained, as if his smile was forced onto his face by invisible strings. Dima must have warned him about what I knew. I wanted to resent Dima for being my father's spy as much as my confidante. I dreaded the day he'd have to choose between us and I'd lose him for good. Maybe that was another reason why I'd ended things between us.

The moment I arrived before him, Dad pulled me into a hug. I sank against his tall, strong form, smelling his familiar aftershave. He pulled back with my cheeks cupped between his big hands and pressed a gentle kiss to each of my cheeks. "*You look good, Katinka.*"

I didn't smile, only stared up into Dad's pale blue eyes. He was only in his late forties, one of the younger Pakhans, and his blond hair still hid the gray streaks well.

"*Dinara,*" I corrected, even though I knew he wouldn't use my second name. When I'd stopped using my first name, Ekaterina, named after Ekaterina the Great, another reason why Dad had chosen to build her palace, he had been heart-broken, and continued to call me by the nickname Katinka. I rarely corrected him anymore, nor did I wear the clothes I preferred when I was around him.

I always chose dresses or skirts in light colors, because he loved seeing me like that. Ekaterina meant pure after all and he wanted to see me in the light, not stumbling into the darkness that lingered deep inside of me. He wrapped an arm around my shoulders and led me inside the splendid mirror-walled foyers with its white and gold décor.

"*Where are Jurij and Artur?*"

"*They are already asleep, and so is Galina.*"

Dad always tried to keep his young wife and my half-brothers out of sight, as if he worried his new family would upset me. I gave him an exasperated look. He needed to stop thinking I needed to be put on a pedestal. I'd been happy when he'd married, and Galina had given him heirs. That meant he wouldn't hover as much anymore and I'd have more freedoms.

"*Are you hungry?*" he asked.

I nodded. Except for vodka and gin, I hadn't consumed anything yet, and it was starting to show in the fuzziness in my brain. Dad snapped his fingers and at once a member of the staff who'd been lurking in the background rushed off toward the kitchen. "*Let's go to my office.*"

Calling the vast room where he worked an office was a mockery. Its sheer size awed most people, and some families of four or five lived in apartments that were much smaller. The gold and white décor carried on, but the furniture was darker. A reddish wood dominated everything, and Dad's desk was the size of a small queen-size bed. We settled on the plush gold and blue sofa that he'd bought from a collector and which originated from the 18th century: Catherine the Great's time. Dad was a man with one foot firmly set in the past and one in the future, maybe that made him so well respected among his men.

A knock sounded and our cook entered with a tray of fresh khachapuri, baked bread in the shape of an almond with cheese and egg filling. She carried it over to us and carefully set it down on the table in front of us before she disappeared again. I reached for a khachapuri, wincing as it burned my fingertips but too greedy for the delicacy of Dad's childhood. The runny egg yolk spread on my tongue, mingling with the saltiness of the cheese and comforting denseness of the dough. Dad had spent the first few years of his life in the Caucasus. I swallowed the first bite then put the bread back down on the plate.

I was done postponing the inevitable, so I met Dad's gaze.

"*Why did you lie?*"

A muscle in Dad's cheek twitched, a sign of his displeasure. Many people would have had reason to cower at this sign of danger, but I wasn't one of them. "*Dima wasn't supposed to tell you.*"

"He didn't. Adamo Falcone did, and then I didn't leave Dima a choice but to admit he knew the truth. You know I can be convincing if I put my mind to it."

Dad chuckled. "Oh, I know. You have the stubbornness and cunning of a great empress."

I sighed. "Why did you lie? You made me believe she was dead. All these years."

"It was for the best. I wanted to protect you."

"That's bullshit!"

Dad's eyes flashed dangerously. "Not that tone around me." He hated when I cursed, and maybe even more when I spoke in English.

I took a deep breath. "Sorry."

"The truth doesn't matter, because what I said is as good as true. She's dead to us, erased from our lives, and out of our reach in Camorra territory."

"Nothing is out of your reach, Dad, if you really want it." He'd dragged his wife Galina out of the furthest corner of the Caucasus, a small village where her parents had hidden her away from my father, despite it being under the control of the enemy.

He shook his head with a rough laugh. "*I'm a businessman and I've survived many attacks to my life, only because I'm cautious. Going to war with Remo Falcone isn't wise. Breaching his territory for a dead woman is insanity.*"

"She's not dead," I whispered harshly.

He cupped my hands. "*She is to me, and she should be to you too. Forget she exists. She's the past and we've left it behind us, haven't we, Katinka?*"

Maybe he had, maybe he *could*. But I saw her in my dreams almost every night, a ghost from the past. I had to see her again, face to face, even if it meant offending Remo Falcone and risking war with the Camorra.

SIX

Dinara

We were cutting it closer than I liked but Dad had insisted I stayed until the morning to grab a few hours of sleep before I took the private jet back to Salt Lake City. He'd tried to convince me to stay altogether. He knew I was taking part in the races and maybe even why, but he had trouble caging me in. Not because he didn't have the means to do so, but because he worried what I'd do without my freedom and a purpose. He trusted I'd eventually return home, not able to go through with my goal.

It was almost 1 p.m. when Dima and I raced back toward camp. Dima hung in his seat. The right side of his face was swollen and blue, and those were only the marks I could see. Dad had him beaten for admitting to the truth about my mother. Guilt burned a fiery path through my insides. "Next time you don't come back with me."

"That'll only postpone my punishment."

"Then don't do things that'll get you punished for me. Maybe it would be best if you didn't follow me on this path anymore. Stay away before my father punishes you worse."

His expression was wounded. "I'll protect you, Dinara. It's my job, my desire."

I sighed. We'd had that conversation before when I'd first decided to join Adamo's races. Dima could be almost as stubborn as I.

We arrived at the camp. Most racers were busy tinkering on their cars, some of which were already set up in a sort of starting formation: ten rows of three cars each.

Last time Dima and I had to start in the last row because we were newbies but due to our good result in the last race, the first race of this circuit, we were bumped up into one of the middle rows. I hadn't bothered reading up on the point system and rules in detail. I always wanted to be first, and for that, I needed to drive fast and risk everything. Easy peasy.

Adamo's car was in the first row, naturally, together with a completely black car I'd butted heads with in the last race. Its owner was an obnoxious, tall rich kid from the suburbs of San Francisco.

I parked my car next to Crank's trailer to ask for my exact position before I weaved into the grid. Dima heaved himself out of the passenger seat, clutching his left side with a groan.

"Are you sure you can race?" I asked worriedly.

"I won't leave your side."

"Looking like you do, I doubt you can keep up with the top drivers today. Seeing as tonight's rest stop and tomorrow's starting point is different for every car, depending on the distance they put behind them in the ten hours of driving, you probably won't get the chance to stay near Dinara," Adamo explained as he stepped down the stairs from the trailer. His dark eyes scanned Dima from head to toe, assessing every injury. Judging by the scars on his body, he could probably evaluate Dima's injuries better than I did.

"I'm fine," Dima gritted out, straightening fully. He and Adamo were the same height, too fucking tall for me. Even my biker boots with their thick soles didn't change the fact that I had to crane my head back. That was the only reason why I missed my high heels.

Adamo shrugged as if he didn't care either way. "Even if you are miles away from Dinara when the race ends, you won't move your car another fucking inch. You hit the brakes at exactly four a.m. like all of us do, got it? And don't try to cheat. We track everyone."

Dima showed his teeth in a dangerous smile. "You're too keen to get Dinara on her own, Falcone. Why is that, I wonder?"

"For no reason that requires your bodyguard services," Adamo said with a hard smile.

I glanced between them. "I don't have time for your bullshit. I have a race to win. What's my position in the grid?"

Adamo motioned inside the trailer. "Crank's got the list. You've got to ask him."

"Go ahead," I told Dima who grudgingly stepped into the trailer but before he disappeared inside, he growled. *"I don't like the way he looks at you. One day I'm going to burn his fucking eyes out."*

I gave him a hard look, and finally he disappeared.

"What did he say? It didn't sound very nice," Adamo said with a hint of amusement. He crossed his arms, accentuating the muscles in them. What maddened me even more than my body's reaction to his assets was the fact that I wasn't sure if Adamo was trying to tease them out of me on purpose.

"Maybe you should consider learning Russian. It's always a good idea to know the tongue of your enemy."

Adamo regarded me in a way that turned my body temperature up by several degrees, an experience I wasn't sure I liked. "Are you an enemy, Dinara?"

I smiled. "That depends on the situation, I suppose."

Adamo chuckled then he shrugged. "We have many enemies. I can't learn all of their languages. Or do you speak French and Italian?"

My smile widened. "Of course. I had tutors who taught me French, English, and Italian, and at home, I spoke Russian."

"Impressive," Adamo admitted. "I only speak Italian and English, but my brother Nino is a walking dictionary."

I distantly remembered the guy with the cold gray eyes, a hazy image from the past, but hard to forget like so many other images from that time. "My French teacher was never really happy with my pronunciation, but I speak and understand it fluently even if I don't sound like a Parisienne lady."

"You don't look like one either."

I raised an eyebrow. "Got a problem with my looks?"

Adamo's eyes trailed the length of me, again lingering on my belly piercing. I'd noticed it before. Maybe he wondered if I had more of them hidden beneath my clothes. I had."Absolutely not. Your looks are more than okay in my book."

"Thanks. That's the kind of approval I needed to feel valued," I said sarcastically, but I had to admit I got a sick kick every time Adamo checked me out. I didn't consider myself as ordinarily beautiful. My appearance with my red hair, freckles, and high cheekbones was too edgy for that.

Dima chose that moment to return. His eyes narrowed to slits as he stepped between Adamo and me. "I got our positions. We should start to prepare everything."

"Mechanics will check if your cars abide by the rules and attach a tracker to your cockpit to make sure you can be punished or disqualified if you drive longer than allowed," Adamo said, giving Dima a meaningful look, before he stalked away.

Dima glared at his back. *"We're next to each other in the starting formation. We should make sure to stay close together, even if one of us is faster than the other."*

I snorted. *"No way, Dima. I'm sorry but I need to be among the first so I can stay close to Adamo. I need more opportunities to extract information from him."*

Dima leaned closer, searching my eyes. "Is this really only about extracting information? I'm not blind."

"Tend to your wounds, or ask someone from the medical team for help. I need to prepare my car."

I walked away. I had never been confronted with Dima's jealousy. He hadn't made a big deal when I'd ended our relationship, nor had he ever tried to win me back. Maybe he'd hoped I'd eventually return to him and now he saw his chances dwindling. I wasn't sure but I hoped he'd get a grip soon. I needed to focus on my plan. I didn't have time to deal with a crazy ex-boyfriend.

Weaving my Toyota through the parked cars and the mechanics, racers and pit girls scattering around them took almost fifteen minutes.

I slammed my palm down on my horn so often that my hand hurt, but eventually I found the marked position. My car was in prime condition so I didn't need to look it over again, and other than some racers I didn't have a team of mechanics. Dima could repair almost anything and I was pretty capable as well.

Instead of wasting time on preparations, I leaned against my car and watched the busy crowd, soaking in their excitement and nervous energy. I'd only seen another female driver but she'd been in the last row. What a shame. More girls needed to trust themselves to play with the big boys. This wasn't a sport that required muscles, only daring and cleverness, and that's something women didn't lack in comparison to men.

Beside me, a guy who looked Mexican leaned against his car. His body was covered with tattoos and he wore a black wifebeater to show them and his muscles off. Like Dima, his hair was in a buzz-cut, but his was dark. He flashed me a grin when he caught me looking. I didn't return the gesture, only nodded. I wondered if the Falcones tolerated gang members or members of a cartel to race as well. They seemed pretty certain in their power over the west. I wasn't here to make friends, and even less to flirt with random guys.

Adamo headed for me and leaned beside me. The guy lost his interest in me at once. "You ready?"

"Always," I replied. "What I'm wondering is how the whole toilet-break business works. Ten hours is a long time."

Adamo gave me a meaningful look.

I scoffed. "Don't tell me there are no official toilet breaks."

"There aren't. You have to decide if you want to lose valuable minutes to relieve yourself."

"Unlike you, I can't pee into a bottle."

"Trust me, even for guys it's not easy to drive and pee into a bottle."

I couldn't help but laugh trying to imagine it, but then my mind drifted off, only conjuring up images of Adamo's naked body. Not a good direction to take before a race. "So you really pee into a bottle?"

Adamo grinned. Whenever he did, he looked more like the dark surfer-boy and not the deadly Falcone brother. I wasn't sure which side of him drew me in more. "Usually I allow myself one toilet break per race, at least in the first five races. The last two races, however…" He chuckled.

"I won't pee into a bottle, but I won't risk falling back just because my bladder is an issue."

"Well, then maybe you should consider using a catheter. But I should warn you. A few very ambitious guys did last year and got a nasty infection."

I scrunched up my nose. "That's taking it a little too far."

"Not if you're in debt with the Camorra, then you better find ways to get money."

"Right. You and your brothers are really clever when it comes to making money."

"I bet your father knows a few tricks as well."

He did. But my father was better at putting up a sophisticated exterior, while the Falcones lived their madness openly. "With a race of this dimension, won't we get into trouble with the police?"

"We might. That depends on the county we're passing. Some are easier to control than others. A few sheriffs are definitely out to catch a few of us. And every year they succeed and one or two land in prison for a while. But like I said, mostly the police turn a blind eye to what's going on. We mainly drive in remote corners of our territory, not to mention in the evening or night."

"Then let's hope we don't get arrested today." I pushed away from the hood when Dima's car rolled toward us.

"I'm sure your father will bail you out if you do," Adamo said with a shrug, but I didn't buy his disinterest for a second. He was trying to figure out how much my father knew of me racing in Camorra territory.

"I don't like to rely on others to save my ass," I said. Dima was stuck behind a crew of five mechanics who were taking care of a car. I wondered how much funds you needed to have a team of that size around you. Money wasn't an issue for me. Dad's black American Express paid for everything and he never asked why I spent too much money, but I wanted to earn my expenses with prize money.

Adamo followed my gaze to Dima. "His ribs are cracked from the way he moves. He won't be able to stick to your side if you don't slow down for him. He'll need breaks."

"Dima is tough, and he knows I won't slow for anyone. I can protect myself."

"If you drive as fast as last time, you won't have to. You'll be at my side, and I can keep an eye on you during the rest hours."

"How chivalrous of you," I said. "But I don't think I trust you, Falcone."

He tilted his head, one corner of his mouth moving up. "Maybe you shouldn't."

I generally didn't trust easily, even if Adamo didn't strike me as a danger—for me at least.

I headed for the trunk of my car and pulled out a half-empty bottle of vodka and opened it.

"Drunk driving might make you reckless but not necessarily faster," Adamo commented.

"I'm not getting drunk, but hard liquor dehydrates my body and makes me pee less. I won't waste time on a toilet break."

Adamo shook his head. "You stop at nothing to reach your goal."

"That's right." For a moment we stared into each other's eyes then Dima broke the moment as he got out of his car. Adamo strode away to the front of the grid where his car was.

My fingers around the steering wheel became sweaty as the minutes until the start trickled by. I'd never driven such a long race. It would be exhausting and explained why every year drivers crashed their cars without outward influences. Even a straight street can become a challenge if you're too tired to keep your eyes open.

From my position in the middle of the field, I couldn't see the pit girl with the flag but as long as the cars in front of me didn't move, I was locked in anyway. It would take a while to reach a better position with more room. Soon the roar of engines rang in my ears and Viper vibrated under me. Dima gave me a warning look. He was worried but he had no reason to be. I could handle my car.

Dust rose up before me, cloaking the cars ahead as they drove off. My foot hovered over the gas and the second the brake lights of the car in front of me died, I slammed my boot down. Viper roared like a wild beast and then we were off. I had to slow almost instantly or risk bumping into the car in front of me.

A start surrounded by all these cars was madness, even worse than the last row.

Time lost its meaning as I fought my way past car after car. Night fell around us and soon the crowd dimmed around me. I wasn't sure how many cars were ahead of me, except for the three I could see. One of them was Adamo's BMW. The other was the black monster from the rich kid. The third belonged to the Mexican guy who'd started beside me. I hadn't even seen him pass me by.

Dima was a few car-lengths behind me with three other cars. I wondered how long he'd be able to keep up. Maybe he could ignore his injuries after only an hour of racing but his pain would only get worse as the time passed.

My assumption turned to reality after five hours on the road. Dima started falling back and then he stopped. I thought he might need a toilet break but instead I watched through the rearview mirror as he bent over and threw up.

For a moment, my foot on the gas eased but then my gaze focused ahead again, on Adamo and the two other drivers in front of me. Dima was tough. He had been a member of the Bratva for almost ten years. He wouldn't give up easily and a few cracked ribs were nothing.

After eight hours, even the cup of vodka and my lack of hydration didn't stop my bladder from feeling full. My eyes burned and the road became blurry on occasion. The deep blackness where the headlights didn't touch my surroundings only added to my body's need for rest. But the distance between me and the three cars in the lead had grown and a break would put me even farther behind, not to mention that it would allow my two pursuers to catch up, or worse overtake me. Gritting my teeth, I tried to ignore the pressure in my bladder. To banish my exhaustion, I turned on the radio, blasting my favorite playlist of Classic Metal from the speakers. Welcome to the Jungle by Guns N' Roses awakened my senses as usual.

Even music wasn't helping anymore as the last thirty minutes of the race trickled by. My need to pee had turned to a painful throbbing in my lower body, and my back and ass were completely stiff from sitting. I hardly felt my fingers anymore. All I could think about was peeing and sleep.

My attention turned to one of the cars in the lead which was slowly falling back. When the last minute of the racing time counted down, it was only a car length ahead of me.

Adamo's car. He'd actually slowed down to spent the night at my side. I wasn't sure if I was flattered or annoyed. The damsel in distress wasn't my favorite role. On the other hand, his company hadn't been unpleasant, but so far we'd never been completely alone. And I realized that's what we'd be tonight—alone—as I stopped the car at exactly four a.m.

SEVEN

Adamo

I didn't plan to slow for Dinara to spend the night at her side. It was a spur of the moment thing when I noticed her car not too far behind me. I didn't lose too much time to the other cars in the lead by letting her catch up with me, nothing I couldn't make up for in the races that followed. And even if I didn't finish the seven-day-race in number one, that wasn't a problem. I didn't need the money and would still earn enough points to stay in the race camp. Dinara opened the door of Viper the same time as I turned off my engine of my car, which I'd positioned right beside hers. She barely glanced my way and instead rushed into the darkness toward the back of her car.

I grinned, realizing why, which reminded me of my own problem. After I'd relieved myself in the darkness as well, I leaned against the hood of my car and stared up at the starry sky. This far outside of civilization the stars always shone brightly. Something I missed whenever I was in Las Vegas. I'd always considered myself a city person until I started living long stretches of time in camp in the middle of nowhere.

Dinara advanced on me and propped up her hip against the hood. "You shouldn't have done that."

I made an innocent face but she narrowed her eyes. Grinning, I said, "I prefer your company to the company of the two assholes in the lead.

And with you, I won't have to sleep with one eye open to make sure no one manipulates my car."

Dinara scoffed. "Who says I won't try to cut through your brake cable? Maybe I'll even stab you when you're asleep. I'm Russian, remember?"

Hard to forget. Dinara's looks had something exotic, especially her high cheekbones. "I'll take my chances with you."

Dinara rubbed her arms. She was only in a tank top and those skimpy jean shorts. I wanted nothing more than to run my palms over her smooth legs peeking out of them. "I didn't pack any food. I don't suppose we can order takeaway out here, right?"

"I come prepared," I said with a chuckle and opened my trunk where I stowed a gas stove and a couple of cans with chili, cream of mushrooms soup, and mac and cheese. "Don't expect too much though."

Dinara scanned my selection. "I've never had mac and cheese before."

I gave her a disbelieving look. "How can you live in the States without trying it?"

"Our cook is Russian. She cooks recipes from my father's home, and I didn't really eat dinner with American families. We stayed among our own."

That sounded familiar. My brothers and I had always stayed among ourselves too, and my brothers still did. "Then mac and cheese it is. Even if it's a poor introduction to the dish. You should try my sister-in-law Kiara's version. It's out of this world."

Dinara smiled wryly in the dim light of my trunk. "Maybe we should wait with family introductions until we've at least shared a kiss."

My pulse picked up, my eyes darting to Dinara's plump mouth, still smiling in that confident way. Fuck. I hadn't considered kissing her tonight, now it would be all I could think about. "There'll be a kiss?" I asked with a slow smile as if I hadn't imagined doing much more.

Dinara took the gas stove out of the trunk and set it down between our cars so it was protected from the breeze before she grabbed a leather jacket and used it as a blanket to sit on. "Do you have a lamp as well? I don't want to keep my door open."

I smirked, picking up the can and a gas lamp, and plopped down on the cool ground. Once it cast its eerie light around us, and the mac and cheese was bubbling, I said, "You never answered my question." I handed Dinara a fork before I turned down the gas flame and poked my own fork into the searing hot mac and cheese.

Dinara did the same and tasted a bite after blowing on it for a while. She chewed a couple of times with a frown. "I don't know what the fuss is about. Our cats get better food."

I laughed. "Sorry my provisions aren't up to your standards."

She laughed too. "I'm not even a picky eater but this is really bad. I don't know if I'll give this another chance."

"Trust me, if done right it's delicious."

"Maybe one day your Kiara can convince me." She put another forkful into her mouth. "Kissing would be a very bad idea considering who we are."

I met her gaze. In the dim light from the gas lamp, the luminous teal of her eyes appeared like the dark green of fir sprigs. "Opponents?"

"That. Among other things. It would be a fateful liaison that's sure to stir up shit in the Bratva and Camorra."

I grinned. "I like trouble."

Dinara shook her head and leaned back on her elbows while I finished the food. "Why did you really seek my closeness tonight? And don't say to kiss me. If you hope to extract information from me, I should warn you that I'm very good at keeping secrets."

"I'm very good at extracting them," I said, leaning back as well so we were at eye level.

Dinara tilted her head. "Are you the wolf in the sheep's hide, Adamo?"

"Do I look like a sheep to you?" I asked, mildly offended.

"I think you hide your Falcone madness better than your brothers do. I bet those surfer curls and charming smiles trick quite a few people into believing that you're the nice guy."

"Maybe I am."

Dinara shifted her weight to one elbow, resting on her side, bringing us even closer. She peered into my eyes and for a moment I was certain she saw everything. "Maybe you want to be. But we are who we are. I am a Mikhailov and you are a Falcone. Our paths aren't on the light side."

"That's the Russian soul being melancholic."

"That's the realist." Dinara let out a yawn and closed her eyes briefly. "What time is it?"

I didn't have to check my phone to know the time. The sun was rising on the horizon, which meant it had to be around six in this part of the country. "Six. Sleeping time."

Dinara nodded. "I'm afraid to ask after the whole toilet break debacle, but do we get the chance to shower during the seven days? I'm not sure I can go without a proper wash and shave that long."

I chuckled. "We have two sanitary trailers with showers that drive around. Sometime tomorrow it should stop here too."

Dinara pushed to her feet and I did the same, which brought us both very close. With a teasing smile, Dinara turned and opened her car, crawling inside. She kicked her boots off and stretched out on the back seat.

The way she lay before me was way too inviting. I wanted nothing more than to crawl inside with her and find out if her belly piercing was the only piece of body art she had.

"Can you close my door?" Dinara's words burst right through my bubble. I did as she asked and after I'd extinguished the lamp, I made myself comfortable on the back seat of my car. It didn't take long for me to fall asleep. Despite Dinara's words, I didn't worry about her manipulating my car.

I woke to the sound of another car and jerked upright, scanning my surroundings blearily. When I spotted the sanitary trailer, I relaxed. A glimpse at my phone revealed it was almost noon and I'd gotten ten messages from Remo, Kiara, Fabiano, Savio, and C.J., most of them wondering why I'd fallen back. Of course, one of the drone cameras had filmed the leading trio. I ignored their messages and climbed out of my car.

When I glimpsed into Dinara's car, she was still stretched out on the back seat, deep asleep. Her palms rested on her belly, cradling a gun. Dinara definitely had trust issues. I, too, had a gun in my car and had kept it under my pillow on the back seat, but I didn't hang on to it as if it were my lifeline. I wondered if she'd thought she might need it against me, or if it was a more general precaution.

I nodded toward the guy riding the sanitary truck. "How long do we got?"

"Ten minutes for two."

I nodded then grabbed a towel and rushed into the bathroom on the trailer of the truck. I didn't wait for the water to get warm, not wanting to waste too much time. Dinara probably needed a bit more time, considering her longer hair. That's something I'd learned living in the Falcone mansion with my brothers' wives.

I resisted the urge to wank off while imagining Dinara taking a shower—the cold water helped with that—and instead hurried through the shower. I towel-dried myself hurriedly before I slipped on boxers and black jeans. The shirt in my hand, I stepped back outside. In the three minutes it had taken me to shower the temperature seemed to have increased ridiculously.

Dinara must have woken by the constant hum of the truck engine because she waited in front of it with fresh clothes and a towel in her arms. She yawned. Some of her mascara had smudged under her eyes and her hair was all over the place, but she still looked eye-catching. A dot of color and excitement in our barren surroundings. Endless sand and stone and dusty roads. "I was starting to wonder if I needed to join you for the shower before the time was up and I didn't get a chance to clean up."

"I took only three minutes. That gives your seven luxurious minutes."

After hearing her suggestion of showering together, I regretted not having prolonged my session.

Dinara moved past me with a small smile. "Thank you. I don't think showering with you would have been a good idea anyway."

With that, she disappeared inside and closed the door.

I pressed out air, unsure how to handle Dinara's flirting because I wasn't sure if she really meant it or was playing with me. Maybe both. But every day I cared a little less about the latter. Two could play a game.

I let the hot midday sun dry my hair even if that increased my curls. Women loved them and I preferred that they made me look different than my brothers.

The driver had already put a bag with provisions on each of our hoods, and I grabbed mine and took a bite of the chocolate muffin as I waited for Dinara to emerge. When she finally did, I almost choked on my bite. She was dressed in her usual jean shorts, boots, and tank top, but for the first time since I'd known her, her top was white and clung to her body. Her hair was dripping water down her shoulders and front, slowly turning the fabric transparent. After a wave at the driver, Dinara headed toward me. My eyes were magically drawn to the outline of her perky breasts through the sheer fabric and the piercing in her left nipple. Dinara grabbed her breakfast and propped herself up against the hood of my car.

The corners of her mouth twitched with amusement. "If it bothers you, wait for the sun to dry my top. It won't take long."

I'd never be able to unsee Dinara's nipple piercing, nor stop wondering how it would be to play with it. I could only imagine how much more sensitive it made her breasts.

"It's a pleasant sight," I said with a smirk once I'd torn my eyes away from her chest.

Dinara let out a laugh before snatching her own muffin and taking a large bite.

"Did it hurt worse than the belly button?" I asked eventually, unable to stifle my curiosity.

Dinara nodded. "Yeah. It hurt like hell, but I've had worse and I really love the result." When I risked another glance at her left breast, I realized the piercing had gemstones on both ends but the fabric didn't allow me to make out more. The sound of a drone camera made us move apart and Dinara slipped inside her car. She'd avoided being interviewed so far and didn't seek the cameras at all.

That didn't change over the next few days. She and I spent three more nights in the same place, but the longer the race lasted the less we talked. Exhaustion was too prominent. But even just sitting beside Dinara in front of the blue gas flame felt right. I enjoyed her company, maybe because she treated me like a normal guy, no reverence or respect. I had a feeling she wouldn't hesitate to kick my ass if I pulled some shit.

I waited for her to bring up her mother or my brothers again but she didn't. Maybe it was tactic and I definitely was still wary of her. She had a reason to be here, and yet I couldn't stay away from her.

On the last two nights, however, I made sure to keep up with the leading duo. Dinara and two other cars followed us not too far away. I finished second, maybe I could have won if I hadn't decided to spend a few nights at Dinara's side, but I didn't regret it. She managed to finish in fourth place. Dima, whose injuries had hindered him as expected, came in as one of the last. He looked royally pissed during the awards ceremony, especially when my name was called as second.

He stepped up beside Dinara who watched everything with crossed arms.

There were seven days until the next race now.

When I stepped down from the winners' rostrum with a bottle of champagne, Dinara headed my way. I shook off a few of the pit girls who came to congratulate me and find out if my stance on fucking them had changed—it hadn't.

"You're not just words and a big name, Adamo. You can race a car, I got to hand it to you," Dinara said.

I grinned. "Thanks. It's not my only talent."

Dinara raised one eyebrow. "Maybe one day you'll show me your other talents."

I took a swig from the champagne then held out the bottle to Dinara. "Whenever you want." Dinara took the bottle and drank a few gulps before handing it back to me and leaning close.

"Maybe after the next race. Until then I'll have to head back to Chicago."

"Next race," I promised.

Her lips brushed my stubbled cheek—I'd cut my beard yesterday because it had become too untamed. Her eyes captured mine and fuck, I was a goner. I wanted to drag her toward my car, set up a tent and devour her.

I hadn't seen C.J. in a couple of weeks and I would have stayed in camp and not returned home after the seven-day-race if I didn't know I had to settle things with her as soon as possible. It didn't feel right to have her in the background when my mind kept revolving around someone else, even if she and I weren't in a relationship. The promise of a kiss and more had lingered between Dinara and me these last few days and I definitely wanted to make good on that promise.

The moment I stepped into C.J.'s apartment she made a move as if to kiss me but I grabbed her shoulders, stopping her. "I—"

"There's someone," she said immediately, smiling knowingly. The hint of hesitation flickered across her expression. She took a step back. As usual, she was only in a negligee and for a moment, I considered taking my words back. I owed Dinara nothing, and C.J. and I weren't exclusive…

Yet, I cared too much about C.J. to keep her in the dark.

"Not really. Not yet. Maybe never—"

She motioned me inside and closed the door. "But your interest is piqued. I think it's so un-Falcone of you to not sleep around even when you're still unsure about the girl."

I sank down on her sofa with a dark laugh. "Don't make me sound like a saint. I'm not."

C.J. covered herself with a bathrobe before she lowered herself beside me. "In comparison to your brothers you are."

"I'm not the guy you first met," I muttered. This was one of the reasons why I didn't often return to Vegas. People always mistook me for the boy I had been, when I'd changed irrevocably over the years.

She smiled wistfully. "I'll miss the orgasms. Sex with johns never does anything for me."

"You should quit and only work in the bar, then you can find a boyfriend who'll give orgasms to you."

She shrugged. "Soon. Until then I can use the money. Will we still see each other?"

I hesitated. I wanted to see her because beside the sex we'd shared many meaningful conversations but I wasn't sure if being just friends would come easily. I wasn't sure about C.J.'s true feelings about me. "I'll be pretty busy with racing in the next few months, but I want to stay friends."

C.J. pursed her lips. "I'm a big girl, Adamo. I can be only friends with you."

"How about we just see how it goes, this just being friends-business?"

She nodded.

When I left her apartment an hour later, a weight had lifted off my shoulders. I realized my sexual relationship with C.J. had stopped me from pursuing Dinara like I wanted to do, but now nothing was in the way anymore.

Maybe Dinara was a bad idea. Most likely even, but I wanted her, and this wasn't about big emotions or marriage. I wanted fun and I had a feeling Dinara was the same way, even if she also had ulterior motives for seeking my closeness.

Dinara

Something about Adamo's behavior was different when he returned from his Vegas trip. He seemed less distant, and the looks he gave me didn't need much interpretation. Adamo wanted to get into my pants. I didn't not want him to try. I was attracted to Adamo. He was the complete opposite of Dima, my only boyfriend, and maybe that made out part of his special appeal. Dima, of course, noticed as well which soured his dark mood even further since his disastrous results in the seven-day-race.

He and I sat on one of the logs arranged around the roaring firepit in the center of camp after the first race since the seven-day-circuit. Many of the other racers were also present, chatting and drinking to celebrate another more or less successful racing day. Dima's injuries had healed and he'd finished fifth, one place behind me today. Adamo had won, which probably made Dima resent him even more.

"If you keep finishing fifth or fourth until the five-day-circuit later in the year then you'll still finish with a decent place for the year."

Dima huffed. "You know I don't care about the results. I'm only here because of you, Dinara. But you make my task of protecting you very hard the way you always run off with Falcone."

"I didn't run off with him. You drove too slowly to keep up with us."

He didn't say anything, only glared into the flames. I accepted a cup with some kind of punch from one of the mechanics. It was too sweet for my taste but the other racers and especially the pit girls seemed to love it. Half a bottle of vodka might have made it tolerable.

My eyes followed a tall form as it approached the scene. Adamo sank down on a log across from me with the fire between us. Our eyes met and a pleasant shiver raced down my back at the look on his face. His dark eyes appeared black in the fire light as they traced my body. I'd never felt like this: as if a simple look could light me on fire. I wasn't sure I appreciated the sensation of my body doing what it wanted.

Adamo raised his cup, toasting me. I did the same and we both took a gulp and grimaced simultaneously. I couldn't help but laugh and Adamo's face flashed with an answering grin.

Dima cursed low under his breath and shoved to his feet. *"I'm off to bed."*

"We don't have a race tomorrow. You don't need to get your beauty sleep," I said, even though I kind of wanted him to leave so I could interact with Adamo without Dima's surveillance. Even if I didn't owe Dima anything, flirting in front of him felt wrong.

Dima nodded in the general direction of Adamo. *"I'm sure he'll keep you company."* He turned and headed into the darkness.

I sighed but didn't follow him. Soon a shadow fell over me. "Is that spot beside you occupied?"

I peered up into Adamo's handsome face and shook my head. "It's yours."

He sank down, closer than Dima had been and our arms brushed. Goose bumps rose all over my body. "The drinks aren't much better than the food," I said with a nod toward the punch.

Adamo shrugged. "This isn't a luxury cruise," he said. "And don't tell me vodka is such a gourmet treat."

"Vodka wins against this sweet atrocity. And what do you know about Russian cuisine? Name one Russian dish."

Adamo narrowed his eyes in thought. "Borscht?"

"That was a lucky guess. Have you ever had it?"

"No. Beet isn't really my thing."

"But mushy pasta with fake cheese sauce is?"

Adamo propped his elbows up on his thighs, his bicep flexing distractingly. My eyes strayed to his marred Camorra tattoo. The handle and tip of the dagger were still intact but the area of the blade where the watchful eye had been was disfigured by burn scars. I knew the general story of how it had come to look like this. The Outfit, an opposing Italian mob family in Chicago, had tortured him but I was curious about more details. Asking for details might prompt Adamo into asking more personal questions, though, and that wasn't something I wanted.

He leaned a bit closer. "What Russian dish would you have me eat if we ever went on a date?"

My heart beat a bit faster. I braced myself on my thighs as well, bringing our faces even closer. "Pelmeni or Pirozhki. Nothing better than sinking your teeth into warm dough to discover a tasty, sizzling filling within." My voice was low, seductive. Not a tone I usually used to describe food, or at any other time.

I didn't mention my favorite khachapuri because that felt too personal.

Adamo nodded and a slow smile spread on his face. "I can't wait to get a taste."

My core tightened, catching me by surprise. Our eyes stayed locked together and if possible, our faces had gotten even closer. The laughter from a pit girl made me pull back. I didn't want people to see us get cozy. "This place is too crowded. And I need a decent drink. How about you join me for a vodka at my car?"

I wasn't sure what I was doing. This had never been part of my plan. Adamo tilted his head. "Lead the way."

I rose to my feet, feeling an unpleasant sense of nervousness. I didn't wait for him and stalked to my car. It was parked at the very edge of camp, cloaked by complete darkness. Dima's car was gone. Maybe he'd parked it somewhere else out of anger, or he'd gone in search of a bar where he could drink himself into a stupor for once. He'd be looking for a long time.

I grabbed the half-full bottle of vodka from my trunk and sat down on the hood of my car. Adamo leaned beside me. After a swig from the bottle, I handed it to him. Our shoulders brushed and my body reacted with a flood of sensations, most prominent and surprising: desire. I swallowed.

Adamo held the bottle out to me. I took it and downed an even longer swig.

"Vodka is starting to grow on me. Maybe I have a thing for Russian delicacies."

I tilted my head toward him. "They are the best."

"I need proof."

Adamo cupped my neck, startling me and pressed his lips to mine. My first reaction was to shove him away, even as my body screamed for more. My fingers curled around his strong shoulders for the shove but instead I dug my nails in and leaned even closer.

Adamo's other hand gripped my hip as his tongue parted my lips, tasting me. His kiss was dominance and fire, and it set me aflame in unexpected ways.

The way our tongues teased each other and our lips perfectly molded together felt as if this was more than a chance meeting. Adamo's hand slid up from my hip, stroking along my ribs, spreading even more fire in its wake. My nipples puckered against my T-shirt. I hadn't bothered wearing a bra because the fabric was loose and my breasts weren't very big.

Adamo's fingertips stroked the underside of one breast before his thumb brushed over my nipple, discovering my piercing. Heat and wetness pooled between my legs at the spike in pleasure. I stifled a moan, trying to rein in my body's overwhelming reaction. His thumb flicked my piercing and a gasp of pleasure burst from my lips. He seemed to control my body with only a few touches. My body yearned for more, my brain demanded control.

Control. *I needed it.*

I jerked free of Adamo's hold and his intoxicating kiss, panting and tingling all over.

EIGHT

Adamo

For a moment, Dinara looked almost frightened but maybe it was the distant firelight throwing dim shadows across her face. It was difficult to make out details so far away from the only light source.

Dinara's red lips pulled into a daring smile that went straight to my dick. "I thought you didn't mix business and pleasure?" Her voice was throaty and breathless. My heart was pounding in my chest and my cock was already pressing uncomfortably against my jeans. I hadn't felt a desire this strong in… ever.

"I don't. Usually."

It wouldn't be the first rule I broke. I had a long history of things I shouldn't do. Dinara seemed a good reason to add another one to the list.

I took out the cigarette package from my back pocket. "What about you? Do you mix business and pleasure?"

Dinara didn't say anything. The fall and rise of her chest were unmistakable even in the dim light streaming from the distant fireplace, our only light source. We were so far out and away from civilization that the darkness was almost impenetrable outside of camp. The headlights of the surrounding cars had all been shut off when their owners had gone to sleep or joined the campfire. Dinara pulled out a joint, her fingers shaking. I couldn't interpret her physical reaction to our kiss.

She lit up the joint and put it in her mouth, causing my mind to create more explicit associations. It glowed brightly as she sucked in a deep breath. After another drag, she handed the joint to me and I took a deep inhale, feeling its effects hum in my veins. I dropped my cigarette packet on the hood for an after-sex-smoke I'd hopefully require. Sex and drugs had been my favorite combination for a while. "You didn't answer my question. Or why did you pull back? I had a feeling you enjoyed the kiss more than a little." Her nipples had been rock-hard and eager for attention when I'd touched them.

Dinara leaned closer and pressed her palm against the bulge in my pants, making me hiss. "I think you enjoyed it even more." I resisted the urge to reach into her pants, even if I knew I'd find her sopping wet, ready to be fucked.

"I did, which is why I don't see why we stopped."

"Because I like things to go by my rules," Dinara said cryptically and hopped off the hood. I thought she'd leave but instead she grabbed my hand and dragged me toward my car, which was even further outside of camp and cloaked in darkness. I followed her and let her push me against the hood of my car. Her face hovered right before mine, her breathing fast and sweet. "What—"

She pressed a finger against my lips, shutting me up.

Dinara reached down and unbuckled my belt with a soft cling, too loud in the starry night. Nothing stirred around us but Dinara didn't seem concerned about getting caught anyway as she pulled down my zipper. I removed the joint from my lips and leaned down to kiss her but she turned her head away. "No kissing."

I bit back my questions, worried I'd stop her from continuing whatever she had in mind. My cock was already eager for her next move. She snagged the joint from my fingers and took a deep drag before she slid it back between my lips. Her hands trailed down my chest and she sank down to her knees, taking me completely off-guard. She tugged at my boxers and jeans until my cock sprang free. I couldn't stop staring at the crown of her head so close to my leaking tip.

Her warm fingers curled around my shaft before she took my tip into her hot, wet mouth. I hissed past the joint then sucked in a deep gust of the smoke as Dinara took me deeper into her mouth until my tip hit the back of her throat. She gagged but didn't retreat. "Fuck," I pressed out. I touched the back of her head but she swatted my hand away and slowly slid my cock back out of her mouth. "No touching. Hands on the hood if you want me to keep blowing you. My rules, not yours. Remember."

I put my palms flat on the car and peered down at Dinara's head moving back and forth as she sucked me. Her tongue circled my tip languidly, licking up my pre-cum. I wished I could see more of her than the scheme of her head. I wanted to see her gorgeous red lips around my tip as she sucked it. This felt like a dream. But even my best drug-induced hallucinations hadn't been anywhere as good as this.

Fuck, her lips on my cock felt like paradise. I moaned when Dinara started massaging my balls as she worked only my tip with her lips and tongue. When she started massaging the sensitive area behind my balls, pleasure radiated through my body and my balls started to tighten. I wouldn't be able to hold out long if she kept it up. I'd been fantasizing about her too long and wasn't prepared for this surprise blowjob.

She pulled her head back, smacking her lips.

I groaned. "I'm close."

Dinara gripped my hips and rose to her feet. In the dim light, the curl of her lips mocked me. "I know, Adamo." She leaned forward and pressed a kiss to my cheek. "Even a Falcone needs to learn patience."

She took a step back. I was frozen, my balls still pulsating, my cock desperate to spurt out a load. With a last smile, she turned around and walked off. I stared at the sway of her hips until her body merged with the shadows and she was swallowed by the dark.

The inside lighting of her car flared up, illuminating Dinara, a tantalizing sight that now taunted me. She slipped into the backseat and before she closed the door, she glanced back at me, then the darkness absorbed her again.

I hadn't been left hanging, or rather *standing* since my first sort-off-girlfriend Harper many years ago. Fuck, she was toying with me. Blood still filled my cock. I was too fucking turned on to hope my erection would disappear any time soon. I clutched my cock angrily and rubbed hard, almost painfully. If someone came by, they'd get a show they wouldn't soon forget.

It didn't take long for me to shoot out my load all across the dusty ground. I shoved my dick back in and zipped up my pants before I kicked dirt over the spot where I suspected my cum had landed. I reached for the cigarette package on the hood but touched cold metal. "Fuck," I growled. Not only had Dinara left me standing here with a fucking boner, she'd also stolen my cigarettes. I was done handling her with kid gloves. In the next race, she'd get to know the real Adamo Falcone on the race track, and next time she'd be the one with a dripping pussy.

Dinara

My spine tingled with animal fear as I turned my back on Adamo, my muscles taut with anticipation, ready to take flight or fight. It wasn't that I expected Adamo to rush after me, grab me and force me to finish what I'd started, but my body preferred to expect the worst. That way people had a hard time catching you off-guard. No steps rang out, nor did Adamo call me nasty names.

I meandered my way past the other race cars until I reached my Toyota. I opened the door, then I couldn't resist to risk a glance over my shoulder at the man I'd left with a raging hard-on. Adamo, too, was looking my way. Even in the dim light I could tell that he hadn't bothered closing his pants yet.

I didn't think it would be this difficult to walk away from Adamo, from sucking his dick no less, but I'd enjoyed the play of power, had gotten high on it. If there was one thing I had trouble resisting then it was a good high. I hadn't expected it to be like this with Adamo, but he filled me with an explosive energy only drugs or racing had done so far.

I climbed into the backseat, kicked off my boots, then threw the door shut, cloaking myself in darkness. I locked the car, reached for the

Glock under the front seat and put it on my belly as I stretched out on my back. Sleeping in the car wasn't comfortable, but sharing a tent with Dima seemed unwise after our recent argument. I didn't even know when he'd be back, or if he'd be back at all. Maybe once things had calmed down. But I actually preferred to keep an eye on my car even at night. Many racers had a lot to lose when they didn't make the podium. The money up for grabs meant salvation for them, a way to pay off their debtors (probably also Camorra, or maybe Bratva) or post bail for a family member. Despair made people do foolish things. I wouldn't give them the chance to slit my tires or cut my brake hose.

I was still wide awake though, so I peered out of the window. Adamo kicked the ground before he, too, climbed into his car. He was pissed. I couldn't help but smile. I wondered what a pissed Adamo would look like, how he'd race.

My body longed to return to him, to continue what I'd begun. My panties stuck to me with my arousal, something I hadn't expected from *giving* Adamo pleasure. I wanted to be close to Adamo but at the same time his closeness shook me up.

My eyes began to droop but I held onto to consciousness for a long time until finally sleep won.

A hard knock at my window woke me. The sun was only just rising over the horizon. My fingers on my gun tightened as I tried to get my bearings. Dima's face peered inside. Frowning, I sat up, wincing at the stiffness in my back from sleeping half sitting up on the backseat. I unlocked the car and Dima ripped open the door at once. A cold gust hit my body. This early in the morning it was really bearable out here in the desert. "What's wrong?" I asked groggily, pushing to the edge of the seat and swinging my legs out of the car. Dima's eyes were bloodshot and dark shadows spread under them. He looked as if he hadn't gotten much sleep, and possibly drunk more than he was used to.

I pushed into my boots and stood.

Dima glowered, taking a step closer. He put one of his hands behind me on the roof of the car, taking up too much room. "*I was there.*"

"*Where?*" I asked, not following his train of thoughts.

"*Last night.*"

I flushed. I hadn't done anything wrong and yet a part of me felt guilty. Admitting weakness wasn't my strong suite, so I got angry instead. "*You spied on me?*"

Dima's face twisted with matching anger. "*You didn't really try to hide it, did you? How could you do this?*"

"*Because I wanted to.*"

Dima shook his head. "*Will you suck every Falcone's cock to get what you want?*"

My eyes widened. I slapped him hard. "*It's none of your business. It hasn't been for a long time. Maybe you should remember your place. You are my bodyguard, Dima. You are working for me. Remember your place, or my father will remind you.*"

Dima stepped back, hurt flickering in his eyes, which I only caught because I knew him better than anyone, but his face turned ice-cold and hard instantly. "*Thank you for reminding me. Don't worry. I won't forget it again.*"

He turned around, and guilt slashed into me. Dima had been my bodyguard for seven years, first one of several but eventually the only. Before that, we'd been friends and after we'd become even closer. He'd never only been a bodyguard and I had never threatened him with my father, or put him in his place.

I was absolute shit at apologizing and admitting faults but my feet moved of their own accord. "*Dima,*" I said, my voice still on edge and not at all apologetic. Damn my pride. "*Wait.*" The apology tickled on the tip of my tongue.

Dima stopped but he didn't turn. Tension lingered in his shoulders.

"*Won't you face me?*"

"*Is that an order?*"

"*Stop this shit! You know I didn't mean it like that. But you have to stop* shoving your nose in my personal business. If I hook up with Adamo, it isn't your business." I hadn't been with anyone else since Dima and I had started dating when I was sixteen, but he and I would never be a couple again. Even when we'd been together, it had never felt right. Though, that might be something to do with my twisted self and not Dima.

He whirled around. "You should know better."

"You're jealous but you need to get a grip."

"Jealous?" he whispered. "Don't I deserve the right to a little jealousy?"

"No. Not anymore."

"Is there a problem?" Adamo asked, appearing tall and slightly sleepy behind Dima. He was only in tight boxers, revealing muscled thighs, and an impressive upper body.

Our argument had gotten loud and woken several people who were now poking their heads out of their tents or cars.

At least, none of them spoke Russian from what I knew so they didn't know what we'd been talking about.

"Fuck off," Dima snarled, his face turning red. I gripped his arm to calm him down but he shook me off.

Adamo grabbed his shoulder, expression hard. "How about you take your anger somewhere else? Calm down before you return. Dinara doesn't need your shit."

Dima jerked free of Adamo's hold, his body tightening in a way I knew too well. He was a martial arts fighter, had been for as long as I could remember and had even killed a couple of men with aimed kicks. There was a reason why my father trusted Dima to keep me safe.

"Dima," I growled, but he wasn't even listening to me. His furious gaze was focused on Adamo. "You have no business getting involved, Falcone pup. This is between Dinara and me, so why don't you return to your bed and stop bothering me." He finally moved as if to turn to me, probably to continue our argument but Adamo grabbed his arm again. He still looked remarkably calm, at least his face, but in his eyes, I could see a dangerous fire I'd never seen on him before, and I couldn't deny it: I was fascinated by it.

Dima whirled on him, trying to land a punch in his face but Adamo must have anticipated the move. He sidestepped the attack and sent a punch into Dima's left side. After that, all hell broke loose. I stumbled back a few steps to avoid becoming a casualty of their testosterone battle. The videos of Adamo's fights I'd watched hadn't nearly done him justice. Seeing him in action right before my eyes, seeing the sweat glittering on his forehead and abs, witnessing the lethal focus in his eyes and the determined precision of his kicks and punches was a completely different matter. It was the difference between seeing a beautiful Fabergé egg on a photo or holding it in your hand, seeing the intricate work put into it up close. Adamo wasn't as breakable as my favorite art piece but he was a masterpiece all the same, and his art of fighting had taken just as much effort, dedication and talent. I'd always thought Adamo was a reluctant fighter, in videos it had sometimes appeared that way, but now as he exchanged punches and kicks with Dima, he looked like he'd been born to fight, as if the demand for blood and violence rang in his veins, called to him like my dark craving often did.

A crowd gathered around us, shouting encouragement and soon exchanging bets. Dust whirled up around the battle, burning in my eyes.

"Stop it!" I screamed, but I wasn't insane enough to step between them. They were like fight dogs. If you tried to get between them, you'd be the one they'd bite.

Crank stumbled toward us, looking taken aback by the violent scene before us. Blood splattered the dusty ground.

He waved at two tall, dark-haired men, probably Camorra members. My suspicion was confirmed when they came closer and I caught sight of the tattoo on their arm.

Even they had trouble separating the two fighters but eventually they dragged them apart. Dima's left eye began to swell shut again when it had only just started to look better after my father had him beaten. His nose was busted too, and dripped blood on his white T-shirt.

Adamo had a cut in his right cheek. He wasn't wearing a shirt, nor shoes, but his skin was covered with blood splatters, and his eyes were wild and hungry. He reminded me of a predator who'd tasted blood for the very first time and had become addicted instantly.

I shook my head. "Was this really necessary?"

The pit girls whispered among themselves, some even gave me taunting smiles. I bared my teeth at them in a dangerous smile that I'd inherited from my father. They averted their eyes and I met Adamo's gaze. He calmed and stopped struggling against the man who held him. "You didn't have to defend me against Dima. He's always on my side."

Adamo scoffed. "It didn't look like that to me."

I glared and turned to Dima who had become very still. I wondered if he was really still on my side but I couldn't imagine it being any other way. His jealousy would have to stop eventually. Maybe I should point out to him that he'd been with a few girls since I'd broken up with him, and I never made a scene because of it.

Dima turned to the guy who held him. "Let me go."

The guy looked at Adamo, which was ridiculous in itself, but of course, Adamo was the highest ranking Camorra member present. He was number fourth after his three older brothers after all.

"Let us go," Adamo ordered in a hard voice, and both men loosened their hold.

Dima stepped back. *"Don't worry about my interference again. I'll attend to business in Chicago from now on."*

I doubted he'd really leave me out of sight. He'd stay close so he could intervene if anything happened but I'd call my father just in case to tell him I'd sent Dima away. Dad would be pissed off and try to convince me to return home, no doubt.

"Dima, let us talk once you've calmed down, all right?"

He didn't say anything, only stalked off toward his car.

"If you miss a race, you risk disqualification!" Crank called but Dima didn't react. He got in his car and drove away.

I sighed.

Adamo wiped the back of his hand over his cut, not taking his eyes off me. Slowly the crowd scattered. I wondered if last night had been worth the fight with Dima. What had it really accomplished except pissing off my best friend, and probably Adamo, too? I hadn't thought it through. I'd reacted out of fear, which was a stupid thing to do. Because I'd felt like losing control, I'd tried to exert control over Adamo in the easiest way I could think of.

Now I'd created a mess, and my body still hummed with desire when I looked at the man before me, especially covered in blood because he'd fought for me.

It was such a damsel-in-distress thing to think, to feel turned on by, but my base instincts were obviously stronger than my stubbornness.

NINE

Dinara

My attention was all over the place during the next race, so even though I started in the front row right beside Adamo, I finished as tenth. Of course, Adamo had played a huge part in my bad result. He'd cut me viciously after the start, so I'd briefly lost control of my car and taken a detour over the bumpy shoulder of the road.

Not that I hadn't done the same to other racers, but so far Adamo hadn't showed me his ruthless side. I had to admit it only made me desire him more. I didn't want to be coddled by anyone. That night after the race the following party was boisterous, and soon most people were drunk or passed out.

I'd only drunk a glass of the slightly less disgusting concoction with peach Schnaps someone had created. Adamo and I had kept an eye on each other all through the evening but hadn't talked. Now that Dima wasn't my shadow, many other racers came by to chat and many of them were more interesting than I'd given them credit for. As the crowd dwindled, I got restless. Something in me called to seek Adamo's closeness but I resisted.

To my surprise, he sought me out when I was heading back to my car. "Already leaving?" he asked, close by, making me jump. I threw him a glance over my shoulder. "Nothing kept my attention."

Adamo caught up with me. "Maybe I can. I bought a bottle of the best vodka I could find in the last liquor store we passed by. How about we share a drink?"

I stopped. After how our last encounter had ended for him, I was wary of his motives. Trust wasn't something I handed out freely. Despite my distrust, I nodded and followed him toward his car, which was far away from most of the others. Dark and secluded.

We shared a drink in silence, leaning against the hood of his car, our shoulders brushing once more. With the music from the party in the background—for once a slower, melodic piece—this felt almost romantic.

"Are you pissed?" I asked eventually.

"Life's too short to hold grudges."

"That's not a motto I live by."

"I bet," Adamo said. He straightened and moved in front of me, towering over my head.

I didn't move, only peered up at him calmly. Slowly he leaned down. "You look as if you want to run. Are you scared of kissing me again?"

"I'm not scared of anything," I muttered. "But I'd rather not have to kick you in the balls because you feel the need to avenge your hurt pride and forget what the word no means."

Adamo braced one hand on the hood, bringing our faces so close together, the heat of his lips seared mine. "I'm fluent in the meaning of no, Dinara. Don't worry. And my pride isn't easily hurt. But tell me, are you saying no to a kiss?"

I should have. Last time, I'd lost myself completely in it, but having Adamo so close, especially his mouth, clouded my judgment. I bridged the distance between us, brushing my lips across his.

Adamo didn't need another invitation. He tore the control over the kiss out of my hands and I let him, too delirious by every stroke of his tongue.

Sleeping with Adamo had never been part of the plan. Maybe if I'd known more about him, about his dark sides, which called loudly to me because they reflected the darkness deep within myself, I could have anticipated it would come to this. His grip on my neck tightened as he deepened our kiss. He tasted like sin and darkness, and he could kiss in a way I'd never considered possible. My body tingled from the simple friction of our lips, from the soft caress of his tongue and the taste of him. Soon the tingle turned into a pulsating need and my panties became damp. I was losing myself in Adamo again, losing control of my body. I snapped back to attention, forcing my mind into stark focus and submitting my body to its command. It had never been difficult. I'd practiced control for years, depended on it.

I reached for Adamo's belt and unbuckled it, snatching my mouth away from Adamo's dangerous lips. I reached for his cock that was trying to break through the fabric of his boxers, but he grabbed my hand and caught my lips in another kiss. "My turn. I have some trust issues when it comes to you and my cock."

I couldn't help but laugh against his mouth but then his hot, skilled tongue traced the seam of my lips before it dipped into my mouth once more. Adamo's hand cupped my breast through my tank. Of course, I wasn't wearing a bra. I was an A-cup so I rarely saw need to do so. Now I wished I had because like last time, Adamo began playing with my piercing, sending bolts of pleasure through my body. Adamo's other hand popped open the button of my jean shorts before it slipped in, stroking over my slit. Like a clam snapping shut to protect itself, my mind did the same, removing myself from the touch. Adamo's hand slid beneath my panties, touching skin, but I witnessed everything through a fog, barely registering the touch. I was in control of my mind and body, focusing on the tattoo on Adamo's forearm, following its intricate lines broken by burn scars. The ugly and beautiful becoming one.

I did what I always did. I drifted off, went through the motions, moaned occasionally, then arched when I thought it was time for an orgasm because Adamo had stroked me for a while. I never had much patience to draw it out. I didn't care if he thought I came too quickly.

Adamo's brows snapped together as he looked into my eyes. Something in his expression shifted from passion to realization then anger.

Adamo slammed his palm down on the hood, snarling, "What the fuck was that?"

I jumped and narrowed my eyes, surprised by his outburst. "What are you talking about?"

"That was fucking fake. Every fucking moan, and that fucking orgasm too. You didn't come, weren't even close no matter how loud you moaned. When I first touched your pussy, it was dripping then it turned dry like the ground below us. I'm not an idiot, and I recognize a female orgasm."

"So now you know if I had an orgasm? You might be a Falcone but you don't know shit about my body."

Heat rose into my cheeks at being caught but I wasn't going to let Adamo put me in a corner. I didn't owe him an orgasm.

Adamo looked livid. "Bullshit, Dinara. Don't lie to me. I recognize a fucking orgasm and that wasn't one," he growled. "Why did you fake it?"

I glared, trying to slide off the hood, but he remained between my legs, his arms braced to either side of my thighs.

"Answer the fucking question."

"I don't owe you shit."

"Is it because you think you can't come with a guy?"

Had Dima talked shit about me? Probably something about me being frigid or something like that. Guilt shot through me. Dima wouldn't badmouth me, and he definitely wouldn't talk about sex with Adamo.

"Fuck off."

Adamo got very close. "Or are you scared of losing control, Dinara?" I tensed because he hit the nail on the head. "You are," he said quietly as if this revealed another piece of the puzzle. The big Dinara Mikhailov puzzle he so eagerly wanted to solve. I wondered what he'd think once he'd fitted the last piece in. I wasn't a masterpiece anyone would show off in a frame. I was a messy thing people kept in the garage or basement.

"I'm not scared of anything," I seethed. I'd lived too many fears to bow to them.

Adamo shook his head, seeing through me like no one ever had. He tilted his head, seeking more of that darkness I tried to bottle up. He wasn't a stranger to horrors knowing his family history, but some things were beyond what people felt comfortable with. I worried that he'd realize I was one of those things.

This wasn't part of the plan. He was a means to an end.

Get a grip!

I grasped his neck and kissed him harshly, wanting to shut him up and stop him from looking at me like that. It made me want things I couldn't afford at the moment, maybe never.

Adamo ripped away from my mouth. He reached between us and slid two fingers along my slit. "I don't want a fucking fake orgasm. I want the real deal and I'm going to earn it, and you will fucking lose control, Dinara."

I'd never come with Dima, but he'd never mentioned it, even though I was almost sure he'd noticed. He wasn't stupid either and knew me even better than Adamo. It wasn't that I hadn't enjoyed many of the things Dima and I had done, but I'd never allowed myself to let myself fall completely, to hand control over my body over to another person. Never again.

I met Adamo's fierce gaze. For some reason, something in him compelled me to throw caution in the wind. "You can lose control with me," he murmured. "You're safe."

I smiled wryly. You're safe was something I'd been told before, but I wasn't that girl anymore and Adamo wasn't a demon from my past. Adamo hooked his hands in my pants and slid them down my legs with my panties, leaving me bare on the hood of the car. I wasn't shy about my body or a prude who had trouble being naked around others. Naked trips to the sauna with family and friends weren't uncommon in my family, and yet, I felt vulnerable as I sat before Adamo. His eyes slid down my body to my pussy. He was right. I was dry like the air around us. The wetness his kiss had conjured had been banished by my fears. I needed that kiss again, that taste of Adamo. I grabbed his collar and pulled him closer. His hand clamped around my neck then finally his mouth pressed against mine, his tongue reawakening my body. Soon a familiar pulsating filled my core. My mind screamed to stay in control and as if Adamo could sense it, he pulled back slightly, his lips still so close they brushed mine when he spoke.

"Stay with me," he ordered, then softer. "Stay." His dark eyes arrested me, held me in the present, no way to escape. He slipped two of his fingers into his mouth, wetting them before he pressed them lightly against my clit. They slid over my bundle of nerves easily with the extra wetness and soon tingles spread through me. He sucked my lower lip into his mouth when his fingers gently slid up and down my slit, scissoring me until every nerve ending in my pussy awakened.

My breathing came faster, my body becoming tenser. A knot was being tightened dangerously with every stroke from Adamo's fingers and he was the only one who could release it. He controlled my body, every delicious sensation I experienced. He gathered the wetness between my folds and spread it over my clit, circling it. His breathing was coming faster now too. He never took his eyes off me as he drove me higher. The sensations became overwhelming, the knot ready to burst. "Yes," Adamo rumbled, his eyes appearing black in the darkness, like they belonged to the devil I'd made a pact with.

He pushed two fingers into me and twisted them. I sucked in a sharp breath, on the edge of falling. My mind screamed for control, my body for release.

With every thrust he twisted his fingers, hitting a delicious point deep within me. My eyelashes fluttered, wanting to lower and sink even deeper into the sensation but I stayed rooted in the moment. His gaze held mine as he fucked me with deep precise strokes. A moan slipped out, not planned, not forced. It fell from my lips like a sigh of relief.

My inner walls began tingling like they'd never done before, began spasming and clenching around Adamo's fingers. I couldn't hold back. Digging my heels into Adamo's ass, I arched back on the hood as pleasure took hold off me, ripping any shred of control from my body. I cried out, clawing at Adamo almost frantically. Adamo pumped his fingers faster, forcing out more moans and cries. I couldn't stop shaking until finally Adamo's fingers stopped. They remained inside of me, like Adamo had wedged himself into my mind, my body, every part of me.

Afterward, my body humming, my breathing raspy, I peered up at the night sky. None of the orgasms I'd given myself over the years had been anywhere as intense. Slowly my senses returned. Adamo hovered over me. "This was an orgasm, Dinara."

I'd lost control. My chest constricted. I shoved him hard and he yielded, taking a step back. A bulge tented his pants. He brought his fingers, coated in my juices to his mouth and licked them clean with a wicked smile. My core clenched, wanting more, completely mesmerized by the sensations slowly dimming in my body. I hopped off the hood, pulled up my jean shorts and panties before I ran off toward my car. Inside of it, with the door closed, my heart began to slow.

Adamo still stood in front of the hood of his car. I'd left him with a hard cock once again. Only this time I didn't feel like the winner of our game. I touched my panties, which were completely drenched then wrenched my hand away and reclined in the seat. "Fuck. Fuck you, Adamo."

Whatever was happening between us could become dangerous, but I knew I wouldn't be able to stay away or rebuild old barriers. I wanted more of what Adamo had given me even if it scared me.

I wasn't a coward, hadn't been raised to be one and wouldn't allow myself to become one, so I didn't avoid Adamo like part of me wanted to do after my flight. Instead I sank down beside him on the log the next evening and held out an unopened cigarette pack to him. It was my peace offering. He accepted it. It took even more courage to hold his gaze because he gave me the feeling as if he could see even more in my eyes than the day before. Every day he unraveled another piece of me, and I was still chipping away uselessly at his barriers. We didn't talk, only listened to the makeshift band a few racers had thrown together. One of the pit girls had an amazing voice, which filled the night with more warmth than the fire. It was long after midnight when most people had gone to sleep. "You have more of that vodka from yesterday in your car?" I heard myself say.

"I drank some of it out of frustration yesterday but there's still enough left," Adamo said in a low voice. We straightened and strode over to his car. People had started talking about us. Rumors made the rounds. We were a small circle, and gossip was impossible to suppress. I didn't care. My reputation was my least concern. This wasn't my home, and those weren't friends or family.

Before Adamo could reach for the bottle, I sunk my fingers into his shirt and tugged him closer. He didn't resist but he didn't lower his head either. Instead he peered down at me. "Not done playing?"

"I'm not playing." At least not the game he might suspect.

"Last time you left me standing there with a boner."

"I did. But I won't do it again."

He leaned closer. "You sure about that? My palms are getting calloused from jerking off."

I laughed but without warning Adamo's kiss slammed me against the car. Passion exploded between us, wiping away any sense of caution. We tore at each other's clothes. Adamo ripped the door open, already pulling down my jean shorts and with it my panties. I shook them off a moment before I pushed Adamo onto the backseat. I wanted, I *needed* to be in control. Adamo's cock stood to attention as he rolled down a condom over it impatiently. I sank down on it and sucked in a sharp breath at the feeling of fullness. It had been more than a year since I'd been with Dima and that had been very different. Adamo's fingers dug into my hips and I started moving my hips. My lips crashed down on his as I rode him. He thrust upward, driving himself even deeper, trying to make me relent control.

My nails dug deeper into his chest, a warning. Adamo gripped my ass cheeks then flipped us over. Falcones never relinquished control. He pushed me into the backseat with his much stronger body and slammed into me. Every thrust of him ripped away another sliver of control. With him on top of me like that, I had no way to win it back.

Losing control. Out of control.

My throat tightened immediately. I clenched and pleasure turned to pain. Adamo touched my cheek and my eyes cut to his. Concern swam in his dark eyes. He saw deeper than he was supposed to, saw things no one should. He wasn't supposed to. "Don't stop," I bit out, not wanting to appear weak. I wasn't breakable or vulnerable, I didn't want him to treat me as such.

My lungs constricted. My body was stronger than my iron will.

Adamo rolled back over, taking me with him, so I was once again on top of him. After a moment to get a grip, I dug my nails into his chest and twisted my hip, driving his cock deeply into me. I bent down, kissing him fiercely, my eyes clenching shut against his inquisitive gaze. His palms cupped my breasts, and his fingers tugged at my piercing. I gasped, my eyes flying open.

"I love that piercing."

My lips fell open when he flicked it again and my pussy clenched tightly around him. I was getting closer and closer, with no way to stop, and for once I didn't try to grapple for control over my body. I let it loose even if it scared me.

Adamo's hips drove upwards as I twisted my hips. I clutched his shoulders, my eyes ripping open as a wave of pleasure tore through me. I couldn't stop it, could only submit to its force. I cried out, my belly constricting, my nipples hardening even more.

I almost blacked out when Adamo's cock expanded under his own orgasm.

Overwhelmed, I fell forward. My face pressed against his chest as I drew in sharp breath after sharp breath. Adamo's hand slid over my back gently. The caress felt good, gave my tumultuous insides an anchor. I allowed myself to enjoy his touch and our still intimate connection.

I could have stayed like this forever, listening to his racing heartbeat, but eventually I sat up. Adamo was still buried in me but he was slowly growing soft. I lifted off him and scrambled backwards and out of the car. Adamo didn't try to stop me. He didn't say anything at all, only removed the condom and knotted it. I fumbled for my clothes in the near dark and awkwardly put them on. They were dusty and stuck to my sweaty skin.

I looked at Adamo, and again part of me wanted to stay, to crawl back into his car and stretch out on the backseat beside him. I trusted that side of me even less than I trusted Adamo.

I wasn't sure what to say. I'd never screwed someone I wasn't dating, and I didn't know how to handle Adamo, or my feelings. Eventually I just turned around to walk away.

Before I was out of earshot, Adamo said, "Good night, Dinara."

TEN

Dinara

Until I saw Adamo again the next day, I wasn't sure how I'd react. If I'd try to bring our relationship back to a less intimate state. Yet, the moment he joined me in the morning with his own bowl as I ate my oatmeal and quietly ate beside me, I knew I didn't want to take a step back. I wanted more.

"Are you okay?" Adamo asked eventually.

I narrowed my eyes. "Why shouldn't I be?"

Adamo shrugged. "I thought you might avoid me now. But it seems I was wrong."

"Would you prefer if I ignored you?"

"I'd prefer if you'd join me at my car tonight again."

I stifled a smile. "Deal."

Adamo and I didn't waste much time when I arrived at his car. We kissed as if we were long lost lovers with limited time to enjoy each other. Maybe that wasn't too far from the truth because time was definitely not in our favor. I was Russian. He was Italian. And even if the racing camp might have blurred some lines, our families were at war.

Adamo moved us backward toward his car and hoisted me on its hood, never ceasing his kiss. His fingers found my piercing then he tugged the shirt over my head and pulled out of the kiss only to lower his lips to my breast. His tongue teased my nipple, flicking the piercing back and force. I released a sharp breath, my legs parting out of their own accord. Adamo pressed a palm against my crotch. I wondered if he could feel my wetness even through the layers of fabric.

My fingers pressed into the hood, my breath coming in short bursts. Every muscle in my body tightened and my heart pounded wildly in my chest. Adamo stepped back and I almost protested until my pride snapped my mouth shut.

Adamo opened the button of my jean shorts then slid them down together with my panties and squatted in front of me. He looked up at me. His face was shrouded in shadows but I knew he was waiting for me to give my okay. After yesterday, his actions had been more cautious. I didn't want him to hold back. I wasn't fragile.

My throat was dry, too dry to speak. I parted my legs wide. I wouldn't half-ass this. I was sopping wet for the man before me. His tongue traced a wet line along my inner thigh, raising goosebumps and making me shiver. I wondered if he could feel the ridges from the past on my skin. So far he hadn't mentioned them. A man with as many scars as he had might have learned to not ask questions about other people's marks.

The night air felt cold against my sopping wet center. I didn't take my eyes off Adamo, didn't lean back. This position gave me a sense of control even if Adamo would soon rip it from me. He moved on to my other thigh and dragged his tongue along my sensitive skin there. "When are you going to lick me?" I asked, but my voice lacked the sarcasm and bravado I'd wanted to put into it. I wanted to feel his tongue on me, in me.

"Soon," Adamo rasped, and his following exhale ghosted over my wet pussy. I bit my lip, tense with expectation and anxiety. The idea of losing control like last time still tightened my chest but my body was calling for more, louder than any doubt and anxiety.

And then Adamo's tongue swiped over my slit slowly, tracing around my clit before he nudged apart my folds with just the tip of his tongue. My teeth sunk into my lower lip as his tip caressed my sensitive flesh, slowly delving deeper until he reached my entrance. My head fell back for a moment, my eyes wide in awe at the sensation Adamo created with a brush of his tongue. He circled my opening, his breathing now more audible.

His lips closed around my sensitive folds, sucking, and I inhaled sharply.

"Do you like it?" Adamo murmured after a while, his voice heavy with desire. As if to emphasize his question, he swiped his tongue upward and nudged my clit.

"Don't talk," I gritted out. "Lick me."

His fingers cupped my ass cheeks and he really dove in. Less gentle, louder. His tongue parted my folds, seeking my entrance, diving in. He flicked up and down, awakening every nerve ending. My lust trickled out and Adamo lapped it up, making me moan. "Do that again," I whispered, almost delirious from the sensations.

Adamo parted me wider and slowly ran his tongue along my opening. My fingers tugged at his hair as I watched him draw out more of my juices and feasting on them. My hips shifted restlessly. Adamo looked up, meeting my gaze as he kept eating me out, his lips shiny with my lust and his eyes hungry for more. My grip on his hair tightened further as my core began to spasm. Adamo closed his lips around my clit as he pushed two fingers into me, and a tremor barreled through my body, taking any semblance of control with it. I cried out, shoving my pussy harder against Adamo's face who accepted the invitation with a growl, sucking harder and plunging his fingers even deeper into me. I rode his fingers and face, almost weeping from pleasure. I didn't care who heard, didn't care about anything but this sense of freedom I felt.

I fell back, completely exhausted. I ran my fingers through Adamo's tousled hair, gentler now as he peppered my pussy with kisses. I blinked up at the sky, wondering what this was. Adamo appeared in my line of vision. I swiped my palm across his beard which was wet with my juices. His expression brimmed with lust and the bulge in his pants was impressive. "Turn around," Adamo said.

I didn't protest. Instead I rolled over until my stomach rested on the warm hood of the car and my ass propped up for Adamo. He stroked my ass cheeks before he rubbed his tip over my opening. I arched against him. "Fuck me, Adamo. Fuck me like you mean it."

Adamo leaned forward, tracing the bumps of my spine with his tongue. His fat tip dipped into me. I tried to move back but Adamo's grip on my hips kept me in place as he thrust into me slowly with only his tip. "Deeper," I gasped.

"Patience. I make the rules."

I reached back, cupping his balls and squeezing. He hissed low in his throat. "That's how you want to play it?" he growled.

"Yes," I rasped as he kept teasing me with his tip.

Adamo retreated and then without warning he slammed all the way into me, filling me to the very brim.

I cried out at the stretchy feeling, on the verge of being painful. Adamo was incredibly thick and long. His tip nudged the sweet spot deep within me.

"Is that what you want?" Adamo asked in a raspy voice.

I twisted my head around to look at his face. "I want you to fuck me until my legs give out and I come all over your car."

His eyes flashed with raw lust and then he slammed even harder into me. His car shook under our fucking and for once I lost all sense of control and it didn't scare me.

Adamo

On occasion I thought I'd figured Dinara out but then something happened that threw me off completely. Like her panic attack when I'd been on top of her when we fucked the first time. We hadn't talked about it, and it hadn't happened again in the two weeks that followed, even though we fucked every night. I was never on top though. Or the fine scars on her upper thighs, I'd first felt with my fingertips then my tongue. When her shorts rode up and the sun hit her skin right, I now saw them too.

Dinara was an enigma I was desperate to understand. I hadn't asked

Remo for more information again. For some reason now that Dinara and I got closer, it would have felt wrong to prod around in her past without her permission. She obviously didn't want to share things with me. Maybe she would eventually.

The heat in the tent was almost unbearable. The sun had been relentless during the day and even the night hadn't delivered much reprieve.

Dinara rolled off me and stretched out on her back, breathing harshly. Our bodies were covered in sweat from sex and the heat.

"Will you ever tell me why you're really here?"

Dinara rolled over on her side, bringing us closer once more. I twisted around to face her. Strands of her red hair stuck to her cheeks and forehead. "I'm surprised Remo didn't tell you everything."

"Remo has a strange set of rules and he likes to play with me," I said, then shrugged. "But I haven't really been trying to extract information from him since this began with us."

"This?" Dinara asked, tracing my disfigured Camorra tattoo. She did so every time after sex, obviously fascinated by its looks or maybe just the story behind it. She cast her eyes up. "What is this between us?"

"You tell me. I think only you know what you really want."

"What do you want Adamo?"

I pushed up on my elbow and traced her cheekbone. She let me, for once not pulling away, not seeking the safety of her own car after we slept together. "I want to get to know you better. Not just your body, but your mind, your past, your darkness."

Dinara smiled bitterly. "No, you don't. Not if you like the version of me you've met so far."

"Let me decide that for myself. I doubt there's anything that could make me see you in a different light. And if its darkness you harbor, I have more than enough of my own, so I don't shy away from it."

Dinara looked up at the tent ceiling. I stroked her belly and played with her piercing.

"What exactly is it?"

She gave me an appalled look. "Don't tell me you don't know what a Fabergé egg is?"

"It's a Russian egg."

She shook her head in exasperation. "It's art and history. Intricate design."

I bent over her belly to take a closer look at the tiny egg dangling from her piercing. It was red with gold décor. "This is an original?"

"It was custom made for me by the same manufacturers who create the bigger Fabergé eggs."

"But why did you choose that for a piercing?"

Her brows crinkled. "It's part of my history. My father gifted a Fabergé egg to me every year since my birth and I keep them in a glass cabinet in my room."

"I'd never pegged you for an art enthusiast, especially this kind of traditional art. You seem more like the Andy Warhol or Jackson Pollock kind of girl."

"You're wrong."

"Because you don't tell me enough about yourself."

"You aren't exactly an open book either."

I inclined my head. "What do you want to know?"

"There are so many things, it's difficult to pick only one," she said but then her gaze darted to my forearm. "Your burn scar. Why didn't you have it lasered and your Camorra tattoo redone?"

Dark shadows from my past took shape. I held out my arm so she could see my tattoo, the knife with the eye and the Camorra motto in Italian. But most of the words were unreadable, twisted and distorted by the burn marks just like the eye. "That day changed me. It awakened a side of me I thought didn't exist. The tattoo in its disfigured state is my reminder and also a warning of what lurks beneath."

In the first few weeks and months after my capture and the torture, I'd woken with nightmares every night. I'd never had my power stripped from me like that before, rendering me at the mercy of someone else. Before that day, I'd thought I was at Remo's mercy and subject to his moods. But afterward, I realized how wrong I'd been. Remo never meant to hurt me. He took care of me in his own twisted way. It took being in the hands of the enemy to realize it.

"Did you never seek revenge for what's been done to you? The pain inflicted on you? The Outfit targeted you to punish your brother. You were still young."

It didn't surprise me that Dinara knew details. After all, Grigory knew all about it, and he obviously didn't mind sharing information with his daughter. Maybe Russian mob bosses didn't coddle their daughters as much as Italians did.

I had occasionally dreamed about revenge, especially in the beginning. I'd spent hours imagining how it would be to have one of my tormentors in my hands and do to them what they'd done to me, but eventually I had stopped obsessing over revenge. "I left the past behind me. I don't need revenge. I don't care what happens with the Outfit. Nino and Remo deal with them. I don't think revenge helps anyone."

"I can't believe you aren't furious," she whispered.

"I am. But I'm channeling whatever anger's still left from that time into racing and fighting. That's enough."

It wasn't quite the truth. That day had awakened something I had more and more trouble suppressing. My dark side—a side I still feared and despised often. The rare moments of acceptance and the peace they'd brought me scared me even more, however.

She traced my burn scar. The skin there wasn't sensitive to touch or pain but the one around it all the more. When Dinara's fingertips trailed higher, discovering a small scar on my bicep and then the scars on my chest, goosebumps rippled across my body. "Are these from your torture as well?"

"Not all of them. A couple. The rest are from fights and my time in New York with the Famiglia."

"I think it's strange that your brother trusted another family enough to send you there. Even when my father makes peace with others, that doesn't mean he trusts them enough to send someone he cares about there."

"I asked Remo to send me there. I needed to get away from my brothers, from their shadow and their protection. In New York, I wasn't treated special in any way. I was a nobody. I had to do the dirty work and their Capo punished me when I messed up."

"No matter where you go, you are never a nobody, Adamo. Even if you're away from your brothers and Vegas, your name carries weight, like mine does. We carry our names as burden and shield. The only way for us to be anonymous is to take on a new name and become someone else."

"Have you ever considered doing that? Leaving your father and the Bratva behind? Starting new?"

Dinara shook her head. "It's in my blood. It's part of my life. I don't like all aspects of the life but I don't want to run from it," she said, tracing my scars.

I told her about every scar and when I finally fell silent, her face was inches from mine. I ran my palm over her upper thighs and the thin scars there, a silent question.

Dinara sighed, turning her face to the ceiling once more. "Sometimes we are our own worst enemy."

I nodded because it was a truth I'd learned in the past. I'd suspected the ridges were self-inflicted. They reminded me of the scars some of my junkie acquaintances had had on their wrists from cutting. "Why?" I asked.

"I took drugs to cover up old pain. But they made me numb in every sense and so I tried to feel something, even if it was pain, as long as I decided what it was."

Something about Dinara reminded me of myself when I hadn't been clean for very long. Drugs were a thing of her past like they were in mine, but I wanted to know the reasons for her addiction. "What kind of old pain?"

Her expression closed off. "The truth about me that your brother hides will change the way you look at me. But tell Remo, I gave him permission to share it with you, if that's what he needs."

Remo never asked for permission, not from anyone. I doubted that was the reason why he'd been holding back the truth from me.

Dinara climbed on top of me, letting her hair curtain my face. "One day you'll have to take me to Vegas with you and show me your city."

"You mean lead you to your mother?"

Dinara's lips brushed mine. "And if I said yes?"

"I don't think it's a good idea, not unless Remo allows a meeting."

"He won't be able to keep her from me forever."

I sighed, raking my hand through Dinara's hair. "I fear you're using me against my brothers. You should know that I'm loyal to them."

"I know," she said simply and kissed me.

I pulled back. "You won't be able to sway me, even if part of me wants to do whatever you ask."

"Shut up," Dinara murmured.

I allowed her to silence me with her lips. I wasn't sure what secret Remo would reveal about Dinara. I hoped it wouldn't make me waver, wouldn't make me want to help her even against Remo. My brother had done some twisted shit in his life, and I feared the thing with Dinara's mother was another on that list. I often disagreed with what my brothers did but I stood by them. What if Dinara's secret made that impossible? Maybe that was why Remo had kept the secret to himself, and maybe now that I was closer to Dinara he'd reveal it for the very same reason. To test my loyalty.

ELEVEN

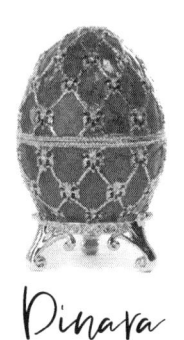

Dinara

MY FATHER HATED MY MOTHER. EVERY TIME I BROUGHT UP HER name loathing edged itself into every hard line of his face. He wanted her dead. No, he wanted her to suffer and die. A simple death wasn't enough for him. As Pakhan he had the means to kill almost anyone, to make their last hours as excruciating as possible, and he certainly didn't have qualms about it.

But my mother was in Camorra territory, at the very center of it in Las Vegas, under the watchful eyes of none other than the Camorra's Capo: Remo Falcone.

Remo Falcone was only a distant memory of a young girl and he was what stood between me and my mother. Impossible to bypass, without help. My father wouldn't help me. Not unless Remo handed him my mother so he could kill her himself. And Adamo?

Maybe Adamo could help, but would he? Using him to get information had been easy, but what I needed from him beyond that....I wasn't sure if I should even consider asking. But did I have a choice?

This was too important to let emotions get in the way, especially when I wasn't sure about their extent. Could anything between us even last?

But unlike Adamo I couldn't let the past rest. It didn't let me. And not pursuing revenge? Impossible.

The past was my burden.

Sometimes at night the memories were fresh and I woke with the scent of my mother's sweet perfume in my nose, my skin covered in sweat. I hated those nights, those dreams, that made me feel small and weak, destroying everything I'd worked so hard for.

The past

"Come on, Mandy," my mother said as she dragged me out of the car and toward a brick building. I didn't like that name. But maybe it wouldn't last. My last five names hadn't. I missed my real name. Ekaterina, or Katinka, how Dad always called me. But it was bad.

"Mandy, hurry!" Her voice was tight with fear. Men had taken us with them, away from the house we'd lived in for weeks now. They had put us into a car and driven us to a place with a big neon sign above its entrance. A woman's legs flashed in bright colors and between them the words Sugar Trap blinked. I didn't fight her hold, only trudged after her. I lowered my gaze to the floor how I had been taught when we walked through a bar. It smelled of alcohol and smoke, but above all, of a heavy perfume, even stronger than the one Mom wore. I almost stumbled when we headed down steep steps. But a man with gray eyes caught my arm. He released me and Mom pulled me even closer.

We arrived in a room without windows. Another man waited inside.

He was very tall, with dark hair, and stood with his arms crossed. His expression terrified me. It promised trouble. But I knew that even a smile didn't mean anything. Pain often followed sweet words and kind smiles. His eyes were almost black and so was his hair. He only briefly looked at me then he narrowed his eyes at Mom and her boyfriend Cody. Cody had a bloody nose. I didn't know why, but I wasn't sad. He was a bad man. A different kind of bad than Dad. Worse, even if Mom didn't see it. Mom hated Dad. She said I needed to hate him too.

"You know who I am?" the tall man asked. His voice was deep and confident.

Mom tightened her hold on my hand. I glanced around. The gray eyed man leaned against the desk, watching me. He didn't smile or glower. He didn't do anything, only looked as if he could see below my skin to the dark parts of me. I stared down at my dirty feet in my flip-flops.

"Of course," Cody said. His voice trembled. My head shot up and I looked at him. I'd never heard that tone from him. He sounded terrified. Sweat glistened on his forehead and he looked about to cry.

"Who am I?" the man asked. He wasn't very old. His voice was low and calm, but Cody's face scrunched up.

"You are Remo Falcone."

"And?"

"Capo of the Camorra." He swallowed audibly. "I've been dealing for you, Sir, for almost six months. But I'm nobody you would know."

Cody sounded so demure. When he ordered me around, he was always confident and angry. Why was Cody so scared of Remo Falcone? If a man like Cody felt that way, I should be terrified.

"You were supposed to sell crack and weed, but I hear you build a little lucrative side-business with the help of the lady over there. Maybe you thought I wouldn't notice because I was too busy establishing power."

Mom's hand around mine was painful. I'd never heard anyone say the word lady with more disgust.

"What's your name, woman?"

My mother twitched. "Eden."

"I'm sure that's your real name."

Mom didn't say anything. Like me she'd had many names in the last few months. "How long have you been doing your side-business in my city?"

Mom looked at Cody.

"I didn't know what she was doing!" he croaked. "Today was the first time, I found out."

"What a coincidence that you happen to find out about it the same day we catch you." Remo nodded toward the gray eyed guy who had set up a laptop in front on the desk and was staring at it. "My brother grabbed a few discs from your place. I assume they won't prove your words to be false, right?"

Cody paled.

Remo turned to Mom again. "How much money did you make?"

"I—I don't know. I never got money."

"You got a roof over your head and enough drugs to forget the past and black out the present too, right?" Remo walked closer to Mom, towering over her and me. "In my city I make the rules, and no one goes against them."

"I didn't know," Mom said. "It was Cody's idea."

Cody glared but lowered his head when Remo turned to him.

"How much further does your business reach? Are there others we should know about?"

"No, it was only us."

"Is he telling the truth, Eden?" Remo asked.

"Y-yes. We only just started."

"Only just started. Sounds as if you had big business plans without involving the Camorra."

Mom tugged a strand of her beautiful red hair behind her ear and gave Remo that smile she usually only gave her boyfriends. "I could tell you about the customers. I'm sure you could make so much more money with it. We were never professional. If you and your Camorra organized everything, you could make millions."

Remo smiled, but it wasn't a nice smile. "You think so?"

"You should take a look at this," the other man said. Remo turned and headed toward the desk. He looked at the laptop for a couple of minutes. Silence reigned in the room. The faces of both men didn't show any emotion as they watched the screen. Remo shoved away from the desk. "Did you sell these videos on the Darknet?"

Cody didn't react. He only blankly stared down at his feet. He looked as if he was praying but I doubted he believed in anything.

"Yes, we did. You could make even more money with it than with your racing and cage fighting," Mom said. She reminded me of the mom she'd occasionally been back at home with Dad.

Remo only stared at me, not saying anything. Mom released my hand and touched my shoulder. I met her gaze. She gave me an encouraging smile. "Why don't you show Mr. Falcone how nice you are."

I nodded. I'd heard those words often in the last few weeks. I looked at

Remo Falcone and he met my gaze. I forced the smile all the customers liked and padded closer to him. My flip-flops smacked loudly in the silence.

At first, I hadn't wanted to do it, but it had only made things worse. Mom had told me I needed to behave then things would be better and eventually I had done what they wanted. It still hurt but Mom felt better when I didn't fight.

"She'll do whatever you want," Mom said.

My cheeks hurt from smiling. Remo didn't look at me like the other men had. He didn't tell me how pretty I was and what a good girl. Suddenly his expression shifted to something dangerous, something wild, and he looked away from me.

He stalked past me and grabbed Mom by the throat. Cody had done it before. It had bothered me in the beginning, but now I felt empty too often. I knew I shouldn't be okay seeing Mom getting hurt but everything in me was hollow.

"Remo," the other man said.

"Are you really trying to give me your daughter for a joyride? You think I tolerate disgusting shit like that in my territory?" His voice became a low hum. "I bet you'd even watch me fuck your kid? You despicable whore wouldn't bat a fucking eye, as long as you get your drugs and are far away from Grigory."

Mom blanched.

"Remo," Nino said firmly, nodding in my direction.

"You really think that shit's still going to damage her after the shit that's been done to her?"

"Dad?" I asked. Mom never talked about him and if she did only to tell me bad things.

Remo's eyes slanted over to me. His fingers still held Mom by the throat. Cody was crying in the background.

"Nino, take the kid upstairs, give her food and decent clothes while I handle this situation."

Mom sent me a begging look. I didn't react. Begging doesn't work, Mom, don't you remember?

Nino appeared before me and held out his hand. "Come on, Ekaterina."

My eyes widened. I put my hand in his and followed him outside. Before the door closed, I heard Mom whimper. "Please don't hand me to Grigory. You wouldn't believe what he'd do to me."

"Probably the same thing I'd do to fucking scum like yourself."

Nino led me upstairs. He picked up a Coke for me at the bar then we headed into a room with a bed and bathroom. I took a hesitant sip from my Coke, then gave him the smile Mom had taught me. He shook his head. "No need for that ever again, Ekaterina. Your father will be here soon, then you'll be safe."

I nodded, even though I didn't know what safe meant anymore. I remembered feeling safe distantly. I remembered lying in Dad's arms as he read me Russian fairytales. Mom didn't allow me to say anything in Russian.

"You can take a shower and I'll ask one of the girls to bring you clothes."

I nodded again. He nodded too. "You're not going to run, are you? I don't want to lock you in."

"No," I whispered. I didn't want to run anymore. Ever since Mom had taken me with her, things had been bad. I wanted them to return to how they used to be.

He nodded, then he walked out.

I looked at the bed, remembering the bed I'd been in less than an hour ago. A bed in Cody's basement. I shivered. The old man who'd been in it with me hadn't come with us. Nino had stayed with him for a while before he'd joined us in the car.

The look in Nino's eyes afterward had reminded me of the look that I sometimes saw in Dad's eyes, or even Remo's eyes just now.

I sank down on the bed and tugged at my white, frilly nightgown. They all loved frills and white. Wrapping my arms around my chest, I waited. I hated the silence. Usually, Mom always allowed me to watch whatever I wanted on TV after the men left, for as long as I wanted. Falling asleep before the TV was better than listening to my thoughts, to the voices of the men my memory kept repeating. Now nothing drowned out the words the old man had said. They replayed over and over again in my head. "Sweet little girl. Good girl. Give Daddy what he needs."

I pressed my palms over my ears, but the voices didn't stop.

The door opened and a woman came in. I kept my hands over my ears.

She looked at me, her eyes big and sad, and put down a heap of clothes. "They'll be too big on you. But better than what you're wearing now, right?"

I blinked at her. She left again and the voice became even louder. I hummed but they were deep in my head, louder than my voice. I rocked back and forth, wanting out of my head, out of my body, away from the voices. I felt so tired. But if I closed my eyes now, faces would join the voices. My palms hurt and my ears rang but I pressed even harder, my nails scratching my scalp. "Stop," I gasped. "Stop."

But the voices kept on whispering. Stop never worked.

The door opened again. Remo stood on the threshold. He stepped inside and I shut up. Humming loudly made people think you were strange. I slowly lowered my hands. Blood and skin stuck under my nails from where I'd hurt my scalp. My pink polish had peeled off in places.

I was momentarily distracted by a red stain on Remo's gray shirt.

"Did you kill Mom and Cody?" I asked.

Remo raised his eyebrows. Dad had always tried to hide everything bad from me, but Mom had told me everything. Remo was like Dad. He had the same dangerous glimmer in his eyes. They were killers. Mom said they were bad, but neither Dad nor Remo had hurt me. The nice men Mom had brought home, they had.

"No, I didn't," he said.

He crouched before me, meeting my gaze. The other men preferred to tower over me. He didn't look sad or as if he felt pity for me. He looked as if he understood me.

"Why not?"

He smiled a strange smile. "Because they aren't mine to kill."

I didn't understand.

"Would you be sad if your mother was dead?"

I looked down at my hands. I loved Mom. But I wasn't sad. Sometimes I even hated her. "I'm a bad girl."

"You're trying to be a good girl so people hurt you less?"

I frowned then nodded.

"Don't," he said firmly.

I looked up.

"Don't ever try to be good to people who hurt you. They don't deserve it."

I nodded because that's what I thought was expected.

"Your father will be here in a couple of hours, Ekaterina. He's going to take you home."

"Home," I repeated, testing the word. I remembered warmth and happiness. It seemed so far away, like the fairytales Dad loved to tell me.

He straightened and looked at me. "Nothing can break you unless you allow it. If you ever return to Vegas, you'll get your chance to end it."

I didn't understand anything. My body was screaming for sleep but I fought it.

"We ordered pizza. You can have some."

I nodded. Then my eyes darted to the TV attached to the wall across from the bed. Remo headed toward the nightstand and took the remote before handing it to me. I immediately turned it on and raised the volume. It was late so all movies were for adults. I stopped when I saw a familiar scene from the movie Alien.

A woman came in with a pizza carton and put it down beside me on the bed. "You're going to have nightmares if you watch something like that," she said to me.

"I like those nightmares," I whispered.

"Become the nightmare even your worst nightmare fears, Ekaterina," Remo said before he and the woman left. I turned the volume even higher and took a slice of pizza. I wasn't really hungry but I stuffed it into my mouth.

My eyes burned with exhaustion but I forced them open, focused on the TV.

A knock sounded. I didn't look away from the second Alien movie. They were doing an Alien movie marathon, and I felt like only if I kept my eyes on the screen would the voices and images stay away.

"Katinka," Dad said softly.

I tore my eyes from the screen, my heart beating faster as I spotted Dad in the doorway, dressed in a black suit and light-blue tie. His face was edged with sorrow. Behind him stood Remo and Nino.

"Katinka?" The name he always used for me sounded wrong. He said it different. It felt different. I didn't know the girl it belonged to anymore. I wasn't her.

Dad came closer. He looked at me different too, as if he thought I was scared of him. Mom had said Dad was a bad man, that he hurt people, killed them, that he'd eventually do the same to her and me. But Dad had never hurt me, not like the men that Mom had brought home so I'd be nice to them.

I dropped the remote on the floor and stormed toward him. The air whooshed out of my lungs as I flung myself against him. He still wore the same Cologne I remembered and his clothes smelled faintly of cigars. He stiffened and didn't hug me back. "I was bad," I gasped out, hoping admitting it would make Dad forgive me.

"Katinka, no," he murmured and then his arms wrapped tightly around me and he lifted me off the ground, clutching me against him. I buried my face against his throat. I felt like crying but I'd stopped crying a while ago. Now I couldn't do it anymore, no matter how sad I was. He cupped the back of my head and rocked me like he'd done when I was really little.

He didn't know what I'd done. If he knew, he'd be mad. Mom had told me over and over again, that Dad would be mad at me, not just at her. He would think I was dirty and bad for what I had to do.

He turned with me on his arms and carried me out of the bar. A black car with Dad's men waited in front of it. Before he walked toward them, he turned to Remo who had accompanied us. "You better keep your promise," Dad said in a voice that held violence.

Remo smiled. Men never smiled when Dad used that voice. "It's not a promise I made to you, Grigory. That promise is for Ekaterina."

I peered at him, wondering what he was talking about.

Dad shook his head. "My daughter won't ever set foot on Vegas ground again. I'll make sure of it. Eventually, you'll have to let me dish out my revenge."

"Dish out revenge on that scum in your trunk. The rest will have to wait for her."

"She won't ever be touched by violence or darkness again, Falcone. I'll protect her from it until my last breath."

"You can't protect her from something that's festering inside of her. Tell her what's waiting for her. Let it be her choice."

Dad didn't say anything, only held me tighter. He turned and headed toward the car. Dad's men didn't look at me. They'd always tried to make me laugh in the past. I hunched on the backseat and Dad took the seat beside me, helping me buckle up before he wrapped an arm around me. He gave me a look that reminded me of the one time I'd broken my favorite porcelain doll. Our housekeeper had fixed her but after that she was too fragile to take her out of the shelf ever again. Eventually I couldn't look at her anymore because when I did, I was only reminded that I couldn't play with her. She made me sad.

"What happened to Mom?"

"She's dead and so are the men who hurt you."

I ducked my head. He knew.

"I'm sorry."

"Don't apologize, Katinka. I'll never let you out of my sight again. Nothing will ever touch you again." He kissed my head. "Soon we'll be home and then everything will be how it used to be. You'll forget what happened."

I never forgot. And things didn't return to how they used to be. I'd become the fragile porcelain doll. Now, back at home in Chicago for a brief visit between races, I felt that way all the more.

I ran my fingertips over the edge of the shelf that held my Fabergé eggs. There were twenty-one of them. Dad had bought one for my birthday every year, even when Mom had taken me with her. He'd given me that egg the day I returned home with him and I'd put it in my shelf to all the others. Everything had been how I remembered it. Only I had changed. Surrounded by the prettiness of my past, I felt out of place, like an intruder in a life I didn't belong anymore.

"Katinka," I tested the word. It still felt as if I were talking about someone else. Tolstoy, our cat, a gorgeous Russian Blue, brushed up to my calf, maybe sensing my distress. I patted his head, causing him to purr.

Dad had tried to make me forget, had moved back to Russia with me for a little while, thinking we could leave the horrors behind, but they followed me.

Eventually, he, too, realized that I wouldn't become the Katinka I'd once been. Every time he'd looked at me with pity or sadness in his eyes, I'd been reminded too. Now he didn't give me that look anymore. I was stronger than I used to be. I didn't need anyone's pity.

I wondered if Adamo would look at me differently, too, once he found out what had happened.

TWELVE

Adamo

My ride back to Vegas was accompanied by a sense of foreboding. Dinara's past obviously held horrors. Possibly created by my brothers. She was worried I'd see her in a different light once I found out but I worried that old resentments for my brothers, especially Remo would rip open. Remo had done too much for me to lose my loyalty, but maybe the truth would destroy our relationship or at the very least set it back to the grudging tolerance I'd felt toward him in my teenage years.

I'd sent Remo and Nino a message that I would be visiting again this weekend before I'd set off from camp but not the reason why. Maybe Remo had an inkling. His messages over the last couple of weeks had revealed his suspicion about Dinara's and my relationship. My brother had always had a sort of sixth sense when it came to sniffing out people's secrets.

I drove toward the Sugar Trap because Remo had asked me to meet him and Nino there. Usually I avoided that place because it reeked of too much despair for my taste. That Remo considered it the best place to discuss whatever he suspected to be my visit about didn't bode well. Stepping into the gloomy light of the whorehouse corridor always gave me a sense of entering a sort of limbo.

The corridor opened up to a bar area of red velvet and black lacquer, which only intensified the hellish vibe of the place. There were poles and booths with velvet curtains and several doors that branched off the main room where the whores took their customers for privacy. Another long corridor, also held in red and black, led to Remo's office.

When I entered the long room without windows, Remo's eyes said he knew why I was there. Nino sat on the sofa, eying me with a hint of disapproval. He thought I sought fights with Remo, but that wasn't the case. But unlike Nino, I had a conscience and it sometimes clashed with Remo's ruthlessness.

"Your visits are becoming more frequent again, but this isn't a simple family reunion, is it, Adamo?" Remo asked, arms crossed in front of his broad chest. He was in workout clothes, probably because he'd kicked the living hell out of the heavy bag hanging from the ceiling between his desk and the sofa. His dark eyes held a hint of suspicion. Maybe it was my own emotion reflecting back at me.

"How are things with Dinara?" Nino asked calmly, trying to be the deescalating presence but accidentally poking the beehive.

I narrowed my eyes. "She's still part of the races and we've been talking often these last few weeks." It wasn't a lie, but certainly not the truth either.

Remo's answering smirk told me he knew. I didn't care. He hadn't said I should stay away from Dinara, and even if he had, I wouldn't have listened. Her closeness called too loudly to me. Getting in bed with the enemy was something he and I had in common.

"You want answers about Dinara. Answers she's unwilling to give you."

"Answers she's *unable* to give me. It seems you are the only one who knows every aspect of her past. You and Nino." I nodded at Nino who kept his usual poker face, not that I would have expected him to show any kind of reaction. His wife Kiara and his kids were the safest bet to tease an emotion out of him. Before his marriage to Kiara, everyone had been convinced he wasn't capable of feelings at all. "Dinara told me she wants you to tell me the truth."

"Is that so? I hope you reminded her that I don't take orders, nor do I need permission. Keeping her secrets isn't only for her sake."

"That's what I thought. If you worry whatever you'll say will shock me or make me resent you for your actions, you're forgetting that I know you, Remo. I know every despicable act you've committed. Nothing could ever shock me when it comes to you."

Remo's face turned hard. "Nino, why don't you gather the info Adamo *demands*."

Nino got up without a word and headed over to the computer on the desk. He threw Remo a warning look. Maybe the secret protected both of them.

"What do you think will you discover today?" Remo asked.

"Dinara went through some shit in the past. Something to do with Grigory and you. Her mother tried to run away with her but you caught them and delivered Dinara right back to her father. You kept Eden for yourself for whatever twisted reason. So maybe Eden and Dinara did something in our territory that pissed you off. We both know you were even more psychotic back in the day than you are now." I remembered the days when Remo and Nino had fought over Vegas, when blood and violence shone in their faces when they returned home from their raids at night.

"I was fucking pissed at the time. Grigory too," Remo said. "I wonder if you think Dinara needs your support against me, and would you give it to her if she asked for it?"

"Are you testing my loyalty?"

"Should I?"

Nino made a small impatient sound. "No loyalties need to be tested."

"He's right. I'm loyal to our family and the Camorra." I held up my arm with the marred Camorra tattoo. "But that doesn't mean that'll stop me from butting heads with you if you're causing Dinara harm."

"I see she got you," Remo said with a dark chuckle.

"Done," Nino said, looking up from the computer screen. Remo gave a jerky nod before he turned back to me again.

"Maybe one day you'll stop suspecting the worst when it comes to me." Remo gave me a harsh smile. "I'm not a good man, but whatever you think about Eden and Dinara, you're wrong." He nodded at Nino then he turned and left.

I frowned at the closed door. I'd have thought Remo would stay to see my reaction, to gauge my loyalty, even if he said it wasn't a test.

Nino raised a USB-stick and motioned toward the laptop on the table in front of the couch. "Might be better if you sit down."

"I can handle it." I'd seen enough death and torture in my life to be hardened for whatever waited on this USB-stick. I snatched the device from his hand and shoved it into the laptop, wanting to get this over with.

Nino didn't leave. He leaned against the wall behind me.

At first, I didn't know what was happening on the screen. The camera was directed at a bed in an otherwise empty room. Was this a video of how Eden started working for the Camorra? Or worse, the video of Remo's first encounter with the woman? I really wasn't keen on seeing him getting it on with Dinara's mother, but it would explain why he left the room.

Then a girl in a white nightgown came into view, definitely not a grown woman. One look at her face and her red hair, and I knew it was a young Dinara, maybe eight or nine years old. A fat guy in only underwear with a mask covering most of his face followed her and my stomach turned, fearing what would come next. The girl shook her head frantically. I couldn't even think of her as Dinara. Then a woman came into view, the same red hair and distantly familiar features. Eden. She talked to Dinara then disappeared from view again.

I wasn't sure what exactly I'd expected. Not what I got. My heart beat frantically, my chest tightening as I kept watching. Bile traveled up my throat. I wasn't sure how long I managed to watch the horror before me. Soon nausea battled with absolute rage in my body.

I grabbed the laptop and threw it against the wall, smashing it. The screen finally turned black and the horrible sounds died. My breathing was harsh as if I'd run or fought a battle, and the spike in adrenaline indicated the same. But I was still sitting in the same spot on the couch. My fingers dug into my thighs, shaking with the need to rage and destroy.

"Remo and I had found out that the Bratva was looking for Grigory's wife. We got a tip that she was in town, so we went looking for her, hoping to blackmail them. What we found wasn't what we expected. Eden and her boyfriend produced these kinds of videos with her daughter and they sold them on the Darknet. We informed Grigory and handed his daughter back to him."

I stared blankly at the destroyed screen. It wasn't enough. The need to destroy more, to rage and hurt was almost impossible to suppress. It was a familiar craving, one I'd felt on occasion over the years—never this potent, this all-consuming, though—and had always ignored. I had barely watched three minutes of the video, had to shut it off before it really began, unable to see the horrors that Dinara had lived. She hadn't been able to stop them. I'd imagined so many horrors, but nothing came close to what I'd watched.

"I always wondered if I'd ever see that look in your eyes."

I dragged my gaze toward Nino, my blood rushing in my ears and pulse throbbing in my temples. "What look?" I barely recognized my voice. It was laced with venom, not directed at my brother.

Nino briefly glanced toward Remo, who must have entered while I'd been absorbed in the horrors on the screen, before he said, "A look I usually only see in Remo's eyes. The hunger for blood and violence. The need for death and destruction. As a baby and younger child, you looked exactly like Remo. And on occasion a similar temper would shine through."

I'd seen photos of my younger self and Nino was right. The older I got the more I'd tried to be different from my brothers, especially Remo. In our time in boarding school in England, I'd gotten the first glimpse of normal people, of their values and their family dynamics, and soon those became goals I wanted to achieve. I thirsted for normalcy, even as my own nature often called for another direction. I wanted to be better, wanted to forgive instead of avenge, to sympathize instead of condemn. I could feel compassion unlike Nino and even Remo. That made my desire to torment others—even if they deserved it—so much worse.

"I guess it's the Falcone blood, right?" I said quietly.

"It can be curse or blessing depending on your viewpoint," Remo said with a twisted smile. He raised a stack of CDs and held them out to me. "We confiscated these when we found Eden and her daughter."

I pushed to my feet, and for a moment I worried my legs would give in, then I walked over to him and took them. I met my brother's gaze. "You put a stop to it."

"Of course," Remo said. "Nino killed the disgusting asshole we found in front of the camera with Dinara, and I gave Eden's boyfriend to Grigory so he could take the revenge he desperately thirsted after."

I nodded numbly. "Why didn't you give him Eden? She deserved death after what she did to her daughter."

Remo's mouth twisted cruelly. "She deserves worse than that. But whatever that is, isn't for you or I or Grigory to decide."

Slowly I began to understand. Remo's messed up logic played out, influenced by our own mother issues. I regarded the stack of CDs in my hand with dread, knowing every one of them stood for a painful moment in Dinara's past, horrors that explained so much, but not everything. Not how that girl on the screen could grow up to become the strong woman I loved to spend time with. "So they all show Dinara with different abusers?"

"Yes," Nino said. "Some of them are on more than one recording. There are ten guys in total and one woman."

My lips twisted with disgust. It was difficult to rein in my emotions. In the past the yearning for a reprieve in the form of drugs would have overwhelmed me in a situation like this, but now the only thing my body called for was blood. Plenty of it and as brutally withdrawn as possible. I wasn't sure if I could quell it this time—if I even wanted to try. "Her abusers, did you kill them as well?"

"Six men and the woman are still alive," Nino said. "We only made sure they would keep their hands to themselves."

"Why didn't you kill them?" But I knew. For the same reason why Remo hadn't killed Eden and hadn't allowed Grigory to do it either, because that wasn't their right.

"Tell Dinara," Remo said. "We know the name of every person on the recordings and their whereabouts. If she wants them, we can give them to her."

"Not to me though," I said wryly. And fuck I got it. For the first time, Remo's twisted psycho logic made sense to me in all its brutal enormity. If he gave me their addresses, I'd pay a visit to each of those fuckers and torture them to death. Wanting to be better than my brothers? Than my nature?

Impossible.

"What if Dinara wants to talk to you?"

"Then she can talk to me in person. No phone calls."

I narrowed my eyes. "Dinara will be safe in Vegas." The words didn't come out like a question as I'd intended but more like a statement with a threatening undertone.

Remo tilted his head. "If I wanted to harm her, I would have done so in the months since she started racing in our territory. I'll blame your disrespect on your emotions for the girl."

"What are you going to do now?" Nino asked.

I swallowed down my first impulse to vow revenge and go on a rampage right away. "Whatever Dinara needs me to do."

Remo met my gaze and nodded. "What she needs will take you on a path you swore to never wade on. It's a path all of us Falcones are well acquainted with. It's paved with blood and death, and once you've walked it, no other path will ever suffice."

I didn't deny it because the call of my inner demons demanding blood and pain was stronger than my drug cravings had ever been. They promised to be even more rewarding and I was eager to believe them. I'd avoided torture and killings for a reason. I enjoyed them too much. Guilt settled in later—when I mourned the person I should have been.

No matter how much I wanted to be different from Remo, I sometimes thought I was more like him than any of my brothers. Nino tortured because it was effective deterrence and punishment as well as a scientific challenge to prolong a victim's death while causing maximum damage. Savio tortured because it was necessary evil in our business. Remo tortured because he enjoyed it, because for him it was linked with pure emotion… and for me it was the same.

"Why don't you spend the night at the mansion? We can all have dinner together and you'll have time to let things settle, to calm down," Nino said in his calm drawl.

I nodded. Dinara wouldn't yet be back in camp either, but even if she were, I needed another day to see her as the woman I'd met and not the scared girl. Maybe one night wouldn't be enough for it. "I need to talk to Kiara anyway."

Nino nodded. Kiara had been abused by her uncle when she was a kid, a few years older than Dinara though, and maybe she could shed some light into Dinara's feelings.

Back in the solitude of my car, the brief glimpses from Dinara's past flared up.

I'd seen Eden as a victim of Grigory's and Remo's cruelty. One man scorned by his woman and another with a hatred toward most women. It had seemed the logical explanation.

When the mansion appeared in front of my windshield, I breathed a sigh of relief. For the first time in a long time, I was desperate for the chaotic atmosphere of my home, for its distracting nature. I didn't want to be left with my thoughts.

The moment I stepped inside, the kids crowded around me, talking all at once, eager to tell me about their adventures and hear my recounts of the last few races. Remo and Nino were already in the common area, sitting at the long dining table with their wives. Neither Fabiano and Leona nor Gemma and Savio were present. Maybe they had date nights.

Kiara was listening to something Nino said, then her gaze cut to me and she smiled kindly. Fina got up and hugged me briefly, her keen blue eyes checking my face. I supposed I was looking out of it. "You're not going to lose your shit again?" she whispered.

I smiled wryly, remembering my teenage ways of dealing with difficult situations. "I'm not a boy anymore."

"You're not," she agreed and stepped back to make room for Kiara while she ushered the kids to the table.

"Why don't you help me grab the food from the kitchen?" Kiara asked.

I nodded and followed her down the long corridor into the vast kitchen. In the past, when it had been only my brothers and me, and our nutrition had mainly consisted of takeout pizza, the room had seemed a waste of space. That had changed since our family had expanded and women, who enjoyed healthy options on occasion, joined us.

When I risked a peek into the oven, I laughed dryly.

Kiara's eyebrows rose. "What's wrong? Is it burned?" She hurried past me and ripped open the oven to check on her casserole.

"No," I said. "It's just that I only recently told Dinara about your mac and cheese after she had her first taste of the dish out of a can."

Kiara closed the oven and turned it off, but made no move to remove the casserole. Instead she leaned against the kitchen counter with a mildly surprised expression. "You told her about our family?"

I shrugged. "Bits and pieces. Not much. But I promised her your mac and cheese would convince her of the dish."

Kiara tried to stifle a smile but failed. "You two spend a lot of time together. It must be serious if you even consider introducing her to us."

Suddenly, I felt on the spot. I leaned against the counter beside Kiara but didn't look at her directly. "We're not serious. We haven't defined what we have. It's more of a friends with benefits situation."

"Like it was with C.J.? Or are you still seeing her as well?" Kiara asked without a hint of judgment in her voice. That was what I appreciated about her. She didn't judge people. She listened and tried to understand.

"No, I ended it with her before I started something with Dinara." I paused, considering my time with C.J. in comparison to what I had with Dinara now. It felt different. I wanted it to be different. With C.J. I'd never considered a future together, never wanted to spend every waking moment with her, but with Dinara…

Kiara touched my arm. "The look on your face tells me it's more than just friends with benefits."

I chuckled. "Considering the reason why Dinara sought me in the first place and what I know now, I'm not sure she would agree with your assessment."

"You think she's being with you to find out the truth about her past and get in contact with her mother?" The hint of protectiveness in her tone teased a smile out of me. Kiara tried to protect every member of the family.

"She didn't know her mother was alive when she joined the races but she definitely hoped to gain information through me," I said. "But I don't think that's why she spends every night with me. She and I both share a drug history. It's like we're connected on a deep, inexplicable level."

I shook my head with a grimace. "Fuck, I sound like a goddamn horoscope."

"You're in love," Kiara said, her eyes alight with amusement.

My alarm bells rang. Falling in love was something I'd tried to avoid since Harper broke my stupid naïve teenage heart. Hurting my feelings wasn't as easy now. No one had been close enough to even try.

"I don't know. But even if that were the case, Dinara is a Bratva princess. Her father is our enemy. I doubt Grigory or Remo are keen on making peace. And after the thing with Gemma's family, it would cause a shitstorm in the Camorra if Remo as much as tried to establish a truce."

Kiara nodded slowly, her expression sympathetic. She touched my arm. "It's not like Remo cares about other people's opinions. If he thinks peace with the Bratva is a tactical advantage, he'll do it. Shitstorm or not." She flushed.

It was always funny to watch Kiara say curse words. It was obvious she felt uncomfortable using them. "And you know he'd do almost anything for you, Adamo."

I sighed. "Yeah, I know." Remo was a family man. He'd lay his life down for any of us. But I was getting ahead of myself. Dinara and I weren't really dating yet. I wasn't sure what she wanted, now less than ever. "Did Nino tell you about Dinara's past?" I asked carefully. I was worried about bridging the subject of sexual abuse with Kiara, reluctant to open up old wounds for her. I still remembered how submissive and fearful she'd been when she'd first joined our family, and it made me furious to think about the horrors both she and Dinara had been submitted to.

"He mentioned it, yes, and he told me you found out today."

"I saw a few minutes from one of the recordings those disgusting perverts did of her." I swallowed, my pulse beginning to pound savagely again.

Talking to Kiara had calmed me but now the fury from before showed its ugly head again. "Remo gave me the CDs with the recordings. He told me he has the names of everyone involved. He wants me to give both to Dinara."

Kiara didn't look surprised. In the past this conversation would have caused her tremendous anxiety but now her only reaction was a subtle tension in her body and her fingers kneading the dish towel. "Remo has his own way of thinking."

"I think he wants Dinara to get revenge. For him it's only natural that she'll want to see her abusers dead, even her mother." I wasn't entirely sure what I felt about this. On the one hand, the prospect of payback excited me, but on the other, I was worried about the consequences for Dinara.

"And what does Dinara want?"

"I have no clue. She didn't tell me. She wanted to know the truth. Once she has it, I don't know what she'll do with it. Maybe she'll ask her father to exert revenge."

"It sounds as if you want her to ask you instead," Kiara said curiously.

She was right, there was no denying it. If Dinara's wish was to get revenge on the people who hurt her, then I wanted her to ask me and not her father, or Dima. The worst thing was it wasn't only because I wanted to help Dinara, a small part of me was also eager for a reason to shed blood. "What do you think is it she wants? You're probably the only one from all of us who understands her."

Kiara didn't say anything at first, her eyes distant as if my words had taken her back many years. Instead of answering, she opened the oven and took out the casserole, obviously weighing her words from the tense look on her face. "Not everyone's way of coping with trauma is revenge on their abusers. It seems like the logical, maybe even only choice from your brothers' and maybe even your standpoint, but some people seek reconciliation and a clarifying conversation over violence. What Dinara needs and desires is impossible to say without knowing her."

I knew Dinara, or at least, I knew as much as she'd allowed me to see so far, but I wasn't sure of her motives. She was a tough girl, so revenge didn't seem completely out of the question. "What about you, Kiara?

Nino killed your uncle in the cruelest way possible. He exerted revenge on your behalf. Did you want to be avenged? Or would you have preferred to make peace with your abuser?"

Kiara's face flickered with pain, and her smile became a bit shakier. These small signs showed me that even after all these years, the events still haunted her. Maybe it was impossible to overcome something as horrible for good. It depressed me to think that Dinara would carry the weight of her past on her shoulders forever. "I could have never forgiven him. I needed him gone, but I could have never done it. I don't think I could have even asked for it, if Nino hadn't decided to do it. He took the decision, *the weight of it*, off my hands. Maybe I could have saved my uncle from his fate but I didn't want to. If he'd lived, I'd have always feared he'd come for me again, even if Nino protected me. To find peace, I needed his death."

"So you're grateful to Nino for killing your uncle the way he did."

"I am, to both Nino and Remo. When I found out he was gone, I felt relief. I never felt guilty over it. It was a necessary step for me to heal."

"Do you think Dinara wanted me to find out the truth so I'd exert revenge for her?"

"I don't know. She isn't helpless like I was back then. She's got her father and his men as support. From what Nino said, her father knows what happened, so Dinara isn't burdened to keep it a secret. She could ask her father to kill her abusers, and he'd do it, right?"

"He'd do it, no doubt, but he'd risk Remo's wrath and retaliation if he shed blood on Camorra territory."

"Remo wants revenge to happen."

"He wants it to happen the way he wants it, and I think for him there's only one person who should shed blood, and that's Dinara. If I'd kill everyone for Dinara, Remo wouldn't do anything to me. I'm his brother. He'd be pissed but that would be all. Maybe Dinara suspects it. Or maybe she'd rather risk my life than that of her father or Dima."

"You think she'd use you like that? To do what she and her father can't do?"

"It would explain why he allows her to race in our territory."

Kiara regarded me with worry in her brown eyes. She let out a small sigh. "I guess there's only one way to find out. Talk to her. Deceit isn't a good start for a relationship."

That's something I'd learned the hard way with my first girlfriend Harper. I'd overcome the deep sense of betrayal and I wasn't the unstable teenager from back then, but if exacting revenge through my hands had been Dinara's plan from the very start, it would definitely leave its traces. Still, for some reason I couldn't imagine Dinara to be deceitful like that. She had been honestly shocked that her mother was alive and she didn't know about the existence of the recordings or that my brothers had gathered the names and addresses of her abusers. Even if revenge had been on her mind, it could only have been an abstract concept.

Kiara smiled. "Talk to her. Tell her what you know and see how she reacts, then you can still decide if you want to cease contact with her."

I nodded. "Dinara was worried that I'd treat her differently after I knew. Now I think, how can I not knowing what I know now? She went through some horrible shit that must have left deep scars."

"Definitely, but when you met her those scars were already part of her. She didn't change. She's still the same girl you met."

I motioned at the steaming casserole of mac and cheese. "If we don't take the food to the table soon, I fear the hungry bunch is going to devour us."

Kiara squeezed my forearm briefly before she grabbed a bowl with salad. I carried the casserole and tried to enjoy a chaotic evening with my family, even as my mind kept whirring with a myriad of thoughts. I wanted nothing more than to hold Dinara in my arms again, even if part of me dreaded the encounter.

THIRTEEN

Adamo

THE DRIVE FROM LAS VEGAS BACK TO CAMP SEEMED TO LAST forever. It was difficult to focus on the street, on anything really, except for the horrible images I'd seen. They'd haunted my night. I couldn't help but wonder how much worse it must be for Dinara. We'd on occasion shared a tent and her sleep had often been interrupted by unintelligible mumblings. Whenever I'd asked what she'd been dreaming about, she'd evaded a reply.

It was impossibly difficult to link that helpless, cowering girl with the fierce and confident woman I'd been spending so much time with. I'd expected a sad story, but not this. Even a night's sleep hadn't managed to calm the raging flood of emotions in my body.

When we'd last seen each other two days ago before she'd left for Chicago and I had driven to Las Vegas, she'd been worried I'd view her in a different light once I knew about her past. I'd thought she was exaggerating. I had been confident nothing could change my opinion of her. Now, I wasn't sure.

Dinara's reaction in the car when I'd laid on top of her, her need to stay in control of her body at all times. It all made sense now. Even before I'd found out the truth, I'd considered her strong, now her strength seemed almost inhuman.

When the first tents of camp came into view, my chest tightened. I was fucking nervous about seeing her again, about doing what I'd promised not to do, about seeing her in a new light. And not just that, a small trickle of doubt about her motives remained. Maybe she would be disappointed if I returned without having killed her mother and everyone else.

A quick scan revealed Dinara's Toyota at the very edge on the west side of camp. I steered my car in that direction.

The moment she spotted me, Dinara headed my way from where she was talking to one of the pit girls. This was the moment of truth.

Dinara

I'd been anxiously awaiting Adamo's return from Vegas, wondering if Remo had revealed my past to him. Part of me wanted him to know, because it would make things easier. Adamo might be more willing to help if he knew why I was doing what I did. On the other hand, I'd enjoyed our time together, the sex and conversations, the way he treated me like his equal. He didn't consider me breakable. I'd proven my strength to him. But once he knew about my past, none of that would matter.

People only saw that one aspect of myself once they found out, as if it was all that defined me. The molested child. The rape girl. It was a big part of me, no doubt, and haunted me to this day, but I didn't want special treatment because of it. I wanted to be treated like anyone else, not someone breakable or vulnerable or damaged. I was neither of those things.

The moment Adamo's car pulled into camp, I excused myself from Kate, the pit girl with the angel voice, who was a kickass cook as well, and headed toward him. My pulse picked up when Adamo got out. One look from him, and I knew Remo had told him enough. As expected, it had changed the way Adamo regarded me. I wasn't only Dinara, Bratva princess and race driver. I was the poor girl from before.

I did a U-turn and stalked back to my car, not in the mood for that kind of confrontation.

I was angry, but beneath that, I was scared, scared of losing the connection

Adamo and I had developed, our easy-going interactions. It was one of the reasons why I loved being part of the race camp. Nobody knew who I'd been before, what had happened. Back in Chicago, everyone did, and despite the years that had passed, it still often showed in the way they looked at me and treated me. How was I supposed to leave the past behind if even bystanders couldn't do it?

I was so fucking scared of having people here look at me the same way, of Adamo looking at me that way. It was one of the reasons why Dima and I hadn't worked out, why our relationship had been doomed from the very start. What had made him appear a safe choice for a relationship in the beginning had ultimately been the nail in our coffin.

Soon steps followed me, and my heart beat only faster.

I hated feeling scared. It reminded me of that girl Adamo now mistook me for. I never wanted to be her again.

"Dinara!" Adamo called and finally caught up with me at my car.

I whirled on him and stared into his eyes, waiting for him to say something, but at the same time so fucking scared of what that would be. Adamo touched my shoulder. Even that simple touch seemed more hesitant than any of our touches in the past.

Adamo watched me not saying a word. He didn't have to. His eyes spoke a clear language—the tongue of pity. I hated nothing more than that. "So Remo told you everything?"

I'd given Adamo the ok, had given Remo the ok, but maybe a stupid part of me had hoped Adamo would let it rest. It was idiotic. Eventually he'd find out. It was inevitable if I wanted to move on with my plan.

Adamo ran a hand through his hair and glanced away. A myriad of emotions swam in his eyes. "Yeah, not everything but enough."

He wasn't telling the truth. There had been a moment of hesitation before he'd answered.

I shoved away from the car. "*Don't*. Don't lie to me to protect me."

I was so tired of people doing it. I deserved the harsh truth, even if it crushed my heart.

Adamo pushed his hands into his pockets. His expression cranked up the compassion.

And I could not bear it. "What exactly did he say?" I seethed, so fucking angry but at the same time bursting with despair. All because of Adamo, of the way he might handle me in the future. I'd never felt anything similar with Dima, as if my heart might splinter.

"Does it matter?"

"Of course, it does!" I sneered. "Can you imagine how frustrating it is to be in the dark about something that concerns you so integrally? Because of the way you're looking at me, I know you're pretty shaken up about what Remo said. He's maybe the only one who knows everything because he's the one who handled everything back then. Even I don't know everything, only the lies and halt-truth that my father, you and your brothers told me."

I could feel the treacherous heaviness in the back of my throat, the prickling at the back of my eyeballs—harbingers of tears. Not going to happen. Crying was a sign of weakness I hadn't allowed myself in a long time.

The craving for relief swelled like the tide, unstoppable, slowly eating away at my resolve like the waves took over the sand. I fumbled for a cigarette, even though I hated the taste, the smell, the feel of the soggy paper in my mouth. I'd never be a smoker because I enjoyed it. But it was better than nothing, better than the alternative. I needed something to soothe my anxious mind, to silence the call of my dark craving.

Adamo came closer, his keen eyes scanning my shaking fingers. Maybe he knew the telltale signs. After all, he was intimate with dark cravings as well.

I steeled myself for his touch but his hands stayed lodged in his jeans. His dark eyes searched mine. Taking a deep drag, I turned my head away, giving him my profile. "I'm not lying," he said, then took a deep breath. "Remo showed me a video of you and what happened."

I felt the color drain from my face, and my throat corded up. Too many years had gone by for me to remember everything, or even the majority of what had happened. I remembered bits and pieces. Nightmarish events that haunted my sleep in disjointed episodes or flashes of still images. I'd worked hard to forget as much as possible, had used alcohol and drugs to speed up the process. "You—" My vocal cords froze up and I couldn't say more.

Anger battled with horror and frustration in my body. Again others knew more about me and my life than I did.

Adamo came even closer, so very careful as if he feared I'd take flight. Running had never solved a thing. "I hardly watched anything. Only a couple of minutes until I realized where it was heading. I couldn't bear to watch further."

I glowered. "You couldn't bear to watch? I lived through what you couldn't even watch."

I wasn't even sure why I was angry about that. A big part of me was glad he hadn't seen more of my horrors. A tiny part was still ashamed when I thought of what had been done to me. It was an ugly voice even years of therapy, drugs and distractions hadn't silenced.

Adamo nodded, his expression kind and solemn at once. I wanted to punch him as hard as I could. Instead I balled one hand to a fist and took another deep drag from my cigarette. My fingers were shaking, letting the smoke rise up in an erratic zig-zag course.

"I know," he murmured in a voice like silk. "I shouldn't have watched it at all without asking for your permission first. This was taken in your personal space."

I scoffed. "Trust me, nobody cared about my personal space back then." I shivered, as remnants of memories flickered at the back of my mind. Words, scents, images that had left permanent marks in my subconscious.

"Dinara, I—" He released a breath.

I met Adamo's gaze. "Say whatever you have to say. I'm not breakable, Adamo. What happened back then didn't break me, whatever happens now and in the future won't break me either." My voice was pure steel, just like the protective coating slowly covering my heart.

"What do you mean?" Adamo asked, looking honestly confused. "I don't have any intention to do something that could hurt you, much less break you."

"The look in your eyes now when you look at me... it means what we had is over."

What we had. We hadn't even put a name to it, hadn't allowed us to define something that went against many odds. I hadn't allowed myself to put too much importance into our liaison. I'd tried to tell myself it was only about having fun and getting closer to a Falcone, but now that I saw our bond crumble right before my eyes, I realized it had been more than just fun. More than I should have ever allowed. More than my father would ever accept.

He bent his head, capturing my gaze with his. His scent, warm and spicy, wrapped around me. "How am I looking at you?"

I laughed bitterly and pointed the glowing tip at his face. "Like this. The same way my father looked at me when Remo handed me back to him. As if I was a broken puppet. Your favorite puppet that you took out to play every day but suddenly it had an irreparable crack, and now you can't ever play with it again because you fear it might break apart if you do. So, you'll put it on a shelf and hardly ever look at it because whenever you do, you're sad about what you lost. That's how you look at me, Adamo. So, go your merry way, I'll survive."

I wouldn't let our relationship continue because Adamo acted out of pity, because he didn't have the balls to end it with poor me.

I was a survivor. I would survive Adamo walking away, not without my dark craving, but I would survive one way or another. Still, my stomach twisted at the thought that this could be our final goodbye—even if goodbye was inevitable for us.

Adamo shook his head. "Bullshit. I never played with you, and I won't go my merry way. We aren't over and I won't allow you to put a wedge between us." He gripped my shoulders, not gentle at all, and my stupid heart pounded with hope. "Nothing changed between us."

And yet everything had. His eyes told the truth. If we wanted a chance, Adamo needed to see me as the girl I'd been before he'd known the truth. He had to see me as a separate being from the poor girl from the video. I wasn't sure if he could. Dad had tried and failed. I never resented him for it. He was my father. I accepted the way he looked at me because we were family. But I wouldn't do the same for Adamo. I couldn't. I needed this part of my life to be only for Dinara, and not poor abused

Katinka. "Then fuck me, Adamo. Fuck me like you would have two days ago and not like I'm breakable." I dropped the cigarette and crushed it under my boot. "Or can't you do it now that you feel pity for me?"

Adamo cupped my neck, heat and anger battling in his eyes. "I don't pity the girl in front of me, Dinara. I pity that girl from the past. But you…you are tough as nails. You don't need my fucking pity."

I nodded, as much to confirm his words as to convince myself that I'd really left every bit of that little girl behind. Deep down I knew she still cowered in a dark part of my brain, small and frightened, threatening to burst forth. I wanted her out of there, and by now I had an idea how to finally succeed.

"Fuck me," I breathed.

Adamo jerked me against his body, his tongue dipping into my mouth. I opened up for him, threw my arms around his neck and molded our bodies together. Adamo squeezed my breast through my tank then tugged at my pebbled nipple. I raked my fingers through his wavy hair, bit down on his lower lip only to sooth it with my tongue a moment later. He pressed his palm against my crotch and I arched against him, wanting to feel his touch on bare skin.

"Get a room," someone called. I was too disoriented from our kiss to know who it was. Adamo grabbed my hand and tugged me along. I followed him, my heart pounding wildly in my chest, my center tingling with need. Adamo dragged me into the old gas station, past a surprised Crank. "Get out," Adamo snarled, and Crank did with a muttered curse. Then we stumbled into the backroom with its old freezer and scattered boxes. The stench of moldy cardboard and something rotten clogged my nose.

Adamo threw the door shut and pressed me against the edge of the freezer, his hands making quick work of my zipper. He didn't bother pulling my shorts down, only shoved his hand into my panties and thrust his middle finger into me. The heel of his palm rubbed my clit as he fingered me hard and fast.

Our eyes stayed locked, my lips parted as Adamo drew moan after moan from my mouth. My arousal soaked my panties, making Adamo's finger slide in and out easily. He added a second finger and slammed even harder into me. The desire in his eyes seared every inch of my skin. No sign of pity, only lust.

I screamed out my release but Adamo hardly gave me time to recover before he shoved down my shorts and hoisted me on the freezer. He pushed my legs apart and took a few deep licks, making me shudder and cling to his hair. Then he straightened and pulled out his cock. He gripped my ankles and propped them up on his shoulders before he dove into me in one hard thrust. He didn't give me time to adept, instead he slammed into me. He leaned forward, bringing my legs closer to my body and changing the angle so he went even deeper. I sucked in breath after shaky breath, my toes curled tightly under the force of the sensations.

Fury and desire had replaced pity, and I became Dinara again, as I lost myself in Adamo's gaze. I dug my nails into his shoulders, my hips meeting him thrust for thrust, and then my lips tore open for a cry as I came again. Adamo slammed even harder into me before he released into me with a low groan.

I closed my eyes, panting. I didn't want this to end. Not today, not tomorrow, maybe never.

Adamo made me want to lose control to him. He made me feel as if I could lose control to him without fear.

When Adamo and I had both calmed down from our release, he met my gaze. His face was covered in sweat and his shirt clung to his upper body. "We're not over," he rasped.

I nodded, breathing harshly. "We're not."

In that moment Adamo looked at me the same way he had before he'd found out the ugly truth, as if I were still tough, racer Dinara to him. I knew there would be moments when this new poignant expression would return but as long as he could make me feel so alive, I could live with the small reminders.

FOURTEEN

Dinara

WE SPENT THE NIGHT IN ADAMO'S TENT TOGETHER. SLEEP evaded me. My thoughts revolved around the events of the previous day, the knowledge that there were still videos of me out there. Now that I knew I remembered the camera always pointed at me. It had faded into the darkness of my memories over the years. Other images had been more prominent.

Adamo's warm scent engulfed me, one of his arms thrown over my waist. His closeness provided the solace I'd never admit I needed. I peered up at the tent ceiling even if it was mostly shrouded in darkness. Only the hint of light drifted over to us, maybe from the fire or one of the cars. The low murmur of voices told me others couldn't sleep either.

"Can't sleep?" Adamo's drowsy voice rang out, making me jump.

"Too many thoughts," I admitted.

Adamo nodded, his nose brushing my cheek. "Whatever you need, I'm here. I know there's a reason why you joined the races, why you sought my closeness, and once you're ready to divulge your reasons, I'm here to listen."

I swallowed, hearing the hint of suspicion in his voice. If I were in his stead, I would be wary of my motives as well, and they hadn't been completely innocent. "Sleeping with you, spending so much time with you, that's not about a plan. I never meant for this to happen. I just wanted to get to know a member of the notorious Falcone clan to cast some light on my past, at least into the corners that my father kept purposefully dark. I thought you'd be the best option. Your brothers' reputations are even less inviting. I never lied to you about my identity. From the start, you knew I was looking for something only a Falcone could give me."

Adamo chuckled. "I'm the least dangerous option, you mean?"

I let out a small laugh. "Walking into Vegas seemed like a bad idea, even in my head, and you fascinated me from the moment I began to research your family."

"What fascinated you?"

"The racing, definitely. But more than that, it was the conflict I sometimes saw in your eyes during cage fights. As if a blood-thirsty part battled with your conscience. You reminded me of myself. My father thinks I belong in the light, but I don't fit in there."

Adamo propped himself up so his face hovered over mine but it was too dark to make out more than the general outline. "The blood you thirst for, is it in Vegas?"

I didn't say anything. Over the last couple of months, my goal had shifted. "I'd wanted to find out more about my past, and I knew only Remo could tell me what my father wouldn't. I didn't have much hope that he would divulge any information. Maybe if my father and he would still cooperate, but now that their relationship has turned hostile, I knew the chances were slim. But I had to take my chances. Part of me hoped, you'd know what I wanted to know."

"What do you want now?"

My heart sped up whenever I tried to determine what exactly I wanted. Deep down only one option sounded satisfying. "I need to do what I'd originally planned. Find out everything before I can really decide what I'm going to do next."

"I have the CDs in my car. Do you want them?"

I quickly shook my head. "Not yet," I whispered. One day I'd try to watch them, but not now, even if they'd show me the cold, hard truth in every disgusting detail. I wasn't ready for that confrontation.

Adamo cupped my cheek. "You want me to take you to Vegas? To meet Remo. Right?"

I'd imagined meeting the man who'd saved me from possibly years of abuse countless times over the years. My father had never talked in very favorable words about the Capo. Now I guessed the reason for it was that Remo had kept my mother and not allowed my father to kill her. I wasn't sure why. It seemed unlikely that Remo Falcone had qualms about ending the life of a woman.

"Yes." Adamo's silence filled the darkness between us. "I know you're loyal to the Camorra and I'm not asking you to betray them. I want to officially meet Remo if he allows it."

"We can drive to Vegas after the next race."

"Won't you have to ask Remo first?" Even if Adamo was the Capo's brother, there were some rules to be followed, unless the Camorra operated completely different from my father's organization, which I seriously doubted. All crime organization were based on a strict hierarchical structure.

"During my last trip to Vegas, I mentioned that you might want to see him to talk. He agreed."

I pushed up. "How did you know? Maybe I'm supposed to assassinate your brother for keeping my mother all these years? You can't know my true motives. I could be lying."

"You haven't revealed your true motives yet, maybe even you don't know them in their full scope at this point, but Remo can protect himself and he's the master of games and cunning. Tricking him is difficult, far more difficult than tricking me."

I huffed. "I think you're putting yourself down."

"Nah, I'm very good at reading people, and even at manipulation if I want to be, it's the Falcone gene, but Remo is the fucking master at it. He might as well have invented it."

"So Remo wants to see me to determine my motives? He's going to find out if I pose a risk to him, you or the Camorra."

Adamo stroked along my arm. "No, I doubt that's why he wants to meet you. Remo kept your mother and the videos for a reason, but he didn't divulge everything to me. You and he both hide part of the truth, and by bringing the two of you together, I hope to uncover everything."

"But you have your suspicions why your brother did what he did?"

"I know Remo. His values haven't changed over the years. They are as twisted and morally doubtful as they used to be."

"It's not like your morals are socially acceptable."

Adamo laughed. "I'm a Falcone. Twisted morals are in my gene pool."

"I wonder when you'll decide I'm not worth the trouble?"

"Oh, I have a feeling you're worth every trouble you might put me through."

I bit my lip, unsure how to respond to that. Every day I spent with Adamo, he grew more on me. I missed him when he wasn't around and I kept thinking about him and how it felt to be with him. I wasn't sure where my path was taking me but I hoped Adamo would join me on it, at least for a little while longer. I didn't dare look too far into the future.

"Dima can't come with us to Vegas. That wouldn't go over well with Remo," Adamo said.

Dima and I didn't talk much but he'd returned to camp with me after my last trip to Chicago. I wasn't sure if it was on my father's orders or if his own protective streak had come through. "Then we'll have to sneak away. I doubt he'll listen to me if I tell him to stay behind. If my father gave him orders to guard me, he won't let anything stop him."

"Then we'll sneak away after the next race. He rarely stays long for the afterparty. And maybe you can slip a couple of sleeping pills into his drink. I can give you something strong."

I shook my head. While I trusted Adamo with myself, I wasn't sure if I should trust him with Dima's life. He was a Bratva soldier after all, and definitely the first one Adamo would kill. "I'll handle it."

Adamo chuckled. "All right. But you don't have to worry. If I wanted to get rid of Dima, I wouldn't do it the cowardly way. I'd beat him in a fight to the death."

"That's a consolation," I said dryly.

Adamo brought our faces even closer and kissed me. The kiss was sweet with a hint of possessiveness. He nipped at my lip before he pulled away. "Why Dima?"

"You mean why I dated him?"

"Yeah," he said. "You and him were together for a few years, right?"

"Three years."

"So why him? At first, I thought he was jealous of us but now I'm not so sure anymore. He definitely disapproves but I'm not sure it's because he wants you for himself or if there's another reason. But you definitely look at him as if he might just as well be your brother and not your ex."

"Are you jealous? I haven't been with him in over a year, and not with anyone else either."

"Just curious. I still think he acts more like a protective brother than a former lover. It's odd."

"More odd than a Falcone and a Mikhailov getting it on?" I asked, trailing my fingers down Adamo's muscled chest and abs.

Adamo chuckled. "Nice try."

I sighed. I'd known Dima almost all my life. He'd been friends even before my mother had taken me away and afterward, he'd been the one whose company I sought as well. Unlike the adults, he didn't look at me with pity and horror. He didn't really know what had happened. That would change later and so would the way he treated me, but he'd always been by my side.

I reached for the cigarette package on the ground beside me and lit a smoke up, then took a deep drag from it. Usually this was a topic that felt too personal, but Adamo and I had reached a point in our…relationship where I wanted to share more of myself. It was a surprising and terrifying realization.

I let out a plume of smoke before I twisted my head around to Adamo "I wanted to be in control, wanted to experience sexuality on my own terms. In the past…" My voice died. I squinted at the glowing tip of my cigarette for a couple of breaths before I could speak again. "The things that were done to me…everything was out of my control. I had to endure the pain, the fear and humiliation. But with Dima, even when it was painful, that was my choice. He let it be my choice. Dima was a safe option. As my bodyguard, he was meant to protect me. Father would have killed him if he'd hurt me. He is my father's man through and through. I knew he'd never do anything I didn't want. With him I could do what I wanted, get the power back that was taken from me as a child."

Sex with Dima had been…freeing in a way because it had been on my terms. It hadn't been forced upon me. Everything was my choice. But it had never felt…right. I'd never really let go of my control so fully until Adamo. Dima and I had been a bond of convenience. Dima had probably hoped it would give him an advantage in the long-term because as an orphan raised by the Bratva his options would have been limited. But he'd also wanted to help me. And for me, it had meant breaking through part of my shackles while also getting my father off my back. Seeing me in a relationship with Dima had given Dad hope that I'd overcome the past and could live a normal life. If I hadn't lived through what I had, I doubt he would have been as thrilled about me dating one of his men.

Adamo nodded, and even though I couldn't see his expression, I warned. "No pity." The timbre of my voice was almost feral.

"No pity. We Falcones don't do pity," he said firmly, snatching the smoke out of my hand and taking a drag himself.

"I almost forgot," I said sarcastically. Adamo kissed me again, his hand sliding over my bare belly, leaving goose bumps in his way. He began to play distractingly with my nipple piercing again. The glow of the cigarette threw shadows onto his face, reflecting in his dark eyes.

"What you said makes sense. I hope I'm not another safe option."

I swallowed a moan as Adamo tugged a bit harder. "Sex with you has nothing to do with a safe option, it's a wild ride that completely rips any semblance of control from me."

Adamo kissed the corner of my lip and squashed the cigarette. "So this is only about sex and dirty orgasms?"

It wasn't. Not anymore. Even if my body constantly yearned for his touch. I raked my fingernails over his chest and abs. "What else would it be about? I really enjoy all the dirty orgasms. You never complained."

Adamo bent over my nipple. "No complaints whatsoever. Every dirty orgasm your skillful mouth and pussy milk out of my cock are very appreciated." He flicked my nipple with his tongue. Then moved lower, his warm breath ghosting over my belly. He buried his face in my pussy, licking up my lust for him. "I don't hear your pussy complain either."

"Shut up," I gasped, and he did while his mouth and tongue played my pussy like an instrument. Losing control had never felt better.

During the race the next day, I had a hard time focusing. One reason was lack of sleep because Adamo and I had kept each other busy until the early morning hours. The other were thoughts of my upcoming meeting with Remo distracting me. I'd be closer to my mother than I'd been in over a decade. The only time I'd ever really seen her had been in nightmares. Would reality be worse?

I wasn't sure if I wanted to see her. When I'd thought she was dead, I'd always wished for a chance to confront her, but now that the option was real and in my reach, my chest constricted at the mere thought. Even if the past still haunted me on occasion, I had it under control most days. What if seeing her would rip open wounds I couldn't close again?

I finished the race in fifteenth place. My worst result so far, but despite my ambition, even that barely registered. All I could think about was that we'd head out to Vegas early in the morning.

Dima didn't join the party after the race and instead hid in his tent right away. I went after him. I wanted to check on him, and I still needed to give him the sleeping pills so he wouldn't get in the way of our plan to head to Vegas. I really didn't need an escort of my father's men at my side. That wouldn't make Remo give up any of his knowledge. He'd kick us out with blazing guns.

"Dima?" I called. I couldn't really knock at his tent. A form shifted inside and eventually the flap opened and Dima poked his head out. He was only in his boxers, a sight I'd seen countless times before, but it felt awkward now. The tattoo of the crossed Kalashnikovs branded his chest—the sign of the Bratva. *"What do you need?"*

I held up the two cups with vodka. "*We didn't share a drink after the race.*"

"*No reason to celebrate, right? We both didn't do well today.*"

Dima had never much cared about succeeding in the races. He'd stayed for me. "*Vodka is right in any situation. To commemorate, to celebrate and just because.*"

The flicker of a smile ghosted across Dima's face before it disappeared.

I handed him one of the cups and he accepted it as he stepped out of the tent. The dose wasn't too high. It would make sure he fell asleep soon and would sleep until the morning. His light slumber would otherwise prove tricky.

We bumped cups before we emptied the vodka in one gulp followed by a hiss. I grinned. It was a homemade vodka from Dad's cook and stronger than the stuff you could buy in stores, especially in the States. Widow maker was one of its nicknames among Dad's men.

Dima scanned my face. "*I'm worried about you, Dinara. Since you found out about your mother, you pulled away from me. I feel like you don't trust me with your plans anymore.*"

I scoffed, even if he'd hit the nail on the head. "You pulled away because you don't like me with Adamo. I gave you room."

"*Don't make the mistake of trusting him. A wolf is still a wolf even covered in sheep fur.*"

"You aren't a sheep either. I don't have any sheep in my life. And don't forget, I'm a wolf myself."

Dima laughed. "*You are.*"

My gaze drifted back to the party. People were dancing around the fire, already drunk on whatever concoction they'd brewed today. Adamo talked to Crank but he kept throwing glances my way.

"*You better return,*" Dima said coldly. "*He's waiting.*"

I sent him an exasperated look but he slipped inside the tent and closed it. The moment I reached the party, someone grabbed my hand and pulled me into a dance circle around the fire. I was too stunned to tell them off. Instead I allowed my body to sway to the music.

Adamo grinned as he watched me. As we passed him by, I grabbed his shirt and tugged him along. For seconds at a time, I forgot what lay ahead and lived only in the moment, existed in the beat. My boots stirred up the dry earth as I danced to the music.

The afterparty was still in full swing when Adamo and I snuck off toward his tent. Nobody got suspicious since we'd done it before. By now our affair wasn't a secret anymore. Luckily, people didn't stick their noses in our business. Most of them had secrets of their own they wanted to cover up. The only one who commented on it at all was Dima. I wondered if he'd mentioned anything to my father, but I doubted it. Dad would have asked me about it if he knew.

It was four in the morning when Adamo and I dismantled the tent and got into his car. Adamo hardly touched the gas and instead let the car roll away from camp slowly. When we were a good distance away, he sped up and we hit the street toward Vegas.

My gaze followed the monotone landscape, only occasionally broken up by Joshua trees or stone formations.

"How long will it take?"

"The ride takes about three hours. Maybe four depending on traffic once we reach Vegas."

"And Remo knows we're coming?"

"I sent him a message. He and Nino will wait for us in the Sugar Trap."

The Sugar Trap…the name rang a bell and eventually the image of a neon sign with spread legs formed in my mind as if dragged out of murky waters. With the memory came a tight sensation in my belly. "Will we ride back right away?"

Adamo slanted me a cautious look. "Maybe you'll need more than just a couple of hours. I booked a hotel for us at the strip. Camorra owned."

"You don't have to spend the night in a hotel with me instead of with your family. I know they don't trust me."

"It's such a burden to spend the night in a five-star hotel with a gorgeous redhead instead of having my family shove their noses in my business and ask me a million questions about you."

My eyebrows shot up. "What kind of questions?"

"My sisters-in-law want to know all about you. A secret girl in my life has them all dying from curiosity."

"Secret girl in Adamo Falcone's life. I like that title."

Before I could think about it, I reached for his hand and before I could pull away again, Adamo linked our fingers. He gave me a knowing smile and silence fell over us. Sometimes I lost myself in the warmth of his eyes. They made me feel as if I could entrust him with every dark secret I harbored.

My pulse spiked at the flood of emotion this realization brought on and looked away. I peered out of the window, trying to recall what I remembered of Remo and Nino Falcone, and Las Vegas. I hadn't understood who they were back then, except the men who'd freed me from my daily hell and given me back to my Dad. For a while, they'd seemed like heroes. But eventually Dad had made it clear that whatever they had done was for business reasons, to create a shaky truce with the Bratva. Dad had lied about mother's death, so I wasn't sure how much of his tales were false too. Yet, the Camorra wasn't really known for their altruistic agendas.

When Las Vegas appeared on the horizon, my belly flipped and my mouth became dry. Over a decade. The girl who'd left this city long ago didn't exist anymore—or so I hoped.

"How long?" I asked, my voice hushed.

Adamo squeezed my hand but even his touch didn't calm me now. "Ten minutes."

Not enough time to brace myself for what lay ahead. Now that I got closer to my goal inner calm seemed impossible to reach.

Ten minutes later we pulled up in front of the Sugar Trap. I pushed open the door, tearing away from Adamo's grip. I drew in a deep breath, fighting against the tightness in my chest. The mere sight of the neon sign brought back memories from the past, from the days and weeks prior to Remo giving me back to my father. Las Vegas was filled with horrible memories for me. It wasn't the only city though. Even before Mother and I had moved here, she had allowed the men who gave us shelter to abuse me.

"Dinara?" Adamo asked carefully, walking up beside me.

"I'm fine," I pressed out before he could ask. "Lead the way."

Adamo took my hand and I let him as he led me toward the shabby black door leading into the Sugar Trap. It was a whorehouse, the first establishment of the sort I set foot inside since that fateful day many years ago, and the place that would determine my future.

FIFTEEN

Dinara

A DAMO OPENED THE DOOR AND HELD IT OPEN FOR ME. I STEPPED into the dimly lit ante-room with its cloakroom and a huge black bouncer sitting at a table. His eyes briefly narrowed on me before they moved on to Adamo and he gave a curt nod.

Adamo didn't say anything, only gave the man a tense smile, before he led me along. My legs felt leaden as I followed him into the bar area of the Sugar Trap where johns could check out the selection of whores and chat with them until they went into one of the backrooms for the actual deed. Now the area was mostly deserted except for a dark-skinned man behind the bar counter, taking stock of the liquor cabinet. It was still too early for customers.

My eyes took in the red leather booths, black lacquer décor and the dance platforms with silver poles. The color scheme hadn't changed nor had the general vibe of the establishment. But it seemed smaller now, and less daunting. For the small, distraught girl from the past everything had seemed so much bigger. Now it was a dingy bar like any other, not so different from the ones Dad had in Chicago. I wasn't allowed to set foot in them but I'd seen photos. I handled all the online presences of the clubs and bars on the internet as well as Darknet for Dad's section of the Bratva. I had a penchant for computer sciences, so it was a way to feel useful and justify the endless amount of money at my disposal.

My pulse didn't slow as we crossed the bar, even if I didn't catch a hint of danger. Adamo threw me another worried look because I'd slowed even more. "We don't have to meet my brothers. We can return to camp."

"No," I said sharply. "I have to talk to Remo."

Some parts of my life, of my past, had remained out of my control, and I needed to yank control back. I needed to talk to someone who'd been there.

Adamo nodded but I could tell he wasn't convinced. He couldn't understand. I wasn't sure if anyone really could. He'd gone through some messed up shit, especially with his mother, but what he'd done, attacking her, had been a spur of the moment thing when it was his brothers' lives or hers. My deepest desires went so much further.

"Let me talk to my brothers before I take you to them, all right?" he said. "Why don't you grab something to drink? I'm sure Jerry will gladly give you whatever you want."

Jerry looked up behind the bar and gave me a quick smile, all white teeth in his dark complexion.

I released Adamo's hand and he disappeared through the backdoor. I headed for the bar but didn't sit down. "Do you have vodka?"

Jerry grinned. "Of course. And a good one if I might say so."

He poured me a generous glass of Moskovskaya, definitely not the worst vodka. I took a sip, my eyes returning to the door where Adamo had disappeared through.

By now, Dima would have noticed my disappearance and would have alerted my father. That was why I'd left my cellphone in my car in camp. I didn't want Dad to track me to this place and send his soldiers to save me, when I didn't want or need saving. At least not the kind of saving he had in mind.

The door swung open and Adamo stepped through followed by two tall men. In my memory both Remo and Nino Falcone had been giants, but now I realized that Adamo was their height. They had seemed so much taller for a little girl. I emptied the glass in one quick gulp, enjoying the burn and the resulting warmth.

Remo's mouth twitched when he followed my actions. His eyes held recognition and the hint of dark amusement. No sign of pity. His brother

Nino's face was completely void of emotions, just like I remembered it. I didn't wait for them to approach me, instead I walked in their direction, my head held high.

I was aware of their reputation, and Adamo's protection would only go so far. They were his brothers, and even if he enjoyed my company, his loyalty lay with the Camorra and his family as it should.

I held out my hand to Remo. "It's been a long time."

Remo nodded with another twitch of his mouth and briefly shook my hand. "Indeed. You changed."

Adamo positioned himself at my side and touched my hip. I briefly glanced his way, surprised by his closeness and his open sign of our togetherness. I couldn't deny that it warmed my chest more than the vodka had done.

Both Nino and Remo glanced at Adamo's move but didn't comment. Dad would probably have attempted to kill Adamo at this display of affection.

"Haven't we all?" I said. "Change is inevitable."

Nino inclined his head and shook my hand. "How about we continue our conversation in the office?"

"That sounds reasonable," I said.

Remo and Nino exchanged a look before they headed back through the door.

Adamo smiled encouragingly, his thumb sliding along my hip. "You are safe in Vegas." His dark eyes held absolutely no doubt.

"I know," I said and briefly kissed him. We followed his brothers, past a long row of closed doors. My belly flipped when I recognized one of them as the door to the room where I'd spent my night. More memories from that day took shape. Cody's face, which had been shrouded in darkness up until this point manifested before my inner eye, and with it came a wave of revulsion.

Remo threw a look over his shoulder before he opened the door to what I assumed was his office. He scanned my face and I steeled myself, remembering Adamo's words about his brother's talent to recognize other people's weaknesses and darkest emotions.

When I entered the office with the boxing sack, desk and sofa, my breath briefly caught in my throat, as the events from a decade ago appeared in my head. Cody's horrified expression, Mother's attempts to bargain with the Capo, and his fury over it. Adamo closed the door with a soft click, but I jumped anyway. I could have kicked myself for this sign of distress because it didn't go unnoticed. All three men registered my jumpiness. If I didn't get a grip, they'd see me as the sheep among the pack, not another wolf.

Adamo rubbed my waist again and while I appreciated his support, and would eventually tell him so, I needed to show strength. I hadn't come this far to cower like the girl I had been in the past. I'd moved beyond her. I had changed.

I gave him a strained smile before I stepped out of his reach and approached Remo who leaned against his desk, watching us with keen eyes. I wondered what Adamo had told him about our relationship and what the Capo thought of it. "Over the years, I made sure to stay up to date on your life," Remo said cryptically.

I didn't show a reaction. As the daughter of the Pakhan who loved to live a flashy life, I was in public more often than I preferred. I'd never hidden, and Dad wouldn't have allowed it either. He wanted me in the spotlight, dressed in pretty dresses for the world to see. Few people dared to speak of the past, even if rumors had spread after my return. "So did I. You and your brothers have kept things interesting over the years."

Remo's eyes flashed with amusement.

"Why would the Capo of the Camorra have any interest in the daughter of his enemy? My life didn't provide the same excitement as yours."

Adamo and Nino watched our conversation but didn't intervene.

"I wanted to see if I was right in my assessment of you."

I narrowed my eyes. "What assessment?"

"If you'd prove as strong as I considered you to be."

I scoffed. "I was a scared child who allowed people to use and abuse her. I wasn't strong. I'm not the same person I used to be. I changed."

Remo pushed away from the desk and moved closer, towering over me, which caused Adamo to tense. I met Remo's gaze unwaveringly. Maybe it was foolish of me not to fear him but I could only see him as the man who'd freed me from my tormentors. "Even back then I saw your strength, even if you couldn't. That you are here today, shows I was right. Maybe you changed on the outside, but deep down you are the same resilient child that survived."

I swallowed, because his words awakened emotions I didn't want to deal with. Adamo took a step closer, and his protective expression didn't bode well. This was between Remo and me. If I wanted to get to the bottom of my past, I needed to talk to Remo alone. I had a feeling he wouldn't be as forthcoming with information as long as I needed Adamo as my babysitter and bodyguard. He was testing me. I cleared my throat and looked at Adamo. "I need to talk to Remo alone."

If Remo was surprised by my request, he hid it well.

Nino exchanged a look with his older brother before he left without another word. Adamo, however, pulled me against his side. "What's the matter?"

"Your brother and I need to talk alone."

"Still don't trust me, hmm?" Adamo asked wryly.

"No," I growled. "That's not it. But the truth I'm going to find out today is my truth. One I want to process before I share it with anyone else. Even with you. It's my past."

Adamo sighed. He leaned in and kissed me. "All right, but remember I'm here if you need me."

He sent his brother a warning look that made me want to ask him to stay after all. When Remo and I were finally alone, silence fell over us for a while. Remo watched me closely, and whatever he saw seemed to please him. "Few of my men feel comfortable in my presence. Most women would rather be locked inside a cage with a fight dog than me, but you ask for a tête-à-tête and don't seem frightened at all?"

"Do I have reason to be scared of you?" I asked.

Again the twitch of his mouth. "I think you already answered that question for yourself before you set foot on Vegas ground."

I shrugged. "I had my assumptions, but of course I couldn't be sure. My father is your enemy. You and him would kill the other if you ever met."

"Your father isn't in the top ten of my enemy list, Dinara. He'll probably live."

My lips thinned. "My father is a strong man with an army of loyal followers."

Remo chuckled. "Ahh, a Bratva princess after all? One could think you don't care for your father's business considering how recklessly you walk into Camorra territory and become part of our racing camp."

"I'm loyal to my father, just like Adamo is loyal to you and the Camorra."

Something shifted in Remo's eyes, and I realized I was treading dangerous ground. "Have you tested his loyalty?"

"I didn't and I won't. Adamo has his place and I have mine."

"But the lines have become blurry, haven't they? You and Adamo have gotten close over the last few weeks," Remo said, and the hint of suspicion and threat swung in his deep voice.

I knew it would be futile to deny it. I wasn't sure how much Adamo had told his brother, and I had a feeling Remo would have smelled the lie. "We have. We share a passion for racing."

"But that's not why your paths crossed, Dinara, am I right? You joined our race camp for a reason."

"I did," I said firmly, not looking away. If I'd lowered my gaze or tried to avoid the topic, Remo would have seen it as an admission of guilt. I was definitely guilty of seeking Adamo's closeness initially to find out about the Falcones and to use him to get in contact with Remo, but sleeping with him or spending so much time with him had never served that purpose. My body and soul had yearned for it. When I was with Adamo, I rarely longed for the rush of drugs that had haunted me for so many years. He was my drug of choice. "My father was always careful to divulge as little information as possible to me about my past. I knew you were the only one who could reveal the parts he left in the dark."

"So you think I'll do that? Why would I reveal information without asking for something in turn? And unlike your father you don't have anything of value to offer."

For a moment I was thrown off. My father had always insisted Remo wouldn't help me with my past. I'd be lucky if I wasn't killed by the crazy Capo. Again I noticed the flicker of challenge in Remo's eyes. Remembering Adamo's words about his brother's manipulation skills, I straightened my shoulders. "My father must have offered you a lot for my mother. There's nothing he'd rather do than kill her with his own hands. But whatever he offered was never enough for you, which means he's got nothing you want. Maybe you are as twisted as everyone says and just want to hold her fate over his head to taunt him, but then the peace which lasted many years doesn't make sense."

Remo's smile widened. "Go on. I'm starting to enjoy your analysis."

"Maybe you waited for me to show up. Maybe my father isn't the one you want to hand information to."

"And why would I choose you, Dinara?"

"Because it's my past. It's my right to know the truth. No one else's."

Remo inclined his head. "Well said."

"So will you tell me everything?"

"I will but first I want to talk about Adamo."

"Adamo's a grown man. He can protect himself."

"Oh, I know, but I have a feeling you might be in need of his help again soon for a path you can't walk alone. He'll do what you ask of him because he cares for you and because it's a path he can't resist. You should be sure that what you want from Adamo doesn't end the day you reach the end of that path, because if it does, you better end it now."

"Adamo and I aren't in a serious relationship. We have fun together. That's all."

Remo leaned closer, and I shied back involuntarily. "Whatever's between the two of you extends beyond fucking. You two share the same vices."

"Adamo and I need to figure it out by ourselves."

Remo gave me a look that sent a shiver down my back. I didn't resent him for his protectiveness of his younger brother. If Adamo ever met my father…things wouldn't be any different. Dad would try to scare him away or at least scare him into treating me right. If he wasn't Remo Falcone's brother, he'd probably even kill him. Maybe he'd do it anyway if he considered it the only option to protect me.

"Maybe we should talk about the reason why you're here now. Ask whatever you want to know."

"Did my father know all these years that my mother was alive?"

Remo nodded. "I never told him otherwise. I had no reason to kill her."

"You didn't, but my father had. So why didn't you allow my father to kill her himself? I can see it in his eyes that he wants to do it. You are the only thing standing in his way," I said.

"Because," Remo growled. "That's your privilege. I told your father I'd keep her in my territory until you were old enough to decide over her fate. I'd have thought you'd come along sooner to kill her."

I froze, realizing the gift laid out before me, the gift Remo was offering. Dad had never mentioned that tidbit of information. Of course, he hadn't. He wanted me in the light, and what Remo was offering led into the depth of hell. "You've kept her for me so I could kill her?"

Kill my mother. I had lost count of the times I'd considered it in abstract fantasies, but I had never been this close. My heart sped up. In the last few days, the idea had taken shape, but the Camorra had always seemed in my way, a barrier I'd have to pass to get what I wanted. Now I realized the only thing stopping me was me. If I wanted to do it, I could find her now and end her life.

"Kill her or do whatever else you see fit for someone like her after everything she's done."

"Broken me?" I clipped, even if it was a tone not fit for a Capo.

"I don't see someone broken when I look at you. And if you think you are, then you should try to fix yourself because no one else can."

I nodded. Dad had tried, Dima had tried, even Adamo was trying but deep down I knew there was only one way for me to get past what had happened.

"What if I want her to be free? What if I want to make my peace with her? Not everyone needs to kill their mother to move on." It was a risky thing to say, but Remo had caught me on the wrong foot.

His expression became dangerous. "That's true. Some people can make peace with their abusers, but our kind isn't able to do it."

Our kind. My father had always tried to keep me away from the darkness but its call had always been loud and clear in my heart. "I never considered killing her."

Remo gave me a look that made it clear he didn't believe me.

"In detail," I amended. "I thought she was dead so I never really considered it a valid option. It was the impossible fantasy of a desperate mind."

"It's not an impossible fantasy anymore, Dinara. It's your revenge. It's in your reach. You only have to take it."

I swallowed. "I can't kill her now. Not yet. I've never killed anyone," I admitted. I'd never even witnessed someone being killed. I had by accident walked in after a killing once when Dad had shot one of his soldiers in his office. But the man had been dead and lying in his blood. I hadn't looked into his eyes in his last waking moments.

Remo shrugged. "No one's without fault."

I snorted. "Some people might see it as a virtue to refrain from killing."

"Those are usually people who've never seen the dark side of life, and tasted how good it can be if you bend it to your will."

"I have seen enough darkness..." I paused, trying to really feel inside of me. I didn't doubt I could pull a trigger if given the right incentive, especially to protect myself or people I cared about. But revenge was a different beast. It stemmed from an even darker urge.

Yet, I wanted to follow its calling.

SIXTEEN

Adamo

I PRACTICALLY BOUNCED ON THE BAR STOOL AS I WAITED FOR Dinara to talk to Remo. It didn't sit well with me that she had to deal with him alone.

"Remo wants to help her. There's no reason for you to be tense," Nino drawled. He sat on the bar stool beside me, regarding me with his usual analytical calm expression.

"Would you have been relaxed to have Kiara in a room with Remo in the beginning?"

"Kiara needed to feel protected and she only trusted me. Dinara seems like a woman who can handle herself. She won't let Remo intimidate her. You don't have to worry." He narrowed his eyes in consideration. "But your comparison proves that your relation to Dinara goes beyond the physical aspect. You care for her on an emotional level."

I tore my eyes away from his. "It's complicated."

"Indeed."

Steps sounded and the door to the back corridor swung open. Dinara was awfully pale when she stepped into the bar. That was a look many people displayed after some alone time with Remo.

I jumped off the stool and hurried over to her. I touched her shoulder, drawing her gaze to mine. "Are you all right?"

Dinara nodded distractedly. "Yeah." She laughed hoarsely. "Or maybe not."

"What did Remo say?"

Dinara held up a piece of paper with a handwritten note. "He gave me the address of the bar where my mother works."

"Dinara," I said slowly. Remo had always wanted to kill our mother for what she'd done to him and my brothers. Revenge had been his driving force. For him it was impossible to comprehend that not everyone followed the same logic as him.

"Take me there," Dinara said, not allowing me to voice my worries. I could feel Nino's gaze on us, probably analyzing our body language to assess our level of emotional connection.

I sighed and resisted the urge to walk into Remo's office to confront him. It would have been hypocritical anyway because avenging Dinara had been on my mind since I'd found out about her past. But I wanted to protect her from it. Nino gave us a curt nod as we walked past him and to my car. Dinara was tense beside me as I headed toward the address. I'd been to the bar only once before. It was one of our shabbier whorehouses, not a place I enjoyed spending time in.

"What will you do when you see your mother?" I asked. I remembered seeing my mother for the first time in years when I was a teen. She was in an asylum, a seemingly broken woman who wanted peace. Back then I'd wanted to move beyond my brothers' constant need for blood and death. I wanted to be better. Instead my desperate attempt to change fate had only thrust me deeper into my predetermined path.

Dinara turned to me, her teal eyes wide. "I don't know."

"I assume Remo gave you permission to kill her."

"He did. He gave me permission to do to her whatever I want. He called it my privilege."

That sounded like my brother. "You don't have to do it. You have options."

"What options?" Dinara whispered harshly. "It's not that I haven't considered killing her. Every night since I found out that she's alive, I've been dreaming about how I'd see her die. Your brother didn't put the idea in my head. It's been there all along." She tipped against her temple.

I took her hand, linking our fingers.

"Did you imagine killing your mother before the day you stabbed her?" she asked.

"For a long time, I believed killing my mother wouldn't change anything. Part of me even hoped we could make peace with her, and become at least a dysfunctional family. I wasn't born when she hurt my brothers. I'd always only heard the stories, and even those were sparse. Remo tried to keep the horrors of the day that my mother tried to kill them away from me. But I needed to realize the horrible impact she had on our family for myself." Nino had once recounted how our mother had cut his wrists, drugged baby Savio and tried to cut Remo as well before she set the room on fire. Remo saved Nino and Savio from a cruel fate. Our mother had still been pregnant with me then, and if she'd succeeded with her devious plan, I would have never even been born. I realized I'd been silent for too long, lost in my thoughts, and so I continued with my story:

"When I saw her that day, trying to kill everyone I cared about and smiling while she did it, I realized what she was. That she was the root of my brothers' problems, of all of our struggles. Our father hadn't been better than her, but he at least was dead and couldn't cast his dark shadow over us anymore. In that moment I wanted to kill her and I never regretted it. I'm glad my brothers did it though. It was their privilege."

"Did it help your brothers to see her dead? To kill her themselves?"

I considered that. I had never really talked about it with my brothers. The topic of our mother's death had been buried with her corpse. She was gone. Maybe my brothers talked about it with their wives but definitely not with me, and I'd never dared to talk about it. Putting the past to rest had been a huge step in finding happiness for me.

"I'm not sure it helped them. It didn't change them. By then we all were already too messed up to find our way back onto a different path, but maybe it gave them peace of mind for a while."

Dinara swallowed. "Peace of mind was what I wanted when I sought you and the truth. I wanted to uncover the ghosts of my past that kept haunting me, wanted to confront them and put them to rest, but I didn't know so many of them were still around."

"You mean your mother and your abusers?"

She nodded. I pulled the car into the half-empty parking lot of the whorehouse and killed the engine but made no move to get out because neither did Dinara. She slanted a cautious look toward the front door of the establishment. It was a simple steel door in a brick building without any windows at the front.

I squeezed her hand. "I'm here."

Dinara gave a more resolute nod and shoved open the door. I released her and got out of the car, following her toward the entrance of the whorehouse. She froze in front of it and turned to me, her eyes frantic. She reached for my gun holster but I stopped her with a gentle touch. "You can't shoot her in the middle of a bar. If you want to kill her, you need to do it somewhere private."

Dinara pulled her hand away, looking lost for a moment. "Will you give me your gun when I need it? I don't have any weapons on me."

"Can you shoot?"

"Dima taught me."

"You can have my gun *if* you need it." I still thought Dinara looked too out of it to make this kind of monumental decision so shortly after having the option handed to her on a silver platter.

"It's my decision," she clipped, her eyes becoming more focused. "My past, my decision. Don't try to stop me."

"I won't," I promised.

She took a deep breath before she stepped into the building, followed closely by me.

The air was thick with smoke, spilled beer and sweat as we headed into the dimly lit bar of the whorehouse. A couple of men sat at the bar, chatting with prostitutes, and half a dozen booths were occupied as well. In some of them the whores and their customers had already moved past chatting. In our better establishment any kind of touching was limited to the backrooms but here things were handled a bit more openly. One of the whores was rubbing a fat guy through his pants while he was pawing at her breasts and slobbering all over her neck.

Dinara didn't seem to notice. Her eyes scanned the room, and I did the same, but didn't spot anyone who could be Eden. "Let's go to the bar counter," I said.

The men at the bar checked out Dinara hungrily but the look I sent them made them avert their gazes hurriedly. The barkeeper, a lanky blond guy in his twenties, came over to us,. "Mr. Falcone," he said with a reverent nod. "What can I do for you?"

"Two vodka, and you can tell me where Eden is."

"She's in a backroom with a customer. Do you want me to get her for you?"

"No," Dinara said quickly.

The barkeeper gave me a questioning look and I nodded. "We'll wait for her. Let her finish her business. But get us those drinks. We'll be over in a booth waiting."

With a hand on Dinara's back, I led her toward a booth in the corner. We made ourselves comfortable and a moment later a waitress delivered our drinks. Dinara looked around, her face hard. "This place is disgusting."

"Are your father's whorehouses better?"

"Most of them aren't, no. But he's got a few more luxurious establishments as well."

Dinara nipped at her vodka then set it down again. I slid closer to her, seeking her gaze.

"Thank you for being at my side," she murmured. "You have every reason to mistrust me or to mind your own business but instead you chose to help me, even when I'm being a bitch."

"You aren't a bitch. You are stubborn and strong-willed."

A slow smile spread on her beautiful face but it dropped rapidly.

Her eyes snapped toward the bar and I followed her gaze. A woman and a man had just stepped back into the bar through the backdoor. The man had his arm wrapped around her waist and she was leaning into him, giving him a flirty smile. Her hair was colored a burgundy red and her skin was tanned, but her cheekbones were unmistakable.

Dinara froze. "It's her."

She sounded small and terrified, like that girl in the recordings. I ran my thumb over her hand, hoping to give her strength. I narrowed my eyes at her mother who was still all over her customer. Hatred burned in my veins. Hatred and a hunger for revenge on Dinara's behalf. I wished she'd ask me to handle the woman for her. I wouldn't hesitate—pretending otherwise would have been a fucking lie. I wouldn't even have qualms about it.

Eden kissed her customer one last time before he walked off, then her pleasant smile fell and she scowled at his back before she turned to the men at the bar with a seductive smile. She hadn't noticed us.

"I need to go," Dinara pressed out. "Now."

She jerked to her feet, her eyes haunted. I stood, grabbed her hand and led her outside as fast as I could. I wasn't sure if Eden saw us, and even if she did, would she even recognize Dinara?

Dinara was hyperventilating when I pushed her down into the passenger seat and squatted before her. I touched her thighs. "Hey. Look at me. I'm here. I can protect you."

"I know," she said between gasps and slowly her breathing calmed and her eyes really focused on my face. "But I need to protect myself. Instead I lose it as if I were still the little girl from back then. I should be strong but I'm not." The despair in her voice and eyes cut me deeply.

"You are," I said firmly. "But you have to give yourself time. You went from thinking your mother was dead to seeing her in flesh and blood. You need time to work things out."

"Take me back to camp," Dinara whispered. "I need to get out of Vegas. I need—" She shook her head. "Just take me away."

I leaned in and kissed her before I closed the door and got in behind the steering wheel. For the first time since I'd known Dinara she looked like the frightened child she didn't want to be perceived as. I could see her struggle to be strong, but the girl from the videos, a shadow from the past, lingered in her eyes.

Dinara was awfully quiet on our drive back to camp. I couldn't forget the haunted look in her eyes when she'd seen her mother. By now, her expression was controlled and her eyes closed off. This was almost worse than before because I didn't know what was really going on inside of her.

After I parked the car at the edge of camp, neither of us moved. "You're not thinking about running back to Chicago for good, are you?"

I realized how much the idea of losing her upset me. I couldn't let her go.

Dinara didn't look at me, her gaze directed ahead. "No, I'm not. I won't find what I need there."

Dima stalked in our direction, as if he was on his way to execute me. My hunger for blood still called loudly to me, so part of me wanted him to try.

"Great," I growled.

"Let me handle him. Stay back please."

Dinara got out and I followed quickly despite her words. Even if I let her deal with him, I'd have her back.

Dima said something in Russian but Dinara ignored him. She walked past him without a word and headed toward her car. That was her way of handling him? I was about to follow her, not wanting her to be alone in the state she was in but Dima barred my way. "Where the fuck did you take her?"

"That's none of your business."

He grabbed my shoulder and I shoved him away, narrowing my eyes. He was starting to seriously piss me off with his disrespect. If it weren't for Dinara, I might have given him a taste of my knife. Maybe that would have stilled the call for blood in my veins.

I had to get a fucking grip.

"You took her to Vegas, didn't you? I told my Pakhan. He's pissed at your brother."

"I'm sure my brother will be heartbroken to hear it," I said sarcastically.

Dima glowered and leaned closer. "The last time she looked this freaked out, she had a relapse and almost died. If something happens to her, I'll kill you."

I got into his face. "She's mine, and I'll make sure she's safe, so fuck off."

"You really think she can ever be yours?" Dima gave me a hard look before he headed after Dinara. I hated that he knew more about Dinara's past than I did. I needed to find out more about her drug history. From my own experience, I knew the call for drugs was still loud in certain moments, and Dinara was pretty shaken right now.

I followed Dima with my eyes and stifled a sigh of relief when Dinara didn't open the car where she had retreated into. Dima stormed off toward his own car, probably to contact Grigory again. Maybe I should ask Remo to send more guards for the races in case the Bratva decided to attack. Before I could decide to approach Dinara, her car drove off.

"Fuck," I muttered. It cost me a lot of restraint not to follow her. She would be pissed if I acted like a stalker. I had to trust that she just needed some time to herself. There weren't any places in our immediate surroundings where she could buy drugs, so she'd have to settle for cheap liquor if she wanted to blank out what happened.

She returned an hour later, and not a moment too soon, because I'd been close to going on a search. I went over to her right away. She leaned against her car but she avoided my eyes and focused on her lighter as she lit the tip of her cigarette. I didn't smell alcohol or marihuana on her.

"I need to be alone right now, Adamo. I know you want to talk but the voices in my head are enough to deal with right now. Just give me time." For a moment, her eyes met mine, asking me to respect her wish.

I nodded reluctantly. "Okay, you know where to find me. Don't do anything stupid without me."

The flicker of a smile crossed her face. "Don't worry."

After a quick kiss, I turned and left her alone, even if it was the last thing I wanted to do. Our next race was scheduled in three days so it wasn't as if I didn't have enough to do. My car needed another check-up and Crank and I needed to go over the statistics of the races.

That night was the first time that Dinara and I didn't see each other since we'd started having sex. It was strange lying in my tent, knowing she was only across camp from me and wondering what she was doing, how she was feeling.

Four days later was a big party because we'd reached the halfway point of our season. After the events of the last couple of days, I wasn't sure if I was in the mood to dance, getting drunk was another matter. That seemed like an enticing option at this point.

I didn't see Dinara in the morning and resisted the urge to seek her out despite the growing desire to do so.

Instead I helped Crank and a few other guys to set up a large firepit in the center for tonight, and bought meat for barbecuing for the entire crowd. The Camorra always sponsored the big celebrations to keep the racers entertained. We earned a lot of money with them after all. When Crank and I unloaded my trunk, I spotted Dinara for the first time that day. She sat on her hood with her arms propped up behind her and her eyes closed. Dima stood beside her and was talking to her, but she didn't give any indication that she was listening to him. She seemed miles away. I could only imagine where her mind was taking her.

Eventually Dima stalked off. I jogged after him and reached him before he could get into his car. "How's she?"

Dima scoffed. "You ask me? I don't even know what the fuck happened these last few days. You took her away and now she's messed up. Did you let her see her mother?"

"Dinara has a right to discover every aspect of her past, even if you and Grigory don't like it."

Dima leaned in, his eyes flashing in warning. "You should be careful, Falcone. Your brothers aren't here to protect you and when it comes to Dinara, Grigory won't care about consequences. He'll rip your heart out and feed it to the dogs if something happens to her."

I smiled darkly. "He can try." I turned, presenting my back to Dima. Did he really think he could scare me? I'd lost count of the number of enemies who wanted to see me and my brothers dead. Grigory would just have to wait at the end of the queue for his fucking turn.

Across camp, Dinara caught my gaze. She must have watched my confrontation with Dima. She didn't look away and so I approached her, taking it as an invitation. She put on her sunglasses casually, but this was a bigger admittance of her emotional turmoil than she probably realized. Instead of asking what I really wanted to know, how she was coping with everything, I said, "Are you going to join the party tonight? It's going to be a blast."

"A blast," she said with a strange smile. "Sounds like something I don't want to miss."

"It starts right before sunset."

It was strange not being closer to her, not touching her, but Dinara still leaned back on her hood and didn't make a move to seek my closeness. If she still needed room to process everything, I'd give it to her. "I'll be there."

I nodded, resisting the urge to rip away her sunglasses to see the look in her eyes. Instead I backed off and returned to Crank. "Trouble in paradise?" he asked when I helped him fire up one of the barbecues he'd built out of an old steal wine barrel.

"Dinara and I enjoy space apart on occasion. We aren't attached by the hip."

"If you say so," Crank said. That was the problem living in camp.

Shortly before sunset, every member of the camp, including pit girls and other women the racers had found in nearby bars had gathered for the party. Flames from the firepit in the center snaked up into the sky and illuminated the night and filled our bodies with warmth. The scent of barbecued meat and marihuana hung heavily in the air. A spicy concoction that made you feel high without a single taste or drag.

I stood at one of the barbecues, turning ribs to keep me busy as I scanned the crowd. Thanks to the barbecues and firepit, the air was still hot and many party guests danced half-naked. None of the girls wore more than a bikini top and hotpants, and even most guys had discarded their shirts by now. I was one of them but so close to the barbecue, a fine sheen of sweat covered my chest despite my lack of clothes.

I froze when I finally discovered Dinara. I'd been looking for her since the start of the party but either she'd hidden in the crowd so far or she joined the party only now. The sun was starting to disappear behind the horizon. I shoved the barbecue tongs at Crank and left my spot at the barbecue to get a closer look at Dinara. The sight was too beautiful to miss.

She danced barefoot under the sinking sun, her red hair aflame in the dimming glow. She was beautifully imperfect—imperfectly beautiful. She was laughter and lightness and happiness.

Our eyes met and for a second she seemed to still, a slight hitch in her charade, then she threw her head back and laughed. She started spinning around herself until she lost her balance and stumbled toward me. She collided with my chest hard, still giggling. Her eyes glowed with forced happiness. No one saw the darkness lingering just beneath.

"Fake it till you make it," she breathed then crashed her lips against mine. Kissing, we tumbled to the ground under the cheers of the crowd. I rolled onto my back, taking her with me. She straddled my hips and let out a battle cry.

I smiled.

Fake it till you make it. I could do that for her, if this was what she needed to get past her demons, past her despair. Her breath smelled of alcohol and marihuana, but she wasn't drunk or high enough to explain her sudden cheer. She wanted to forget, to be happy and she was determined to force it.

The crowd began to dance in a circle around us and Dinara leaned down again for a lingering kiss. She was usually less open with public displays of affection, but I took her up without hesitation and kissed her back, wanting everyone to see that she was mine—now and for however long she let me.

"Dance with me. Help me forget tonight," she rasped, her eyes almost feverish with despair. "Let's just be us tonight. Not anyone's daughter or brother. Let's be in the moment. No past, no future."

I clapped her ass in response, causing the crowd to roar with delight. Dinara's eyes flashed with indignation, then eagerness. I grabbed her hips and sat up. "Just us." I kissed her harshly before I nodded at one of the female dancers. She grabbed Dinara and pulled her into the dancing circle. I jumped to my feet and joined them. We danced until our feet hurt, until our surroundings became blurry from alcohol and the joints that were passed along.

Dinara never strayed from my side, our bodies molded together as we danced to the beat. Feeling her body pressed up against mine and seeing the fire in her eyes, desire for her flamed up in me and soon my cock dug against her belly. Her eyes lit up with lust. I leaned down, kissing her ear. "I need to fuck you now, Dinara."

"Then fuck me," she said. I lifted her off the ground and her legs wrapped around my hips as I carried her away from the party. Hiding wasn't an option anymore. Everyone knew about us by now, and I wanted them to know. I wanted the whole fucking world to know about Dinara and me, even the Bratva and her murderous father.

The next afternoon, Crank approached me as I was on my way to take a shower. My head was throbbing with a headache. Dinara and I had kept each other awake until the early morning, and even returned to the party in between our alone times. I couldn't even remember the last time I'd been this shitfaced. The last thing I wanted was to talk to anyone, especially because Crank's expression told me I wouldn't like what he'd have to say. "Trouble?" I asked, waiting on the first step to the washroom trailer for him.

He grimaced. "I heard that Dinara asked around for drugs, Adamo."

My eyes darted across the camp toward my car and the tent where Dinara and I had spent the night. I didn't see her anywhere so she was probably still asleep. "What kind of drugs?"

"She wasn't picky. But cocaine or heroin were her preferred choices."

I nodded slowly. There wasn't a rule against drugs during the races. Several racers were loyal customers of the Camorra's drug dealers, mostly ecstasy and LSD though. And I knew that many people had been high on more than weed last night. I didn't get involved in this side of our business. It was too risky for me to be around harder drugs, even if I'd been clean for many years. I'd learned not to trust easily, least of all myself.

"I thought you might want to know," Crank said.

"Did anyone sell her shit?" I growled.

Crank gave me a crooked smile. "Nobody dared to do it before asking you for permission, seeing as she's your girl."

I didn't contradict him, even if Dinara probably hated being branded as mine—or anyone's for that matter. "Good. I'll go talk to them to make sure they keep their drugs under wraps."

After a quick shower, I went to one of the racers who also worked as our drug distributor and told him to make sure no one in Camorra territory dared to sell anything to Dinara. Word would spread soon. She was mine and whoever dared to provide her with stuff would pay with blood.

I headed back to my tent but Dinara had disappeared so I went in search of her and eventually found her at her Toyota.

She leaned under the open hood of her car, tinkering with the engine. Her long legs peeked out of her jean shorts and the soft bumps of her spine invited my tongue to trace them, but I held back my need to be close to her. We had issues to discuss first. Noticing me, she straightened and narrowed her eyes. "What's wrong?"

I leaned against the car, trying to stifle my annoyance. She acted as if last night hadn't happened and was back to her distant self. But the paleness of her skin and the way she squinted into the light revealed the truth of last night's revelry. "This is my race, and people tell me things. Nobody deals with drugs unless they have the okay from the Camorra."

"I know. That's why I asked someone if they could buy me stuff. I anticipated that I'd have a hard time getting anything myself because people seem to think you can decide what I do or don't do."

"You didn't come to me."

"You wouldn't have sold me drugs, or would you? Judging from your pissed look, I'll get a lecture now. I'm really not sure if I have the brain capacity after last night."

"No, of course I won't let you buy drugs! I took the shit myself. Heroin, cocaine, even crystal. I know what it does to the body. It ruins you. Your body, your mind, everything."

Dinara

I laughed bitterly. "I have danced with the devil before. I know what it does." Part of me was glad for Adamo's concern but the bigger part felt caught and defensive. I was so tired, from last night, from trying to forget my twisted feelings. At the party and with Adamo, I'd forgotten about my mother for a few hours, but this morning everything had slammed right back into me. I couldn't escape reality, at least not for long, not without my old vices.

"How long have you been clean?"

I closed the hood and sighed. "Almost a year now."

Worry and frustration battled in Adamo's eyes. "And now you want to throw it out of the window, for what?"

I'd thought the exact same thing the first night after our return from Vegas, alone in my tent after everyone had refused to sell me stuff. For a moment I'd considered driving to the next big city, a place where nobody recognized me, much less knew that I was Adamo's girl, how everyone around here called me. With the last shreds of my resolve, I'd stayed put and spent most of the night staring at the ceiling of my tent, too afraid to fall asleep and be haunted by new memories, awakened by my recent trip to Vegas. Becoming clean and staying clean had been a struggle. This was the longest I'd succeeded to stay away from drugs since I was fourteen and I'd almost thrown it all away because of my mother. She'd ruined my life once and I'd almost given her the power to do it again. I was furious at myself, but as usual too proud to admit it.

I glared. "You can't even imagine what kind of images my mind's been replaying since I saw my mother. So much buried shit has come up. It's eating away at me, and I know the only way to stop it is to knock myself out with drugs."

Adamo moved closer. I could tell that he wanted to touch me, maybe even hug me, and I wanted him to, but still I didn't move. Last night our bodies had joined, fueled by passion and exhilaration, now every touch would be filled with emotions I didn't want to deal with. "The memories come back twice as bad once the effect wanes off, Dinara. You can't escape them. I tried too."

Fuck, it took every ounce of restraint not to fly into his arms. I wanted to be held by him, but I didn't want to look weak. Though, it was probably a little too late for that. In Vegas, I'd completely lost it. Seeing my mother had twisted my insides, had made me feel like a little girl. She'd changed so much over the years since Dad didn't pay for her beauty treatments anymore and she worked as a cheap whore, but my mind had pulled up past images.

"What am I supposed to do?" I asked quietly, moving a bit closer to him.

"Whatever it is, I'm there for you, but you don't need drugs, Dinara."

"You don't know what I need. You can't. Not until you've lived what I have. The only thing that makes the pain go away for a while are the drugs."

"It doesn't have to be that way."

He was right. I'd fought too hard to get where I was now. Adamo touched my cheek and I leaned into him. "We'll figure out a way for you to move past this shit. Together."

I nodded. "Together."

SEVENTEEN

Adamo

DINARA JOINED ME IN MY TENT THAT NIGHT, BUT SHE WAS RESTLESS. "Can we go somewhere else? Somewhere away from everyone where we can sleep outside without our tent? I feel like everything's closing in on me." Her voice was hesitant.

"Of course," I murmured.

We packed everything and drove my car about a mile away from camp. Tomorrow wasn't a race day so it wasn't a problem. We set up our sleeping bags and pillows on the ground until we created a spacious bed under the stars. For a while, we sat beside each other, staring off into the darkness. In the distance lights from camp illuminated the horizon, but soon those would die as well. I'd set up the gas lamp behind us on the smallest possible flame to create just enough light so we could see our faces. "I've been thinking about watching the recordings you gave me but I'm scared. If seeing my mother already unsettled me so much, what will seeing all those guys and what they did, do to me?" She snapped her mouth shut, regret passing her face. In the months since I'd known Dinara, I'd learned one thing about her: she hated admitting weakness, or what she perceived as weakness. I linked our fingers.

"If you want, I can be present when you watch it," I said, even if the thought of seeing Dinara's abuse turned my stomach over. Watching a few minutes had already been too much. But for Dinara I'd do it.

She twisted her head around to me. "I don't think I want you to see me like that, not more than you have already seen." She shook her head. "Fuck, this is so messed up."

"I could burn them for you. If Remo hadn't given them to me, you would have never known they exist. Just pretend you never found out."

"He wanted me to have them so I can see my abusers and decide over their fate. Your brother is all about Judgment Day, isn't he?"

I chuckled. "Not in a religious sense, but an eye for an eye is definitely his style. Though he wouldn't settle for an eye. He'd take the eyes, the tongue and at least one organ before he'd consider it even."

"What would he do to my abusers?"

Probably the same thing I'd been fantasizing about. It was ironic that I'd spent most of my life trying to be better than Remo. "Torture them until they beg for death, until every part of their body is broken and their mind too. He'd make sure the other abusers would find out what's happening so they'd piss their pants knowing they were next. He'd work his way up from the least guilty fucker to the number one, keeping the best for last." My voice rang with eagerness and dark hunger. I raked a hand through my hair, my blood pounding in my veins.

Dinara regarded my face. "Sounds like you gave it plenty of thought."

I smiled twistedly. "I'm a Falcone. Twisted shit is in my blood."

She scooted closer and leaned over me, pushing me back. Her hair curtained our faces as she straddled my hips. She became serious. "There's only one other thing that can help me move on. Not drugs, and definitely not forgiveness."

"Tell me." But deep down I knew what she wanted, what she'd ask of me, and with the same certainty I knew I wouldn't deny her. Fuck, I wanted it to happen. I *shouldn't* want it so much.

"Help me kill her, help me kill every single one of them." She kissed me harshly then reached between us and rubbed me roughly through my pants. Gripping her neck, I returned the kiss with even more force. With a growl, I flipped us over and shoved down her shorts before I unzipped my pants. Sliding her panties to the side, I slammed into her in one hard stroke. She arched up with a moan. We locked gazes and in hers lay trust and an emotion we both couldn't admit to. Only our pants and moans filled the emptiness as our bodies joined. More than the physical aspect I could feel how this moment brought us closer on an emotional level.

Afterward we lay beside each other, both of us silently watching the starry sky. Dinara took out a cigarette and lighted it then took a long drag before holding it out to me. I'd been trying to stop smoking again, but today wasn't a good day to begin this quest, and I doubted the next few weeks would be better. I took the butt and inhaled deeply.

"And? Will you help me?"

I blew out a plume of smoke, blacking out the beautiful night sky. "Yes."

There was no hesitation in my voice, not a flicker of doubt in my mind.

Dinara rested her head on my shoulder and I wrapped my arm around her. "I've never killed anyone. Not even really hurt anyone."

I couldn't say the same. As a Falcone, it had fallen upon me to become accustomed with violence from an early age. "If you can't do it, I can do it for you."

Dinara propped her head up. "No, I don't want to use you as my assassin. That was never the plan. Fuck, when I came here to find out more about my past, I didn't think it would end with me making a plan to go on a killing spree with you."

I searched her face. I couldn't detect a hint of a lie in her voice. "But you were curious about me and my brothers killing our mother."

"Of course, I was. If you meet someone who's stabbed their mother, it's bound to be the most interesting thing about them, even if your life probably entails many interesting incidents."

"Your father is Pakhan. Your life certainly hasn't been boring either."

Dinara's mouth pulled into a tight line. "Dad tried to give me the life of a princess, or rather life of a tsarina. My wardrobes are filled with more dresses than I can ever wear and I own jewelry that's worth many millions. There's staff for every little demand in our home. I attended balls in Russia and parties in Chicago. I lived a boring life."

"It sounds like you lived the life of someone else. I can't imagine you in a ballgown, exchanging pleasantries with stuck-up people."

"I felt like an impostor."

"Then why did you do it? Why didn't you tell your father that wasn't you."

"He knows that's not me, but he hopes that's who I could become. He thinks it's a sign for my continued suffering that I don't enjoy meaningless revelries like many other girls in our circle do. He thinks he could fix me by showing me that side of life. And I humor him because it makes him feel better. I see it as my job, and I get paid very well."

I chuckled. "That's one way of looking at it. But waltzing over dancefloors was only a small part of what you did."

"Dima took me on adventures, to races and parties, to parts of Chicago I shouldn't be setting foot in."

"But your father knew."

"Dima is his man. He tells him everything, but Dad accepted the untamable part of me and allowed me to live it, as long as he didn't have to witness it."

"Maybe he'll eventually accept that this is who you are, untamable and strong, because you want to be, and not as a sign of past horrors."

"Maybe," she agreed but doubt filled the word. "You mentioned that your brother has the names and addresses of the men who molested me."

"I'll call him in the morning and ask him to email them to me."

"He'll probably be pissed if he finds out I'm dragging you into this mess with me."

Remo was all for vengeance and bloody vendettas, especially if they involved horrible mothers, but he was certainly weary of Dinara's motives. He thought he still needed to protect me when I was perfectly capable of protecting myself.

"I've been considering asking Dima to help me, maybe even my father. They both would kill every person who hurt me."

I frowned. "I told you I'd help you. There's no reason for you to ask anyone else, especially because Remo won't be happy if your father breaches our territory."

"I'd do it to show you that I'm not here because I need your help. I don't want you to think what's between us serves the purpose of making you help me. That's not the case. I wanted information, that was it. Now that I have it, I wouldn't need you anymore, especially now that I know that Remo is willing to give me all the info I need to get revenge."

"Ouch," I said dryly. "Good to know you don't need me anymore." I gave her a sarcastic smile.

She rolled her eyes. "You know what I mean. I'm here because I enjoy being with you, the sex, the talking, everything. I'm here because I want to be."

I raked my fingers through her hair, enjoying the silky feel of it against my skin. Dinara had the softest hair I could imagine. "There's no place I'd rather be than at your side, even if it involves brutal revenge."

Dinara sighed. "What about after? When the revenge part is over. We are who we are."

"You've said it before," I murmured. "How about we take one day after the other?"

"Deal," she said before she became silent for a couple of minutes. The tension entering her body told me her thoughts had drifted back to the past. "I think we need to make them watch the recordings when we confront them—before we deal with them."

"That serves two purposes. They'll be reminded of their sins and you'll be angry enough to exact revenge."

Dinara huffed out a dark laugh. "Do you think I'll need further encouragement to kill them?"

"If you've never killed, maybe. The first kill is always the hardest."

"Was it for you?"

"It was during an attack to save my own and my brothers' lives, so I didn't have time to think. I just pulled the trigger. My hardest kill was the one after, the one Remo had me do to become a Camorrista. He made me angry at the guy before I had to shoot him. It made things easier."

"I suppose it does. I don't think anger will be an issue, but what if I freeze up like I did with my mother? What if I become this helpless girl who can't do anything?"

"I'll be there to shake you out of it. If you really want to kill them, then I'll make sure you can do it."

"Fuck, we're both twisted, you realize it, right?"

"I made my peace with it," I said with an ironic smile. "Have you considered how you want to kill them? With a gun, quick and easy, or with a knife, more personal and given that you don't have experience stabbing someone, more painful. You'll probably need a few stabs to kill. Do you want to torture them in advance? Or do you have another death in mind?"

Dinara pressed her forehead against mine. "Maybe it's a bad sign that none of what you just said freaked me out."

"If me saying it would already freak you out, then we don't have to hunt your abusers down."

"Yeah…" Dinara breathed out slowly. "I think shooting our first victim would be best. That way I can get my first time over with quickly. I don't think I could just shove a knife into someone, much less several times. Maybe I'll consider it for the later kills."

"I can show you how to do it. We could practice on the corpse of the first victim."

Dinara laughed. "Now I'm a bit freaked out."

"Bad enough to run away from me?" I murmured. In the past I'd always kept this part of me safely hidden, especially when I was around girls but even around my family. With Dinara, I felt as if I could finally reveal this twisted, morbid side of myself.

"Never," she said firmly, nipping at my lower lip.

Eventually Dinara fell asleep in my arms and like so often before, she mumbled and twisted in her sleep. I brushed a strand of hair from her forehead, wondering if this path we'd embark on was the right choice for Dinara, if it would dispel her nightmares or only add new ones.

Dinara

We left camp right after the next race. Adamo had printed out the list with the addresses of my abusers. I scanned the names but they didn't mean anything to me. They'd never introduced themselves with their real names. The names didn't hold the horrors of the past, but I knew their faces would. Even if they'd changed over the years, I'd recognize their eyes. Those always haunted me the most. The eagerness ... the hunger...

Adamo and I checked into a shabby motel at the interstate right outside of Reno, a place more fitting for our journey than a nice hotel.

We'd only spend a night here before we'd finally set out to find the first person on our list tomorrow. My very first abuser. I stared up at the grayish-white motel ceiling, listening to Adamo taking a shower.

It wouldn't be difficult to find him. He owned a hardware store in Reno where he worked six days a week. He was known as a sex offender. Since a conviction shortly after he'd abused me and a few years in prison, he had lived a solidary life. No family living nearby and if Adamo's contacts were right, no close friends either. Adamo had done plenty of research since he'd received the list. He was determined to help me. His own demons powered him. Demons even more blood-thirsty than mine.

Adamo emerged from the bathroom in a plume of steam with only a towel wrapped around his narrow waist. Usually the sight of his abs and muscled chest always got me in the mood but today my mind whirled with too many thoughts of what lay ahead.

"You cut your hair," I said quietly. Even to my own ears, my voice sounded strange, as if I was lost in another dimension.

Adamo came toward me and perched on the edge of the bed. I touched his short hair, gone the curls I could sink my fingers into.

"It's easier to clean up. Things might get messy soon."

He meant bloody. Soon things would get bloody. "Is blood difficult to wash out of hair?" I asked hoarsely. "Maybe I should cut my hair too."

"No, keep your hair. I love it." His brows furrowed. "Are you worried about tomorrow? He won't escape, and if I can't restrain him, which I doubt, I can still call reinforcement."

"I'm not worried about that. I saw you fight Dima. I know you can handle even a capable fighter. I'm worried about myself."

Adamo stretched out beside me, cloaking me in his fresh herbal shower gel scent. The bed creaked under the additional weight. "How you'll handle the situation?"

I nodded and pointed at the new gun on my nightstand. Adamo had gotten it for me. "I held it in my hand this morning and imagined pulling the trigger while looking into the asshole's eyes. In my imagination it felt good, it was easy, just a twitch of my finger, nothing more."

Adamo leaned close, his lips brushing my ear. "If you're asking if it'll be as easy in reality, then I have to say probably not. We won't know until the moment. Maybe you'll pull the trigger without a second thought, or maybe you'll realize you can't follow through with our plan."

"I have to."

I didn't want Adamo to be my executioner. I couldn't put that burden on anyone else. "It's my revenge. I should do it. With you at my side, I can do it."

Adamo's dark eyes met mine. "We can stop at any point. We don't have to finish every name on that list. This is about helping you cope with what happened, not make it worse. And if you need me to do it, I'll handle them all for you."

If I'd only needed an executioner, I could have asked Dad to hunt down every single of my abusers. He would have gladly done it. He too yearned for a way to avenge me, and maybe even himself. That men had dared to lay hand on the daughter of a high-ranking Bratva member was like a slap in the face, even if my abusers didn't know who I was.

The next morning, before Adamo and I set off to find guy number one on our list, we settled in front of his laptop to watch the disc with the recording of me with today's target. The screen lit up with the image of a bed and a young version of myself perching on its edge with her hands in her lap, her eyes cast down. It was like watching someone else but I knew that would change the moment I started the recording. The girl's horrors would become mine. The video would become reality in my head, would draw up memories of scents and sensations from the dark corners of my mind. I'd be dragged right back into the past. Adamo waited for me to hit play, his eyes kind and his expression patient.

I only stared at the screen, my body frozen. Past Dinara had her hair in pigtails, something that many of my abusers favored.

"We don't have to watch," Adamo said. "You know what happened. We know he's guilty. There's no reason to torture yourself with images from the past."

I didn't react, only stared at the screen. The problem was these images had haunted me almost every day since Dad had picked me up in Vegas over a decade ago.

"Or if you don't want me to watch I can go for a walk until you're done."

Panic rushed through me at his suggestion, so I grabbed his hand, linking our fingers. "No," I whispered harshly. "I can't watch it alone. It's bad enough that I relive it in my nightmares every night all alone."

He squeezed my hand and my heart clenched with a mix of emotions at his support. Adamo had absolutely no reason to help me, but here he was. He was trying to keep his emotions under control for me but in his eyes, I could see many of my own emotions. The absolute hatred toward my abusers and the determination to exert revenge, and beneath all of that, an emotion both Adamo and I couldn't risk given our families, our backgrounds…our futures. I'd been trying to ignore my feelings but looking at him now I couldn't deny that I was falling for Adamo. It was absolutely insane and I was glad that our revenge plan would keep me too busy to consider the insanity of my heart's choice.

I focused on the screen and hit play, my body tightening even more. The first guy on our list walked into the room. His smile was overly kind as he approached my past self, but beneath it, lingered eagerness and hunger. Soon his face appeared before my inner eye, no longer on the screen. My grip on Adamo's hand tightened as I tried to keep my face neutral, wanting to be strong, even as revulsion and terror battled in my insides. My throat corded up and cold sweat broke out on my body, plastering my clothes to my body. When the man sat down beside young Dinara on the bed and touched her leg, I hit the pause button, stopping the video. I released a harsh breath, my pulse racing in my veins as past fears drove up my adrenaline. "I can't watch it."

"It's okay. We can still dispose of all the discs."

I shook my head. "We'll take it with us to him today. I want him to watch it, even if I can't do it."

"All right," Adamo said simply. I kissed him before I scooted to the edge of the bed.

"Let's go now." I needed to move before I lost courage. Locked into this motel room I felt like a caged animal.

Adamo didn't hesitate. He stuffed the disc and the laptop into a bag before he followed me. He'd asked if I wanted him to pack material for torture but I had said no. Killing another person would be challenge enough. Torture was out of the question, even if every single of my abusers deserved it. I wanted them dead. That would be enough.

Adamo parked at the curb across from the hardware store where the guy worked and also lived in a backroom. It was already late in the afternoon and the shop was supposed to close in half an hour. We didn't talk as we sat together in the car. Adamo had grabbed a bag with donuts but I couldn't force more than a bite past my corded-up throat. My heart hadn't stopped pounding since we'd watched the first few minutes of the video. I felt as if I were the prey and not the hunter.

My hands were clammy, and I was glad for Adamo at my side because he looked remarkably calm.

"It's time," he said eventually, and I realized that almost thirty minutes had passed without me realizing it. "He'll close the shop any minute now."

"Okay," I croaked.

Adamo grabbed my chin and forced me to look into his eyes. "We should go now so we can slip in as last-minute customers. Breaking in poses the risk of alerting the police. This isn't Las Vegas, we don't have every police officer on our payroll."

I swallowed and nodded, but I couldn't move. Tears of anger at myself welled up and I blinked them back. "I—"

"I'll go alone and kill him for you, unless you don't want me to do it?"

I wanted my abuser dead, I wanted to do it myself, but maybe I was too weak to do it. I gave the tiniest nod, even as I hated myself for it. Adamo gave me a kiss and got out of the car before he grabbed the bag from the trunk. He jogged over to the hardware store and not a minute too soon. A guy had appeared at the door to turn the sign to closed. Adamo flashed him a charming smile and was allowed inside. Both men disappeared from my view and soon after Adamo hung up the closed sign before he headed back out of sight again.

I glared down at my hands, furious at myself for allowing someone else to dish out my revenge.

EIGHTEEN

Adamo

I'd seen Dinara's inner struggle in her eyes and wasn't surprised that she couldn't go through with our plan. I'd expected her to lose courage. It was one thing to wish for revenge, to imagine killing someone, but it was a whole different matter to actually go through with it, to see the life drain from someone's eyes. Even if Dinara was a Bratva princess, she'd never been part of the brutal sides of business. Her father had protected her from it, the same way I would protect her if she wanted me to. Killing someone got easier with time. In the beginning it had been harder for me more than it was now.

As I closed the door of the hardware store behind me and watched the bastards unsuspecting smile, eagerness took hold of me. Dishing out revenge on Dinara's behalf wasn't a burden. It would be satisfying in so many ways. Maybe I could even keep pretending that I wasn't enjoying it.

I turned the lock and then gave number one, the first name on our list, a dark smile.

His expression fell, fear flaring up in his eyes. Maybe he thought this was a robbery. He wouldn't be that lucky. He was older than on the videos but it was him, no doubt. Even if Remo hadn't provided me with the whereabouts of our targets, I would have recognized the man before me. The mousy face, the same unshaven appearance. He stumbled backward toward his sales counter, probably to ring an alarm. I chased after him, grabbed his arm and jerked him to the floor. He lost his balance and fell to the floor with a cry of pain. His wide blue eyes met mine. "I don't have much money! You can have it all."

"This isn't about money," I said as I circled him. I shouldn't be enjoying this as much as I did. I'd always resented Remo for playing with his victims.

Confusion flickered in the man's eyes. I pulled my gun and the color drained from his face. I calmly walked back to the shop door and turned the sign to "closed" before I returned to number one. Following Dinara's request I hadn't packed any torture instruments, but a hardware store was the land of milk and honey for someone like me.

"I hear you like little girls."

He looked caught before he quickly shook his head. "That was a long time ago. I changed. I paid for what I did."

I took out the laptop and showed him the first image of Dinara on the bed.

"You sure as hell didn't pay for what you did to her."

Horror entered the man's eyes. Being confronted with your own depravity must have stung.

"But you will," I promised. "This girl on the screen. Her name is Dinara and she wants you to die. She doesn't want me to torture you but maybe I'll do it just for myself."

I had dreamed about it last night.

A knock sent a wave of tension through my body.

The man cried out, "Help! Call the police!"

I kicked his right side, on level of his kidney and liver, silencing him effectively as he gasped for breath. When I spotted Dinara at the door, I relaxed and went over to her. I unlocked the door and let her in. A brief glance down the street told me that nobody had noticed anything yet.

She stepped in hesitantly, still a spooked look on her face. I wasn't sure if it was a good idea that she was here. It was fucking selfish, but I was worried she'd change her mind and spare the asshole.

Her eyes moved past me to the man on the floor who was holding his side, crying. His teary gaze settled on her. "Please help me."

Slowly Dinara moved toward him and stopped right over him. "Do you remember my face?" she whispered.

The man shook his head frantically.

"That's funny because I see your face and every revolting inch of your body every night when I close my eyes," Dinara said, her voice cracking.

"I'm sorry! I swear. I changed. I was a bad person back then, but I don't do this anymore. I paid for my sins. I was in jail."

"For hurting other girls like me," Dinara said. "Girls whose nights will forever be haunted by nightmares."

I stepped up beside her, touched her shoulder to show her my support. She trembled under my touch.

"Please don't kill me. Don't I deserve a second chance?"

I gritted my teeth, wanting nothing more than to smash his face so he'd shut up. I could see the hesitation in Dinara's face. It took all of my control not to try to talk her into killing him. This was her decision. I had no right to force her in a certain direction only because I was a twisted fuck who wanted to torture and kill the guy before me.

Dinara tore her eyes away from the man. "Do you think he says the truth? Do you think he changed?"

"I doubt it," I said. "Do you want me to search his living quarters? Maybe we can find something."

Dinara gave a small nod. I wasn't sure if new proof would really matter. This was an internal battle for Dinara, one between her dark side and her good side. I'd fought the same battle.

I handed her my second gun. "If he makes a move, you shoot him."

I wasn't sure if she would but from the look on his face, the asshole believed she was capable of killing him and that was all that mattered.

I headed to the backrooms of the store that he used as his apartment. I didn't want to find proof of his continued depravity because it would mean more girls had suffered but at the same time, I wanted to find something that would convince Dinara to continue with our plan. Something that would tip the scale in favor of her dark side.

After twenty minutes of searching, I found images on his computer that left no doubt that he still harbored the same disgusting desires from the past, even if he wasn't in the photos. They looked as if he'd downloaded them from the Darknet. I went back into the store. Dinara stood a few steps away from the man, the gun trained on him. Her eyes darted to me and I gave a nod. "I found photos."

Another almost imperceptible nod.

Number one glanced back and forth between Dinara and me. "They are just photos. I never touched a kid since I came out of jail."

"The kids in those photos were touched by other perverts like yourself so you could wank off looking at those photos," I growled.

I stepped close to Dinara and she lowered the gun. We moved a few steps away from the man. "What do you want to do now?"

Dinara swallowed audibly, conflict dancing across her tense features. "I want him dead. I want to be the one, but…I just don't know if I can. It's like something is still holding me back."

"You've never done this before. It's only natural that you hesitate."

I didn't remember the moments prior to pulling the trigger on another human for the very first time. It had happened too fast, no time to let my conscience speak up. I sometimes wondered if it would have. In the weeks after my kill, I hadn't so much been bothered by my conscience but the lack thereof.

"Can you show him the video? I want him to remember what he did, and maybe it'll give me the courage to go through with what I want."

Number one hadn't moved an inch as if he hoped we might forget he existed.

I removed the laptop and the disc from my bag and set everything up on a shelf so the asshole got a good look at the screen. After a nod from Dinara, I turned the recording on. This time neither Dinara nor I hit pause. Instead we watched every soul-crushing moment of the video. I wanted nothing more than to turn the screen off, or better yet smash the fucking thing like I'd done with Remo's laptop, but I stayed rooted to the spot. The only movement I allowed myself was the occasional sideways glance to Dinara who seemed to be lost in the images, her gaze distant and her body taut with tension. How hard must it be for her to relive those moments?

I glowered at the asshole on the floor who had lowered his head as if he couldn't bear to watch. Fury raced through me. I grabbed his head roughly and jerked up his chin, forcing his attention back on the laptop screen. "I know what I did! I don't need to see," he whimpered, closing his eyes, and my fury multiplied, turned feral. "You will open your fucking eyes or I'll staple your eyelids to your fucking brows. I'm sure I can find a stapler somewhere in your shop."

His eyes flew open and he didn't dare looking away from the screen again. I was glad when we neared the end of the recording. The sounds and images had turned my stomach, and I just wanted to help Dinara move past those horrors.

Dinara looked like a wax figure of herself, pale and perfectly motionless. This was meant to help her, but what if it didn't? What if this only fulfilled my own twisted hunger for blood?

Dinara

The images of the screen became blurry and my mind took over, replaying my memories so much more vividly than the video.

Every sensation washed through my body, every pain and odor, every sound and image. They flooded my body like an unstoppable avalanche, dragging up buried emotions. Shame and revulsion, fear and despair, but above all: anger. Anger at the man before me. When the screen turned black and past-Dinara's ordeal was over, I lowered my gaze to the cowering man before me. He begged me with his eyes, pretended to be a victim, when he was a monster who'd ruined my childhood to satisfy his own needs.

I'd remembered his eyes and his words, the names he called me and the name he wanted to be called, even before I'd watched the video. I remembered his low breathing, his aftershave and the sweat underneath it. I moved closer, took a deep inhale. Even his aftershave was still the same. A new flood of images, the same I'd replayed before, wanted to flare up for a repeat performance, but my mind fought the onslaught.

Revulsion welled up in me, followed by panic, but I didn't allow it to take root, and finally anger ruled over everything else. My hands were shaking and my throat was tight as I set down the gun on the counter. Adamo watched the move with a frown. My blood seemed to pulsate with fiery anger as I stepped up close to Adamo, my breathing coming in quick bursts. Our eyes met and his held a myriad of questions. He thought I couldn't shoot my abuser. Maybe he even thought I'd show him mercy and let him live. I'd considered it when I'd first stepped into the hardware store and seen the pitiful guy but whenever the thought had tried to take root, every fiber in my body had fought it and the voice calling for retribution had chanted louder. I took a deep breath and slanted another look at the man. Hope had entered his expression and he gave me another begging look. Over a decade ago, nobody had cared about what I wanted, about my begging.

No mercy.

Without thinking about it, I reached for the knife in Adamo's chest holster, curled my fingers around the cold handle. Adamo didn't stop me as I withdrew the sharp blade with a satisfying hiss.

I'd never used a knife in a violent way and I wasn't sure what I was doing as I stumbled toward my abuser. He tried to scramble backwards but I followed. My heart beat in my throat and my surroundings became a blur as I lunged at him. He brought his arms up, tried to fight me off but I lashed out at him with the knife. Flung it at his flailing arms, his upper body, every inch of him I could reach. He tried to fight me off, and Adamo's voice rang in the back of my head, but the man's screams drowned it out. I couldn't stop, even if I didn't even see what I was doing. My vision was blurry with tears and blood. My palm and my thigh stung, my cheek throbbed, but my hand with the knife still arched down on my abuser until I was dragged away and someone was holding me tightly in their arms despite my struggling.

I gasped for breath. Every intake stung in my chest.

"Shhh, Dinara. Everything is okay. Calm down. He's dead. Calm down."

Adamo's soothing voice waded through the fog clouding my brain and slowly I came to myself. Adamo ripped a piece off his shirt and wiped my face with it. I closed my eyes, allowing him to clean me. When I opened them again, my surroundings came back into focus. Shock crashed down on me as I saw the sight before me. The man lay in a large puddle of blood and his corpse was littered with stab wounds. His hands, his arms, his chest, his face, his throat…the blade hadn't spared any part of his upper body. *I* hadn't spared a part of his body. I had done this.

I released a shaky breath. Slowly I looked down at myself. Adamo's arm was still wrapped around my waist and I sat between his legs, his warm chest pressed against my back. My bare legs were smeared with blood, and my jean shorts were completely soaked with it. I raised my hands, also covered in red. The knife clattered to the floor and the sound made me flinch. My shirt, my hair…everything was covered in blood. And the shred of fabric Adamo had used to clean my face and eyelids was now red. I blinked, stunned by what I had done. "Why did you stop me?" I said, but my voice sounded distant, as if something was blocking my ears. Maybe more blood. I shuddered.

Adamo took my hand and turned it so I saw a long but shallow cut in my palm then he pointed at another deeper cut in my calf. "You cut yourself in your state and I didn't want you to seriously injure yourself. He's been long dead."

I nodded. "I don't know what got into me. I just lost it…"

Adamo pressed his cheek against mine, even though I was a mess. "Maybe this is a start. Maybe this is your way of releasing the pain you have bottled up."

There was no pain now. No memories. No fear or anger or hatred, only numbness and a blissful calm.

"What do we do now?"

"I have to call our local cleaning crew so they can come over and take care of this."

I laughed hollowly. "I guess it's a good thing this is Camorra land."

"It makes things easier. Vegas would be even better, but our men will clean this up and dispose of the body. Nobody will be able to trace anything back to you or me."

Adamo got up then held out his hand. I took it and allowed him to pull me to my feet. My legs felt shaky. Now that the first wave of adrenaline waned off, my palm and calf throbbed where I'd cut myself. The realization that my blood mingled with the blood of my abuser sent a new wave of revulsion through me and I couldn't suppress a violent shudder. Adamo touched my arm, seeking my eyes. "Dinara?"

"I have to shower. I need to get rid of his blood." I sucked in a deep breath, realizing I was close to panicking, something we really couldn't use right now.

"You could shower in the back?"

I shook my head jerkily. Just the idea of using the same shower my abuser had used made me feel even sicker. "In our motel," I pressed out.

"Okay," Adamo said slowly, as if he was talking to a frightened child, and maybe that was exactly the impression I gave off. "I need to call the crew first and we need to clean up a bit and find something to cover our bloody clothes with. We can't cross the street looking as if we'd bathed in blood."

I nodded, even if my desire to flee was getting stronger by the second.

Adamo picked up his phone for two quick calls before he appeared in front of me again. I was busy staring at the remains of my abuser. "I was worried I couldn't kill someone. Worried I wouldn't be able to pull a trigger. Instead I slaughtered him with a knife. This is so much more messed up than shooting someone."

Adamo stroked my cheek. "It's more personal. What this man did to you was very personal, and you paid him back in a personal way as well. It's not that strange if you think about it."

"I think most people would disagree with you. Nothing we do is normal."

"Who cares?"

"Yeah," I whispered.

Thirty minutes later, we left the hardware store. Adamo, who looked less like a bloody mess, had gotten the car and parked at the curb right in front of the hardware store. His clean-up crew was already busy sorting out the mess I'd caused. They'd even brought me new clothes to wear instead of my own for the ride back to our motel. I'd awkwardly freed my hair from the blood in the sink of the customer bathroom, but my skin was itching all over. I needed to shower as soon as possible.

The moment we entered our small motel room, I headed right into the bathroom and closed the door. I needed a few minutes to myself to process everything that had happened. As the hot water streamed down my body, I closed my eyes and let the tears I'd held back, stream down my face. For a long time, I didn't move and with every passing moment, and every tear I shed, I felt a little lighter, as if the murder had lifted a weight of my shoulders. There still remained plenty of ballast on my soul, but it was a beginning.

NINETEEN

Dinara

AFTER MY SHOWER, I CHANCED A GLANCE AT MYSELF IN THE mirror. I'd missed a spot of dried blood near my temple. I reached for a towel and rubbed it away. My eyes were calm, not full of adrenaline or haunted, no sign that I'd killed a man in a blood-thirsty rage less than an hour ago. Turning away from my reflection, I stepped out of the bathroom, my hair still damp and only a towel around my body. Adamo was on the phone, nodding as he listened to what the person on the other end had to say. "All right, thanks. Good work."

Adamo looked up and rose from the bed before he approached me. He cupped my cheeks in his warm palms, his eyes searching mine without saying a word for what felt like forever. I let him, found inner peace as I lost myself in his gaze. The brutal events of the day hadn't left a trace in his eyes either. "You okay?"

I searched inside myself for a feeling of unease, of a deep unsettling sensation, but I was calm. I shook my head and pressed myself against Adamo. "I'm fine."

"That's good. The crew got rid of the body and cleaned every inch of the store. Nobody will suspect anything. It'll take a while before anyone will notice he's gone and hopefully the police will just think he moved away to avoid the rumors."

I nodded, but my mind had already moved on from the man I'd killed to the next name on the list.

Adamo pulled back. "Let me take a shower, then we can talk some more."

He headed into the bathroom but unlike me he didn't close the door.

I stretched out on the bed and turned my phone on. I'd turned it off since yesterday to avoid calls from Dima and my father. As expected, my mailbox was overflowing with messages from both of them. As if Dad could sense my phone being turned on, he called again. Taking a deep breath, I picked up.

"Dinara, where the hell are you? Are you all right? Do you need help?"

The words were fired at me rapidly, making it difficult to understand them. "I'm fine. I don't need help. I'm dealing with matters."

"What kind of matters?"

"Nothing for you to worry about, Dad. Honestly. I'll be back in Chicago soon. Just give me some time and space."

The more time I spent with Adamo the less I wanted to return to Chicago. I felt out of place there, now more than ever, and while I missed Dima, he and I had moved apart over the last year.

"I have been giving you plenty of time and space recently. Few men in my position would allow their daughters to walk around in enemy territory. That's where you still are, right?"

"Yes, but you know I'm not in danger."

"Do I? You're hunting the past and that's never a good thing."

"Nobody holds grudges better than you do, Dad, and nobody clings more stubbornly to the past. I get that from you."

He made a displeased sound. "Dima should be at your side. You aren't meant to be alone."

"I'm not alone," I said.

Dad scoffed. "You think a Falcone is going to protect you? Don't make the mistake of becoming too friendly with them, Dinara. It's a slippery slope."

"What did Dima tell you?"

"I saw a video of you and the youngest Falcone dancing and kissing." The last was said with blatant contempt.

Once I'd made sure the shower was still running, I said, "*You don't have to worry. There's nothing between us. He's a means to an end. Not more. He helps me get what I want.*"

Guilt settled in the pit of my stomach for lying to my father like that, and for talking about Adamo as if he didn't mean anything, when every day we were together, he captured more of my heart. I was glad that he couldn't hear me talk like that. Even though, Adamo couldn't talk Russian, I didn't want him to be present when I spewed such hurtful lies.

"*And what is that?*"

"To kill the past."

"*Don't let this man drag you into the dark.*"

If anything, I was dragging Adamo into the dark. But even that didn't ring quite true. It felt as if we were going this path as equals, hand in hand, driven by our demons. "Promise not to send Dima to get me, or I'll dispose of my phone and you won't be able to talk to me until I'm done."

"*I want daily messages telling me you're okay, and I'll track your whereabouts. If you don't message me a day, I'll send men over, even if it means war with the Camorra.*"

I sighed. I knew that tone and that it was futile to discuss the matter further with him. "All right."

The shower was turned off in the bathroom. Luckily, I could hear a knock in the background on Dad's end. Dad was silent for a moment, as if he was listening to someone. "*I have to go, Katinka. Be careful.*"

"Always." He hung up and I lowered the phone with a deep sigh.

"Bad news?" Adamo asked carefully, leaning in the doorway with only a towel wrapped around his hip.

"My father worries about me."

"Will he send men?"

"No, as long as I give him daily updates that I'm alive, he won't act. He trusts me."

"But definitely not me," Adamo said, walking toward me. "And he won't ever do it."

He was right. My father wasn't a man who trusted easily, and certainly not a member of the Camorra. "It doesn't matter. As long as I trust you," I said.

Adamo sank down beside me. "And do you trust me?"

"Would I be here with you if I didn't?"

Adamo shrugged. "Maybe I'm your only option."

I shook my head. "I could do this on my own. I know the addresses of every person on our list and after today we know that I can go through with killing them, so if it was really just about convenience, I wouldn't need you beyond this point."

Adamo smiled mirthlessly. "Then why am I still here?"

"I don't need you to kill them, but I need your support, your encouragement. When you are close, I just feel better, more secure in who I am."

"You don't need me but you do," he murmured.

I sighed. "Maybe it doesn't make sense."

"Maybe you just need to admit that you need me. Today you acted out of an impulse, and completely lost control. You didn't pay attention to what was happening around you. If the same thing happens next time, you'll need me to make sure nothing happens while you're in your zone."

"Like hurting myself."

"Or someone walking in on you. I doubt you would have noticed if someone had suddenly walked into the hardware store."

"You're right. It was as if I was possessed." I leaned closer to Adamo. "Okay, I need you, but I don't want you to think that's why I want to be with you."

"Then why do you want to be with me?"

"Why do you want to help me? Why do you do this for a girl you have sex with?"

"You're not just a girl I have sex with."

"And you're not just a guy I have sex with."

Adamo smiled crookedly. "One day one of us has to be brave and put a name to what we have."

"Do we?" I whispered. Adamo lay back on the bed and pulled me against him, one arm wrapped around me. "Who's going to make us?"

"Maybe we'll want certainty at some point, or maybe eventually our families will want answers, more answers than we have at this point."

"That's not something I want to think about now. I want to live in the moment. Right now the only thing I want to focus on is revenge and how we can make every person on the list pay for what they did to me, and other children."

Adamo ran his hand lightly over my upper arm. "Even if you killed in a rush today, that doesn't mean you won't be haunted by nightmares of the murder. Maybe they'll cease eventually, maybe they won't. I just want you to be sure you can live with them, especially if we continue to hunt down your abusers and more deaths are added to your conscience."

I let out a bitter laugh. "Will they be worse than the nightmares that have been haunting my dreams since I was a little kid? I doubt it. So if you ask me, these new nightmares will be a damn improvement to the horrors of my nights right now."

Adamo's arm around me tightened. "Fuck. I really wish I could have tortured the asshole today. I actually considered doing it before you showed up."

I propped myself up. "The next name on our list…he was one of the worst. I mean, every experience was horrible but some were nicer about it."

Adamo gritted his teeth. "Nice isn't a word I'd use to describe the atrocities those perverts did to you."

I swallowed. "And they'll all pay for what they did. But the next guy on the list, he was bad, really bad. He liked to hurt, and I…" Killing my abusers was one thing, but torturing them was another matter. Even some of my father's men couldn't watch torture, could I? And not just watch, could I torture someone myself?

Adamo tilted his head to catch my gaze. "You want to torture the asshole?"

My lips parted, but a wave of nerves washed through me. "I want him to suffer before he dies."

"He will if you want it. I can do it."

"I should at least be part of it. This is my revenge and I don't want to be a coward."

"It's not about being a coward. Torturing someone takes a lot out of you. It's different than the act of killing. You have to face the victim's despair, pain and begging, have to relish in it and use it as another tool of suffering for them."

"How many have you tortured? I know Remo and Nino are famous for their special talent, but I didn't hear any stories about you."

"I tried not to get involved in torture except when it was absolutely necessary. Both Nino and Remo wanted me to gain some experience but eventually they stopped forcing me to participate in these sessions."

If even Adamo, who was a Falcone, couldn't bear to torture someone, how would I be able to do it? "If it bothers you, if it gives you nightmares, then I don't want you to do it, not for me. If I want them to suffer, I'll have to do it myself. I won't ask you to do something you hate."

Adamo chuckled darkly, and pressed a fierce kiss to my lips. "It's not that I hate it or that it haunts me in nightmares, Dinara. I enjoy it too much, that's the fucking problem. I relish in the act of causing others' pain, at least when I think they deserve it. I wish it were different, but I'm messed up. And the people on our list, they all deserve it so I'll have a fucking great time doing it."

"So you didn't partake in torture because you liked it too much?"

He nodded. "Yeah, I quickly realized that I had the potential to be as good and creative as Remo, but I never wanted to be like that. I thought I could be better." His smile became darker. "But I'm not, and the next asshole on the list will learn it the hard way, if you let me."

I swallowed and gave a jerky nod. Adamo kissed me and wrapped his arms even more tightly around me. I could hardly breathe, but I only hugged him back with the same force. After the events of the day, after everything we'd just discussed, my body rang with the need to be as close to Adamo as possible. I didn't care if it made me look weak or needy. Adamo made me feel as if it was okay to not be strong once in a while. He pressed a kiss to my forehead and I closed my eyes, feeling safe.

The next morning, we headed out for the next stop on our roadtrip: Sacramento, the home of number two on our list. Even though this was my path to vengeance, Adamo and I were in this together. I was glad that I didn't have to take this difficult journey alone.

The windows of the car were rolled down as we took the Interstate

80 to Sacramento. Warm air tousled my hair and my eyes were closed. The low beat of a rap song blasted from the speakers. Adamo's fingers around mine kept me rooted as they always did when images from the past replayed in my head. This time they hadn't overpowered me. I'd summoned my personal demons to find the right mindset for what lay ahead.

Adamo parked in front of the house of number two and killed the engine. The house wasn't how I'd imagined it. I'd expected a forlorn, unkempt place. Something that reflected my own dark feelings whenever the face of *him* replayed in my memory. He had been the fear of my past.

Goosebumps rose all over my body. The front yard was immaculately kept, with perfectly trimmed lawn and a beautiful white porch. This looked like a place of happiness.

"Are you sure he lives here alone?"

"Not alone, no. He shares the house with his mother, but he doesn't have his own family."

"Does she know?" I asked.

"Yes, she gave him an alibi in a case but he was convicted anyway."

I nodded, wondering how she could live with what her son had done, but she wasn't my concern. "But she isn't home now?"

"No, she works in a gas station. We're clear to go in."

Clear to go in. I smiled wryly. "You make it sound as if we're a SWAT team."

"We're going to kidnap him, so we have to be as stealthy."

"This is a good neighborhood so people will report suspicious behavior."

Adamo shrugged. "We'll be fine. Let's wait here for him to return home from work."

We sat in silence for almost an hour before a car pulled into the driveway and a short but heavily overweight man got out. His hair had thinned and turned gray, but even from afar his face sent a shudder through my body. My fingers clamped around my knees and my breathing became uneven as my pulse sped up. I was torn between the urge to run and the desire to attack. "Dinara?" Adamo said softly.

I dragged my eyes away. Adamo's brows furrowed. "You are safe. The roles have switched. You aren't his victim. You will be his judge."

"I know," I said, and the words said aloud banished the fear from the past into the darkest corner of my mind where little Katinka still cowered helplessly. Today she'd get justice.

TWENTY

Dinara

My fingers shook with nerves and excitement when Adamo dragged the struggling man into the basement of a Camorra storage. Considering that his death wouldn't be quick, Adamo had chosen the place for its remote location. The walls were thick and would contain my abuser's screams.

I had never hurt someone on purpose before Adamo and I started our vigilante journey. There had never been a reason to do it. I wasn't someone who enjoyed seeing people in pain. It didn't give me a kick, or even fascinated me.

Adamo was different. I occasionally caught the flicker of eagerness in his dark eyes when we'd discussed possible torture methods that we could try on number two. Adamo had called them by their names in the beginning but I preferred to give them numbers. It made them appear less human and more like the monsters that haunted my nightmares.

The basement was dank and the stench of something rotten and piss hung in the air. Maybe rats. A few smaller puddles of water littered the floor where the ceiling leaked.

"We could have used one of the Camorra torture rooms. They are better equipped and cleaner," Adamo commented as he shoved the struggling man toward the wall. He collided hard with it and fell to his knees with a pained gasp.

"No," I said firmly. I'd already accepted too much help from the Camorra, and technically still was, even if Adamo didn't do this in his capacity as a Camorrista but as my... lover. Boyfriend? I pushed the thought away.

Number two turned around and stumbled to his feet. His eyes sought mine. They lacked emotion and I vividly remembered the blank look in them as he'd laid hands on me many years ago. He'd paid extra. I remembered that too. My mother hadn't wanted him to see me again but eventually Cody convinced her because the money was too good. Three encounters... three horror-filled hours. I didn't remember much of them, as if my mind had blacked out parts to protect me.

Adamo held the knife out to me, a smaller, curved blade, not meant to kill, but maim or skin. After he'd pinned my abuser on the ground, Adamo used duct tape to bind the man's hands and feet together.

The man struggled against his restraints, and for the first time, true fear flashed in those pitiless eyes. I nodded with a bitter smile. "That's what I felt."

I remembered the choking fear, the daunting panic and eventually the heart-breaking realization that I was helpless. That even my mother wouldn't stop him. But today I was the one in control. I approached him slowly, my fingers around the blade tightening.

"Do you remember me?" I asked.

The man's brows furrowed as he scanned my face. "No! I swear. This must be a misunderstanding."

It wasn't. I recognized him and the Falcones had made sure he was the right person. There would be no mistakes, no regret, no mercy.

I glanced at Adamo and gave a short nod. Adamo unpacked his laptop and set it up in front of the man. "Watch it closely," Adamo said, fury tinging his voice. Violence twisted his expression. I took strange consolation in the realization that even if I'd fail, Adamo would be there to do what I couldn't.

The video began and the man's eyes widened with surprise. I stepped back, allowed him to watch the videos of us. On occasion, eagerness flickered in his eyes and my stomach tightened at his obvious excitement over what he'd done to me many years ago. I wanted to believe that people could change, that they could better themselves, but so far Adamo's and my experiences proved the opposite. Adamo leaned against the wall to the man's right with balled fists. It was obvious how difficult it was for him to hold himself back. Every time my abuser showed signs of enjoyment, Adamo's body rocked forward.

I turned the video off when I couldn't bear another second. I allowed myself a few deep breaths to steal myself, to lock little Katinka away deep inside my mind before I confronted my past tormentor. "Do you remember me now?"

His gaze snapped up to mine. He didn't say anything but the nervous back and forth of his eyes told me he was trying to think of an excuse. I lifted the knife. He began struggling against his restraints again and screamed at the top of his lungs for help. I flinched at the volume, goosebumps rising on my skin. I stepped closer and held the knife right in front of his face. "Stop screaming," I whispered harshly. My voice wasn't as strong and threatening as I wanted it to be.

The man didn't stop. He struggled even harder, almost topping over backwards with the chair Adamo had tied him to. "Shut up," I rasped.

The man didn't even seem to hear me. I was air for him. I slanted a look at Adamo. He knew how to handle situations like this. I couldn't ask for help, my tongue too heavy, and luckily, I didn't have to. Adamo pushed away from the wall and pulled his second knife. In two long steps he appeared beside me, grabbed the man's hair and pressed the blade against his throat. "Shut up, or I'll cut off your fucking tongue," he snarled, sounding so terrifying that even my body involuntarily leaned away from him for a moment.

Adamo relished in what he did. His eyes held the same euphoric rush I remembered from taking drugs. I wondered if his fall would be as steep once the rush waned off. I remembered the bleak, depressing hours afterward, and the increasing yearning for the next fix. When would Adamo need his next fix?

Adamo's gaze slanted to me, frantic, eager, hungry. "He's yours."

Mine. Mine to judge. To torture. To kill.

I lifted the knife, scanned the sharp blade. Holding my breath, I jabbed the knife into his thigh. My eyes widened, my knuckles turning white around the handle, shocked by my own actions. The man cried out harshly, eyes wide and agonized. Blood soaked the fabric around the blade, which was still buried inside his leg.

"Twist it," Adamo murmured, voice compelling.

I tightened my hold but didn't move. Adamo covered my hand with his. "I can help."

I nodded. He guided my hand, turning the blade clockwise.

The screams escalated, buried themselves in my head and raised goosebumps. My body revolted against my actions. I shook my head and Adamo released my hand. I jerked it away from the knife.

"Do you want me to do it?" Adamo asked.

I took a step back. I didn't look at number two, only at the man I was falling for more every day. He wanted to help me, but beyond that he thirsted for the violence. He wanted this, needed this, maybe as much as I did.

"Yes," I whispered.

Adamo fixed number two with a bone-chilling look. A hunter ready to tear into his prey. Adamo ripped the knife out of number two's leg before he sliced it across his abdomen, creating a shallow cut. Painful but not lethal.

I backed away, and watched, fascinated and terrified by Adamo, by his focus, his eagerness, his skill.

I couldn't help but wonder if I was the reason for the awakening of his bloodlust, if my request had broken through his walls and unleashed an unstoppable hunger.

"Adamo," I whispered eventually. He dropped the knife, his eyes darting to me. It took a heartbeat before they really saw me.

"He's yours now," he said in a raspy voice.

I nodded and grasped the gun. Pulling the trigger was easy, and strangely enough felt almost like an act of mercy.

Adamo

The shot rang in the dirty basement, followed by utter silence. I breathed harshly, trying to come down from my euphoric high. My pulse was pounding wildly in my veins and I felt almost invincible and overall: exhilaratingly alive. Slowly I became aware of Dinara's presence again. She stood a few feet from me. She'd watched everything without a word, every second of me losing control. I must have looked insane as I'd lost myself in the blood revelry. Fuck. I couldn't believe I'd let it consume me like that.

I met Dinara's gaze, expecting the worst: disgust and maybe even fear, but I found only realization and the hint of shock. Dinara lowered the gun and put it back into the bag with weapons. I sat back on my haunches, wondering if I should explain myself. But what could I say to justify my actions? I was a twisted fuck. A bitter smile twisted my lips as I met Dinara's beautiful eyes. "One monster killing another, a terrifying sight, hmm?"

Dinara tilted her head. "You are not like him."

"But I'm a monster. If I were you, I'd want to get as far from me as possible."

Maybe I finally needed to come to terms that I couldn't be better, that my nature would never allow me to achieve the level of goodness I'd wished for when I was younger.

She shook her head, as her expression filled with gratefulness. "No. You do this for me. That's something I won't ever forget. And I sure as hell won't go anywhere, Adamo."

"I do this for you, yes, but a small part also does it for me, because I want it."

"That's okay."

I laughed hoarsely. "Okay?"

"Yes, because even if you enjoy it ultimately, you do it for me. If that isn't proof for..." She trailed off, looking almost embarrassed.

"It is proof," I agreed. Proving to Dinara how much she meant to me was why I was here. It was why I started, but it wasn't why I kept going once I lay my hands on my victim. Once I'd begun my dark task, I was lost, lost to a deep yearning and dark hunger. I staggered to my feet. My legs felt unsteady as if I'd ridden a rollercoaster too often. This after torture sensation came closer to a drug rush than anything ever had, and anything ever could.

Dinara grabbed a towel from my bag and handed it to me. I took it. My hands were coated in blood and my clothes were soaked. They were ruined. I remembered when Remo and Nino had returned home like this and I'd feigned disgust when I'd really felt fascination.

Dinara watched me calmly, and I wondered what she saw. I remembered the sick fascination I'd felt when I'd first seen Remo and Nino in action. Even back then part of me had wondered how it would feel to lose myself in something as depraved but I'd fought it, had resisted for as long as I could.

Dinara scanned the remains of number two. If the sight unsettled her, she hid it. Once my hands were clean, I touched her arm, drawing her attention back to me.

"I'm fine," she said quietly. "I'm glad you did what you did. He deserved it, but it's not something I can do. I realized that now."

"You don't have to. I can if you want me to." I wanted to feel this high again. Dinara could probably see it in my face.

"I don't want to be the reason why you lose control," she said.

A dark laugh burst out of me. I touched her cheek. "You really think it's your fault I'm like this. That's the Falcone gene and my bloody upbringing, not you."

Dinara pressed a soft kiss to my lips. "Let's get out of here. I don't want to give him another second of my life. He got what he deserved. He's the past now."

After calling the clean-up crew, Dinara and I headed back to our motel. It was better than the dump in Reno, but definitely not a place that invited you to stay longer.

Dinara sat cross-legged on the bed when I emerged from the bathroom after a long shower. She was staring down at the list with her abusers. She had already crossed off number two. I sank down beside her. "I wonder how I'll feel once we can cross off the last name."

That was her mother's name. We hadn't discussed her end yet. Dinara avoided the topic. No matter how much she hated her mother, killing her would be different to every other kill. "You'll feel freed," I said. It was the outcome I hoped for.

"How do you feel?" Dinara asked, changing the topic as usually when we discussed the end of our vendetta.

I scooted closer to her and wrapped an arm around her shoulders as I considered my feelings. I didn't feel guilty, not even slightly. He'd deserved everything I'd done. "Good. Back to normal."

Dinara raised her eyebrows. "Normal isn't a word I'd use to describe you."

"Ditto," I said with a grin, but I became serious when I saw the honest concern in Dinara's eyes. "This is about you, not me. We're doing this so you can bury your past and find peace. What I'm feeling isn't important, but I'm not lying. I feel fine. The better question is how you feel?"

Dinara frowned as if she was listening into herself. "It's surreal, all of this. For so long, these people haunted my nightmares, and I could do nothing, but now I'm no longer the victim, and it feels good. I want to keep going."

"We will keep going, but I think it's good for us to have a break for a few days before we move on to Vegas."

When Dinara and I first had made the list and discussed our revenge plan, we'd agreed to return to camp after the first two kills to drive two races before we'd head to Vegas where the rest of the abusers lived. It would give us time to cool off, and would keep the speculations in camp to a minimum.

"I know," Dinara said. "But now that we've begun I hate to stop."

"You don't want time to doubt our actions?" I guessed.

Dinara shrugged. "Maybe. I can't imagine my conscience becoming a problem, not with the way I'm feeling now, but I…" She sighed. "I don't know. I don't want to risk it. I want all of them to get what they deserve."

"They will, because my conscience sure as hell won't become a problem."

Dinara smiled strangely and kissed me. "To think that I'd ever fall for an Italian mobster—" She snapped her lips shut, eyes going wide.

The high from the torture was nothing to what I felt now.

I opened my mouth but Dinara clapped her hand over my lips. "Don't say anything. Not now."

My eyes crinkled in amusement. Kissing her palm, I nodded my agreement. Slowly, Dinara lowered her hand.

"I never thought I'd fall for a Bratva princess either," I rushed to say.

Dinara kissed me hard. "Shut up, shut up. I don't want to talk emotions, not now. Not yet."

"After everything we've done, and everything we plan to do, you're scared of emotions?" I teased. Her eyes begged me to shut up and this time I did. Instead I pulled her against me and showed her with my body what I felt. No words needed.

TWENTY-ONE

Adamo

DINARA AND I RETURNED TO CAMP AND PARTICIPATED IN THE two following races, but our hearts weren't into it. The list occupied our thoughts. It was futile to pretend otherwise. We headed for Las Vegas the morning after the second race, unable to push our vendetta off further. We were both antsy.

We paid for another shabby motel on the old part of the strip. A place like that felt more fitting to our quest than a five-star hotel. We wouldn't be returning to camp until every last name on our list was crossed off, no matter how long it took. The races could wait.

The next few kills went smoothly, without torture. Easy kills that Dinara executed with a gun. I held back my own cravings for blood, allowing her to do this on her own terms. Worse than resisting my thirst for blood was watching the recordings. Every minute burned itself into my head and sometimes even followed me in my nightmares.

Dinara lay stretched out on the bed beside me after we'd crossed off number six, completely naked, and gorgeous beyond words. Seeing her like this and remembering the recordings I'd seen of her was difficult to put together. Dinara had survived horrors I couldn't even comprehend, and she'd become fierce and determined, but also kind. So many people would have turned jaded after what she'd gone through.

We hadn't discussed our emotions again, had skidded around the topic carefully, but watching her now, the desire to express my feelings was almost irresistible.

Dinara's eyes told me she knew what I was thinking. "Not yet," she whispered.

I smiled wryly. "When?"

"Not yet," she simply said.

Torture made my blood sing. I was still high, euphoric, but no longer lost in a trance. Dinara had captured my full attention. The way she'd unleashed her pain. The last few kills had been almost emotionless. Dinara had shot every abuser with a bullet in the head. Cool and controlled. But today had been different. As with her first kill, Dinara had lost herself in the need for revenge. Maybe it was because we'd faced two abusers, a married couple, who'd both abused Dinara. Her anger had mostly been focused on the woman. I had lost count of the time Dinara had stabbed her. She'd ferally attacked once I was done, had killed as if possessed.

Now silence had fallen in the cell below the Sugar Trap.

I was frozen as I looked at Dinara.

Blood coated her lips, a streak of color against her pale skin. Even the flaming red of her hair paled in comparison.

She lay motionless on the cold stone floor, her wide eyes directed at the ceiling but unseeing of what lay before her.

I dropped the knife. It landed with a clatter, blood splattering around it. For a second a sliver of my face reflected in the only clean spot on the sharp blade. For the first time in my life, I understood the fear people harbored when they heard my name. *Falcone.*

Today my expression justified their terror.

Bloodshed was in my genes. All of my life, I'd fought this craving deep in my veins, had dimmed it with drugs and alcohol, but its call had always been present, an undercurrent in my body that threatened to pull me under.

I hadn't let it. I'd thrown myself headfirst into its depth, had followed the current to the darkest part of my soul. For so long this day had been my greatest nightmare, a fear beyond measure. But fuck, today felt like a rebirth, like a homecoming to my true self.

My palms were sticky with her blood and it felt perfect. I had never before killed a woman, much less caused one pain on purpose, but after watching the recording, she'd become faceless to me, a mere target I needed to eradicate.

No street race could ever compete with the thrill, the absolute high of a kill, and even less with the power rush of torture.

Denying one's nature is living a lie. Only drugs in all shapes and forms had made it possible. No more.

People finally had a reason for the nickname they gave my brothers and me.

The monsters of Las Vegas.

My monstrous side had come out to play but the revelry had only just begun.

Remo and I were similar in looks, but that wasn't our most striking similarity. His cruelty and brutality had appalled me most of my life because it reflected a part of me I despised. Today I made peace with him and me.

I had Dinara to thank for that.

She turned her head and blinked at me, her chest heaving. "Will it always be like this?"

"Like what?" I asked hoarsely. I wasn't even sure why my throat ached. Unlike our victim I hadn't screamed. I had hardly said anything at all.

She drew in a deep breath as if she needed time to sort her thoughts, to form the right words. "I'm equally horrified and disgusted by what we did as I'm feeling exhilarated and empowered. Will it always be like that? This conflict tearing at my chest because I lost myself completely to the bloodlust. Just pulling the trigger is different, but this...this personal kill..." She sighed.

I moved closer to her and sank down on my knees beside her. "I don't know."

She searched my eyes. "What do you feel, Adamo?"

I considered lying, masking my true feelings. "Not horror. Not disgust." My gaze strayed toward the corpses, waiting for a flicker of regret, any kind of emotion a normal person would feel, but there was nothing, only the need to repeat what I just experienced. When I looked back at Dinara, realization filled her expression. The monster was difficult to hide once you took it out to play. "You like it more every time we do it."

I smiled darkly. "You know what they call us Falcones."

Remo and Nino would be so proud of me if they could have seen me like this. Pride goes before a fall. I'd always given them shit for what they did, for what they enjoyed doing, and now here I was.

She pushed into a sitting position and reached for my hand, linking our fingers. Our palms stuck together with the blood of our victim. "I couldn't have done this without you. I can't go on without you."

"You want to stick to our plan? Even your mother?"

"Yes," she said without hesitation. "I want to make them pay, every single one of them. They must bleed."

I squeezed her hand. "And bleed they will, Dinara. Their screams will drive away the ghosts their actions left in your soul."

Dinara shook her head with a small smile. She pressed a kiss to my lips. It tasted of blood and tears, and even that didn't disgust me. "Poet and killer. You never cease to surprise me, Adamo." Her eyes shone with resolve. "I think I'm falling for you."

Surprise washed through me. "What happened to not yet?"

Dinara shook her head. "Why should I be scared?"

There were probably a hundred reasons why our emotions should scare us, but I didn't give a damn about a single one of them. I cradled her neck, pulling her closer. "I'll go every step of the way with you. I'll give you the justice you deserve, even if it takes my last breath."

"No," she whispered. "Neither of us is going to give their last breath for these disgusting creatures. We are going to live when their blood has long been spilled."

I kissed her again, harder this time, my tongue parting her lips. My hand roamed her back.

Dinara pulled away with a shake of her head. "I can't. Not like this." She motioned at her blood-covered state. "Not beside them." She nodded at the bodies. "Could you?"

I wished the answer would have been no but my veins pulsed with the remnants of adrenaline from the kill and desire. I could have fucked Dinara right here on the cold, blood-soaked floor. I pushed to my feet and held out my hand. "Don't ask questions if the answers could scare you."

Dinara gripped my hand and I pulled her to her feet. She touched my chest, nails digging in. "I won't ever be scared of you." Her face moved very close until it was all I could see. "Because your monster won't ever hurt me."

I nodded, because that was true. "Let's take a shower and grab something to eat. We have a long day tomorrow."

Dinara slanted a look toward the corpses. "What about them? Don't we have to get rid of them?"

I took out my phone and called Nino. He and Remo were upstairs in the office and would handle the situation. "It'll be dealt with."

Dinara nodded. We headed upstairs, covered in blood and strangely elated. On our way out of the bar, we ran across Remo and Nino. Remo met my gaze, but he didn't say anything. I gave him a small nod. Today, maybe for the first time ever, I really understood him, and he saw it in my face.

"We'll deal with the corpses," Nino said matter-of-factly.

A nervous energy surrounded Dinara as we stepped out of the Sugar Trap but the closer we got to the car the calmer she got. She opened the passenger door, and released a small laugh. "We really did it. We're almost done with our list."

Only one name remained, a name we avoided mentioning.

I could practically see the weight falling off her. Euphoria was banishing any hint of anxiety. For now her demons were put to rest. They weren't gone for good however. I was intimately familiar with demons of the past. They'd come back to haunt her, but they would have lost some of their power over her.

"We did, and we won't stop until you got what you want."

We got into the car and I hit the gas, racing away, out of the city. Dinara reached over, her palm covering my cock through my jeans. I slanted her a questioning look. Her lips dragged into a teasing smile, but in her eyes, darkness mixed with lust. Fuck, and it turned me on. I would have fucked her right there with the dead bodies.

She rubbed harder. I slowed the car, wanting to pull over. She shook her head. "Keep driving. Fast."

I chose side streets that were less crowded at this time of the night. My foot pressed down on the gas again.

Dinara nodded and lowered her eyes to my bulge. She unbuckled her belt and scooted closer before she opened my zipper. After a bit of fumbling, my cock sprang free and she took it into her mouth.

I hissed at the feel of her wet heat. Her tongue rimmed my tip before she sucked me even deeper. One of my hands tangled in her red mane as her head bobbed up and down. My eyes were fixed on the street ahead, racing through the near darkness.

I moaned when Dinara sucked only my tip while her hands palmed my balls through the jeans. The wet sounds of her mouth working my cock filled the car. My fingers tightened in her hair when I hit her throat. She pulled back slightly only to work my tip even more feverously with her mouth and tongue. My fingers locked tighter around the steering wheel as the first treacherous pulsating took hold off my balls. Dinara sucked me harder, her fingers massaging my balls into orgasm, and then pleasure shot through me and I released right into her mouth.

Groaning, I pumped my hips, my foot on the gas slacking, while Dinara milked me dry. "Fuck," I growled as I almost swerved the car off the street. Dinara raised her head, smiling darkly, her lips coated with my cum. Her tongue darted out, licking it up.

"Your turn now," I rasped, steering the car toward the side of the road.

She grabbed the wheel, pushing the car back on the street. "Keep driving. Fast."

I shook my head. "Can't eat you out while I'm driving. Even my driving skills aren't good enough to drive blind."

She grinned wickedly. "Finger me and drive."

I sped up once more as I watched Dinara slide down her pants and thong in one move, revealing those sexy lean legs and delicious pussy with the trimmed red hair. She gave me a look that told me she knew the effect her body had on me. She leaned her back against the door and propped up one leg against my thigh, giving me a prime view of that sopping wet pink pussy.

"Eyes on the street, Falcone," she said with a daring grin.

"How am I supposed to focus on driving if your pussy's tempting me?"

"You're a big boy. You can deal. Now get me off."

I chuckled as I returned my eyes to the street. I reached out and cupped Dinara's knee, then slowly trailed my hand up her inner thigh.

"Faster."

"The car or my fingers?"

"Both," she hissed, grabbing my wrist and pressing my fingers against her wet pussy. I groaned at the feel of her welcoming heat, knowing it would feel perfect around my cock.

I slid two fingers into her. She moaned, her walls clenching around my fingers.

Soon Dinara's hips rotated frantically, driving my fingers deeper into her pussy. The lights of Vegas came into view and soon we passed buildings and crowded sidewalks.

I fingered Dinara even faster until she cried out, her inner muscles clamping like a vice around my fingers. I kept fucking her but slowed. My foot on the gas eased too and soon the blur of hotels and people became distinguishable. Dinara leaned her cheek against the glass, peering out with parted lips. I curled my fingers, causing her to moan and fog up the glass. I pulled into the parking garage of a random hotel and parked at the side. The moment the car stopped, I shoved my seat back.

Dinara didn't hesitate before she climbed on my lap and lowered herself on my cock.

The passengers of passing cars gave us white-eyed looks. It was only a matter of time before their reports would lead security or even the police here. I grabbed Dinara's neck and pulled her down for a kiss while my other hand palmed her firm ass as she rode me. Our bodies seemed to become one and our surroundings faded to the background.

We clung to each other almost desperately, as if this was the last time, we could ever be close.

When we returned to our motel room that night, our mood was solemn. We'd almost reached the end of our list, and with it the end of our vigilante journey. After that we'd have to return to our normal life, or as normal as our life could be. We crawled into bed together, both on our backs, our arms touching.

"What are we going to do after the last kill?" I asked.

Dinara blinked up at the ceiling. "I hope I'll feel freed."

"I hope so too, but that's not what I meant."

She rolled over to face me, her smile solemn. "I know. I suppose you will return to the race camp?"

"The season is as good as over and with all the races I missed, I can't make a top ten position anyway."

Dinara nodded. She stroked her fingertips along the stubble on my chin and cheek. "So you'll return to Vegas to celebrate Christmas with your brothers?"

Christmas seemed lightyears away, even if there was only a month until Christmas eve. "That's the plan, yes," I said slowly. "But I thought you could join me."

Surprise crossed Dinara's face. "You want me to spend the holidays with your family?"

"With me and my family," I corrected. "Does it really come as such a shock to you that I want you at my side, even during the holidays. We've spent night and day together over the last few months, and to be fucking honest, despite all the brutal shit our adventure entailed, it was the best time of my life."

"Then you should reconsider your life choices," she said with a wry smile, but her eyes held tenderness. "It says a lot about me and you that it was also the best time of my life. We're fucked up."

"So what?"

"Once we're done with the list, you'll still be a Camorrista and I'll still be the daughter of the Chicago Pakhan. Is there a way this can work?" Her lips brushed mine and her eyes held hope and anxiety.

"If we want it to."

"My father doesn't want war with the Outfit. That would hit too close to home, but if he agreed to a truce with your brothers, that might very well lead to a war declaration from the Outfit."

"We don't fight over the same territory," I said. "Your father rules over the Great Lakes. We don't have to declare truce to ignore each other's existence."

"You think ignoring each other's existence is enough for you and me to be an official couple? Where would we even live? We couldn't live in Chicago together because that would cause trouble."

"Not to mention that the Outfit would have a field day if they got their hands on me again to finish what they started."

Dinara stroked the scar on my forearm absent-mindedly as she continued, "And me living in Las Vegas would look just as bad. No matter what we said, people would consider me as part of the Camorra and suspect a truce between your family and mine, which would have the same result. War between the Bratva and the Outfit."

The Outfit had strong ties to the political elite in Chicago and Illinois. Even if the Camorra and Bratva fought together to in attack it would mean a lot of unwanted attention. That wasn't something we wanted or needed. But I wasn't willing to give Dinara up over mob politics.

"I want us to be together. If we both want it, nothing can stop us."

Dinara leaned her forehead against mine. "Let's talk about this once we're done."

She still couldn't say it. The last name on our list was Dinara's biggest challenge.

"It won't be easy. Maybe you can't go through with it. And that's okay too. That doesn't mean you failed or that you're still shackled by the past."

"I have to do it," Dinara whispered. "I have to kill her."

I kissed her temple. Whatever it took to help Dinara, I'd do it.

Dinara

Before I could go through with killing my mother, I needed to return to Chicago. Adamo was reluctant to let me leave, but ultimately, he understood and accepted my need to talk to my father.

I stepped into the foyer of our mansion. For a moment I only inhaled the familiar scent. I'd hated living in this golden cage and yet I always missed it. Or maybe I just missed Russia.

Dad waited in his office. Even the tsar couldn't have had a more magnificent workspace. Dad looked up when I entered.

Bloodshed was his profession. I had no illusions regarding the atrocities he was capable of. If you wanted to become anything in the Bratva, you couldn't afford a conscience. But I'd always been his little girl, a precious doll he wanted to keep away from the terrors of his business.

Now I'd shown my true colors. I'd tortured and killed. I was a Mikhailov.

He didn't get up from his chair, only leaned back, regarding me closely. "You worked with the Camorra to dish out the revenge I could have dished out for you. Why would you ask the enemy for help but not your own father?"

Disappointment and anger rang in his deep voice. His eyes hit me with the full force of his disappointment. I walked toward him, my high heels clicking on the parquet. The Russian lady costume barely hid what truly lay beneath, a broken, messed-up murderer.

"Because you would have never allowed me to be part of the killings. My only chance to dish out revenge was to seek other allies."

Dad hit the desk with his palm and shoved to his feet, towering over me. "Because I didn't want blood on your hands. I wanted to protect you from the evil of this world. And the fucking Falcones throw you right into the abysm of hell."

I met his furious gaze. Grown men fell to their knees before this man but I'd never been scared of him. Maybe I was a fool for thinking I was safe from his cruel side. "Protecting me now, against my will I might add, won't make the past undone. I know you feel guilty for being unable to protect me back then."

The fury multiplied, his eyes practically burning up with rage but behind it guilt flared up.

"The Falcones never had the power to throw me into any abyss, because I've been living in a fucking hell for years, from the moment the first bastard raped me."

Dad gripped one of the expensive Fabergé eggs from his desk and tossed it against the closest wall. It shattered with an earsplitting crash and every beautiful piece fell to the floor. The word rape was one we'd skidded around so far. We knew what had happened but somehow putting a word to it had threatened to make it worse. I took his hand, stepping closer. "You can't save me, Dad. No one can. I need to claw myself out of the abyss my mother threw me into."

"Don't speak that name."

"Killing those men felt good, so good. Their pain took away some of my own."

Dad cupped my cheeks, searching my eyes as if he hoped to find the little daughter that he'd dressed in princess dresses. But that girl was dead, died many painful deaths to be reborn as something vile and vengeful. "If I could make undone what's been done to you, I'd kill every single of my men just to get my little Katinka back."

My eyes prickled. "I know. But she's dead, and now I'm going to make sure every single person who killed her will be too."

"A father never wants his daughter to become like him, not if he's a man like myself."

"I'm glad I'm like you in this regard. I'm glad I could hold the knife that executed the kill. I'm glad I'm not the princess in need of a prince to settle her scores."

"But you got help from the Falcone prince, didn't you?"

I nodded. "He helped me track them down. But it was me who killed them. They're all dead. Now only my mother is left."

"I should be the one to kill her, not you. Killing a woman, killing your mother, will leave scars. Scars I don't think you should inflict on yourself."

I smiled emotionlessly. "She's the worst monster of them all. That woman is the reason why I'll never know what the word "mother" really means. Killing her will set me free."

Dad stroked my cheek. "I hope it does. I really hope it does, but if I've learned something over the years, it's that revenge rarely sets us free. It only shackles us to new demons. Sometimes those only join the old ones. I can't lose you, Dinara."

I pulled back with a frown. "You think I'll run off with Adamo, join the Camorra."

"That's not the loss I worry about." His fingers curled around my forearm.

"I didn't try to kill myself. And I haven't been cutting myself in a while." Despite the many years that had passed since my slip, Dad couldn't get over it and I felt guilty because of it, but I was trying to live a new, better life.

Dad's eyes became distant. "When Dima found you in a puddle of blood with foam around your mouth, I thought I'd lost you."

"I won't overdose again, Dad. I'm clean. You know no one's going to sell me shit in your territory anyway."

"What about Camorra territory?"

"Not there either, trust me. Adamo made sure of it."

"Adamo," Dad repeated, a dangerous gleam in his eyes. "What's really between you and this Falcone boy?"

"He's not a boy, Dad."

Dad just kept staring into my eyes. "Is it serious?"

"What would you do if I said yes?"

"You're going to be torn between two worlds."

"It's the same world, just different sides."

"Exactly. You know I can't allow you to date the enemy. Nobody will understand it."

"They don't have to, as long as you do."

"Do you realize in what position you put me? Allowing you to keep wandering around in Camorra lands puts the business at risk. Moscow won't be happy about that."

"I don't know anything about your business, and even if I did, I wouldn't tell anyone."

"If the Camorra used you as bait, they'd have me in their hands and you know it."

I smiled wryly. "You know Remo better than I do, and even I know he'd never use me like that."

"That man doesn't have a kind bone in his body, Dinara. There's a reason why he controls the west without a hiccup."

"There's a reason why you're Pakhan, Dad. Still you live by certain rules. One of them makes sure you're allowing me to do what I do even though you disapprove, and the same rules have Remo Falcone see me as off-limits as well."

"Having men like us in your hand, that's a powerful position to be in, I hope you realize that," he murmured, cupping my head. "I'm gifting you with more freedom than I'd ever allow anyone else and not because of these rules you mention."

"Because of pity," I guessed.

Dad smiled wistfully. "Oh, not pity either. The girl before me today doesn't need my pity." He kissed my temple. "Love's a fool's game. Don't play it."

"I need to return to Vegas to finish what I started."

Dad's lips thinned. "Don't lose yourself. Don't give your mother any power over you. She deserves to die and be forgotten."

TWENTY-TWO

Dinara

THE LAST FEW KILLINGS HAD BEEN EASY, EASIER THAN THEY should have been, but maybe killing lay in my blood like Adamo always claimed it lay in his.

Today was different though, and nothing about it would be easy. I felt even more nervous than before the very first kill. Adamo squeezed my hand, his gaze seeking mine, trying to determine if I was okay.

I wasn't sure what I was feeling. My emotions tumbled all over themselves, and I'd thrown up what little I'd had for breakfast. This was the summit I had to climb. Every kill until this point had been mere preparation for this day. When I'd talked to Dad yesterday, he'd offered to kill her if I couldn't go through with it. Adamo, too, wouldn't hesitate to take this burden off my shoulders, but I couldn't allow either man to kill for me. This was between my mother and me. She was the one who'd sold me to the highest bidder, who'd ripped me away from my home and my father because she wanted freedom. Dad had never revealed the details of their relationship—until last night.

He'd met her as an escort but their sexual encounters had ended in my mother becoming pregnant with me, and my father insisting she kept me. Later, he forbade her to work as an escort, sent her into a rehabilitation clinic and forced her to live in his mansion, so I had a mother. He'd wanted me to have parents but my mother had never wanted to have me, to be a mom, to be clean. She wanted her life back and when it became clear my father wouldn't give it to her, she used me as a means to punish him and to get what she wanted.

"Dinara?" Adamo asked, worried.

I snapped out of my thoughts. We were parked in front of the apartment building where my mother lived. She'd tried to run away yesterday after she must have found out about the murders, but a Camorra soldier had kept watch over her place. Now she waited for us to arrive. I wondered if she knew that she'd share the same fate as every other name on our list or if she hoped for mercy.

I grasped the door handle. "I'm ready." My voice sounded resolute, determined, calm—the opposite of what I was feeling.

Adamo and I took the elevator up to the third floor then headed toward the last door on the left. A dusty, stale stench lingered in the corridor and the carpet had seen better days. Adamo knocked. I balled my hands into fists to stop them from trembling. I'd waited for this day for a long time but now I was terrified. A middle-aged man, the Camorra soldier, opened the door and let us in. Adamo went in first and I followed after a moment of hesitation. The place wasn't what I'd expected. I'd thought it would be a sad, dirty place, but the apartment was clean and newly furnished with plenty of glass, fake marble, and golden décor. Black and white photos of my mother in lingerie hung at the wall over the white leather couch. I didn't find a sign of myself anywhere in the apartment. My mother had probably forgotten about my existence.

When I spotted her, a shiver raced down my spine and the desire to leave became almost unstoppable.

Last time I had only seen my mother from afar. Now only a few feet separated us. I remembered that Dad had compared my beauty to my mother's when I was very little, before he never spoke of her again. Beauty still lingered under her wrinkles and the frown lines around her mouth and forehead. She was dressed in an expensive-looking dress, with immaculate nails and hair. A cigarette burned in the ashtray on the glass table in front of her. Her eyes darted between Adamo and me, anxiety lining her face.

"Katinka," she said softly, as if she was happy to see me, as if she had any right to call me by the name she'd ripped away from me.

"Don't," I seethed. "Don't use that name. I'm Dinara now. Or maybe you want to use one of the many names you chose for me while you let one man after the other rape me?"

She blanched. I could see how she was trying to come up with something to say. She reached for the cigarette and took a shaky drag. I'd never smoke again. Her jittery energy told me that she needed something stronger than tobacco. Drugs. I couldn't believe I'd followed in her footsteps and also fallen trap to addiction. I swore I'd never touch anything ever again. I'd never become the despicable woman before me.

"Dinara," she began hesitantly. "I never meant for you to get hurt. I was in a bad state of mind. I was full of despair."

I staggered closer to her, furious tears stinging in my eyes. "Despair?"

"Your father—"

Her familiar, too sweet, too strong perfume penetrated my nose, bringing up vivid memories that almost made my legs buckle. "My father forbade you from taking drugs. He wanted you to take care of me. He provided for you so you could be a mother to me. He gave you money so you didn't have to sell your body anymore."

"I never asked for any of this. I was happy with what I had."

I swallowed hard. She didn't seem guilty at all.

"I didn't know what those men did to you. They hurt you, not me."

I couldn't believe her audacity. "There are recordings of what happened. You are in many of them, telling me to be nice to those assholes. You recorded what happened. You knew, don't pretend you didn't!"

"I—I was drugged. Those men pressured me."

"You can blame them or my father but you are the true monster, Eden. They at least didn't know me. You should have loved me."

She made a move as if to stand but Adamo sent her a warning look.

"I was too young when I gave birth to you. I didn't even want to have a child," she said, glancing from him to me. The cigarette between her fingers had almost burned down.

I pressed my lips together, remembering Dad's words. My mother hadn't wanted me. She'd wanted to get an abortion but Dad didn't allow it. He wouldn't allow her to get rid of his child. I didn't resent her for not being ready for a child, not even that she'd wanted to abort me, but I hated her for how she'd used me, how she'd let other abuse me only so she could live the life she wanted. That wasn't something I could ever forgive.

"A mother is supposed to protect her child from all harm, not throw it in its way. I loved you. I trusted you, and you destroyed everything. You ruined my life."

She motioned at me. "You are here now and you look strong."

"I'm here because of Dad, because he protected me."

"Don't become like him, don't kill me, Dinara. I can leave the States so you'll never have to see me again."

"Maybe you can run from what happened but I can't. It'll always be a part of me."

Mother slanted an assessing glance at Adamo, as if she wondered if he might be her salvation. She didn't know him. He was the last person to expect mercy from.

"Did you ever have nightmares because of what you did to me?" I asked.

"Remo Falcone made sure I couldn't forget what happened," she said, but she didn't say it as if this had caused her distress on my behalf. Her voice rang with self-pity. She met Adamo's gaze. "He's your brother. You know how he is. Have you told her?"

"Whatever my brother did is nothing in comparison to what you did to your own daughter," Adamo growled, his eyes flashing with violence.

My own hunger for blood answered. I wasn't sure why I was still talking to my mother. Maybe deep down I hoped she'd realize what she did, how she broke a young child's trust and ruined my life, but I wouldn't get the satisfaction of an honest apology. My mother was incapable of seeing her mistakes.

I took the gun from the holster under my leather jacket. My mother jerked to her feet with raised hands. "Please, Dinara. You won't feel better if you kill me. You'll be guilty."

"Guilty?" I rasped. "As guilty as you feel for what you did to me?"

I raised the gun, pointed it straight at her head. Her frantic eyes searched the room for an opportunity to escape, to save herself. My finger on the trigger shook. I only had to pull the trigger to end this but I was unable to move. I wasn't sure what was holding me back. I didn't love the woman before me, but until this point, a tiny, silly part had hoped everything would turn out to be a big misunderstanding, that there was an explanation that would prove my mother's innocence. I knew that wouldn't happen, but my heart had foolishly clung to hope. I'd wanted to find a mother I could love, a mother I could forgive. The woman before me wasn't that mother.

I turned away, unable to look at her. Adamo touched my shoulder, searching my eyes. "I can't," I said almost tonelessly, lowering the gun.

"Do you want me—"

"No," I said quickly. I put the gun down on the side table.

From the corner of my eye, I noticed my mother approach us hesitantly. "You won't regret it, I swear. Now that you decided to spare me, Remo will let me go, like you said. I'll leave and never come back. But..." She licked her lips. "Your father will hunt me. I'll need some money to reach Europe and create a new life for me over there."

Adamo's expression shifted to absolute fury. "Are you asking Dinara for money?"

Eden took a step back. "If she wants me to live and not have my death on her conscience, I need some money to escape Grigory."

New tears pressed against my eyeballs. "Just like you needed money last time but back then you couldn't ask me for it, so you sold me to old men who molested me."

I began to shake, anger and utter despair battling inside of me. I ripped the knife out of its holster and whirled around. With a hoarse cry, I smashed the blade into her chest. Her eyes widened and her lips parted in a silent cry. Then she crumpled to the ground, taking me with her because I was still clutching the knife. I landed on my knees beside her. I released the knife, gripped her shoulders and began to shake her.

"How could you do this to me? How? How?" I screamed. My tears blinded my vision and my throat was raw from screaming. "How? Why didn't you love me enough to protect me? Why?" I kept shaking her and screaming but she couldn't answer me, and no matter what she'd have said it would have never given me the answer I wished for.

I released her and curled up, my face buried in my hands, which were sticky with her blood. I sobbed and shuddered. "Why didn't you love me?"

Adamo knelt down beside me and wrapped an arm around me, pulling me against him. "She was a monster and never deserved to be your mother. You are lovable and I love you."

I froze against him, sucking in a shaky breath. I lifted my face. I must have looked a mess with blood, tears, and snot on my face but Adamo's expression was full of love. "You love me?"

"Yes, even if I'm breaking our keeping it casual pact. I don't care. I won't hide my emotions. I fucking love you and you better deal with it."

I let out a strangled laugh. "I love you, too." I kissed Adamo but when I pulled back his lips were coated with blood. My eyes sought the corpse of my mother right beside us. Her blood was slowly spreading under her body and her lifeless eyes stared at the ceiling.

I sagged against Adamo, adrenaline fading and leaving a strange sensation of emptiness. I'd done it. We'd done it. Killed every single tormentor on my list. Even my mother. I'd expected euphoria and relief, and there was a flicker of relief but stronger was the uncertainty. What now? All my life, I'd thriven to uncover my past and then to punish those who'd abused me. Now that I'd succeeded, I had to focus on my future, on new goals and figure out what I really wanted.

I reached into my jean shorts, and took out the crumpled piece of paper, dotted with blood. I'd kept it in my pocket since we'd started our path of vengeance.

We were done with our list. It seemed forever ago that we'd killed the first man on the list. Every second of every day had been dominated by thoughts of revenge. It had occupied my every thought, my night and days, and now, that we'd reached the end, a feeling of "what now?" took hold of me.

Adamo stroked my back. Neither he nor I made a move to get up from the blood puddle gathering around us, soaking our clothes. It was still warm. "It's over," I whispered, almost awed.

Adamo kissed my temple. "Now you can move on."

I searched his eyes, wondering what we would do now and if it would be as easy as he said.

I glanced at my mother. No, at the woman who had given birth to me. She wasn't really a mother and had never been.

"The clean-up crew will deal with her. You can forget she ever existed," Adamo said. "Let's get out of here." He got up and held out his hand to me.

I nodded, even if I still felt trapped in a daze, and allowed him to pull me to my feet. Adamo called the clean-up crew and led me toward the door. I chanced a last look at my mother before I left. I'd wanted her dead and I didn't feel any regret over killing her, but the euphoria and sense of freedom didn't come yet.

Adamo

We returned to our hotel and entered the building through a back entrance because we looked rough covered in blood as we were. The staff turned a blind eye to our state. Las Vegas and especially our hotels were under our total control. Everybody who worked for us knew better than to show interest in suspicious behavior.

Dinara headed into the bathroom and I followed her. She hadn't said anything since we'd left her mother's place.

She sank down on the edge of the bathtub and kept looking at her blood-crusted fingers, flexing them as if she didn't trust her eyes. After our last few killings, euphoria and excitement had been our dominating feelings. With every crossed-off name on our list, another weight seemed to have lifted off Dinara's shoulder. Not today though. I perched beside her. "She deserved death."

"By our standards, definitely," Dinara said.

"Not just by our standards. I think many people would agree she deserved to die after what she did." Social norms and average morals were something neither Dinara nor I had many experiences with, but child abuse was a crime most people wanted to see punished as harshly as possible. "Do you regret killing her?"

Dinara finally looked up from her hands, her brows puckering as she considered my question. "No. I don't feel any remorse. I would have kept thinking about her if I'd known she was alive. I could have never really moved on. And not just that. If I'd kept her alive and suffered because of it, Dad would have taken matters into his own hands eventually. He would have moved heaven and earth to kill her in your brother's territory and that would have only caused trouble. I don't want our families to be at war."

"It's not like we're at peace right now."

"Not at war either. As long as we ignore each other, there's a chance for us to be…" She trailed off, her expression shutting off.

I grabbed her hand. "For us to be together," I finished. Dinara's eyes bored into mine. A few tiny blood splatters dotted her cheeks and forehead, her hair was a mess, and her skin was pale, and yet she looked more beautiful than anyone I'd ever seen.

"Yeah," she agreed quietly. "What now? I feel as if there's a void opening up before me right now where a purpose had been before."

"Now we take a shower and get a good night's sleep, and tomorrow we return to camp."

Surprise crossed Dinara's expression as if she hadn't even considered the option of returning to camp.

"You want to return to camp, right?"

A tired smile spread on her face. "It's the only place I want to be right now."

I woke in the middle of the night to an empty bed. Searching the room, I found Dinara in front of the panorama windows. She let her gaze stray over the flickering lights of the Strip below us. I got out of bed and joined her. A lost look lay in her eyes, as if she were looking for an anchor to hold on to. I touched her back and she gave me a tired smile over her shoulder.

"I couldn't sleep."

"Nightmares?"

She shook her head with a small frown. "No, not really. I just feel a little lost. I'd thought I'd kill the past by killing my abusers, but it still lingers in the back of my mind, not as prominent as before but still there."

Healing would take more than killing her mother and abusers, and above all, it would take more time. I led her back to bed and we lay down, my arms around her waist. I could feel the unrest in her body.

"Maybe you should talk to Kiara," I said eventually.

"Your sister-in-law," she said, starting to pull away. Her defenses rose into place. "And why should I?"

"Because she experienced something similar." I hadn't discussed this with Kiara, but she was one of the kindest, most helpful people I knew, so I was sure she'd help Dinara.

Dinara swung out of bed, her back to me. She took a cigarette from the packet and slipped it between her lips but she didn't light it up. Instead she scowled at the tip. She flipped the lighter almost angrily and finally lit up her cigarette. I sat up as well so I could see her face but she was squinting at the burning tip. Finally, she turned to me, her eyes hard. "And what would that be?"

"She was abused by her uncle when she was a kid."

Dinara let out a bitter laugh and took a deep drag of her cigarette, blowing out the smoke slowly. "Did her mom get cash for selling her little daughter too? Was she raped by a dozen guys, sometimes while her mother watched?"

"I know you didn't experience exactly the same but that doesn't mean she doesn't understand the trauma you went through. Maybe talking to her will help you."

She glowered at me. "Do you handle trauma the same way Remo or Nino do? The shit that happened in your youth, the death of your mother? No, you don't. But for some reason people think that all rape victims are the same, as if we all deal with the shit the same way. As if all of us want pity and be coddled as if suddenly we're frail."

"I don't coddle you nor do I fucking pity you, and I most definitely don't think you're frail."

"But when you found out, that's exactly what you thought."

Anger rose in me. I snatched the cigarette from her mouth and snuffed it in the ashtray. "I didn't fucking know what I was thinking. I was shocked by the shitshow Remo lay down at my feet."

Dinara rolled her eyes. "You were shocked by what you saw? I lived that shitshow."

I ran a hand through my hair with a sigh. I grabbed Dinara's hand and to my surprise she let me, even allowed me to link our fingers. "I know. Fuck, Dinara, I want to help you."

"And you are, and you already did by helping me take out these assholes one after the other."

"You think that's enough?"

She stared into my eyes, not saying anything for a long time. "I don't know but it made me feel better, at least temporarily. I guess I'll just have to determine what I want now, and how to live with the demons I can't kill as easily."

I could see a weight falling off when we left Las Vegas behind. The city would always be associated with painful memories for her. Linking our fingers, I caught her attention. She gave me a distracted smile.

"Do you feel different?" I asked.

"Different than before we started our vendetta?"

I nodded.

She considered that. "Yesterday I would have said "no". It felt as if I was falling into a black hole, but I'm starting to realize what we accomplished. The people who hurt me and other girls are gone. My mother is gone and they can't ever hold power over me again."

"You'll feel even better after the upcoming race."

Her smile became less tense. "I really missed racing. I never thought it would grow on me so much."

"You never thought I'd grow on you so much either," I joked, wanting to lighten the mood further.

Dinara rolled her eyes but then she leaned over and distracted me briefly with a kiss. "You caught me by surprise. That won't happen again."

"I already have your heart."

"You do, now you'll just have to keep it," she said teasingly. She sank back against the seat, her shoulders relaxing for the first time since yesterday.

"Now that I have it, I won't give it back."

Dinara's gaze became distant. "We'll just have to convince our families."

"It's our life. They'll have to accept our choice."

Dinara gave me a look that made it clear it wouldn't be as easy as that. I knew she was right, but we'd already gone through so much and I wouldn't let anyone tear us apart.

TWENTY-THREE

Dinara

BEING BACK AT CAMP ACTUALLY FELT LIKE RETURNING HOME. I loved my childhood home in Chicago, but it had always felt like a prison of sort. When I lived there, I had to abide by certain rules. Dad's soldiers and the staff required that I reflected a certain image. Not to mention that Dad preferred to see a version of me that had little resemblance to the real Dinara.

Kate, the pit girl with the beautiful voice greeted me with a hug when I ran across her on my way to the toilet trailer. I could see us becoming friends in the long run, if I stayed in camp and really started seeing it as my home. If she'd heard what had happened, she didn't let it show. I couldn't believe that no one had spread rumors.

I never made it to the trailer because Dima headed my way. I hadn't seen him in weeks. I hugged him. "I missed you," I admitted.

His expression twisted with apprehension when he pulled back. I braced myself for what he had to say. "We should return to Chicago now. There's no reason for us to stay. Falcone and the races served their purpose. We don't need either anymore."

I allowed my gaze to take in the tents and race cars, soaking up the buzzing excitement of the day before a race. I didn't want to leave. I wanted to become a part of the camp, just because and not for any other reason. I wanted to be with Adamo. "Why should I return to Chicago?"

"Because that's where you belong," Dima muttered. "This isn't your home. Don't overstay your welcome, Dinara. Remo Falcone might have tolerated your presence so he could play with you but now that the game is over, he'll want you off his territory as soon as possible."

"Nobody played with me. He gave me an option and I grabbed it. Only because it was an option Dad and you disapprove of doesn't mean his motives were bad. He gave me what I wanted."

Dima made a face. "He's good at manipulation. I have to admit it. Remo used you to exact revenge that your father wanted."

"He might have wanted it but it was mine to begin with. Not his, or anyone else's."

"And yet you shared it with Adamo instead of me or your father."

"Because neither of you would have allowed me to get my hands dirty. You would have taken matters into your own hands. Maybe you would have allowed me to watch but definitely not to partake."

"Because what you did can destroy you."

"But it didn't," I said firmly. "I don't have nightmares, and I don't feel guilty."

That wasn't quite true. I had nightmares but they were better than the ones that had haunted me in the past. They didn't wake me in a cold sweat with a pounding heart.

"I won't return to Chicago now. I'll finish the season—"

"Your father wants you back in Chicago, so that's where I'm taking you. You got what you wanted, now you have to come to your senses."

I narrowed my eyes. "Are you going to tie me up and kidnap me?"

"Your father won't accept a no in this case, and he'll blame Adamo if you don't show up in Chicago tonight."

I gritted my teeth. I didn't want to provoke my father. He'd been pissed about my vigilante quest but had allowed me to do what I needed to do, but I had a feeling he wouldn't be as tolerant if I ignored his order this time. I didn't want to turn him against Adamo. I wanted him to like Adamo, to accept him as the man I loved, no matter how unlikely that was.

"I'll have to talk to Adamo first," I said. Dima didn't bother hiding his disapproval but I didn't care. I wouldn't sneak away. Adamo deserved to know what was going on. I turned on my heel and went in search of Adamo. I found him, as expected, at Crank's trailer, probably discussing last-minute details for tomorrow's race. He gave me a distracted smile but his face morphed into a frown when he saw my expression. He said something to Crank who nodded before he jogged toward me. "What's wrong?"

It was strange how well Adamo knew me. I'd always prided myself on my poker face, but after everything Adamo and I had been through, we knew each other's fake expressions and the true meaning behind them. It was scary and comforting all at once.

"I need to return to Chicago—tonight."

Adamo froze. "Why? You'll miss tomorrow's race."

"I know. But my father insists that I'll return to talk to him. He's given me the time to do what I needed to do but now his patience is running thin."

Adamo regarded me silently for a couple of heartbeats. The hint of worry and suspicion flared up in his eyes but disappeared so quickly I would have missed them if I didn't know him just as well as he knew me.

"I'll be back as soon as possible," I said firmly. "But I need to straighten things with my father first. I don't want him to send the cavalry and create more tension between our families."

Adamo touched my hips, pulling me closer. "Maybe he won't allow you to return."

"The only way he could make me stay is to lock me in and that's something he'd never do." To me, at least. Because of what happened to me, Dad hated to force his will on me, which was why I had more freedoms than most girls I knew.

"If you don't return, I'll drive to Chicago and get you myself."

I scoffed. "Don't you dare. That would be insanity. Dad would kill you on sight. Trust me to handle my father. He won't force me to stay. I know him."

Adamo still looked doubtful but he nodded anyway. "All right. I trust you. Promise me to hurry."

"I will."

"Dinara!" Dima called across camp, impatience ringing in his voice.

I sighed. "It's time for me to leave." Adamo pressed his lips against mine and kissed me passionately. When he pulled back and released me, Dima's expression had darkened even more.

"Did you tell him goodbye?" Dima asked when we got into the car together.

"It wasn't a goodbye. It was a see-you-later."

Dima sent me an exasperated look. "That's not what your father wants."

"It's what I want," I said sharply.

Chicago felt even less like home than last time. I'd transformed over the last few months. I didn't bother changing into new clothes before seeing Dad. My boots, tattered jeans, and biker jacket were me and I didn't want to pretend I was someone else.

Dad's face flashed with surprise when I entered his office. He scanned my outfit, obviously disgruntled. For him, women should wear dresses and skirts to emphasize their femininity. He got up from his desk chair and strode toward me to pull me into a tight embrace. "It's good to have you back now. I couldn't stop worrying about you while you spent time in Camorra territory."

I gave him a tense smile. He thought I'd returned for good, that I wouldn't return to camp, to Adamo.

"Dad," I began, pulling back.

Dad's eyes tightened. "Your place is here, with your people, with your family."

"I'm a grown-up, and grown-ups eventually move out and live their own life. You know that I never really felt like I belonged in our circles. I don't want to schmooze the wives of oligarchs and politicians, or pretend I give a damn about the newest limited-edition bag from Louis Vuitton.

I want to be free and do as I please. I don't want to fulfill my role as a Pakhan's daughter. I never did. You have Galina and the boys for that. You don't need me."

Dad took a step back, his shoulders stiffening. I could tell that he was hurt by my words. "I gave you all the freedom you need, more than any other girl in your position would ever be allowed. All I ask is for you to be loyal."

My brows snapped together. "Of course, I'm loyal. That I want to spend the year as a race driver in Camorra territory doesn't mean I'm not loyal to you. I love you Dad. I'd never betray you."

"You want to be with the Falcone boy."

"He's not a boy," I said. "And yes, I want to be with him. It's not like we're going to marry. We just enjoy spending time together."

Dad stroked my cheek as if I were a delusional child. "This can't work Dinara. You will be torn between two worlds, worlds that'll never merge. I don't want open war with Dante Cavallaro, but if I make peace with the Camorra, his arch-enemy, that'll be the result. He's acquired some very important political alleys these last few years and it'll hurt my business if they start to turn their attention on me."

"I'm not asking you to risk war with the Outfit, or to make peace with the Camorra. I'm not part of the Bratva, and if I stop doing our websites, then I won't have any involvement with our business at all. There won't be a risk of me revealing anything to Adamo, not even by accident. He and I don't even discuss business details anyway."

"Dinara, you are a Mikhailov and people will judge you as one. You lived a fantasy for a few months but now you have to face reality. A Mikhailov and a Falcone can't be together. I can't allow it."

I took a step back. "You can't or you won't?"

Dad smiled joylessly. "It doesn't matter. The fact is that you can't see Adamo Falcone again."

Anger rushed through my veins. "You're asking me to stop seeing Adamo?"

"I'm not asking you. You won't see him again and you won't set foot on Camorra territory."

"You can't order me around like that. It's my life. I always respect you but you need to respect me as well."

Dad's face became hard. "You can stop seeing him, or I'll find a way to move him out of the picture in some other way. It's up to you, but the end result will be the same. Adamo Falcone won't be a part of your life."

My mouth fell open. "Are you threatening to kill him?"

Dad perched on the edge of his desk, his business expression replacing the look he usually gave me. "I'll do what's necessary to protect all of us." His voice didn't leave room for an argument. For him the matter was settled and my opinion was irrelevant. This side of him wasn't new to me, but usually I wasn't on the receiving end of it.

I glared. "You aren't protecting me by keeping me away from Adamo! I thought you wanted to see me happy but you're obviously only concerned about business."

"If open war breaks out in Chicago, everyone's going to be at risk. You, Galina, the boys, my men. I have responsibility that goes beyond your infatuation with a boy you hardly know."

I couldn't believe his nerve. He didn't know the first thing about Adamo and me. He'd never wanted to know and I'd been careful not to tell him too much. Why poke a beehive? "Adamo saved me. He gave me what I needed to forget the past. He brings me happiness in the present and he makes me excited for the future. Isn't that more than a silly infatuation?" For the longest time, I'd tried to pretend I wasn't in love with Adamo, had feared any kind of commitment, but now that I was past the point of denial, it made me all the more furious to have others question feelings I'd battled for months. "I'm not someone who allows emotions easily. You know me, Dad. If I tell you that I want to be with Adamo, then that means something."

"Do you really think his family will allow him to be with you? Their traditions aren't ours. They'll never fully accept you, never trust you."

I wasn't sure. Adamo had assured me his family would accept me. They weren't as traditional as the other Italian mob families. After all, their Enforcer was married to an Outsider, which if you looked at it, was a bigger risk than having a relationship with someone from an adverse crime organization. I'd been brought up in a world of violence and bound by strict rules. I knew how to keep a secret, no matter how dark. I could lie into the face of a police officer without batting an eye. Even if Adamo and I had been brought up on different sides, our lives were similar. "I'll cross that bridge when I reach it, but that's my problem, not yours."

Dad stood and grabbed my shoulders gently, his smile wistful but his eyes were relentless. "I'll do whatever's necessary to protect you, Katinka. Don't force my hand."

I didn't doubt for a second that Dad would kill Adamo. He wanted to protect me at all costs. That he wouldn't step on the Outfit's toes by doing so was a side-effect not the reason. "You're trying to make up for the past because you couldn't protect me from my mother and the men who molested me, but you can't undo what's happened, and certainly not by ruining my life now."

Dad's fingers tightened around my upper arms. "You have Dima. You two were happy together. If you want to protect Adamo, you'll stay. He's young. He'll find a new love, someone he can actually be with. Or do you actually think you can live in Las Vegas with him?"

Las Vegas was out of the question, would always be, but Adamo didn't want to live there either.

Yet…

"Katinka, be reasonable," Dad said softly. "Some things aren't meant to be. If you miss racing, we can try to set something up."

I tore away from his grip, unable to bear his closeness. Without another word, I stormed out of his office. My eyes burned but I didn't cry. I almost bumped into Dima in the lobby. He must have waited for me and now he'd probably keep an eye on me to make sure I didn't leave the house. Red-hot fury sizzled in my veins. I charged toward the front door, determined to leave. I'd take a car, because Dad had probably given orders to all our pilots not to fly me anywhere.

I didn't get far. Dima grabbed my forearm, jerking me to a stop. I whirled on him, furious and desperate.

I didn't want to lose Dad, or Dima. I didn't want to never see my half-brothers again either. But giving up Adamo? I wasn't sure I could do it. "Let me go," I hissed but Dima didn't loosen his hold.

"Dinara," he murmured imploringly, the voice that was usually balm on my anger. "Think before you act. Do you really want Adamo to die? Do you think he'd want to die for you?"

I froze.

"Would you want Adamo to insist on being with you if Remo threatened your life because of it? Would you die for a relationship that might not even last years?"

I didn't even have to think about it. The answer rang loud and clear in my heart. Yes, I would risk my life to be with Adamo because I loved him and because he'd already done so much for me. Dima seemed to see the answer in my face because his expression fell but he still didn't release me. "Are you sure his answer would be the same? He might have helped you get revenge but that never really posed a threat to his life. But if your Dad puts him on his death list, his days are counted."

Few people survived for long if Dad wanted them dead. My mother had because of Remo Falcone's intervention. Adamo had the Camorra at his back, but he was an easy target when he lived in camp, and Dad had made it clear he would risk war with the Camorra this time if necessary. My shoulders sagged. The idea of being separated from Adamo hurt but the fear of him being killed was even greater. Maybe Dad and Dima had a point. Adamo and I hadn't been together for long, and the majority of the time we'd been too cowardly to even put a name to what we had. I couldn't decide for Adamo to risk his life. No, I definitely didn't want him to risk his life.

"I need to end it face to face, Dima. I won't do it over the phone. That's a bullshit move after everything he's done for me."

"Your father won't allow you to return to camp. He suspects you might stay."

"Talk to him. If I do it now, I'll only make things worse. I'm too angry. Tell him you'll make sure I'll return."

"I *will* make sure you return," Dima said firmly. "Because if you don't, your father will relieve me of my head. I really don't want to die so you can traipse about with Falcone. Stay here. Don't you dare run off."

I felt empty as I watched Dima set out for my father's office. Last night,

I'd allowed myself to imagine a future with Adamo. It had been blurry, with many variables, but I had been happy and free. If I stayed in Chicago, I'd never be either, not without Adamo, not as the Dinara that Dad wanted me to be.

Dima returned five minutes later. "He agreed, but he made it very clear that he'll send men after Adamo if you aren't back home tomorrow for lunch."

"I'll be back," I said.

When Dima and I sat in Dad's private jet for the second time that day, my stomach sank. Adamo deserved to be told the reason for breaking things off in person, but the idea of actually telling him, of being close to him for one last time, it split my heart in two. What if I couldn't say goodbye?

Adamo

Dinara's message telling me she would be back soon raised my alarm and the moment Dinara showed up in camp early the next morning with Dima, I knew something was up. She looked exhausted and as if she was bracing herself for a battle.

I had barely slept the night. I hurried toward her, eager to clear things up. Dinara got out of the car but Dima didn't. He stayed behind the steering wheel, looking stoic as usual. I grabbed Dinara and kissed her. For a moment she tensed but then she threw herself into the kiss, oozing despair and passion. I cupped the back of her head, pulling her even closer. It felt as if we hadn't seen each other in forever.

Eventually Dinara jerked away and staggered a step back. Her cheeks were flushed. The dazed look in her eyes quickly morphed into apprehension, then determination. This wasn't good.

"What's wrong?" I murmured. We were a good distance away from Dima but the windows of the car were down and I didn't want to risk him overhearing our conversation in case he was part of the reason for Dinara's tension.

"Nothing," she said quickly, but her voice proved her answer wrong.

"I didn't think you'd be back in time for the race tonight. I worried it would take you days to convince your father you were safe here."

She looked away briefly and when she met my gaze again, her walls had come up, locking me out of her mind and heart.

"Dinara," I said imploringly, taking her hand. "Tell me what's going on."

Her eyes locked on mine then she pulled her hand away. "I didn't return for the race tonight. I won't race again. Racing was always only a means to an end, and so were you." Her voice wavered when she said the latter.

"Liar," I growled, stepping closer again. I wouldn't allow her to put distance between us, not physically and not with words either. We'd gone through too much. We were both haunted by inner demons—demons only we could understand. Maybe we'd been born on different sides but fate had thrown us together because we were meant to be, because no one would ever see the world the way we did. "If I was only a means to an end, you wouldn't be here right now. You would have left without an explanation or ditched me over the phone. But you are here, Dinara. Why?"

She held my gaze, trying to appear resolute and emotionless, but I'd seen every emotion in those green eyes and knew her too well to believe her charade.

"I simply thought you deserved to find out in person after everything you did for me. I'm not ungrateful, even if I used you for my purposes."

I smirked. "You need to do better to convince me."

Dinara glared. "It doesn't matter. I'm not here to convince you, Adamo. I'm here to inform you about my decision. This is the last time you'll see me. I won't stay in camp, nor will we ever meet again. I belong in Chicago with my people."

"Your people? The people that want you to dress up as a fake version of yourself? The people who only know one side of you, but not every aspect of yourself, not the dark parts only I got to see."

Dinara reached into her pocket and took out a smoke. Her fingers were unsteady when she lit it up.

"I thought you wanted to stop?"

She shrugged. "It wouldn't work."

"The not-smoking or us?"

She took a deep drag and glanced at her boots. "Both." She peered back up at me. "Listen, Adamo. This is a courtesy. I won't explain my reasons. What we had was fun as long as it lasted but it was never meant to be forever. You have to accept my decision. But even if you don't, it won't change a thing. Dima and I'll fly back to Chicago today and I'll return to my old life, and so should you."

"We aren't the same people from our old lives. We changed."

"I should go now. This is pointless," Dinara clipped and tossed her cigarette to the ground then stomped it out with her boots.

Despite her words, she didn't move a muscle, as if she was rooted to the ground.

I took a step closer. "You can trust me with anything, Dinara. Didn't I prove that over and over again in the last few months? Tell me the fucking truth. Is this because your father doesn't want you to be with me?" I asked in a low voice.

Dinara looked away, obviously fighting to keep her expression neutral. "We always knew that our relationship had an expiration date. We're from two different worlds."

I positioned myself right in front of her, cupped her cheeks and forced her to meet my eyes. She narrowed them to keep me at a distance but I knew her too well for that. What we'd done these last couple of weeks, killing and torturing together, overcoming past demons, that had given me a key to look past her barriers, just like she could look past mine. "Maybe our families are from different worlds, and on different sides, but we aren't. Our life as we've led it over the past year has been in a world of our own."

"Exactly," she whispered. "But we can't stay in our own bubble or world or whatever else you want to call it. We got family and we belong with them."

"We belong with each other. It's where we found happiness. I won't give you up and I know you don't want to give me up. Did your father threaten to kill me if you didn't break it off?" Dinara had her own head and I doubted she would allow anyone, not even her father to forbid her from seeing me, but if she feared for my life that would change things.

She closed her eyes, trying to lock me out but I kept stroking her cheeks with my thumbs and eventually she covered my hands with hers. "I hate that you know me so well, that you know how things work in the messed-up world I live in. I should have never let you in."

"I didn't give you a choice," I said quietly. "Just like you didn't give me one either."

Dinara let out a harsh breath and opened her eyes. This time it was harder to gauge her emotions. She was really giving it her all.

"So he did threaten to kill or at least seriously hurt me if you kept seeing me?" Dinara always talked with respect and love about her father. I'd never met the man, but even Remo and Nino seemed to respect him to some degree. Though, that was probably a testament to his ruthlessness and brutality, both character traits my brothers appreciated.

It was obvious he was important to Dinara, had been the most important person in her life for a long time. If Grigory was willing to risk war with the Camorra, willing to raise Remo's wrath, because both would be guaranteed if he laid a hand on me, then he must really mistrust me, or have a closer relationship with the Outfit than we thought. Whatever it was, he'd be a difficult nut to crack. Considering Dinara's love for her father, killing him seemed like a bad idea.

"Your family doesn't mind us being together?" she asked.

"Remo has never been someone who played by the rules. He trusts me so he accepts my choice. Of course, he'd never confide any business details relevant to the Bratva while you were present, but he won't stop me from seeing you. My main work is racing and it'll stay that way. It's not like I'm at the base of Camorra business in Las Vegas. I don't even have to live there."

She scoffed. "Racing is one of your most important businesses and how can you be sure you'll be happy living the nomad life forever?"

"We'll figure something out, and I don't care how, but I won't give you up, you hear me?"

Dinara took a step back but I followed. I wouldn't let her do this. "Don't make this harder on us than it needs to be. I won't risk your life."

"I don't care. It's my life to decide on. And I'm willing to take a risk because what we have is worth it."

"You can't decide alone, and for me, the risk is not worth it, Adamo. And it's not just your life on the line. This conflict could endanger my father, Dima and the rest of my family. Nothing is worth risking so much, least of all a relationship based on something as twisted as revenge and blood-thirst."

She made a move as if to turn and return to her car but I grabbed her wrist and pulled her against me. She didn't resist, but despair flashed in her eyes. "Let me go. You have to accept my decision. And let's be honest, in a year or maybe less you'll have found a new girl to get cozy with, someone who doesn't have the Russian mafia at her back, or who's as messed up as I am."

"I like your kind of baggage and your messed-up brain. I want you, and no one else."

I lowered my head and kissed her fiercely and for a moment she kissed me back with the same passion, only fueled with despair, then she ripped away. "It's over, Adamo. Accept it. Move on. It's what I'll do." She stumbled toward the car.

"Does returning to your old life include getting back together with Dima?" I asked, jealousy raging in my body. Fuck. I wanted to ram my knife into Dima's stupid face. He was pretending to be busy with his phone, but I wasn't buying it for a moment. He was paying close attention to what was going on between Dinara and me.

Dinara stiffened but when she faced me her expression was cold. "Maybe. But from this day on, it's none of your business." She ripped open the door of her Toyota.

"You can't run away from what we have, Dinara. We both know that emotions, dark or light, follow you wherever you run."

Dinara swung herself into the car and slammed her door shut. She turned to Dima and said something. He briefly glanced my way. He didn't look triumphant but I still wanted to kill him. The engine roared up and then Dinara's Toyota raced away, only leaving a cloud of dust behind.

"Fuck!" I snarled as I watched her drive away. My breathing was harsh and my heart galloped in my chest. I closed my eyes, trying to calm myself down. I needed to think. Right now, my first impulse was to take our Camorra jet and fly to Chicago to put a bullet into Grigory's head, and into every fucker's head who thought he could keep me away from Dinara.

After a few more deep breaths, I pulled out my phone and called Remo. Usually Nino was the person I called to ask for advice. He was the voice of reason after all. "Adamo—"

"I need your advice," I interrupted him.

"I thought Nino was your advisor of choice."

I didn't say anything. Of course, Remo would put his finger into the wound.

"That you choose me to give you advice tells me you already made up your mind and need encouragement for an irrational and emotionally charged endeavor Nino would disapprove of."

"I hate that you read people so well," I muttered. He was right as usual.

"I assume this is about Dinara. You and her completed your list, so your reasons to be together have to be evaluated anew."

"That sounds like Nino."

"No one's been on the receiving end of Nino's logical advice more often than me. I can anticipate his advice without talking to him."

"And yet you always do whatever the fuck you want."

"Just what you have in mind," he said with dark amusement.

"Dinara ended things between us because her father threatened my life." I fell silent. I wasn't a kid anymore, but Remo's protectiveness hadn't really caught up on that yet.

"Did he now?" Remo asked in a voice that rang my alarm bells.

"I don't want you to handle him. This is my problem, Remo. Your involvement could end things with Dinara for good. I'll deal with Grigory."

"If Grigory lays a hand on you, he'll pay the consequences, Adamo. You are my brother and I'll rip his Russian ass apart if he touches you."

This was Remo's way of showing he cared for me. I knew that now, but I couldn't allow it. "I'll handle things. If I want to win Dinara back, I'll have to show her how serious I am."

"You plan to go to Chicago."

"Yes. I have to. If I risk my life, she'll realize I won't give her up no matter what."

"And you expect me to give you the okay for this suicidal bullshit?" Remo growled.

"You would do the same if our roles were reversed. You never cared about your life when the people you love were involved. You allowed Cavallaro to torture you for me and Serafina. A painful death was as good as certain, but you didn't care. Now it's my turn to follow in your manic footsteps."

"You are becoming too much like me, Adamo," Remo said.

"I thought you'd be happy."

"You were supposed to be the good Falcone."

I scoffed. "We both know that would have never worked."

"You might have to kill Grigory," Remo said.

"If I kill him, Dinara won't ever forgive me. I'll have to convince him—"

"Or die."

"That's not the outcome I'm hoping for."

"It's not an outcome I can allow, you realize that."

"I want your promise that you won't go on a killing spree if things don't work out. I'm the one who's intruding on Grigory's territory. If he decides to kill me, he's got every right to do so."

"And as your brother, I have every right to seek revenge."

"Remo," I gritted out. "I don't want you to avenge me. If her father got killed as well, that would break Dinara."

"If she really loves you, she won't allow her father to kill you, and if she can't stop him, she should be happy if I kill him."

For Remo, many things were black and white, especially where loyalty was concerned. Deep down, I hoped Dinara wouldn't allow her father to kill me, but above all, I wanted to convince him of my feelings for his daughter.

"If Greta fell in love with an enemy, could he stop you from killing him if his love for her was true and if he tried to prove it to you by risking his life?"

"No," Remo said without hesitation.

"Even if that meant Greta would never forgive you?"

"Greta can't be separated from Nevio, nor should she be separated from her family. We are her safe haven. I'd never allow anyone to take that from her, not even for love."

"Okay, maybe Greta wasn't the best example, but Dinara doesn't have trouble adapting to new surroundings. She loved living in camp with me."

"But being with you still means you're taking her away from Grigory. He lost her once before and he hasn't forgiven himself for it yet. Allowing her to be with you means putting her at risk in enemy territory, away from his power."

"I'll have to give it a try," I said imploringly.

"Do what you must, you are an adult. But tell Grigory that I'll destroy everything he holds dear if he touches you."

"Will do," I said, even if I had absolutely no intention to follow through.

After my conversation with Remo, I was determined to go through with my plan. This was insanity but if that was what it took to convince Dinara and her father that we had to be together, then I'd do it.

I rented a private jet instead of taking one of the Camorra's. If I showed up with a Camorra jet, Grigory might consider it a threatening gesture, but I wasn't here as a Camorrista. I was here as Adamo.

A taxi took me to the Mikhailov palace. The moment I walked toward the gate and told the guard my name, he rang the alarm. Within a minute, several Bratva guards and Dima rushed down the driveway.

Dima shook his head, an incredulous expression twisting his features. The gates swung open and the guard shoved me toward Dima. I didn't resist.

Dima grabbed my arm in a crushing grip, bringing his mouth close to my ear. "What the fuck, Falcone? Are you crazy? You must realize that even your name can't protect you in Chicago. This isn't Camorra land. Grigory will be pissed and kill you."

"That's what you've been waiting for, right? So this'll be a good day for you."

Dima shook his head, muttering something in Russian under his breath. "You are an idiot. Dinara will be devastated if something happens to you."

My heart skipped a beat hearing her name. "Dinara and I love each other."

Dima nodded. "I know, but Grigory won't care. He wants Dinara in Chicago, he wants her safe. Sending her off with a Falcone isn't something he can accept." Dima patted me down and removed my knives and guns, and handed them over to the other guards who trained their guns on me.

"Are you alone?" Dima asked.

"Yes."

"Usually I'd say you're lying because it's absolutely idiotic to come here without a backup, but I believe you. You've got more guts than I thought."

Dima dragged me along the driveway toward a magnificent palace and then inside the building. It was something straight out of Russia, a palace so full of splendor that even I was awed despite having grown up in a huge mansion. The States and even the Camorra seemed light years away in this place.

"Maybe you can put in a good word for me, if you want Dinara to be happy," I joked.

Dima gave me an amused look. "If Dinara hasn't convinced him yet, then I definitely can't do it. And if you think that Grigory will listen to you, then you're the biggest fool I know."

Dima knocked on a massive wood double-door with gilded decorations. Business seemed to be going splendidly for the Bratva.

"*Come in,*" a deep male voice said in Russian. I'd worked my ass off to learn the language whenever I had a moment to spare but I was still far from being fluent. But I understood enough and could even communicate on a basic level. I'd wanted to surprise Dinara with it. Now I could only hope it would appease Grigory enough to save my life.

Dima shoved open the door and led me into a vast office. I'd seen photos of Dinara's father on the internet but this was the first time I saw him in person. He rose from his desk chair and walked around the massive piece of furniture, his expression harsh. He was a tall man and judging from the look in his eyes, he didn't have any interest in listening to what I had to say. I was a threat in his eyes. For his daughter, for the Bratva, for his business. He wanted me gone, as far away from Dinara as possible, and that I'd showed up today, made him want to kill me.

Maybe it was a sign of disrespect in his eyes. Remo would have respected someone who risked his life in such a suicidal way. But Remo's way of thinking was different from most people. Still, I had to hope that Grigory would realize what this meant.

That I was willing to risk everything for his daughter. Maybe it would save my life. Not that saving my life was my top priority. I wouldn't leave unless I could be with Dinara.

TWENTY-FOUR

Dinara

When I'd been with Adamo, time had often flown by and I'd often wished to slow it down, had wanted to savor our moments together. Now that I'd never see him again, I wished I'd really enjoyed every second of our togetherness without hesitation or reservation.

Alone in my room, every second seemed to drag and I just wanted to speed it up, but to what avail? What was there to look forward to? I'd returned to my life, but I wasn't the same Dinara who'd joined the race camp at the beginning of the year. After experiencing love and joy and passion with Adamo, my emotionally detached existence in Chicago was unbearable. In the past, I would have opted to create fake euphoria with drugs but now I knew they wouldn't come close to what I'd felt with Adamo.

I traced the shelves with Fabergé eggs with my eyes. They always gave me a strange sense of peace. I could spend hours looking at their intricate designs. For this very reason, I'd set up a cozy armchair in front of the glass cabinet and this was where I'd spent the last hour. Peace didn't come, though. Even art couldn't stop my thoughts from whirring.

My phone beeped. Glancing down at the screen, I saw that it was a message from Dima.

Adamo is here. In your father's office.

I sat up fully and stared at my screen in horror.

This isn't funny!

He didn't write back. What if this wasn't a joke? Dima wasn't really someone who made jokes about something like that, or at all. I rushed out of my room and stormed down the staircase. Adamo couldn't be here. Even he wouldn't be this reckless, would he?

But deep down, I knew that he would. Adamo was fearless.

He was the guy who'd joined me on my vendetta without a second thought, who loved the thrill of racing cars at their limit, who wanted to date his enemy's daughter no matter the cost.

Damn it.

I didn't bother knocking and just burst into Dad's office, where I hoped to find Adamo. As long as Dad hadn't let the guards take Adamo down into our basement, there was still hope, no matter how small. Then I froze because Adamo stood in the middle of the room. Dima and two of my father's guards lined his sides. Adamo's head swiveled around and he gave me a smile. What the hell was he smiling about? Did he want to die?

"Have you lost your mind?" I asked, horrified. Dad's expression made it clear that he'd hoped I wouldn't find out about Adamo's arrival. Disposing of him would be more difficult with me here.

Adamo shrugged. "I lost my heart," he said wryly.

I could have killed him, but more than that, I wanted to kiss him and press myself against him, and never let him go. These last couple of days without him, thinking that I might never see him again had been hell. I'd hardly slept because I'd lain awake wondering if I should just leave Chicago for good and return to Adamo. But fear of my father's reaction had held me back. I hadn't wanted to risk Adamo's life. Yet, now he was here signing his death warrant for me.

"Dad," I said, turning to my father. "Just let him leave. He's probably high or drunk. He won't even remember anything tomorrow. He doesn't know what he's doing."

"I'm perfectly sober and haven't been high in many years, Mr. Mikhailov. And I'm absolutely sure of what I'm doing. I'm here to ask you to allow your daughter to be with me, to be free to live the life she wants," Adamo said in broken Russian, but Dad's face flashed with surprise, which he quickly masked with anger. I stepped into the room and closed the door, keeping a close eye on both my father and Adamo.

"You can't keep me away from your daughter, unless you stop my heart from beating."

Dad looked as if that was exactly what he'd do. He'd killed so many people in his life, some for hardly any reason at all, and Adamo gave him so many reasons. "Showing up here takes a lot of bravery, or maybe it's just insanity. That's something the name Falcone has stood for in a long time."

"Dad," I tried again, and finally he met my gaze. His expression showed regret, as if he'd already made up his mind and knew what it would do to me.

I staggered forward but one of his men held me back. "Dad," I whispered desperately. "If you do this, I can't forgive you."

"You should leave, Katinka. This is between me and Adamo."

"No," I growled. "It's not. This is about my life, about my heart. You can't dismiss me as if I'm a little child."

Dad motioned at one of his soldiers who made a move as if to grab my arm and lead me away. I slapped his hand away. "Don't you dare!"

I reached inside my pocket, my fingers closing around my phone. Maybe I should leave and call Remo. But what purpose would that serve? He wouldn't be quick enough to send help.

Adamo took a step closer to my father. I didn't detect a hint of fear in his expression, there was only determination. "I waded through blood for your daughter, and I'll do it again, even if it's my own, because Dinara is worth shedding every last drop of my blood for. I won't give her up, no matter what you do or what you say. And if it takes torture and death to prove my feelings for your daughter, then that's what I'm willing to do. I love her and no force on this earth can shake that, so if you don't want me to be with your daughter, if you want me to give her up, then you'll have to end my life today."

I sucked in a shaky breath, unable to process the words Adamo had said. Dima had lived to protect me. He, too, would have died for me, but his loyalty had been for my father, and one reason, maybe even the main reason for his willingness to die for me, had stemmed from his duty toward his Pakhan, but Adamo risked everything only because of me. He opposed my father in his own territory for me. He accepted death to prove his love. I'd tried to marginalize my feelings for the man before me, had tried to tell myself they'd wane with time, but now that Adamo showed the courage to proclaim his feelings in such a risky manner, it would have been absolutely cowardly of me to pretend I didn't love him. I didn't want to be without him, not another day. The last few days had been hell, filled with a new kind of nightmare of losing Adamo every single night. I'd woken bathed in sweat, with my heart beating in my throat.

I felt shaky under the force of my emotions, under the display of emotion on Adamo's face. He loved me fiercely. Recklessly. Definitely foolishly.

I slanted a look at my father, terrified of his reaction to such a forceful appearance. Dad expected respect as Pakhan and was used to people showing it to him. Of course, Adamo wasn't one of his subjects but I wasn't sure how much that mattered to him.

Instead of the dreaded fury, respect flickered in his eyes. Respect for Adamo's words. Even Dima looked less hostile toward Adamo. Surprise and relief washed through me. Maybe we could get out of this in one piece. If Dad hurt or killed Adamo, I doubted I'd heal again.

"You speak Russian," Dad said matter-of-factly. I could have laughed at his conversational tone as if this wasn't a hearing determining Adamo's fate. "I suppose your brother Nino taught you to handle Bratva soldiers that crossed your path during your races."

"I learned it for Dinara. To show my respect for her heritage, and yours."

Dad kept his expression cold and hard, but I knew him better than almost anyone else. He liked Adamo, as much as a Pakhan could like a Falcone, and a protective father could like his daughter's lover.

"Dad," I said firmly as I headed toward Adamo. One of Dad's men tried to stop me, but I sent him a glare and walked past him. I took Adamo's hand and faced my father with him as a unit. "I love Adamo, and I, too, am willing to wade through blood for him. I won't let you kill him. If you want to protect me, if you want me to find happiness and be in the light, then you'll allow Adamo and me to be together. I can't live without him. *I won't.*" The last was a threat Dad understood too well. The day I'd almost died of an overdose haunted him to this day and even if I hadn't tried to kill myself, Dad never really believed that. I hated blackmailing him with something like that. I wanted to live and wouldn't try anything like that, but he didn't know. He always worried about me.

Dad scowled at his soldiers. "Out. Now."

Dima raised his eyebrows. "Are you sure? One of us could stay…"

"I'm perfectly capable of protecting myself against one enemy, Dima. Now follow my order."

Dima sent me a searching look, as if he considered me another enemy for my father, but then he left.

I wasn't Dad's enemy, would never be, but I'd stop him from killing Adamo. Once it was only the three of us, Dad walked around his desk and sat down in his chair. That he had turned his back toward Adamo could be a sign that he didn't consider him a threat, a game of power and testosterone, but it could also be a signal of peace. I begged for the latter. I didn't want either of the most important men in my life to get hurt, especially not by each other's hand.

"You're an idiot," I whispered, looking into Adamo's eyes.

Adamo smiled wryly. "I know."

Dad tapped his fingers on the desk, his eyes lingering on my hand in Adamo's. "There won't be peace with the Camorra. That ship has sailed after the last few attacks." Dad spoke in English, and my pulse slowed a bit more. Dad was trying to make Adamo feel more comfortable by talking in his mother tongue.

"I'm not asking for peace. I'm asking for the chance to be with your daughter."

"How are you going to be with my daughter if you're on different sides in a war? That could become a problem. Unless you hope to take her from me and make her a part of your Falcone clan and the Camorra."

Behind Dad's cold mask, I recognized his worry about losing me. Family meant everything to him and even though he had Galina and his sons, he needed me to be part of it as well.

Adamo raised his eyebrows. "Dinara isn't really part of the Bratva, is she?"

Anger flashed in Dad's eyes but Adamo continued unfazed. "But I have absolutely no intention to take Dinara from you, not that she would let me. She'd kick my ass, because she loves you and wants you in her life."

Dad's gaze met mine and for an instant, uncertainty flared up. The hint of doubt festered inside of him. I held his gaze, hoping he could see that I couldn't imagine a life without him in it, but neither could I imagine being without Adamo. I didn't have many people in my life I really cared about and I wanted those few as close to me as possible.

"Dinara's happiness is and has always been my main concern," Dad said firmly. "I won't forget that you helped her bring justice to the monsters of her past."

"I'd do anything for her." I squeezed Adamo's hand. Words like those had always seemed a meaningless promise to me but now I knew he meant them absolutely.

"Leave the Camorra?" Dad asked with a cocked eyebrow. I sent him an incredulous look. He knew Adamo would never betray his brothers, not even for me, and if I asked that of him, I wouldn't deserve his love anyway. We both needed our families in our lives even if we could never become one big family.

Adamo gave my father a knowing smile. "Are you suggesting I could join the Bratva?"

Dad didn't say anything, only scrutinized Adamo with an unreadable expression.

The Bratva would never accept a former Camorra soldier in their rows. No matter how well Adamo would learn to speak Russian, he'd always be an alien—the enemy.

Before I could voice my thoughts, Adamo said, "I think we both know that I'd never find a home in Chicago and I have absolutely no intention to leave my family or the Camorra. Both are part of my identity, of my very being. Leaving the Camorra would be like leaving myself behind and changing who I am. Your daughter loves the man I am today, not an alternate version of me."

Adamo's dark eyes slanted to me and I gave him a nod. I didn't want him to change. I wanted the man I'd met.

"Then what do you suggest? It seems we're at an impasse, stuck on different sides of a war. Dinara would be torn between us."

"I won't be torn. It's not like there is an open war between the Bratva in your territory and the Camorra. The Las Vegas Bratva doesn't have strong ties to your organization."

"We don't need a truce. We need an agreement of mutual ignorance. A simple non-aggression pact," Adamo said.

"The line between a truce that could bring me the wrath of the Outfit and a non-aggression pact seems fleeting."

Adamo shook his head. "A truce often entails cooperation. We agree on co-existence. We don't help you against the Outfit. You don't help us against the Outfit."

"You can't come to Chicago as you please in that case. Outside of my home, you won't be protected from attacks. My men won't help you if the Outfit tries to kidnap you again."

Adamo smirked. "The Outfit won't capture me again. I was a naïve boy when they did. And if they'd ever catch me, the Camorra would come to my help. I wouldn't need the Bratva for that."

Dad leaned back in his chair. What Adamo suggested was a shaky arrangement. If something happened to Adamo, I'd move heaven and earth to convince my father to send his men to save him, and Adamo would undoubtedly use his Camorra soldiers to save me if something happened. Lines would get blurry. Even this co-existence pact might compel the Outfit to act if they considered our arrangement a threat to their business.

I didn't really care about the Bratva beyond the fact that Dad's life depended on their success.

"Where would you live? How would you be together?" Dad asked, turning his attention back to me. "Live in Las Vegas, with the Camorra clan? That would be hard to explain to my men. Co-existence only goes so far." Dad's men admired him. They trusted his judgment, but he had a point. If I got too cozy with the Camorra, that wouldn't sit well with them. Dad's only option then would be to officially declare his disapproval and cast me out.

The point was moot anyway. I shook my head forcefully. I didn't want to live in Las Vegas. The city held too many horrors for me. Little Katinka lingered in too many dark corners, ready to spring her memories on me. I met Adamo's gaze, wondering if he expected me to move to Vegas with him eventually. His family was very close. His brothers all shared a mansion, and they probably expected Adamo to join their co-living at some point.

Of course, Dad picked up on my uncertainty. He pushed to his feet and smoothed his dark suit. "I'll give you two a moment to talk. I want answers when I return so I can make a decision."

Dad walked past us and left the room.

I whirled on Adamo and slapped his chest hard, glaring. "What the hell has gotten into you? Have you lost your mind waltzing into my father's home? He could have killed you on sight!"

"He didn't," Adamo said with a slow smile as he wrapped his arms around my waist and pulled me against him. Didn't he realize in how much trouble he was?

"He might still do it."

"No, he won't."

"So now you can look into the future?"

Adamo leaned down, his lips pressing against mine. I softened and kissed him back. I'd missed him these last few days. Now that I could touch him again, I wondered how I could have ever considered living without his touch, his smile. Adamo drew back. "Your father wouldn't have listened to everything I had to say and given us alone time if he had made up his mind to kill me. He trusts me with you, and that's a big deal considering you are obviously very precious to him."

"Maybe he wants to give us time to say goodbye," I said. Yet, I had to agree. Dad didn't dislike Adamo. It was more than I'd ever dared to hope for.

"So what do you say? Do we want to be together?"

I gave him a condescending look. "Of course. But Dad wants a solution that won't cause him trouble."

"He wants your happiness. That's his top priority even if it shouldn't be." I pursed my lips. Adamo laughed. "It's true. The head of a crime organization should never prioritize his family over business. But Remo's the same way. Maybe that's why they grudgingly tolerate each other despite the eternal conflict between Italians and Russians."

"He won't accept me going to Las Vegas with you."

"You don't want to live in Las Vegas anyway," Adamo said gently.

I sighed. "You're right. I won't ever like that place. Not after what happened. Even if we killed the monsters from my past, that doesn't eradicate what happened. It's still in my head."

"I know. I didn't experience your horrors but even I still occasionally have nightmares about my kidnapping and the torture."

"But won't your family expect you to live with them in the mansion?"

"I think they know that I never really wanted that. Even before I met you, I lived the majority of the year in camp. I prefer the nomad life. Organizing the races is a part of the business I enjoy dealing with."

"But that was before you discovered your love of torture. I'm sure your brothers can use your newfound talents in better ways."

Adamo chuckled mirthlessly. "Trust me, my brothers have enough expertise torturing people. They don't need my help. And it's not that I discovered my talent for torture through our vengeance trip. It's been something I've been battling with for a long time. It's a dark craving I've been feeling for a long time, and it was why I really consumed drugs. They mellowed out this urge. They turned me into the person I wanted to be but the effect never lasted long."

"If that's the case, are you sure you can live without the thrill of blood without resorting to drugs to mellow your urge?"

Adamo thought about it. "Yeah. I feel like the urge has lessened since I allowed myself to live it for a little while. Suppressing it, only increased the craving. I guess I just need to allow my dark craving out to play on occasion to keep it in check. What about your dark craving?"

"It's there. It'll always be, I guess, but I won't give in. Not after I saw how it dictated my mother's life."

"Good," Adamo murmured.

"But we still didn't make a decision about our future."

"It's easy. We live in camp. The races take place nine months of the year, so we'll have to follow the circuit anyway. I want to keep racing. What about you?"

"Oh yes," I said with a grin. I missed the thrill of racing. I even missed the chaotic atmosphere in camp.

"We could buy a motorhome to have more room. That would allow us to create a home for us without settling down in a place. We could visit Las Vegas on occasion and if your father ever doesn't want to kill me, we could visit Chicago as well. Otherwise we'll just have to split up for our family visits."

"You think your brothers will agree to that?"

"Once Gemma and Savio start popping out babies, my brothers can use the additional space. And Remo's twins probably won't ever move out, so they need rooms as well. If I only require one room for visits, that gives my brothers the chance to create living space for their kids. It's a win-win situation if you ask me."

It sounded like the perfect solution. I still wasn't convinced his brothers would agree, but maybe we could convince Dad as a first step and get Adamo out of Chicago in one piece.

"Can you imagine living in a motorhome with me, or is such a living arrangement not fit for a Bratva princess?" Adamo asked in a low voice, pulling me even closer and cupping my ass.

I cocked an eyebrow. "I prefer freedom and being with you to a palace. What about you, Camorra prince?"

Adamo grinned. "I've been living the nomad life in a tent and car for a couple of years now. I don't need much."

He lowered his mouth to mine once more, his tongue teasing my lips apart. His hand on my ass moved even lower until his fingers stroked over my crotch. I moaned into his mouth and stood on my tiptoes to give him better access. Of course, Dad chose that moment to return.

I quickly stepped back from Adamo, my cheeks heating. Being caught by my Dad was something that made even me blush. Adamo smiled as if he hadn't just fingered me through my jean shorts.

I was glad for Dad's poker face because he didn't give any indication that he'd noticed us getting it on.

"And?" he asked neutrally.

Adamo explained our planned living arrangements to my father, making everything sound perfectly reasonable. When he was done, Dad nodded. "That could work. But who guarantees Dinara's safety?"

"Nothing will ever happen to Dinara. When we killed her abusers, I was her protector. Neither Dima nor you were there but Dinara was always safe."

I gritted my teeth, hating how they discussed me as if I weren't present. "I don't need constant protection. I'm capable of staying away from danger and if necessary, to defend myself. I can kill someone."

Both Adamo and Dad ignored my protest. "If I entrust you with my daughter's safety, you better make sure you don't disappoint me, because if something happens to her, I'll find you and torture you to death with my own hands, and believe me they are very capable."

"Dad," I muttered.

"If something happens to Dinara, which it won't, I deserve everything you have planned for me and gladly accept my fate," Adamo said.

I shook my head. "You two are impossible."

Dad gave Adamo a curt nod, which was the extent of approval he was probably capable of. "I won't kill you today. Right now, I'm willing to give your relationship with my daughter the green light. Don't make me change my mind."

"I won't," Adamo promised.

"Does that mean Adamo and I can return to camp tomorrow?"

Dad nodded, but I could tell he still had trouble letting me go. I released Adamo's hand and went over to Dad to hug him tightly. "Thank you," I whispered. His decision was a risk. If anyone but me would have started something with an Italian, or worse a Camorrista, he would have killed them on the spot, but for me, he was willing to accept even that.

"Everything for you, Katinka," he said in a low voice before he kissed my temple.

"I suppose we'll have to live in sin forever," I said with a relieved laugh as we headed out of my father's office. Considering how conservative great parts of the Italian mob were, being together without being married would cause a scandal, but our relationship was scandalous on so many levels anyway.

"So you're saying you'd say no if I ever asked you to marry me?"

I sent Adamo a warning look as I led him through the lobby. "Don't you dare pop that question. We haven't even dated for a year, and even then would be way too soon. I'm not even sure I want to marry at all, definitely not before I'm thirty. There's really no reason to tie the knot."

I wasn't in a hurry to marry and had never really thought about my future in detail. I loved Adamo, but that didn't mean I wanted to marry.

Adamo and I were allowed to spend the night together in my room, which obviously surprised Adamo judging by his expression when I didn't give him a guest bedroom.

"Dad knows we're having sex, so keeping us apart for a night seems pointless."

The moment I closed my door, Adamo pressed me against it, kissing me. I pulled away. "I shouldn't reward you for almost getting killed."

"I'm very alive," Adamo said.

I slipped past him toward the cabinet with my Fabergé eggs. Adamo followed me.

"You handled my father very well. Few men know what to say."

"I don't know your father, but I know men like him. I've grown up among my brothers, and trust me when I say no one's more homicidal than Remo."

"But Remo is your brother. He wouldn't kill you. Nothing's holding my father back."

"You are," Adamo said as he wrapped his arms around my waist from behind. "Those eggs are beautiful, but we can't take them with us to camp."

I huffed. "They stay here. They are too precious and beautiful to ride around in a motor home."

"You are as precious and beautiful."

I nudged him with my elbow. "Compliments won't get you sex. I'm still pissed that you risked so much. I would have never forgiven myself if my father had killed you. Nor would I have forgiven him."

Adamo slipped his hand under my shirt, playing with my belly piercing, as he nodded toward the Fabergé egg in the center, the most expensive piece in the cabinet and the first egg Dad had gifted to me. "That's your belly piercing."

"It is. It's my favorite and I love to have it close no matter where I am."

Adamo nodded then his hand slipped lower. He popped open my button before he glided into my panties. His fingers found my clit and began rubbing small teasing circles.

I bit my lip, leaning back against him.

"I don't need compliments to get sex," Adamo said in a low voice before he nibbled on my throat. His fingers stroked open my folds, scissoring my sensitive skin.

"My father might consider it disrespectful that you can't restrain yourself even for one night," I panted.

Adamo chuckled. "I won't tell him. Will you?" He pushed two fingers into me.

"No," I gasped.

That night I lie awake in Adamo's arms for a long time, not haunted by worries or fears. I imagined our future together and I was excited about it. Nothing was really holding us back now.

TWENTY-FIVE

Adamo

When Dinara and I returned to camp the next day, it really felt like a final homecoming. Crank gave me a wave and a thumbs up when he spotted Dinara. I had already called Remo last night to make sure he didn't attack Chicago when he didn't hear from me for too long. I really didn't want my tentative understanding with Grigory to be undermined. I hadn't given him details about my agreement with Grigory but knowing Remo, he probably suspected something. My brothers knew I preferred camp life to staying in Las Vegas anyway.

Dinara shone with happiness when we set up our tent between our cars. It wasn't a splendid home, but it was all we needed at the moment. Once the season was over in two weeks, we'd have time to buy a motorhome for us.

I didn't miss the many curious or even apprehensive looks from fellow drivers or pit girls.

"Do you think they know why we were gone so often these last few months?" Dinara asked.

"They know something. I should have known that rumors would spread eventually."

"I think some of them will think twice now before cutting you off during a race. Nobody wants to get tortured and killed," Dinara said wryly.

"It's not like I'm a different person."

"You are to them. Because of your easy-going personality it was easy for people to forget that you're a Falcone. Now they realize that one of the monsters from Vegas actually walks among them and it makes them nervous."

I could tell that this amused Dinara a great deal. "I hate that name."

"But it serves its purpose. It's better to be feared than to be liked in the mob business."

I laughed darkly. "Indeed. That's Remo's credo. I guess it was inevitable that I'd fulfill my family's fate at some point."

"People in camp will get a grip eventually once they see that nothing has changed. Until then you'll have an easier time to make up points."

"There's no way I can make up the points I lost in the last few races, nor can you. We'll have to go through qualification races next season."

Excitement flashed in Dinara's eyes. "I love a challenge."

"I think people see you in a new light as well. The apprehensive looks aren't only for me."

Dinara glanced around and people quickly looked away. "I doubt they fear me for myself. Women are always underestimated."

"Anyone who underestimates you is a fool."

"I really missed this," Dinara said when we sat on a log around the fire with the rest of the camp, drinking beer and eating chicken wings that burned my taste buds. Country music blared from the speakers set up around the perimeter.

"Yeah, it's a strange little world of our own where we can bend the rules."

Dinara moved her legs in rhythm to the country beat. I grinned challengingly. "I never took you for a country girl."

She took a sip from her beer, a slow smile spreading on her gorgeous face. "I'm a multilayered personality."

I chuckled. "No kidding." I wrapped my arm around her shoulders and she leaned her head against my shoulder. "It's strange to think that this will be our home from now on."

Dinara shrugged. "We'll be free. I don't think there's anything better in the world."

"Yeah," I murmured. The first people started dancing around the fire as their alcohol levels rose. "Did you talk to Dima?"

Dinara sighed. "I didn't see him before we left. I suppose he avoided me. Maybe he feels that I betrayed what we had."

"But you weren't a couple anymore. He was your bodyguard."

"He's always been more than that. But Dima is loyal to my father and he can't follow me on this new path. He'll always serve my father until he dies or gets killed doing his duty. Maybe he thinks it's my duty to stay in Chicago and be the Bratva princess my father always wanted me to be."

"But it's not who you want to be. If Dima ever really loved you, he must realize it."

Dinara raised her head. "What Dima and I had wasn't really love, I realize that now that I'm with you."

"Because you love me."

Dinara gave me a strange smile. "You really want me to say it more often, don't you?"

I kissed her. "Oh definitely."

The dancing around us got wilder, stirring up dust. Many people began singing along to the songs, most of them without having a clue about the actual lyrics.

"Let's join them," Dinara said, setting her beer bottle down on the ground.

"I thought you'd never ask." I shoved to my feet and pulled her along with me. When we joined the dancers, a few of them hesitated, obviously still unsure about us after the killer couple rumors Crank had told me about, but soon the music and alcohol carried away their tension and we became part of the camp again.

Dinara laughed as we stumbled along to the music in an uncoordinated but fun line-dance formation. Her eyes locked on mine, her face illuminated beautifully by the fire. This wasn't fake happiness. No pretend laughter. Darkness was a part of both Dinara and me, but we'd banished it to a faraway spot in us. It didn't rule over our lives.

It was almost three in the morning when Dinara and I finally went to bed in our tent. We weren't drunk but a gentle buzz filled my body. After making love, we fell asleep in each other's arms.

Dinara's tossing and turning, and unintelligible mumbles woke me from my own nightmare—the same one that haunted me for years, but other than in the past, I didn't wake covered in sweat and with my heart beating in my throat. The nightmare had altered since Dinara and I had started our vengeance trip. Now I always managed to free myself from my restraints eventually and fought my torturers. It seemed my nightmares now allowed me my revenge.

Dinara's breathing slowed once she woke and I kissed her cheek. "I wish the nightmares would have died with my abusers," she whispered into the dark.

"Eventually they will fade or maybe they'll change," I said then told her about my own altered nightmare.

"I'm still surprised that you never sought revenge against the people who tortured you. You have the Camorra at your back."

"Revenge against the Outfit, especially their Capo and his Underbosses wouldn't change anything, it would only continue an endless spiral of violence and revenge. You could end everything by killing your abusers, but in a war, revenge only leads to more violence. What happened to me wasn't personal."

Dinara let out a strangled laugh. "I think getting tortured is pretty personal."

"It wasn't about me, it was about Remo. My pain was revenge for Remo's actions, and if I took revenge in turn it would lead to a new act of revenge from the Outfit."

"A never-ending spiral of violence."

"I want to live in the present and for the future. The past is the past."

"For the first time in my life, I want the same. The past is dead, and I'm really excited about our future."

"It's going to be a crazy ride in many ways."

Dinara hummed her approval.

"There are only two more races before the season's over and most people will return to their families for Christmas. Only a few stay in camp, like Crank, and celebrate together."

"We don't celebrate Christmas in December. The orthodox Christmas is in January, so maybe I'll stay in camp until January."

Over my dead body. "I want you to celebrate Christmas with me and my family in Las Vegas."

She froze in my arms. "I'm not part of your family. I'm sure your brothers and their families don't want me there."

I hadn't asked my brothers yet but I loved Dinara and wanted to spend the holidays with her. I doubted Kiara and Serafina would have anything against it. Remo was very protective of our mansion, so I wasn't sure about his reaction. And then there were Savio and Gemma. They both were absolutely easy-going under normal circumstances but half of Gemma's family had been killed by the Bratva, so they might be biased in their opinion of Dinara. I kept those thoughts to myself. I would find a way to convince my family that Dinara wasn't a threat. "My family should meet you and what better way to do it than for Christmas? They'll love you like I do."

"I'm not someone who has a long list of fans. I'm not one of those sweet, always smiling girls everyone wants in their family."

"Trust me, you'll fit in perfectly with your personality. Don't let me celebrate Christmas alone. There's nothing more depressing than being surrounded by happy couples and families while being alone."

Dinara was quiet for a long time then she sighed. "All right, but please make sure I'll be welcome. I really don't want to intrude on your family time."

"You are my family," I murmured.

Dinara pressed herself closer to my body and kissed my throat. "I love you."

The next morning I called Remo. He was the first person I needed to convince. To my surprise, he wasn't against my suggestion. "Bring her along. Kiara will be ecstatic to cook for more people."

"I expected more resistance from you," I admitted.

"If you trust Dinara, I trust your judgment. Not to mention that both Nino and I know her, and doubt she'll pose a risk. She's got more reason to be grateful toward us than to hate us for an enmity between mob families that doesn't really concern her."

"What about Savio and Gemma?" I asked.

"Talk to Savio. If he's against it, I can't allow Dinara to join us."

"I understand," I said. "Thanks, Remo. I know I often didn't show you my gratefulness for what you've done, but I won't ever forget what you did to give Dinara justice. I'll try to be less of a dickhead toward you in the future."

"That's a start," Remo said wryly. "Now clear things with Savio."

"Yes, Capo." I hung up and dialed Savio's cellphone. He picked up after the tenth ring.

"This better be good," he muttered. "You're interrupting my marital duties."

I could hear Gemma hissing something unintelligible and something that sounded like a slap. Savio chuckled.

"I need to talk to you about Christmas," I said.

"Okay? I'm not on the organization committee for Christmas. Ask the girls."

"It's about Dinara. I want to bring her along to celebrate Christmas with us."

Silence followed on the other end.

His voice had lost its usual ease when he spoke eventually. "Remo mentioned that you and she are still together. I thought things would end after you finished your killing spree."

"We love each other," I admitted, even if I felt exposed admitting this to Savio. He and I didn't usually share our deepest darkest emotions.

"Loving the enemy seems to run in the family."

"Dinara isn't the enemy. She was never really part of the Bratva."

"Her father is Pakhan. Our women are part of our world by association even if they aren't inducted." It was strange to hear Savio so serious and it told me that this was a difficult topic for him and Gemma.

"Dinara left Chicago to be with me."

"Good for you."

"I know you have every reason to hate the Bratva, and Gemma even more so, and that's why I want to ask if you'll be okay if I bring Dinara along."

"That's not my decision," Savio said, then his voice became muffled, as he probably described the situation to Gemma. I didn't know Gemma as well as Kiara, but she'd never struck me as someone who'd judge people easily.

"Okay," Savio said without warning.

"What?"

"It's okay for you to bring her along. Gemma and I won't judge Dinara before we meet her. We'll give her a chance."

"Thanks, Savio," I said honestly.

"I don't have time to keep chatting with you. I need to satisfy my wife." He hung up and I shook my head with a smile.

I found Dinara tinkering with her car for the race tomorrow. She raised her eyebrows. "You look thrilled."

"I talked to my family. They want you to join us for Christmas."

"You sound relieved, so you weren't sure they would."

I wrapped an arm around her waist. "Savio and Gemma were a bit of an unknown, but they want to meet you."

"To see if I'm a threat?"

I grinned. "Everyone's curious about you. And I think you'll like Gemma. She's into cage fighting."

Dinara frowned. "I'm not into fighting."

"But you are into racing, which is also a male-dominated activity."

Dinara rolled her eyes. "I don't need a dick to kick ass on the racetrack."

"Oh I know," I said. "So will you celebrate Christmas with me and my family?"

Dinara gave a resolute nod but I could tell she was nervous. "I survived your father and you'll survive my family, don't worry."

"That's a consolation."

Dinara

I'd never celebrated Christmas in December. Not that I was a big fan of the holiday in general. I'd always only celebrated it for my Dad and later for my half-brothers.

Adamo had told me so much about his family that I felt as if I already knew them. I wondered how much they knew about me. I wasn't someone who got nervous easily or who was anxious before meeting new people. I was definitely more of an extrovert even if I didn't have any trouble being alone either. I knew not everyone liked me, and I could live with it, so I wasn't worried about becoming Miss Popular. I was however nervous because this wasn't just a random meeting. This held meaning. It constituted that my relationship with Adamo was serious for both of us. So far we never really put a name to it. We lived it. But this was a new step in our relationship.

When we pulled up in the driveway of the magnificent white mansion, my palms actually became sweaty. This was important for Adamo, and in turn, it was for me.

"Nervous?" Adamo asked with a smirk after we got out of the car. He grabbed the huge bag with presents from the trunk before he stepped up to my side.

I rolled my eyes but gladly accepted his outstretched hand as moral support. "Do I have reason to be? Everyone's okay with me being here?"

Adamo gave me a look that made it clear he thought I was being cute. I nudged my elbow into his side. "Do you think there'll ever be a chance for me to meet your father for a relaxed family meeting? Maybe celebrate your orthodox Christmas together?"

That Dad hadn't killed Adamo when he'd shown up on our doorstep had been a miracle. He was very protective of Galina and his sons, so I doubted he'd allow Adamo to be in their presence any time soon. Maybe Remo didn't consider me a risk to his family, but Adamo was a Camorrista, a Falcone, and for my father to not regard him as a threat would take a long time, if it ever happened at all.

"Let's take this one step at a time, okay? He didn't kill you last time. That's a good start but we shouldn't overstrain our luck too much. Let's give him time to get used to the idea of you being a constant presence in my life. Right now, he probably still hopes our relationship fails."

Adamo stopped in his tracks, eyebrows cocked and the same smirk on his face. "And? Would you bet on us?"

"We aren't a safe bet," I said with a wicked smile. "But who wants safe when they can have what we have." I grabbed his collar and pulled him against me for a kiss. Adamo wrapped his arms around me.

Loud kissing noises disrupted the moment. Adamo and I pulled apart. Adamo groaned and narrowed his eyes at a trio of boys who lingered in the open doorway, watching us. The tallest boy with black hair stormed toward us and gave Adamo a grin before he faced me with a cautious glint in his eyes. "Who are you?" he asked—no, *demanded*.

Adamo nudged him forward. "That's none of your business, Nevio. And you better watch your mouth or you'll be in trouble."

Nevio pressed his lips together but didn't look guilty at all as he slanted me another look. The boy was maybe eight years old but definitely had the sass and confidence of a grown-up. Despite his rudeness, I liked the kid. If I ever had kids, I'd prefer them to have their own head and not let adults or anyone else trample all over them.

I raised my eyebrows at the kid. The two other boys showed more restraint but obviously distrusted my presence as well. They didn't resemble Nevio. I assumed they were Nino's kids.

"Are our presents in there?" Nevio asked, pointing at the bag. That seemed to pique the curiosity of the two other boys as well and they swarmed in on Adamo.

Adamo shrugged. "That depends on your behavior."

"Nevio, Alessio, Massimo!" a woman shouted, her impatience ringing loudly in her voice. The boys turned on their heels and dashed back inside, leaving Adamo and me alone.

I let out a laugh. "Will the rest of your family give me a similar welcome?"

Adamo linked our hands again. "The kids aren't used to strangers visiting the mansion. Remo doesn't usually allow visitors. He's very protective."

I nodded, realizing what Adamo was telling me. That Remo welcomed me into his home was a big deal. "He trusts your judgment of me."

Nino strolled over to us where we waited on the porch. "Won't you come in?"

"I wanted to give Dinara the chance to change her mind after the rude welcome from Nevio."

Nino gave me a halfway welcoming nod before he turned to Adamo once more. "What did he do?"

"He demanded to know who she is. Didn't you tell the kids?"

Nino shook his head. "We told them you'd be bringing your girlfriend along. It caused quite the stir because you never presented someone before."

Adamo had mentioned that he'd never been serious enough about anyone to submit them to his family's presence. That he trusted me enough to take me filled me with warmth.

"Let's go," Nino said. "Kiara prepared dinner. We don't want it to become cold."

Adamo and I followed Nino through a long corridor into a huge room that seemed to serve as the common area of the mansion. Adamo had mentioned that every brother had his own wing where they lived with their wife and kids. Even Adamo still had his own wing even though he lived in camp most of the year.

The common area was already crowded with the Falcone clan. Half a dozen kids buzzed about, creating an impressive noise level. Three boys and two girls. Everyone turned to us as we stepped into the room. Adamo had showed me photos of his family but I wasn't sure I'd be able to keep the names of the kids straight. At least the adults were easy to remember.

The third dark-haired man had to be Adamo's brother Savio and beside him his sex bomb of a wife, Gemma. I was happy with my body but even I felt a flicker of inadequacy upon seeing her curves. Part of her family had been killed by Bratva so her hesitant expression didn't come as a surprise. I met her gaze and gave her a tense smile. I wouldn't feel guilty for something I wasn't responsible for. My father had assured me that he hadn't had a hand in the attack. But even if he had, I wasn't part of his business. That our families would never sit around a table and play happy family had been clear from the very start.

"Welcome to our home," Remo said. Even his body language was different from our previous meetings. A hint of tension in his limbs spoke of his protectiveness and caution. I wasn't a threat in his eyes or I wouldn't be here but trust wasn't part of our relationship yet. Adamo squeezed my hand and tugged me closer to his family. The table was already set but no one had taken their respective seats yet.

Remo's wife, who reminded me a bit of Grace Kelly, sent her son Nevio a warning look before she came toward me and smiled. The first completely friendly gesture of my visit, not that I had reason to complain. After all, my father almost killed Adamo.

"Hi Dinara, it's wonderful to finally meet you. We almost gave up hope that Adamo would bring you here. He's been very secretive about his relationship with you," Serafina said.

"We needed time to figure things out for ourselves before we told others details," I said with a smile of my own.

"That makes sense," Leona, the wife of Fabiano, the Camorra Enforcer and not-blood-related brother of the Falcones, said.

"Dinner is ready!" a dark-haired woman said as she headed our way. I recognized her as Nino's wife, Kiara. For some reason, I felt my cheeks heat when I remembered Adamo's suggestion to talk to her about my past. It still didn't sit well with me that he thought a similar past of abuse meant Kiara and I could give each other life advice. Every person had a unique way of coping with trauma. She seemed to have found her safe haven in her family, living a traditional role of providing for her huge family. I wasn't someone who wanted safety and continuity to deal with my past.

I wanted thrill and adventure. Kiara made a beeline for me and gave me a bright smile. She looked genuinely happy to see me. She pulled me into a hug. I stiffened at first because I hadn't expected it. My family was more reserved. We rarely hugged, especially not people we barely knew.

After a moment of surprise, I forced myself to relax but she pulled away instantly and gave me an embarrassed smile. "I'm sorry. I didn't mean to spring my hug on you."

"Don't worry. It's nice to meet you."

Kiara was a gorgeous, petite woman with the kindest eyes I'd ever seen. She was someone I'd have imagined as the docile wife of a pastor, not a notorious and undoubtedly sociopathic mobster like Nino Falcone.

"Nino, can you help me carry everything to the table?" Kiara asked before she and her husband disappeared.

"I'll help you as well," Gemma said, rushing after them. Maybe this wasn't as easy for her as Adamo had thought. He looked at his brother Savio but I couldn't read the look that passed between them.

I greeted Leona and Serafina who welcomed me without reservation. They too seemed honestly interested in meeting me. After greeting the women of the family, Adamo led me toward Remo and Nino as well as Fabiano and Savio. Fabiano shook my hand with a tight smile. I hadn't expected a warmer welcome from the Camorra Enforcer, but he wasn't hostile so I took it as a good sign. My stomach tightened when I finally faced Savio. "Hi," I said stupidly. I wasn't sure why I felt uncomfortable. I wasn't guilty by association.

Savio scanned me from head to toe. I was in my beloved biker boots but instead of ripped jeans or jean shorts, I'd opted for a more festive plaid skirt, black tights, and black leather jacket over a black long-sleeved body. "I should have known my emo kid brother finds himself an emo rocker chick."

I blinked. "The role of Ken and Barbie in the family are already taken so we had to settle for the emo couple," I shot back before I could think it through.

Remo cocked an eyebrow with that look of dark amusement always lingering on his face.

Savio actually spluttered with laughter. He clapped Adamo's shoulder hard. "Now I know why you chose her."

I stifled a pleased grin. Adamo gave me a shrug but I could see the tension leaving his shoulders. "It wasn't a choice. Dinara is a force to be reckoned with. I didn't have a choice but to fall for her."

My face heated. I sunk my nails into his hand in warning. He wasn't supposed to embarrass me. Talking emotions in front of people really put me on the spot.

After a couple of minutes, Kiara, Nino, and Gemma returned with casseroles and pans, and we settled around the table. The kids still eyed me with a mix of caution and curiosity. The presents would hopefully sway them toward me tomorrow, but I wasn't sure how to handle Gemma. She had avoided me so far.

I occasionally cast a glance at her during dinner. Luckily the rest of the Falcone clan chatted animatedly with me about racing. We avoided any mention of Russia or Bratva until Leona asked, "How do you celebrate Christmas in Russia?"

I hesitated, glancing at Gemma and Savio. I didn't want to open old wounds, but Gemma looked up from her plate and met my gaze. She gave me a small smile. I relaxed and gave her a grateful smile in turn. "We celebrate on January seventh. In my family we cook twelve dishes that represent the disciples of Jesus, but that's not how everyone in Russia does it. We have a multitude of traditions in our country."

More questions about Russia soon rained down on me. I was relieved that my heritage wasn't the pink elephant in the room anymore.

"I'd love to see the Bolchoi ballet one day," a tiny girl with the same black hair and dark eyes as her twin Nevio piped in. Her name was Greta if I remembered Adamo's instructions correctly, and she looked like a precious doll with her symmetric facial features, big eyes and porcelain skin.

"I saw them a few times in Saint Petersburg and Moscow. My favorite ballets are the Nutcracker and Swan Lake."

Greta smiled shyly at me, briefly meeting my eyes before looking away. "Mine too."

At once, everyone became even warmer toward me as if this little girl's verdict held particular significance. Adamo patted my leg then interlaced our fingers under the table.

By the end of the night, I was completely relaxed. I didn't feel like part of the family yet, but I hadn't expected that. Yet, I enjoyed the chaotic coziness of the Falcone home.

It was a different kind of Christmas than we celebrated in Chicago and I loved this new experience. I wanted Adamo to be part of our traditions as well, but I worried what Dad would do to him if I brought him home with me. While I was safe in Las Vegas with the Falcone clan, I wasn't sure if Adamo would be safe in Chicago. Dad could still change his mind any day.

After Christmas dinner, we all moved toward the sofas. The beautifully decorated Christmas tree towered over us and illuminated our surroundings with the gentle glow of the electric candles. Before I could sit down beside Adamo, Gemma approached me.

"I'm sorry that I was rude and didn't welcome you right away. Christmas is hard for me..." She swallowed. "But I shouldn't vent my sadness on you."

"I'm sorry for what happened to your family. I hate that mob business kills so many innocents."

"Thank you," Gemma said with a small smile. "I'm glad Adamo found you. I've never seen him so happy before."

Adamo was talking to Fabiano, but I could tell that he was half-listening to my conversation with Gemma.

After Greta did a short ballet performance that Kiara accompanied with the piano, Kiara began to gather up the dishes. I helped her and carried a stack of plates over into the kitchen. I wondered if Adamo had mentioned a conversation to her as well. It made me feel awkward. I wasn't embarrassed about my past but I preferred for people to judge me for my actions today and not for something that was done to me more than a decade ago.

She noticed my curious gaze and leaned against the kitchen counter. "Adamo always seemed so restless when he came to visit, especially during the Christmas holidays, but today for the first time since I've known him, he looked as if he exuded calm. He's arrived. You are his anchor and no matter where you two live or if you keep traveling with the racing camp, he's found his home in you. That's wonderful. We all need something that gives us roots so we can grow for the future, and you are each other's roots."

I bit my lip, my throat clogging with emotions. "Thank you, Kiara. I never meant for it to happen. I didn't think I could really trust someone like I trust Adamo."

Kiara nodded. "I never thought I could experience what I have with Nino, but the past doesn't have to define us. We shouldn't let it."

"Yes," I agreed.

The door swung open and her two sons rushed in. They pressed up to her. "Mom, can we have cookies before bed?" the shorter boy, Massimo asked.

"It's Christmas," Alessio reminded her.

Kiara laughed, and I fell in as well. They reminded me of my half-brothers. When sweets were concerned, they could be quite cunning.

A moment later, Adamo came in with a couple of empty glasses, but it was obvious that he was checking on me. He wrapped his arm around my waist, pulling me against him.

"I'm fine," I said before he could ask.

Adamo nodded. "I knew you'd be."

I stifled a smile. I'd always wanted someone at my side who knew I could handle myself, who didn't treat me like a damsel in distress, and I'd found that person in Adamo.

TWENTY-SIX

Adamo

SHE STOOD AGAINST THE HORIZON, ILLUMINATED BY THE sinking sun, completely naked except for her biker boots. Her red hair glowed like flames in the last rays and her pale, beautiful body appeared almost pearlescent. I got out of the tent and watched her a bit longer.

She was so fucking gorgeous. She turned and met my gaze. A smile broke free on her face. It wasn't one of the fake smiles, weighed down by darkness from the past. It was a free, honest smile. That didn't mean she didn't still harbor darkness. We both did. It was what made us understand the other so well. But we controlled our darkness now, like a tamed beast behind iron-bars. Sometimes we let it out to play but mostly it slept peacefully in its corner.

I still felt as stupidly in love with Dinara as I'd been when I'd rushed to Chicago to convince her father. We'd grown closer, Dinara and I, and even her father grudgingly tolerated me. We'd even celebrated the orthodox Christmas together in Asper for the first time this year.

Dinara bit her lip in that teasing way she had, turning fully to me so I could see the length of her naked body. One of her hands cupped her breast, teasing her piercing, as the other slowly slid down her belly to the apex of her thighs with the soft patch of red hair. Blood rushed down my body, gathering in my cock. She and I always took time away from camp, so we could fully enjoy each other's company.

I strode closer to her, taking her in and the way she stroked herself. When I stopped right in front of her, she was panting softly, her lips parted. Two fingers worked her clit, spreading wetness all over it. I grabbed her hips and sucked her pierced nipple into my mouth. Her fingers moved faster on her clit and she let out a sharp moan. I sank down slowly, tracing my tongue over her belly before I arrived at eye level with her pussy. Her fingers circled her bundle of nerves and her lust had already gathered all around it. The sight of her glistening folds made my mouth watery. I leaned forward and teased her fingers and clit with my tongue, tasting her sweet arousal. Her fingers didn't cease the circling of her clit. Instead, they soon began to fight my tongue for dominance. After she came, I pulled her down on my lap. Making love to her still felt like a revelation every time.

Afterward, we watched the night sky as we reclined on the hood of my BMW and drank ice-cold beer.

"In the past, I would have needed a smoke to really enjoy the moment," Dinara murmured.

"I don't even miss smoking anymore."

"Me neither. You and racing give me the highs that I need," she said with a teasing smile. I touched her cheek, unable to believe how lucky I was, how ridiculously happy.

And then it hit me. This was the moment I'd been waiting for. Of course, I wasn't prepared, but it didn't matter. I didn't want to wait to get a ring. This was the right time and I hoped Dinara would see it too. I slid off the hood and sank down on the dusty ground before Dinara.

She sat up slowly, her eyes widening briefly, then disbelief took hold of her face. "What are you doing?"

I took her hand with a grin. "We made it to five years, even though you thought we wouldn't. I think we're still going strong. I'd bet all my money on us making it to fifty years."

Dinara bit her lower lip, stifling laughter. "Considering our risky lifestyle, I doubt we'll live that long."

"I know you aren't thirty yet, so your second requirement isn't fulfilled, but I can't wait another five years. I'd say we're good to go…" I fumbled inside my jeans pocket and pulled out a discarded silver chewing gum wrapper.

Dinara let out a disbelieving laugh but didn't comment. I formed the wrapper into a makeshift ring, then took her hand again. "Dinara Mikhailov, will you marry me?" I held up the wrapper ring, which glittered in the headlights, making it look more sturdy than it was.

"You are out of your mind!" Dinara exclaimed, but her eyes were soft and she had trouble fighting her smile.

I lifted the ring a bit higher. "I'm afraid I need an answer."

She closed her eyes for a moment and when she opened them again, she said, "Yes."

I pushed the wrapper ring on her finger, then staggered to my feet and wrapped my arms around her. I kissed her fiercely as she pressed close to me. "For a second I worried you'd say no."

"For a second I considered saying no. I really love our life of sin, without commitment, free-spirited and wild."

I looked into her eyes. "Then why didn't you?" Dinara and I had never seriously talked about marriage. She wasn't like some girls who dreamed about a big wedding and a princess dress. If I'd had more time planning this moment, I probably would have gotten cold feet. But she had said yes, to me, to us, to forever.

Dinara

Adamo grinned as if he'd won the jackpot. I stretched out my hand and admired the silver wrapper ring around my finger, not answering his question yet. "I'm glad you put so much effort into our engagement ring," I teased him. I didn't really care. I rarely wore jewelry, even though I owned a shocking amount of it, all gifted by my father or family in Russia. I hadn't taken any of my jewelry with me, and I didn't miss it. The only things I really wanted to have with me were my Fabergé eggs, but a motorhome wasn't a good place for valuable pieces of art.

He ran a hand through his unruly hair. He always cut it at the beginning of the season but allowed it to grow in the months that followed. "I thought you didn't care about jewelry."

He actually sounded worried. "I don't," I whispered. "This is the perfect ring for us."

Adamo chuckled. "I'm not sure I agree. You'll get a better ring soon." He paused, raising his eyebrows. "But you didn't answer my question."

Why did I say yes? For a long time, I'd been against marriage, considered it superfluous and restricting. The mere idea of binding myself to a person like that had made me nervous, but when Adamo had popped the question, my body hadn't reacted with a cold sweat or feeling of nausea. It had felt inexplicably right. "Because I can't imagine ever living without you again, so we might as well make it official. I realized we were already committed, and marriage to you doesn't mean we can't be wild and free-spirited anymore."

"I think that's the sweetest thing you've ever said to me," Adamo joked.

I boxed his shoulder before I kissed him hard. "I love you, and I love being reckless with you, and I know we can keep being reckless even when we're married and that's perfect."

"And I love you." He took my hand and inspected the ring he'd put together. "We can go ring shopping next time we pass a city."

I pursed my lips in thought. I couldn't really see myself with a wedding ring. "Do we have to get an actual ring? Can't we get something else that shows we're together? Or maybe we just don't have anything but the love in our hearts."

Adamo smirked. "Nice try. I want a sign of you being mine for everyone to see."

"You'll be mine too, remember?"

"I don't want to forget."

I wrapped my arms around his neck. "No ring. But if you have a better suggestion, I might be open for it."

Adamo thought about it for a while before a grin spread on his face. He still managed to look like a boyish daredevil when he gave me that look. "How about we get a wedding tattoo? Nino could do the design and inking."

My brows rose in surprise. I actually liked the idea. "Why not? At least that way we can't lose it."

"Perfect."

"You realize we can't have a big celebration, right?" The Camorra and Bratva still barely tolerated each other, and so far Adamo's and my unusual relationship hadn't caused my father any trouble, but a wedding feast that involved both our families might change that.

Adamo shrugged. "I don't really care about a big party. This is about us. For all I care, it can only be you and I, and it would be the perfect wedding."

"We could marry in one of those chapels in Vegas. You know, the ones where Elvis seals the bond."

Adamo obviously had to stifle laughter. "Not Elvis, but we can marry in a chapel in Vegas if that's what you want."

"It would fit, don't you think?"

Adamo dropped his forehead against mine, smiling crookedly. "A girl who hates Valentine's Day, who hates rings and who doesn't want a nerve-racking wedding feast. I'm pretty sure you were heaven sent."

"I seriously doubt it. If anything, heaven dropped me on earth because I didn't behave."

"I like it when you don't behave," Adamo murmured.

"I know." I pulled him on top of me.

Adamo

A week later, Dinara and I traveled to Las Vegas to spend a few days with my brothers and their families, and tell them about our decision. Of course, the second we announced our plan to marry, Kiara already fantasized about planning the wedding.

Dinara gave me a panicked look, so I spoke up before my sisters-in-law called a wedding planner. "Dinara and I don't want to celebrate. We just want to elope in a chapel around here. No big deal."

"Oh," Kiara mumbled, exchanging a look with the other women.

"You realize you're breaking quite a few hearts here, right?" Remo said, but he looked like he didn't care. He'd never been one for the big celebrations, and probably wouldn't have had any kind of wedding ceremony if Serafina hadn't wanted it.

"For us, it's not about the celebration, it's about the promise we give each other," Dinara said carefully.

"Considering the difficulty of having your family and ours under one roof, your decision is wise," Nino said.

Dinara nodded quickly. "Yes, that's another reason why we didn't want to make a big deal of it. It's just for us."

"We don't want a ring either," I said. "Instead we want you to create wedding tattoos for us."

Savio flashed Nino a grin. "Then you'll have tattooed almost every member of our family. It's becoming a heart-warming tradition."

I scoffed. "A bull tattoo over your dick isn't the most heart-warming sign."

Savio sent Gemma a cocky look. "The sight of my bull always warms Gemma's panties and heart, right?" She punched his abs, causing him to grunt.

"I hope you don't want your wedding tattoos in similarly shady places," Nino said dryly.

Dinara laughed.

"Don't worry," I said.

"When are you going to marry?" Kiara asked. I could tell she was bummed about not getting to organize a big wedding.

"Tomorrow," Dinara and I said at the same time.

Kiara smiled hopefully. "Can we be there?"

Nino touched her shoulder.

"I think the lovebirds want to be alone," Remo said.

I nodded. "We really don't want to make a big deal out of it." Inviting my family to the wedding wouldn't go over well with Grigory, and there was no way we could have him at the ceremony in Vegas without causing a major scandal, and most likely bloodbath.

"At least, have someone record the ceremony," Kiara begged.

"I think there's a package we can book that includes photos and even a video," Dinara said. "I could check." She pulled out her phone but Remo waved her off.

"They are going to take photos and record everything if you ask them to. You'll be a Falcone."

Dinara and I exchanged a look.

"Actually," I said. "Dinara will keep her name. Like we said, we just want to marry as a sign for us, not for outward appearances."

"That's reasonable given the situation with Grigory," Nino drawled.

I laughed. "I knew you'd agree."

Kiara shook her head, looking honestly disturbed. "You two are the least romantic people I know. Nino at least pretends to be romantic for my sake."

"At least, they both don't have a romantic bone in their body," Serafina said.

Dinara shrugged. "Our idea of romance is sharing a beer on a car hood after kicking each other's ass during a race."

I pulled her against me and kissed her temple. "Perfect."

When Dinara told her father about our decision that night, his excitement was limited. Not so much because she chose to marry me. I think he'd made his peace with me at this point, but he was appalled by the fact that his precious daughter would marry in a cliched chapel in Vegas. But he, like my family, had to accept our decision.

The next morning, Dinara and I followed Nino into a room that he'd prepared as a makeshift tattoo studio.

I was nervous if Dinara would like the tattoo I'd chosen. I'd searched the internet for days for possible options. Most of them were just tattooed rings but that would have been the too obvious choice. Dinara and I wanted something more subtle, not for everyone to see.

Nino pulled out the sheets with his design of our wedding tattoos. He pushed the sheet with the tattoo for Dinara's palm over to her and the other sheet to me. Dinara scanned the drawing of an intricate lock in the shape of a heart then glanced over to my sheet with the matching key.

"Do you like it?" I asked when she didn't say anything. She nodded with a slow smile. "Can you do something this delicate on a small scale like a finger?" she asked Nino, who frowned in response.

"I thought we could ink it into our palms. That way the key and the lock always merge when we hold hands. The downside is that tattoos in palms only last up to a year so we'd have to redo them regularly," I said quickly. I hadn't discussed this with her yet. It was meant as a surprise.

Dinara nodded immediately. "That's actually perfect, because it means that we have to renew our vows every year." She paused. "I feel bad that you're the romantic in our relationship."

"I'm glad your expectations are low when it comes to romantic gestures, trust me."

Dinara and I exchanged a grin. Nino looked impatient. "So I assume you are both fine with me tattooing the designs into your palms?"

"Yes," Dinara said, and I nodded.

"I should warn you that the palm is a tender spot and the tattoo is going to be at least uncomfortable, maybe even painful depending on your level of sensitivity."

"I don't think either of us is very sensitive to pain anymore," I said dryly. I'd gone through torture at the hands of our enemy and more broken bones than I cared to recount during fights or race accidents. And Dinara had lived through enough shit as well. Not to mention that she had a nipple piercing, which Nino of course didn't know.

"Who wants to go first?"

"Me," Dinara said without hesitation and thrust her hand at Nino who disinfected it thoroughly.

He took the tattoo needle but didn't begin right away. "If you need me to stop, just say so."

Dinara nodded but she didn't say anything as Nino tattooed the intricate design into her palm, only watched with fascination. While I admired my brother's tattoo art, my gaze often wandered to Dinara's gorgeous face, unable to believe that we'd actually say yes to each other today. When Nino was done, she held up her hand between us. The skin was red but it was obvious that my brother had created something magnificent.

"Your turn," Nino told me.

I held out my hand but didn't take my eyes off Dinara who gave me a small smile. When the needle pierced my skin, I twitched once. It was uncomfortable like Nino had said, but nothing close to the pain I'd felt before, only this time the end result was worth every second of discomfort.

After Nino was done with my tattoo, he nodded in satisfaction before he turned into warning mode again. "Try to keep the wounds clean and no hand-holding or tattoo merging in the next few days. The result will suffer if you get an infection."

"We'll behave," I told Nino sarcastically.

He gave Dinara a look. "I hope you're the sensible of the two of you."

"I love racing and got my belly pierced in a dingy back-alley place that also sold second-hand cell phones."

Nino sighed and got up. "I think you two are a good match."

"We are," I agreed.

Three hours later we stood in front of an Elvis imitator after all. Dinara and I had chosen matching outfits of our favorite leather jackets, ripped jeans, and white tees, no fancy shit. But I'd stuffed a white rose into the pocket of my jacket and Dinara held a bouquet of white roses in her hand. A single flower was also woven into her red hair, creating a beautiful contrast.

After we'd said our vows and kissed longer than was appropriate, I carried Dinara out of the chapel and toward my BMW. I lowered her into the passenger seat, then gave her another lingering kiss before I closed the door and took my seat behind the wheel. "Ready for happily ever after with me?"

"So ready," Dinara said. I hit the gas and we shot out of the parking lot with a loud clattering. The kids had insisted we string a dozen cans to the exhaust pipe.

We let the windows down, turned up the music—"Highway to Hell"—which seemed like the perfect ironic touch to our day and raced through Vegas. Soon we left the city behind us to find a remote place for our first night together as a married couple. We had everything we needed to make it the perfect honeymoon. Each other, cans of macaroni and cheese for nostalgic reasons, and a six-pack of ice-cold beer.

EPILOGUE

Adamo

DINARA SENT ME A CHALLENGING LOOK, COCKING ONE PERFECTLY groomed red eyebrow in an exaggerated way.

One corner of my mouth twitched up and I mimicked her expression.

"I'll kick your ass Falcone," she called over the roar of the engines.

I answered by letting my car howl. "Not if I kick your ass first, Mrs. Falcone."

Officially, Dinara was still a Mikhailov, but she'd soon realized that everyone considered her a Falcone in camp and in Vegas. Eventually, she'd stopped correcting them.

The pit girl raised the start flag. I tensed with eagerness, the thrill of the upcoming race rushing in my veins. This was the first race of the seven-day-circuit, and Dinara and I stood in the first row due to our excellent results so far.

When the pit girl dropped the flag, Dinara's battle-cry-like laugh burst through the roar of the engines. I grinned as I slammed my foot down on the gas pedal.

My heart pounded, my pulse hammered in my veins, and I felt high on freedom and adrenaline. Dinara and I raced together for almost fifteen years now but we still relished every second of a race. Dinara tried to push me off the road when she cut in front of me in the first bend but I held against it. My smile widened. It was on. There was nothing better than a wife who could kick your ass in a race.

Dinara won the first day, but I was right behind her so we could spend the night in the same spot. It had become a beloved ritual.

"Did you wait for me?" I joked when I got out of my car.

Dinara snorted. "I'm not nostalgic!" She disappeared behind her trunk to relieve herself, and I hid behind an assortment of rocks to do the same.

Dinara scanned the horizon when I joined her a couple of minutes later. I kissed her plump lips. "They'll be here soon, don't worry."

"I know," she said, but she didn't stop searching the area. Finally, the outline of our huge motorhome appeared in the distance. It had its own shower and toilet, a kitchen, living area, and plenty of sleeping room.

The horn sounded a few times as usual before the motorhome pulled up beside our cars. The door on the driver's side swung open and Aurora hopped out of the motorhome, her blond hair in a messy ponytail. "Roman refused to take a nap. He was too eager to watch the race," she said with an apologetic expression.

"Don't worry," I said. "He can be as stubborn as his mother."

Dinara sent me a warning look before she headed for the passenger side and climbed up to free Roman from his child seat. He wrapped his short legs around her waist as she came toward me. His dark hair was all over the place. It had grown in the last few weeks and fell into his eyes, but he hated having it cut so we just gave up. Maybe he'd eventually grow tired of it being so long.

"I'll cook dinner," Aurora called as she headed into the back of the motorhome. When our son was born four years ago, we'd wondered how we'd manage to keep racing. Dinara had paused for a year and just supported me, but then she'd missed it too much. The standard races weren't a big problem. Dinara's friend and former pit girl Kate could watch Roman during that time but the seven-day circuit was a bigger problem. Luckily Aurora, Fabiano's and Leona's daughter, was fascinated by racing and wanted to earn additional pocket money, so she played our babysitter for a few weeks during the summer holidays. This was the second year she helped us out after begging her father for over a year to allow her this job. I had to swear to him to protect her with my life, which I would have done anyway. Fabiano was like family, so Aurora was too.

I set up a small fire in front of the motorhome. Dinara and I sank down in front of it with Roman between us. He'd fallen asleep the moment he was reunited with us. No surprise considering that it was four in the morning. His nap and sleeping routine always got messed up during this week. Aurora carried our breakfast over to us. Hash browns, bacon and eggs sunny-side-up. She yawned and gave us an embarrassed smile.

"Go to bed," Dinara urged. She too looked exhausted. I was beyond that point. My head felt as if it was filled with cotton candy.

With a wave, Aurora disappeared in the motorhome and after a few minutes the lights went out.

"I wish we could sleep in our bed," Dinara mumbled.

"Yeah." I stroked Roman's unruly head. We'd chosen his name because it worked in Russia and Italy, so we didn't offend either of our families. "But the rules are the rules."

Dinara rolled her eyes. "I get it. We all have to sleep uncomfortably to have the same conditions." Fifteen minutes later, the three of us huddled together in our shared tent. Roman hadn't woken. I admired him for his ability to fall asleep in a heartbeat and continue to sleep no matter what happened around him. With him between us, Dinara and I fell asleep. This had become a tradition for us. One of us always gave in and drove a bit slower so the other could catch up and we could have family time in the evening. Dinara and I were competitive but we didn't really race to win. We raced because it was our life.

Dinara's breathing evened out. She'd fallen asleep with her chin resting against Roman's head and a peaceful expression on her face. Having Roman had really turned us into our own little family. We'd worried if it would be a problem to keep up our nomad life with a child but Roman never knew another way of living. He loved being fawned over by all the pit girls and getting to ride in all the cool race cars. And since we had him, my brothers and their families occasionally visited camp, even if Dinara and I tried to visit them as often as our tight racing schedule allowed.

Late the next morning, during our second breakfast, Aurora, Roman, Dinara and I sat around our kitchen table in the motorhome together and ate the khachapuri that Dinara had made.

"My father bought a new lodge near Aspen, a bigger one," Dinara said as she checked her messages on her cellphone. Our main contact to our families during the season was via phone. Dinara saw her father and half-brothers even less frequently than my family. And her contact with Dima was limited to occasional text altogether. She showed me the screen with several photos of a splendid timber lodge.

"The last one was already too big for us. You told him that we won't add more kids to our family, right?"

"I did, but I think he prefers to ignore it. Once Jurij and Artur start giving him grandkids we'll be off the hook."

"That can take a decade."

"With so much space, we could all celebrate together. A big Falcone-Mikhailov Christmas," I joked. The Bratva and the Camorra still only tolerated each other. There was no cooperation. Dinara's and my marriage hadn't changed that, not that we'd advertised our union. We didn't want to stir up trouble in Chicago. Over the last decade, we'd established a routine. We celebrated Christmas with my family in December and then we celebrated again with Dinara's family. Because her father didn't want me to set foot in Chicago, he'd bought a lodge in Aspen where we could celebrate together and enjoy a ski and snowboarding holiday. It was a compromise that worked well and Roman was ecstatic over getting presents twice.

"I think it's really cool that you celebrate Christmas twice," Aurora said. "What do you say, Roman?"

"Yes!" he agreed enthusiastically.

Dinara and I exchanged an amused look. She took my hand under the table, pressing our tattoos together.

Dinara

Roman clapped enthusiastically as he watched the awards ceremony. Aurora had to hold his hand tightly to stop him from running around.

It was only the second time that I'd managed to win the seven-day-circuit. In the past my constant pee breaks had destroyed any chance at winning, not to mention that Adamo and I often waited for each other in the first few days to spend the night together.

When I stepped on the winner's rostrum, Roman clapped even harder, beaming all over his face.

Adamo climbed up on the rostrum beside me. He'd finished in third position. I gave him a coy look. So far he was still in the lead when it came to total wins, but I had every intention to catch up with him eventually.

After the ceremony, Roman rushed over to us and threw himself into my arms. I swung him up and he thrust his arms up over his head, as if he too had won. Adamo smiled broadly at me. Despite our competitiveness losing against each other never stung, even if we teased each other mercilessly in the days that followed. The winner always got the bragging rights and the loser promised retribution.

"You beat Dad, Mom," Roman reminded me, before he turned to Adamo to say in a gravelly voice. "Sorry, Dad."

Adamo tousled Roman's unruly hair. "Don't worry, buddy. Next time Dad will win again."

I sent him a look that made it blatantly clear that wouldn't happen.

"I want to race too!" Roman declared.

"Maybe next year," Adamo said with a wink.

Over my dead body. This was one of the times where I wished Adamo and I hadn't passed on our recklessness. Adamo always joked I was being overprotective, and he was right, but I just couldn't help it.

Together we climbed down the rostrum, and I accepted the congratulations of fellow racers and many pit girls. Funnily enough, these girls had become much nicer to me since I'd given birth, probably because they didn't see me as competition anymore now that I was a mom. Not that I'd ever competed with them for their prey—the bachelor racers. I'd only had eyes for Adamo from the beginning.

I still rocked jean shorts and crop tops, even if I had to have my belly piercing removed due to an infection during pregnancy. I now wore the tiny Fabergé egg as a pendant around my neck. Adamo had actually had the idea and gifted the necklace to me shortly after I'd given birth to Roman.

"I'm starving," I said as I followed Adamo who cleared a path through the buzzing crowd, which was already prepping everything for the huge party that always followed the seven-day-circuit.

An hour later Adamo, Aurora, Roman, and I were square in the middle of the celebrations. A fire roared up into the sky and blasted us with heat. I held Roman's hand tightly as he tugged to get closer to the raging flames.

"Someone was too fond of fire accelerant," Aurora mused as she sipped at her Coke. While Adamo and I weren't a stickler for rules, we'd given our word to Fabiano that we'd watch his daughter closely, so we didn't allow her to have any alcohol.

A couple racers had checked Aurora out when she first appeared in camp, but one look from Adamo and a gentle reminder from me that her father was the Camorra's Enforcer stopped any interest the male camp population might have had in her.

Roman yanked even harder at my arm and pointed at the flames with his free hand. "I want to watch the fire!"

"You can watch it from here," I said, then turned to Adamo. "I wish he was less reckless."

Adamo chuckled and wrapped an arm around my shoulders. "Did you really think a kid of ours would be the cautious type?"

Aurora hid a smile behind her can of Coke. A moment later she joined the dancing crowd. She'd borrowed one of my crop tops and combined it with baggy jeans and white sneakers covered with drawings in permanent marker, looking as if she belonged here and not in an elite high school. Adamo's vigilant gaze followed her briefly, but when he saw that she was surrounded by pit girls, and that the guys kept a respectful distance, he locked eyes with me again.

Roman's frustration rose as I kept him in place. His dark eyes sent me a reproachful look, as if he couldn't believe I dared to restrict his desire for freedom so shamelessly. Adamo hoisted him up over his head and positioned him on his shoulders. I used my now free hand to grab a beer from the drinks table and took a sip while Adamo began to rock to the music, moving closer to the fire, much to Roman's delight. His excited laughter made me smile and I followed along, my body losing itself to the fast beat of the music.

Adamo and I celebrated like this for two hours before we took our leave shortly before midnight with a sleeping Roman. He hung limply over Adamo's shoulder, his mouth slack in sleep.

Our days of partying until the early morning hours until we stumbled toward our tent in a drunk haze were over since I'd become pregnant with Roman. Now two beers already created a buzz in my body that only half a bottle of vodka had done in the past. Aurora followed us since she wasn't allowed to party by herself. "Can you get him ready for bed?" I asked. "We'd like to watch the stars for a bit." Aurora smiled affirmatively before she took Roman from us and went into the motorhome.

Adamo smoothed his palm around my bare midriff. "Watch the stars, hmm?" His low voice and the kiss he planted on my neck sent a pleasant shiver down my spine. I slanted a look at the motorhome but the door was closed and Aurora wasn't anywhere near the windows.

"It's a beautiful night," I said with a shrug, nodding up at the sky.

"Indeed," Adamo said as he tugged me along toward our parked cars. "How about we do a little joyride to a more secluded place to *watch the stars.*"

Smiling, I pushed past him and slid into the driver's seat. "The winner drives."

Adamo raised his hands, palms facing my way. "All right." As always, the sight of his tattooed key warmed my heart.

After a few minutes of driving, the lights of the celebrations weren't visible anymore. I parked the car off to the left of the road and turned the lights off, bathing us in darkness.

Stepping out into the cool night, I took a deep breath. I loved living in camp, the chaos and noise. I loved Roman, his stubbornness and recklessness. But I also loved these small slices of alone time that Adamo and I carved out for ourselves. I hopped on the hood of my car and Adamo pushed between my legs almost right away, slinging his arms around my waist and jerking me against his body. His erection pressed against my crotch, making me moan. We hadn't had the energy to sleep with each other in the last seven days, but the thrill of winning had awakened my libido.

"You deserve a prize for winning," Adamo murmured. "Lie back."

I lowered myself to the still-warm hood. Adamo's lips and tongue traced my belly as his fingers opened my pants and slid them down. Peering up at the sky, the myriad of stars twinkling beautifully against its black canvas, my lips parted in a low moan as Adamo's mouth found my center. I fought the urge to close my eyes as the pleasure rose higher, tightening a knot deep in my core. I came with a cry, the stars in the sky blending with the lights bursting before my eyes as the sensations overwhelmed me.

Soon Adamo wrapped his arms around me once more, pulling me up against him, and we made love. The stars became meaningless as our gazes locked. We didn't look anywhere but at each other until we came and lay spent on the hood, wrapped up in each other, my leg thrown over Adamo's hip.

"How long do you think will we continue to live this nomad life?" I asked breathlessly.

Adamo kissed my hand then my cheek. "Until we're old and gray, or old and bald in my case."

"You have thick hair. You won't go bald."

Adamo chuckled. "That's your main concern."

I nudged him hard. "You think we can still race cars when we're eighty? I doubt we'll win a single qualification race."

"Do you want to settle down in a nice suburb?"

"Yeah, right," I said sarcastically, then yawned. It had been a long day but lying in Adamo's arms under the night sky, listening to the soft whoosh of the wind and the occasional chirp of a cricket was too good to exchange it for sleep.

"Let's just take it one day at a time. That always worked really well for us, don't you think?"

"It worked perfectly," I said. "I still can't believe we're here today, married with a child, without a war between our families at our back. Maybe it's karma's way of making up for the shitshow that was my childhood."

"Maybe," Adamo murmured. "Or maybe you just fought for your happiness, like I did."

"I am happy," I said—sometimes it was still hard to believe. "As a teen, I always thought I'd end up as a depressed, chain-smoking mid-thirty single lady with a drinking problem who'd die of lung cancer or a liver cirrhosis."

Adamo burst out laughing. "Our emo teen selves would have had a field day together. I thought I'd either die of an overdose or because Remo killed me."

"I guess it's good that we didn't cross paths during that time."

"I'm just glad that we met. I can't imagine life without you in it."

I brought my face even closer to his. "Every day since you've been in my life has been better than any day before we met."

I kissed him and he pulled me even closer until I could hardly breathe, but I clung to him. "There won't ever be another day without you in my life."

THE END

Please consider leaving a review. Readers like you help other readers discover new books!

If you want to be among the first to get updates on books, please join my Facebook group: Cora's Flamingo Squad
www.facebook.com/groups/172463493660891

For bonus content and news, subscribe to my newsletter!
corareillyauthor.blogspot.com/p/newsletter.html

OTHER BOOKS

The Camorra Chronicles:
Twisted Loyalties (#1)
Fabiano
Twisted Emotions (#2)
Nino
Twisted Pride (#3)
Remo
Twisted Bonds (#4)
Nino
Twisted Hearts (#5)
Savio

Mafia Standalone Books:
Fragile Longing
Sweet Temptation

Born in Blood Mafia Chronicles:
Luca Vitiello
(Luca's POV of Bound By Honor)
Bound by Honor
(Aria & Luca)
Bound by Duty
(Valentina & Dante)
Bound by Hatred
(Gianna & Matteo)
Bound By Temptation
(Liliana & Romero)
Bound By Vengeance
(Growl & Cara)
Bound By Love
(Luca & Aria)
Bound By The Past
(Dante & Valentina)

ABOUT THE AUTHOR

Cora is the *USA Today* Bestselling author of the Born in Blood Mafia Series, the Camorra Chronicles and many other books, most of them featuring dangerously sexy bad boys. She likes her men like her martinis—dirty and strong.

Cora lives in Germany with her family and a cute but crazy Bearded Collie. When she doesn't spend her days dreaming up sexy books, she plans her next travel adventure or cooks too spicy dishes from all over the world.

Printed in Great Britain
by Amazon